# The Duchess
# of Carbon County

# *The Duchess of Carbon County*

## Kat Martin

**Five Star**
**Unity, Maine**

Five Star Romance
Published in conjunction with Kat Martin.

Cover photograph by Alan LaVallee

July 1997
Standard Print Hardcover edition.

Five Star Standard Print Romance Series.

The text of this edition is unabridged.

Set in 11 pt. Times by Minnie B. Raven.

Printed in the United States on permanent paper.

**Library of Congress Cataloging in Publication Data**

Martin, Kat.
    Duchess of Carbon County / Kat Martin.
      p.  cm.
    ISBN 0-7862-1105-9 (hc : alk. paper)
    I. Title.
  PS3563.A7246D83   1997
  813´.54—DC21                            97-9390

c-1

*To my mother,*
*for her years of unwavering love and support.*

# Chapter 1

April 15, 1878
Keyserville, Pennsylvania

The deafening roar, then the echo of the blast awoke her.

Heart beating like a frightened butterfly, she sat bolt upright in her narrow iron bed, her mind fighting images of grinding timbers, billowing clouds of thick black dust, and the terrible earthshaking rumble of the mountain as the mine caved in.

Elaina McAllister took several calming breaths and glanced at familiar surroundings: the high-ceilinged room, the chipped blue porcelain pitcher on the scarred oak stand beside her bed, the sienna-hued daguerreotype of her father. Only a dream. The end of a hazy nightmare that had haunted her since childhood.

Running her slim fingers through the dark hair curling at her temples, Elaina brushed the still-damp strands away from her cheeks. The dream, now no more than an indistinct memory, faded completely with the sharp rap at the door and the gust of cool air as it opened.

"Sorry, Laina honey." Ada Lowery, skirts flying, bustled noisily into the room. "The dinin' room's fillin' up in a hurry this mornin', and Lizzy Miller's brother says she's sick. I ain't sure I believe him, but you'll have to come down early." The gray-haired woman handed Elaina a light cotton wrapper, little protection against the brisk morning chill. Padding efficiently toward the window on tiny squarish feet, Ada parted the threadbare curtains, pushed open two rippley glass panes, and hustled back across the room.

"I'd best git back to the biscuits and mush, honey. I'll see you downstairs." Rosy-cheeked and smiling, Ada pulled the door closed behind her.

As Elaina swung her long, slender legs to the floor, she felt a surge of affection toward the buxom little woman. Robust. That was how Elaina thought of Ada. Robust and unflagging. And a very dear friend.

Because yesterday had been her nineteenth birthday, Elaina felt a little different today, a little more in charge of herself. Even working extra hours couldn't dampen her spirits. She would wear her yellow batiste, she decided, to match her sunny mood. The dress dipped a little too low in front, but Ada, who was the hotel manager, thought the scoop neckline was good for business.

"What harm could there be in givin' them poor miserable miners a little somethin' to brighten their day?" she would say, smiling broadly and patting Elaina's cheek. Elaina had never really liked the idea. If she had her way, she'd have worn something a little more modest while serving the men their meals.

After a hurried toilette that ended with a last glance in the mirror to check her appearance, Elaina headed down the two flights of stairs to the dining room, noticing once again the flowered paper peeling from the walls of the old hotel and the dark stains that marred the ceilings. Several windows were cracked and the cook stove smoked up the kitchen. Sometimes Elaina felt the old place called out to her, cried out to her for help. When the rusted plumbing dripped water on the once-gleaming floors, Elaina imagined the drops were tears.

Elaina sighed. When her father had owned the Hotel Keyserville, it had been a showplace. It sorrowed her to see it in such a state of disrepair.

As she neared the dining room, Elaina heard the echo of voices and whiffed the aroma of fresh baked biscuits.

"Thanks fer hurryin', honey." Ada pushed open the swinging door, brandishing a wooden spoon that threatened to drip pancake batter on the just-swept floors. "They'll be poundin' on the tables if'n we don't get 'em fed soon." Ada grinned, used the back of her hand to swipe at a few stray tendrils of gray hair, and ducked back into the kitchen.

Used to the men's impatience, Elaina tied an apron over her dress and quickly set to work. Once elegant, the dining room was now merely serviceable. Ornate brass chandeliers still hung from the

8

ceiling, but several of the frosted glass shades had been broken, and the room was now lit with a bit of a glare. Fresh white tablecloths spoke of the room's cleanliness, and Elaina's addition to the stark surroundings, a single pink or red rose from the bushes near the side of the hotel, adorned each rough-hewn table.

"Mornin', Miss Elaina." Josh Colson seated himself in a rickety straight-backed chair while his nine-year-old son, Johnny, climbed up beside him.

"Good morning, Josh, Johnny." Elaina smiled down at the little red-haired boy, and he glanced away shyly. After taking their orders, she brought Josh a steaming mug of coffee and Johnny a mug of cocoa. She liked the Colson family. The men reminded her of big red-headed bears, and the women were polite and friendly.

"Do any good this morning, Josh?" she asked. "I heard you had a meeting with Ben Taylor." Taylor was foreman at the Blue Mountain Mine.

"Nah. Same old story. All we get is excuses and delays." Josh clenched his fist.

"I'm sorry, Josh. I really hoped this time —"

"They got us over a barrel and they know it. We gotta work to feed our families. Either the miners' con rots us or we starve to death. Not much of a choice, is it?"

Elaina swallowed hard. Why did she always feel so guilty? Hoping to make him smile, she patted little Johnny's hand.

"Need some butter over here, miss," a burly miner broke in. Elaina obliged, waited on several other customers, pouring coffee and clearing away their dishes, but kept up her conversation with Josh.

"Even that wouldn't be so bad," Josh was saying, "if the shifts were shorter and the tunnels safer. Safety. That's the most important thing."

"Maybe things'll change, Josh." He looked at her as if to say there was a snowball's chance in hell and finished the last of his eggs.

Most of the customers had eaten and left by the time Elaina picked up the last two half-eaten platters of sausage and flapjacks from a table near the window. She was off work now until the noon meal, a scant hour away, and looking forward to a moment's peace.

She was less than halfway to the kitchen when the jingle of the bell above the door drew her attention to a tall dark-haired man who stood in the doorway. He paused just inside the entrance, his pale blue eyes taking in every nook and cranny while his clothes and air of confidence set him apart from the miners who frequented the hotel. As he hung his broad-brimmed black felt hat on a peg beside the door, Elaina caught the gleam of silver on the band.

Still carrying the platters, she slowed her steps, the man's dark looks striking a distant chord. Surely it couldn't be, she thought, but her heart pounded and her eyes frantically searched for another glimpse of the man's compelling face. As he spotted a table in the corner with eyes that missed nothing but paid her little heed, Elaina took a few more uncertain steps.

When he turned in her direction, she was sure her heart would stop. For a long, dizzying second the plates teetered precariously on the palms of her trembling hands. Then they crashed to the floor. Broken china, greasy bits of sausage, and clumps of flapjack slid across the pine planks.

Ignoring the tangle of glass and food at her feet, and the surprised stares of the last remaining customers, Elaina ran, skirts flying, as fast as her long legs would carry her, into the arms of the astonished dark-haired man.

"Ren!" she breathed as she hugged him, arms wrapped tightly around his neck. She clutched him fiercely, afraid he might fade, just like her dreams.

"Hold on a minute, miss," he cautioned, but she heard only his husky voice.

"I prayed someday you'd come back," she said. "I just knew you would. Is Tommy with you?" She glanced toward the door, then self-consciously to the mound of broken dishes. "I was just so surprised to see you —" She kissed his sun-brown cheek and smiled up at him. "How long can you stay? When did you get here?"

He smiled wryly. "Much as I'm beginning to wish it were otherwise, I'm afraid you've mistaken me for somebody else." Gently he unwound her arms from behind his neck and set her away from him.

"Don't you recognize me?" she asked, crestfallen.

10

"I'm sorry to disappoint you, miss, but I'm not . . . what was his name?"

"Ren," she said, trying to read his expression. "But you must be Ren. You look just like him . . . I think."

"You think?" His pale eyes glinted with mischief. "How long has it been since you've seen this fellow?"

"About nine years." She knew exactly how long it had been. October first, just less than nine years ago. She would never forget that day. But the boy she'd known only briefly was another matter indeed. She eyed the stranger and began to have her doubts.

He grinned broadly, a flash of white against his darkly tanned skin. "And you think you would know this man after all that time? A man can change a heap in nine years."

Elaina followed the line of his gaze and realized it rested on the swell of her bosom above her scoop-necked dress. Swallowing hard, she felt the warmth in her heart spread rapidly to her cheeks.

"You're not teasing me, are you? I mean . . . you're really not Ren?"

"Sorry. No, I'm not Ren. But I appreciate the kiss." He ran a long-boned hand across his cheek, and she reddened even more.

"I feel so foolish," she said as one of the kitchen boys arrived with a mop and pail to clean up the mess. Gratefully she smiled at the youth and felt more foolish than ever. Nine years *was* a long time. Besides, Ren was probably married by now with a whole passel of children. Seeing him again was just a silly schoolgirl dream.

When she returned her attention to the stranger, she found him smiling indulgently, as if she were a child, and Elaina's temper flared. "Well, if you're not Ren Daniels, who are you?"

His smile broadened. "Name's Dan Morgan. Pleased to make your acquaintance, Miss . . . ?"

"McAllister. Elaina McAllister. Morgan, you say?"

"That's right."

"Dan Morgan?" she repeated. There was something familiar about the name, but she couldn't quite remember what it was.

Suddenly she knew. "You're Black Dan!" It was the name the newspapers had dubbed him, in their typically dramatic way. "You're the gunman Dolph Redmond hired."

"At your service, Miss McAllister." He inclined his head in a

11

mocking bow, but his eyes had turned vague and distant.

Of all the men she could have mistaken for Ren! Stepping away, she took a long, cool look at him. He was as tall as Ren — no, he was taller. His shoulders were wide, definitely broader than Ren's, and she didn't remember Ren's waist ever being so narrow. Though the gunman's hair was as dark as Ren's, it was graying at the temples and not quite as unruly as she remembered.

And his eyes were different. The stranger's eyes were blue, just as Ren's had been, but not sparkling and full of life. These were the color of the sky on a hot day. Light blue — and hard. And there were tiny wrinkles near the corners, though she didn't believe the man had yet reached thirty. A long scar began behind his ear, ran down his neck, and disappeared beneath his collar, making him look every bit the dangerous man he was and convincing her completely that this man was not her Ren. This was the gunman, Dan Morgan. A man who was here at the mine owner's request — paid to stop the miners from staging a walkout. The kind of man Elaina McAllister despised.

"Care to join me for a cup of coffee?" he asked.

Elaina bit her lip in an effort to stifle the scathing retort on the tip of her tongue. It didn't help. "Not on your life. I know why you're here, and I think you're . . . you're despicable!" As she whirled to leave, Morgan caught her arm and pulled her up short.

"I don't care what you think about me personally, Miss McAllister — as long as you stay out of my affairs." Morgan watched the color drain from the girl's flushed face. He hated to frighten her, but he really had no choice. "You just do your job and I'll do mine. Now, how about that coffee?" When he released her arm, she lifted her chin in a gesture of defiance, and a memory of that same bravado nine years ago flashed through his mind. Settling himself at one of the tables, he watched her stiff-backed figure as she marched toward the kitchen.

He hadn't expected to see her. Hadn't been sure she even still lived in the town. He certainly hadn't expected her to recognize him after all these years.

He smiled to himself. She sure had turned into a pretty little thing, not all gangly and coltish like the child he remembered. He figured she must be somewhere near nineteen, then wondered if

12

she'd married. The notion felt strange. Even with her growth from child to woman — all gentle curves and a tempting bosom — it was hard for him to think of her as more than a little girl. Her eyes were still that tawny golden color, only now they seemed bigger, and softer.

Morgan felt a wave of guilt. God, he hated to lie to her. He owed the girl his life! It didn't seem right to deceive her, no matter what the reason. But the less she knew, the better off they'd both be. He thought of the last time he'd seen her, almost nine years ago. The memory burned like a white-hot iron. Little Lainey, he had called her. That was how he'd thought of her that night in the mine. The night he would never forget.

Elaina set the mug down in front of Morgan a little too hard, and several drops of coffee ran over the edge. She didn't bother to wipe them up. To hell with him and his threats! No wonder Dolph Redmond had hired him. He was just the kind of man Redmond and Dawson admired, the kind who threw his weight around and talked tough.

She helped the kitchen boy finish cleaning up her mess, then retrieved the morning paper, the *Sentinel*, from a stack beside the door. Determined to take a break, she poured herself a mug of coffee, seated herself, opened the paper, and scanned the headlines. But try as she might, her mind refused to decipher the printed words. Though she pretended to read, her look strayed repeatedly to the imposing figure across the room.

He was dressed just as she'd expect: open-neck white shirt, soft black leather vest, snug-fitting breeches that disappeared into shiny black leather boots. A staghorn-handled revolver rested menacingly in the leather holster strapped to his muscular thigh.

When the bell above the door signaled the entrance of another customer, Morgan's dark, finely arched brows narrowed. His angular jaw clenched almost imperceptibly as the man who had entered scrutinized him from a table beside the door. Well-defined cheekbones caught shadows as Morgan sipped his coffee.

The gunman was definitely handsome, Elaina thought — in a ruthless sort of way — and, with that exception, he certainly looked a lot like Ren.

Reynold Lee Daniels. The best looking boy in Carbon County. Every girl in school had been in love with him, and every father had warned his daughter about Ren's less than honorable intentions. At ten years old, she had watched him from afar. She had not been immune to his charms, but she was younger than the rest, so he'd ignored her completely. Until the night she dug him out of the coal mine — the night she couldn't forget.

It had been cold that October evening in 1869. She had torn her dress climbing trees, so her mother had sent her to bed early. But voices arguing in the downstairs parlor roused her curiosity. She heard the angry words even through the walls of her room.

"It's time you shut your mouth, McAllister, and listened," a deep voice said. "You gave up your say in mine affairs when you borrowed that money from us. Now, Dolph and I say we blow the tunnel at dawn, and we don't give a damn whether you like it or not!"

Determined to see who it was, Elaina tiptoed to the top of the stairs. In the parlor below, Dolph Redmond and Henry Dawson, her father's partners, were arguing bitterly with her father.

"Please, Henry, listen to me," her father was saying. "Those two boys are still alive in there. You know it and so do I. We heard them tapping when we were in the crosscut. Several others did, too. My conscience will not allow me to condone murder — at any price!"

Everyone in Carbon County knew about the cave-in at the Blue Mountain Mine. Henry Dawson said a pocket of methane gas had exploded. That had been four days ago. Since then, fifty miners had been rescued, ten of those badly injured. Eight had come up dead, and two remained trapped in the mine — eight-year-old Tommy Daniels, Elaina's best friend, and his older brother, Ren, who'd just turned eighteen.

Elaina pressed her face between the carved mahogany balusters of the stairs, her single thick dark braid tickling her cheek as it swung across her shoulder.

"How can you justify killing two innocent boys just to save a few dollars?" her father said, his face pale. He squeezed his hands together and paced in front of the fireplace, leaving mud on the thick Persian carpet.

14

"It ain't a few dollars and you know it," Dawson said, chewing his stubby cigar. "It could take days, maybe even weeks, to git them kids outta there. They was workin' A level instead of E like the others, so they ain't down as deep, but they's farther in."

"What were they doing in there?" her father asked.

"They was crevicing," Dawson said.

She knew that meant wedging themselves into crawl spaces too risky to dynamite and too small for a grown man to fit into, digging the coal out by hand from the narrowest cracks. It was the meanest job in the mine.

"We needed somebody small, so we sent the young 'un. And that older boy's a troublemaker, so we made him go, too. We was hopin' to make him quit." Dawson's ruddy face had reddened even more. "Odds are they'd be dead afore we could git to 'em, anyway. The damn mine's near busted now. We can't afford to lose any more money." He slammed his hand down on the mantel, and Elaina jumped as if a gun had been fired.

"How do you intend to explain the boys' death to the others?" her father pressed.

"Most folks will assume they're dead by now, just like them others," Dawson answered. "Only Ned Marlow and Jack Dorsey heard the tapping. A little extra in their wages'll keep 'em quiet. As much whiskey as they down, nobody'd believe 'em anyway." With his short legs firmly planted, Dawson glared up at her father. "The miners need work too bad to give us much argument. 'Sides, those Daniels boys ain't got no kin left 'round here."

Dolph Redmond spoke up for the first time. "You should have stayed in New York, McAllister. We could have used that extra capital you might have raised. Instead, you came running back here at the first sign of trouble." He shifted his position on the velvet settee and uncrossed his thin legs.

"Personally," he continued, "it won't hurt my feelings one bit to see those two troublemakers disappear. That older boy spends half his shift trying to convince the other miners that conditions in the mine aren't safe anymore, and the young one goes along with him."

"Well, obviously they aren't safe!"

"That's no longer your affair," Redmond softly warned.

Her father ignored Redmond's warning. "If I remember correctly, the boys' father died in a similar accident four or five years ago over at the Middleton Mine when you two were running things there."

"Yeah, Ed Daniels was a troublemaker, too. Always fightin' for miners' rights — higher pay, shorter shifts, that kinda thing. See where it got him, don't ya?" Dawson removed the stubby cigar from his mouth and spat into the brass spittoon beneath the clock on the wall.

"How soon did you blast after that cave-in?"

Redmond smiled, his lips a thin red wound.

Dawson balled a fist but kept it near his side.

Grampa McAllister's cherrywood clock ticked heavily, the only sound in the room.

"Why didn't you just fire the man?" her father finally asked.

"You oughta know that by now. Them hard-rockers is a close-knit bunch. A firin' leaves hard feelin's. Better to make things tough enough so's the man'll quit. Ed Daniels weren't smart enough to know when to give up." Dawson moved closer, his barrel chest heaving.

"Gentlemen, please." Dolph Redmond stepped between the two men. "There's no need to stir up the past. These things happen. It's just part of doing business."

"Then it's settled," Dawson said. "Time's money and we've lost enough already. We put fire in the hole at first light. If the buggers git out afore then, so be it."

"I want no part of this." Her father sank down on the settee, his face hollow and pale. "You men are murdering those boys."

"Relax, McAllister. Nobody's murdering anybody, and I don't want to hear any more of that kind of talk, if you know what's good for you — and for your family." Redmond smoothed a wrinkle from his immaculate blue suit, then gestured at Dawson, and both men moved toward the door.

Elaina still remembered Dolph Redmond's last words: "All miners take risks. Besides, there's hours left till dawn."

She had returned to her room in tears and cried until she was numb. Hours later she'd thought of something that just might save her friends. . . .

A second jingle of the bell above the door drew Elaina's thoughts

16

from the past. As she rose and headed toward the first noon arrivals, she glanced again at the gunman, her sympathy for the miners' cause stronger than ever. Maybe it was time she did more than just sympathize. More than just wish conditions would improve.

Maybe it was high time indeed.

# Chapter 2

Over the top of his steaming mug of coffee, Morgan watched the men he had come to see walk into the room and head directly toward his table.

"Mr. Morgan?" Dolph Redmond extended a pale hand. With black hair slicked back from a too-high forehead and ears too close to the sides of his face, Dolph Redmond reminded Morgan of a rattlesnake — without the decency to sound a warning.

"I'm Morgan." He unwound his lanky frame and accepted the handshake while his cold gaze brusquely assessed the three men.

"I'm Adolph Redmond. My friends call me Dolph."

"Mr. Redmond," Morgan responded pointedly.

"This is my partner, Henry Dawson, and his son, Chuck."

Morgan shook hands with the other two men. Redmond was the tallest, the most expensively dressed, and, Morgan figured, probably the brains of the operation. Dawson looked a little like a former bare-knuckle fighter. He was short and stocky, and his bulbous, veined nose said he was a man who enjoyed his whiskey. The son had his father's powerful shoulders and arms, but stood eye to eye with Morgan, who was at least five inches taller than Henry.

"We're glad you accepted our invitation, Mr. Morgan," Redmond said.

"That remains to be seen, Mr. Redmond." Morgan lifted a corner of his mouth in a mirthless smile. He wasn't worried about the men remembering him. He'd been considered dead around these parts for nearly nine years. He'd bet he had a plot in the cemetery. After an accident, even if the bodies of the victims weren't recovered, the Blue Mountain Mining Company provided a headstone to mark the symbolic grave.

"Let's go into the office where we can speak a little more

privately," Redmond said, pointing toward the door with a delicate finger ending in a finely manicured nail. "Chuck, have Elaina bring in some coffee."

The men moved on into the hotel's inner office. Redmond seated himself behind a carved oak desk, and Morgan took a chair facing him, as did Dawson and his son. The room was furnished with few frills: the desk, the chairs, a brass desk lamp, and an ornate floor lamp with a red-fringed shade. Faded pictures of the hotel as it had once looked lined one wall, along with sketches of what appeared to be plans for expansion. They, too, were yellow and faded. Lowell McAllister, it seemed, had had grand plans for the Hotel Keyserville.

While he waited for the men to make themselves comfortable, Morgan again assessed the men. He remembered the younger Dawson from his youth. Two years Morgan's senior, Chuck Dawson had been self-centered, dishonest, and conniving. He'd been caught cheating the miners at cards more than once and been suspect in several cases of missing wages. When he'd dragged Betsy Pierson behind the schoolhouse, only his father's money had saved him from punishment.

From the looks of things, Chuck Dawson had changed little. He'd grown taller and filled out in the shoulders, but unlike the older Dawson whose ruddy complexion, round face, and balding head gave him an almost jolly appearance, the younger man remained thin-faced and sallow. With his patrician nose, sandy hair, and generous mouth, he would probably be considered handsome, in a slick sort of way, but personally Morgan thought the man had too much the look of a jackal.

"Well, Morgan," Redmond began. "Let's get down to business. We invited you here to help us with a little problem. As you probably noticed on your way into town, coal mining is our main source of income. Dawson and I own the hotel and the general store and a few other odd businesses, but the real money's in the mining. We've been through some tough years lately, but times are changing. The coal market's due for an upswing, and we intend to be ready."

A thousand questions raced through Morgan's mind, starting with what had happened to the McAllister family and their interest in the Blue Mountain Mine.

Ten years ago, he and his brother had gone to work at Blue

Mountain after the cave-in at the Middleton Mine and the death of their father. At that time Lowell McAllister had owned the mine as well as the hotel and general store. The following year McAllister had taken on Redmond and Dawson as partners, but he'd still controlled the majority interest in the mine as well as his other assets.

Morgan eyed the three men warily. "Go on" was all he said. He settled his long-legged frame a little deeper in the uncomfortable brown leather chair.

"Well, some of the miners have been stirring up trouble again. Happens every once in a while, but this time it appears it may be a little more than we can handle." Redmond offered a thin cigar. Morgan declined, and Redmond lit one for himself.

"Damn miners don't know when they got it good," the older Dawson put in. "They got it a damn sight easier'n they used to. Leastwise they got Sundays off. Some of their pappies used to work a seven-day week."

Morgan stiffened. Seven ten-hour days a week, unsafe working conditions at the Middleton Mine, and the resulting accident had killed his father. He had not forgotten. Things had been better at Blue Mountain — at least until McAllister took on Dawson and Redmond.

Morgan ran a hand through his dark, wavy hair and forced the hatred from his sky-blue eyes. "And just what would you gentlemen suggest I do about this little problem of yours?"

Henry Dawson broke in before Redmond could speak. "The miners is havin' a meetin' tomorrow mornin'. Walkin' off the job for it. Costin' us time and money. We ain't gonna stand for it. We want them stopped once and fer all. We want you to attend that little meetin' wearin' that big hog leg of yers. Just make sure they know anybody makin' trouble will be dealin' with you — and with that iron on yer hip."

"If that doesn't discourage them," Redmond added, "maybe we can arrange a little accident to demonstrate our sincerity."

Morgan clenched his teeth. He'd been right. Things in Keyserville hadn't changed a bit in the last nine years. If anything, they'd gotten worse. "How much is this show of sincerity worth to you boys?" he asked.

Chuck Dawson spoke up for the first time. "How much you

figure you're worth, gunman?" His dark eyes squinted as he leaned forward in his chair.

Morgan betrayed no emotion. "I'll expect double what you offered in the letter. Half now, half when the job is done. This little problem of yours seems a whole lot bigger all of a sudden."

As he pursed his lips, Dawson's sandy brows drew together; then he relaxed against his chair. "You'd better be worth it, gunman."

"Name's Morgan," he reminded the man coldly. "Dan or Mister."

The sound of the door opening interrupted the exchange. Elaina McAllister entered the room carrying a tray laden with mugs and a pot of coffee. The radiance on her face that Morgan had seen earlier had disappeared, replaced by what he read as a mask of careful control.

Chuck Dawson rose from his chair to help her set the tray down, his hand lingering in a possessive manner on her arm. Morgan couldn't be certain, but he thought he saw her flinch. She watched Dawson warily, with a look that sent a chill up Morgan's spine. Where was the spunky little girl who had braved the depths of an abandoned mine to save her friends? Where was the fiery woman he'd seen? Now her gentle amber eyes looked only wary and resigned, like those of a caged beast.

"Mr. Morgan," Chuck Dawson was saying, "may I present my fiancée, Miss McAllister."

Morgan was glad he was sitting down. His breath seemed so tightly lodged in his throat he had to force himself to release it. It was all he could do to keep his voice even as he steeled himself, came to his feet, and nodded a greeting. "Pleased to make your acquaintance, Miss McAllister."

Of all the unmitigated gall, Elaina thought, reading the tension in the hard planes of the gunman's face. He thinks I'm afraid of him! Just because he kills people for a living doesn't mean he can frighten everyone. For a moment she felt a surge of spirit and lifted her chin. Then she met the brooding dark eyes of her fiancé, and the same revulsion that had plagued her these past few years knotted her stomach into a hard tight ball. Feeling Chuck's fingers move absently up and down the length of her arm, she stiffened, then carefully numbed herself to the feeling, as she'd taught herself to do.

Glancing toward Morgan, she noticed the .45 slung at his hip and focused her mind on the introduction being made. "I'm sure the pleasure is all mine, Mr. Morgan," she replied sarcastically, her gaze frosty as she searched his light blue eyes. Then she felt Chuck Dawson's moist palm at her waist and suddenly wanted nothing more than to be out of the room.

"Thank you for the coffee, my dear," Dawson said dismissively. "I have a meeting at the mine this afternoon. Maybe I'll see you this evening."

Elaina nodded, glanced at Morgan, and fled the room.

Morgan sat back down. He hadn't missed the relief that swept over the girl as she'd closed the door behind her. He owed that girl. Owed her his life. He was going to find out what the hell was going on in Keyserville if it was the last thing he ever did.

Glad for the clanging pots, scraping silver, and pounding mallets of the hotel kitchen, Elaina picked up a serving spoon and stirred a pot of beef stew that was bubbling on a back burner of the huge black stove. As long as she was busy, she didn't have time to think, though it was hard not to dwell on her grim future as Mrs. Chuck Dawson.

"Laina honey, who is that man!" Ada Lowery pointed toward the inner office. Living, as she did, in a small suite of rooms off the kitchen, Ada missed little of what went on in the hotel.

"That's Black Dan himself," Elaina said, putting the lid back on the stew pot. Then, taking her place beside Ada, she picked up a knife and started peeling an onion.

"Lord A'mighty, he's a hard-lookin' sort. Tougher'n a boot, I'll wager. Kinda handsome, though, if he'd lose that scowl of his." Ada, too, picked up an onion and set to work.

The kitchen was warm and humid; a kettle of beef stock for gravy and soup boiled next to the stew. The windows were fogged with steam, and the dampness made tiny dark brown ringlets curl around Elaina's face. Absentmindedly she shoved them behind her ear.

"He looks a little like Ren Daniels," she told Ada.

"Who?" Ada's eyes were beginning to tear from the stinging onion juices.

"Oh, just a boy I used to know. I've mentioned him before. The one I had such a fancy for when I was a little girl. Surely you remember. I probably drove you crazy talking about him when I first moved in here. His younger brother, Tommy, was my best friend." She and Tommy had played together whenever she could escape her mother's endless round of socializing — teas, recitals, church functions — and her own numerous hours of lessons — piano, singing, ballet, French. It had been through one of the abandoned tunnels she and Tommy used to play in on the far side of Blue Mountain that she'd been able to find the boys that night in the mine.

She wondered for the thousandth time in the past nine years where the two boys were. What had become of Tommy? Had he grown up to be as handsome as his older brother? She'd met Ren only a few times, when he came to walk Tommy home from school. Ren had insisted Tommy go to class while he worked extra hours in the mine to support them. Ren took care of Tommy after their parents died, and Tommy adored him.

Elaina finished peeling the onion and picked up another. Her eyes, too, were beginning to tear. The women looked at each other and laughed good-naturedly.

"Good thing the men can't see us," Elaina joked. "They'd be sure we were crying."

Ada Lowery grew serious. "You sure you ain't gonna be cryin' up a storm if you go through with that weddin' Chuck Dawson has planned? He ain't gonna be put off much longer."

Elaina sighed. Ada was right. Chuck had been pushing for the wedding for over two years. Lately he'd become adamant. In three weeks their engagement would be official, and Chuck had already warned her not to plan on a long engagement.

"I don't have any choice," Elaina said defensively.

Ada shook her head. "Life's nothin' but choices, honey, and this is the most important one you'll ever make."

"We've been all through this, Ada. Henry Dawson's the last man on earth I'll be indebted to."

Ada harrumphed but said nothing. Elaina picked up another onion.

When her father died, he'd left behind dozens of staggering debts, most of them owed to Redmond and Dawson. The men had taken the McAllister mansion as partial payment, but Dawson had insisted Elaina and her mother remain in the lovely old Victorian house when by rights they should have sold it to pay off some of the debts. He'd take care of whatever they owed Dolph Redmond, he'd said.

Elaina could still hear her mother's deathbed words: "You've got to set things right, pay him back somehow, clear the family name." Elaina had heard the words so many times they still rang in her ears.

"Some debts can't be repaid," Ada interrupted, and Elaina wondered, not for the first time, if reading minds was one more of the buxom woman's many talents.

" 'Sides, the way old man Dawson takes care of you ain't nothin' special. You work for yer keep, same as me."

"It doesn't matter. I owe him and I intend to repay him, for Mama *and* for me."

Ada shook her head. "I just wish there was somethin' I could say to make you change yer mind."

"Nothing's going to change my mind, Ada. I won't be beholden to him. Besides, maybe somehow I can make things better at the mine." Secretly, she hoped that after she and Chuck were married, she'd be in a position to exert some influence over working conditions at the mine, make some improvements. It was a long shot, but it was a chance she was willing to take.

Ada just shook her head. "Yer blasted pride'll be yer downfall, honey."

Elaina ignored her, turning out the next onion with renewed vigor. She owed Henry Dawson, and though she felt no love for Chuck, she was going to repay her obligation to Henry the only way she could — by marrying his son, as she knew he wished. Elaina grabbed a dish cloth and dabbed at her eyes, suddenly glad for the onion tears that disguised a few of her own.

Dan Morgan unpacked the few articles of clothing he'd brought on his trip east, shrugged out of his shirt, and sat on the edge of the bed to pull off his boots.

Thoughts of the beautiful woman he'd seen today stirred images of the courageous little girl who'd saved his life nine years ago. She

24

was beautiful now, but no more beautiful than she had looked to him that day in the mine.

"You saved our lives, Lainey," he'd said to her. "We'll never forget you." Or the men who did this, he'd added to himself. His black hair was matted with dirt and coal dust, and all he could think of was making the mine owners pay.

"What will we do now?" Lainey had asked, brushing coal dust from her skirt as she got up from the ground.

"*We* aren't going to do anything. Tommy and I are leaving."

Tommy looked stunned.

"It's too dangerous for us to stay here now," Ren explained. "We know too much. If someone discovered the truth about what happened here today, it could raise questions about the accident at the Middleton Mine. Redmond and Dawson can't afford to let that happen. And that makes it too dangerous for Tommy and me to stay."

"Can't we just go to the sheriff?" Lainey asked.

"Who'd believe us? Besides, they'd just claim I was stirring up more trouble between the miners and the management. There might be another so-called accident."

"I guess you're right," she admitted, "but I still don't want you to go." She smiled sadly, then blushed beneath his close regard.

"You mustn't tell anyone you saved our lives, Lainey. Let them think we're dead." He was tired and dirty, wet, torn, and ragged — and he now knew for certain his father had been murdered.

For the first time Ren noticed the girl's bleeding fingers. "God, Lainey." He kissed her bloody hands as he knelt beside her, tipping her chin up with his hand. "You're the bravest little girl I've ever known. Maybe someday Tommy and I can make this up to you. I don't know how, but maybe someday." He kissed her dirt-smudged cheek and hugged her briefly. His brother did the same.

"Bye, Lainey," Tommy said as great tears rolled down his cheeks, leaving trails of white where the coal dust had washed away.

"I'll miss you," she had whispered. He could still remember her forlorn figure as she clutched her ragged, dirty skirt, picked up her lamp, and headed home.

Morgan smiled and dropped his other boot on the floor. Elaina was certainly not the ragamuffin he remembered, though her circumstances remained a mystery.

Not for long, he thought, vowing to begin looking for answers in the morning. Reaching for the black leather vest that hung at the head of the bed, Morgan removed a small address book, a newspaper clipping, and several business cards — the only papers that could identify him — from the inside pocket. Carefully, he slid them beneath the mattress. His encounter with Elaina had shown him the need for care, but Morgan wasn't worried. Being careful was part of his job.

The new day dawned clear, though a harsh spring wind bit with icy spines into anyone unfortunate enough to be out-of-doors.

On the street below her window, the breeze blew bits of paper and tugged at the skirts of the women who passed by, their heads together in quiet conversation. Everyone in Keyserville had heard about the miners' meeting at the town meeting hall. After her encounter with Morgan, Elaina had decided it was time she made her own feelings known. It wasn't like her to speak out, to voice her opinions, especially to a roomful of men, but that was exactly what she intended to do. She'd already cleared the time with Ada, who secretly sympathized with the miners.

Pulling her window closed against the chill that suddenly shook her slender frame, Elaina thought about the dark-haired stranger who looked so much like Ren. Black Dan had been the talk of the town when rumor leaked out that he'd been sent for. Morgan was a hard, cruel man, and she wondered how she could ever have mistaken him for the lighthearted, carefree Ren.

At least he forced me to take a stand, she thought as she battled a fresh jolt of nerves. Choosing a warm blue wool jersey dress with a ruffled front and simple gored skirt she hoped would help her make the right impression, Elaina closed the door to the old armoire. With trembling fingers, she pulled the dress over her head, adjusted the lacy cuffs and the modest neckline, then used her mother's silver-handled brush to arrange her hair, pulling it up on the sides and securing it with combs, but leaving it loose in back, hanging almost to her waist.

After grabbing a woolen shawl, she pinched her cheeks, said a short prayer the miners wouldn't notice how nervous she was, and headed down the stairs. She knew Redmond and Dawson would be furious, but there was always the slim hope she'd get by without them finding out she was going to the meeting. Whatever happened, she'd worry about the consequences tomorrow. Just this one time, in memory of her father, she had to let the men know how she felt.

# *Chapter 3*

Head held high, Elaina walked down the two flights of stairs, out through the double mahogany doors, and along Broad Street toward the meeting hall.

Though Keyserville was a small town, two-story brick buildings, false-fronted shops, and canopied mercantile establishments lined the street. She could see J. P. Sidwell's Livery just up ahead, and noticed several miners' wives whispering in hushed tones in front of Walzheimer's General Store.

By the time Elaina reached the town hall, the meeting had been under way for more than an hour. She figured her timing should be just about right. With the wind whipping her skirts, she paused for a moment at the top of the stone steps to bolster her courage; then she straightened her shoulders, tossed back her head, and opened the door.

Josh Colson, who headed the grievance committee, stood at the lectern. Every seat in the hall was filled, and miners stood along both walls.

"We've got to stand together!" Josh was saying. He banged the lectern with his fist, and a murmur of agreement filled the hall. As the door creaked shut behind Elaina, he glanced up, his pause drawing the miners' attention. The room calmed to a quiet hush as the men realized a woman had entered the room.

"What's she doin' here?" Jacob Vorhees wanted to know.

"Yeah," another took up the cry, "who invited her?"

Elaina's heart pounded. This was going to be even harder than she'd imagined.

"She's Chuck Dawson's girl. Git her outta here!" a burly, bearded miner demanded.

"She's probably a company spy!" one of the younger men chimed in.

28

Elaina gripped the folds of her jersey dress, feeling close to tears. Why had she come? They weren't going to listen to anything she had to say. All she was doing was making a fool of herself. She bit her lip and turned to leave but stopped when she heard Josh Colson's voice above the noise.

"Wait a minute, boys, wait a minute. I know Miss McAllister, and so do a lot of you. She wouldn't have come here without a darned good reason." The men quieted a little. "I vote we hear what she has to say."

"He's right," Mike O'Shannessy and some of the others agreed. The room began to still as the men settled back down.

"You got somethin' to say, Miss McAllister?" Josh asked.

Elaina swallowed hard. Taking a deep breath, she marched up the aisle to the front of the room. When she reached the lectern, Josh smiled at her reassuringly. With her heart pounding so hard it thumped against her ribs, she turned to face the men. It was one of the toughest things she'd ever had to do. Her palms were damp, her knees shaking, and the remaining color had drained from her cheeks.

"I didn't mean to cause any trouble," she said hesitantly. "I just thought . . . I mean . . . some of you knew my father." When she heard the men's muttered acknowledgment, a bit of her courage returned. "If you worked for him before he took on Redmond and Dawson as partners, then you know working conditions weren't always as bad as they are now. My father was concerned for the miners' safety. He knew long hours only increased the risk of accidents. He kept the equipment well maintained; he didn't believe in taking shortcuts that might cost lives." Before she could continue, a flash of light at the back of the hall signaled the opening door. The tall man who entered settled his broad-brimmed black hat a little lower across his brow. His pale blue eyes held hers, and for a moment she couldn't remember what she wanted to say.

Why had he come? she wondered. Did he intend to stop the meeting? She forced her mind back to the words she wanted to say, and her heart resumed its uneven beat. The rumble in the crowd ceased as she picked up her train of thought.

"I came here today because I wanted you to know that I think what you're trying to do, what you're trying to achieve, is right. You deserve a day's pay for a day's work. You have the right —

no the obligation — to insist on safe working conditions." The men shouted their approval. Elaina stiffened her spine and went on, determined just this once to speak her mind. "My father believed that — and so do I!"

She glanced toward the back of the room and saw the tall man lean nonchalantly against the wall, his big .45 resting ominously on his hip. His cool look infuriated her. How dare he come here and try to intimidate these men!

Lifting her chin, she leaned over the lectern, searching each man's eyes. "And if you have to fight for what you know is right, then so be it!"

Cheers and whistles of approval thundered through the hall. Josh Colson grinned at her and squeezed her arm. Gathering her skirts, she headed back up the aisle to the entrance, hearing the miners' applause and feeling shaky all over. Dan Morgan, his eyes unreadable, flashed her a mocking smile and touched the brim of his hat in a tiny salute as she passed through the door.

She closed it firmly behind her, then collapsed against the heavy planking. She'd finally done it! She'd taken a stand at last. She knew her father would have been proud. Then her mind echoed the last words she'd spoken: "If you have to fight . . . so be it!" and her feelings of accomplishment fled with the icy breeze.

God, what had she done? She'd only meant to give them a little moral support, tell them how her father would have felt. She certainly hadn't meant to encourage violence. It went against everything she believed in.

Pulling her cloak around her, Elaina headed into the wind, thinking again of her words and of the terrible conditions at Blue Mountain. In the anthracite region a man a day lost his life to the mines. Maybe violence *was* the only way to change things.

With shoulders not nearly so straight, she walked back to the hotel, allowing herself for the first time to think what Henry Dawson and, more important, Chuck Dawson would do when they found out. The thought sent shivers down her spine.

Chuck was a domineering bully, even more unreasonable than his father. The older Dawson, she'd learned, acted only out of self-interest, a desire to retain the wealth and power he'd accumulated over the years. Henry had been kind to her, she grudgingly admitted. He said she was like the little girl he'd always wanted and never had.

The younger Dawson enjoyed hurting others. His cruelty was what disturbed her most about becoming his wife. She'd seen the way he treated the miners, even the young boys who worked at the mine. She remembered the time one of the little nippers, boys who worked the doors that controlled the air flow into the shafts, had fallen asleep at his post. Chuck had taken the seven-year-old deep into the mind, removed the boy's lamp, then left the child alone in the darkness all day and late into the evening. When the child had finally been brought to the surface, he was so frightened he could barely speak.

Remembering the incident, Elaina shuddered and hoped she could make Chuck change his ways.

Dan Morgan stayed at the hall only long enough to make his presence known and make clear the threat it implied. He had a meeting scheduled with Dolph Redmond and the two Dawson men. They were going out to the mine. He hated the role he was playing, but he knew it was the only way he could discover what was going on in Keyserville.

Outside the hall, he untied the black gelding he had hired, mounted, and headed toward the hotel. He smiled as he thought of the woman at the hall. She was Dawson's fiancée, yet she'd taken a stand against him. Morgan was only a little surprised; even as a child, she'd fought for the underdog. And he'd learned years ago that it was the quiet ones a man had to watch. Their fire was all underneath, where it counted. Elaina had come through for the men today, just as she had for him nine years ago.

Morgan nudged his horse into a walk, ignoring the curious glances of the people on the street while his thoughts remained on Elaina. What a beautiful woman she'd become — slim straight nose, ruby lips a man could damn near taste, petal-smooth skin. She was just a little taller than most of the women he knew, but not too tall. And you couldn't miss that figure. High, round breasts, tiny waist — he could easily imagine her long, slim legs and gently curving hips. And that hair. Long and thick, the color of sable. Red-brown highlights glinted every time she moved. Damn good thing he was almost a married man. The last thing he wanted was to seduce the woman who had saved his life!

"How'd your little show go this morning, Morgan?" Chuck Dawson was waiting on the front porch of the hotel as Morgan rode up.

"Just the way you planned," Morgan answered, "but those boys don't look as if they'll be easily dissuaded." Dawson clenched his fist, and Morgan felt a chill as he thought of the man's hands on Elaina's high, full breasts.

"Then we'll just have to use a little more persuasion." Dawson mounted his horse. "We're meeting my father and Dolph Redmond out at the mine."

Morgan nodded, and the two men headed out of town just as the meeting hall began to empty. The surly looks on the miners' faces clearly spoke of the outcome of the meeting.

"You better watch your back, gunman!" a voice in the milling crowd threatened as Morgan rode past.

"Git outta town and leave decent folks alone!" another voice called out.

Morgan wished there were some other way to handle the situation. He hated to go against the very men he wanted to help. If there were any other way . . . but there wasn't. In the long run, this would be best for all concerned.

Riding in silence, they continued down the street and into the countryside, while familiar landmarks — a shabby old miner's shack, a covered bridge he used to play beneath — brought memories of his early years. But the memory he couldn't forget was the night before he left Keyserville: October 1, 1869.

He and Tommy had been trapped in the darkness for more than four days. The candle atop Ren's cap had gone out in the blast, and Tommy's had lasted through only the first eight hours. After that they'd existed in total darkness. Ren's overalls and shirt were soaked clear through from the water dripping off the ceilings; his skin had become soft and loose, chafing constantly against the rough material of his clothes; and the dampness from the earth beneath him seeped into every bone in his body. He was stiff and sore, and the bruises he'd received from falling timbers throbbed unbearably.

"Ren? Do you think we're going to die?" Tommy's small voice

sliced through the blackness like a knife.

"Don't be foolish," Ren answered, wanting desperately to keep up his younger brother's spirits. "Just keep tapping. I'll start again when you get tired."

"I'm so cold . . . and I'm scared." Tommy groped in the darkness until he finally found Ren's hand.

Ren held it tightly. "They'll find us soon, Tommy. I'm sure of it. You just have to be brave a little longer."

"I'll be brave, Ren, I promise."

The despair in his brother's voice tore at Ren's heart. "I know how hard this is, Tommy — Papa would have been proud of you — but we can't give up."

"I won't give up, Ren."

"Good boy. Now just keep tap— What was that?" Ren stiffened, straining to hear the sound.

"What?" Tommy listened, too.

*Tap, tap, tap.*

"That!" Ren felt his way blindly across the narrow chamber to the opposite wall of the cavern.

*Tap, tap, tap.*

"There it is again. And it's close!" Ren remembered how his heart had leapt. "Tap back a few times," he'd instructed. "Then help me dig."

Tommy had tapped a rapid staccato. Even in the dark, Ren had felt his brother's smile.

As the men rounded a bend in the road, Blue Mountain came into view, a quick reminder that Ren was now Dan Morgan. Redmond and the elder Dawson waited near the front gate.

The mine looked much the same as he remembered: a huge mountain of earth, scarred and debauched. Deep holes penetrated the sides of the mountain as if it had been endlessly violated, and rusting mine cars stood forlornly beside the main entrance. Narrow iron tracks ran into the hillside awaiting the heavy, rumbling burden of the loaded coal cars.

It all seemed just as forbidding as he remembered, only now, as they moved inside the main shaft, he could see that the timbers needed replacing and the equipment clearly showed a lack of main-

33

tenance. Morgan's mind again filled with grisly images of the past — days buried in the dank, cold depths of the mine, men dead and dying, screaming in agony beneath the fallen timbers. He had trouble concentrating on the conversation.

"Well, whaddaya think of 'er?" Henry Dawson wanted to know.

"Sorry, 'fraid I don't know much about mining," Morgan lied. "Looks dark and cold to me."

Dawson laughed. "That's what all you Johnny-come-latelies say. Takes a real muckman to work in them tunnels!"

Morgan thought how right the man was. He'd given up mining nine years ago, except for some financial investments, and never regretted it once.

As they moved a little deeper into the tunnel, Morgan could smell the dank air moving out of the shaft. All was quiet, the miners still in town. Only a few mules brayed from their dark stable beneath the earth. Mules were a necessary part of the anthracite mining industry. They pulled the heavy coal cars up and down the tunnels, moving the coal to the surface. Some of the animals were never allowed to see the sunlight. It interfered with their ability to work in the suffocating depths.

Morgan had heard of mules who went crazy when they saw the light after being kept for years in the tunnels. They wouldn't return to the mine no matter how much they were beaten. Morgan understood their feelings. Sometimes mules were smarter than men.

The four men left the mine and headed for the company's headquarters building to continue their discussion. Redmond wanted to hear the details of the morning's events. Morgan filled him in, careful to omit any mention of Elaina's passionate speech. As Morgan took in Chuck Dawson's sallow complexion and dark brooding eyes, he wondered what the man would do to Elaina when he found out.

The meeting continued for more than an hour, each man offering grisly suggestions as to how Morgan should handle the problem of the miners. A walkout would be far too costly. Losing one day was more than they'd planned on. And giving in to the miners' demands was out of the question. It was far cheaper to pay Morgan's fee and keep things the way they were. Morgan assured them he'd take each idea into consideration. Secretly, with every new and deadly sug-

34

gestion, he damned the three to hell.

When the meeting ended, all four men mounted their horses and headed back into town. It wasn't far, and the countryside was pleasant: green forested hills and deep ravines interrupted by gently tumbling streams. He recalled scenes from his childhood, drawing his attention astray. Wasn't it just around that bend he'd made love to Prudence Mayfield, the mayor's daughter? Memories of ripe ivory breasts and a slightly too-wide bottom drew the pull of a smile.

As he returned his attention to the present, he glanced ahead and caught a flash of sunlight on metal and a slight movement in a copse of trees. His senses alerted, he reined up his horse just as a series of shots rang out and a fiery, burning sensation tore through his chest, the impact of the bullet nearly knocking him from the saddle. At the instant the black horse leapt toward cover, a second bullet slammed into his thigh.

Though he fought to stay in the saddle, great waves of pain swept over him, numbing him with the force of a blow. Gripping the horn so hard his fingers ached, Morgan battled the beckoning darkness. Then he pitched forward, plunging into the rocks at the side of the road.

"Damn!" Chuck Dawson dismounted hurriedly and crouched among the boulders, Redmond and Henry Dawson close behind. The shooting had ceased after the first few shots, and they saw no sign of the man who'd been hiding among the trees, but, to be certain of their safety, they waited a few minutes longer before moving into the open.

"He's long gone by now," Henry Dawson said. The men rose cautiously, checked again for any sign of their attacker, then approached Dan Morgan's crumpled form.

"Anybody get a look at him?" Redmond asked.

"Too damn busy tryin' to save my own hide." Henry Dawson spoke the thoughts of all three.

"He still alive?" Chuck pointed to Morgan, and the men knelt beside the injured man. Redmond felt Morgan's pulse.

"He's alive. At least for now. We'd better get him to the hotel and fetch Doc Willowford."

Saddle leather creaked, but the big black gelding stood stock-still as the men threw Morgan's unconscious body across the horse. All

35

three mounted and rode at a fast pace toward town, leading the big black behind them. Chuck went to fetch the doctor, and the two older men carried Morgan into the hotel.

Elaina opened the dining room door just as Redmond and Dawson entered the lobby. She paled at the sight of the blood-covered stranger who, only hours before, had mocked her at the hall.

"He's been shot," Dolph Redmond informed her with an almost casual air.

His even tone made her bristle. Did the man have ice water for blood? Closing the door behind her, she walked along beside the wounded man.

In his unconscious state, Morgan's hard features had softened. His dark hair fell across his brow, and Elaina thought how much like Ren he looked. How handsome and vulnerable. Suddenly Elaina felt a terrible responsibility for the tragedy. Had she been the cause of the gunman's injuries? She'd been afraid her speech would incite the miners to violence. Could the man's condition be partly her fault?

Chuck Dawson pushed through the front doors. "Doc Willowford's out delivering a baby."

"Put him in the room next to mine," Elaina said. Though the third floor had never been finished, there was one empty room adjacent to hers and another down the hall.

Chuck looked skeptical.

"Do as she says," Redmond ordered. "Maybe she can keep him alive and we'll get some use out of him yet. He ought to be good and mad if he lives through this." Both Dawsons smiled.

"Sometimes yer a whole lot smarter'n you look, Dolph," Henry said.

Chuck's expression mirrored wholehearted agreement.

Elaina passed the men on the stairs and dashed ahead to ready the room, then hurried to her own room for a pitcher of water and the other items she needed. When she returned, she found the stranger on the bed and the elder Dawson removing the man's boots.

"Why don't you leave him to me?" she said. "If I need your help, I'll come down and get you." Though she could have used their assistance, just being in the same room with the three men made her nervous.

36

Redmond nodded his agreement and motioned the others to follow.

"You'd better tell Ada to find someone else to work the dining room for a while, if you want this man to live," she warned.

"I'll take care of it," Henry Dawson assured her. "You just git that gunman back on his feet."

The men left quietly, and Elaina relaxed a little. Glancing down at the deathly pallor of the man lying on the bed, she began to assess his condition. She'd always been a fair hand at doctoring. It was just something she had a knack for. Even Ada couldn't heal a sick boarder the way Elaina could. It had been a passion of her grandmother's. Elaina had followed the skinny little woman around whenever she had the chance, so Grandma McAllister had left her healing book to Elaina when she died. Over the years Elaina had gotten better and better at it, considering she'd had no formal training. People had confidence in her. Next to Doc Willowford, she was the best the small town had to offer.

Elaina washed her hands in the basin on the bureau, then unbuttoned and opened the man's blood-soaked shirt. Taking a hard look at the wound, she determined the bullet had gone into the area just below the shoulder. It was difficult to tell whether or not it had punctured a lung, but his blood didn't look frothy. Still, with the shallow way he was breathing, she couldn't be sure.

Elaina took her scissors to the gunman's bloody shirt and eventually was able to get it off. Then she realized the man had a leg injury as well. No wonder he looked so pale. He must have lost a lot of blood.

Elaina walked into the hall. At one end a huge closet lined with shelves was filled with bedding, towels, and clean sheets. It was dark inside, so she carefully propped open the door. Just the thought of being in the room with the door closed and no light prickled her with fear. Quickly she removed a sheet and hurried back to the injured man, shredding the sheet into bandages along the way.

The chest wound was going to take some time, so she decided to deal with the leg injury first. Stuffing some of the clean sheeting into the shoulder to stem the bleeding as best she could, she moved on to the leg wound.

For an instant she hesitated, her hand poised above the buttons

37

of the gunman's snug black breeches. She'd cared for injured men before. Why did removing this man's clothes seem different? Because he looks like Ren, her mind said. Because you've dreamed of the body beneath Ren's clothes. Forcing the ridiculous notion aside, she worked the buttons, cut away some of the blood-soaked material, then worked the breeches down over the gunman's narrow hips and muscular thighs. As she removed his bloody woolen underwear, she said a prayer of thanks the man was unconscious.

Though she hated to admit it, Elaina had never seen a finer specimen than the one on the bed. Lying naked, his body looked lean and hard, his waist narrow, his hips taut. She tried not to notice the dark hair curling across the width of his chest, forming a thin line down his flat stomach to protectively surround his male organs, but she'd seen only one other man completely naked, an injured miner from Middleton, and the sight of this man was more than intriguing.

*Intriguing!* What in God's name was the matter with her? The man was near dead and here she was staring at his physique! Wiping away more blood, she probed the leg wound and discovered the bullet had exited through the back of the thigh. The leg wound should be simple, as long as it didn't fester — and with her grandmother's herb dressing she was certain it wouldn't.

After thoroughly cleansing the bullet hole, she fished through her small leather medicine bag and found some powdered dog daisy, useful for control of the bleeding. She sprinkled some in, along with some alder bark to keep the inflammation down, placed a compress on the wound, and quickly swathed the leg in bandages.

"Anything I can do, Laina honey?" Ada Lowery stuck her head in just as Elaina was pulling the bloody wrappings from the wound in the man's wide chest.

"Thanks, Ada. It looks like this could get a bit rough."

"You know I never been much good at doctorin', but I'll do whatever you say." She moved to the man's bedside. "Lord A'mighty! Ain't he a dandy. Ain't seen a man built like that 'round these parts in a coon's age."

Elaina flushed. At least she felt a little more justified in her earlier reactions. "Ada, you're terrible," she chided without looking up from her task.

"Kinda reminds me of my dead husband Jake — in his prime, I mean. 'Course Jake was about three inches shorter'n this one." Ada grinned broadly. "Not where it counted, mind you."

Elaina laughed aloud, glad for a break from the tension. "Here." Grabbing the older woman's hand, she pulled her into position. "I'm going to probe for the bullet. I don't think he'll wake up, but you'd better get ready to hold him down just in case."

Ada nodded.

Elaina washed her hands a second time and carefully set out the herbs she would need. Though the room was cool, perspiration beaded her forehead.

With infinite patience, Elaina probed the wound. Ada pressed her weight on the man's upper body but he didn't stir. The bullet was deeply embedded just below the collarbone, but it was easy to locate, and no other damage had been done. As she pulled the offending lead from the wound and the man's breathing continued evenly, Elaina breathed a sigh of relief. She finished her cleaning, applied the herbs, and bound the wound tightly, smiling with satisfaction at her handiwork. If all went well, the man would live.

Then Dolph Redmond's words crowded her mind: "He ought to be good and mad if he lives through this." She wondered for the miners' sake if she had done the right thing.

# Chapter 4

Six hours later Dan Morgan opened his eyes and squinted through a haze of pain. He tried to lift himself up off the bed, but a wave of dizziness forced him back into unconsciousness. Clouded images of a woman with red-brown hair leaning over him occasionally pierced the haze.

Morgan slept fitfully, waking sometime later when he thought he saw a man in a dark gray suit beside his bed. Again he drifted into unconsciousness.

It was the gentle warmth of the sun's rays against the mat of crisp hair on his chest that finally awoke him late the following morning. Slowly opening his eyes, he allowed them to adjust to the sunlight that filtered into the room. As he heard the sound of footsteps near his bed, he blinked several times, trying to purge the fuzzy images. Then the rounded swell of two full breasts peeking above a dainty scooped neckline came into view as a dark-haired girl leaned over him. For a moment he thought he might be dreaming. Then, for the first time in two days, he lifted a corner of his mouth in a half-hearted smile. Raising a shaky hand, he gently cupped a ripe, full breast.

A shriek of outrage let him know for certain he was awake. He chuckled softly as his hand fell harmlessly back to his side.

"Well, Mr. Morgan, I see you're going to live," came the caustic retort of the woman with the shining hair.

He let the words sink in. Morgan. She'd called him Morgan. The name held no meaning for him, no sense of recognition. He tried to remember, but no thoughts came to mind. Nothing.

"Morgan," he repeated, saying the name aloud, though his voice sounded thick and fuzzy. "You called me Morgan." Still nothing. He no longer smiled. Instead, his eyes darted around the room, noting

40

the peeling paper on the walls and the stains on the ceiling. A plain wooden bureau with an oval minor above was cluttered with towels and bandages. Otherwise the room was empty and spotlessly clean.

"Well, that's your name, isn't it?" the woman retorted, still smarting from his rude behavior.

He lay quiet for a moment. "I don't know . . . I can't seem to remember. Where am I?"

The woman's anger faded. She stepped closer to his bedside. "You're in the Hotel Keyserville," she told him, placing a gentle hand on his forehead. "You don't have any sign of fever. Are you sure you don't remember?"

He struggled, making every effort to form some thought about the past. Licking his dry lips, he sighed and fell back against the pillow, a knot of despair tightening his stomach. "Not a thing."

"Doc Willowford was here late yesterday evening. He said you took a nasty hit on the head when you fell off your horse. I guess it was worse than he thought. I'll have him come up and take another look at you."

"My name's Morgan, you say?"

"Yes, Dan Morgan. You're in Keyserville, Pennsylvania. You were shot yesterday morning. Dolph Redmond and Henry Dawson brought you in. I'm Elaina McAllister." Elaina smiled ironically at the sudden twist of fate. She'd worried about the gunman's anger at the miners for the shooting. Now Black Dan couldn't remember enough about what had happened to be mad. At least the men would get a slight reprieve from whatever punishment Morgan intended to mete out.

"How are you feeling?"

"Pretty rocky. You been taking care of me?"

"I was the only one available."

"Thanks."

"You'd better get some rest. Don't try to do too much too soon." She smiled down at him and felt a small tug at her heart. How could such a hard man look so helpless? She shook her head at the notion. There was nothing helpless about Dan Morgan, or at least there wouldn't be as soon as he got back on his feet.

Elaina was checking the bandages on Morgan's chest when the door to the room flew wide. She felt the usual chill as Chuck Dawson entered, his eyes narrowed and hot, his face drawn and red. Instead of his customary stiff greeting, he just clenched his teeth and stared at her.

The gunman eyed the two of them, but said nothing. She knew he had little strength and the less he exerted himself, the better off he'd be. Her gaze returned to her intended.

"Hello, Chuck," she said, trying to keep her voice even. She had never seen quite that look in his dark eyes before. With cold certainty, she realized he'd heard about her speech at the meeting hall, and a trickle of icy dread snaked down her spine.

"Is something wrong, Chuck?" she asked, trying to sound nonchalant.

"You know damned well there's something wrong!" He moved toward her ominously. "You went to that damned miners' meeting yesterday, didn't you?"

She didn't answer.

"You told those miners you agreed with them." His eyes looked like angry black pits. "After all my father and I have done for you, you told them they were right and we were wrong!" His voice sounded shrill. His fists clenched and unclenched with the effort to control his temper.

Elaina flinched a little with every word.

"I will not have it, Elaina. You're going to be my wife. I won't have you making a fool of me in front of the whole damned town!" Taking another step forward, his face a mask of rage, he slapped her hard across the cheek with the palm of his hand.

Elaina clutched the corner of the bureau to steady herself, feeling a sudden rush of tears and the salty taste of blood. She swallowed hard and looked away, wiping at the blood in the corner of her mouth. What had she expected? She'd done exactly as he said. What she didn't expect was to see Dan Morgan's attempt to raise himself up off his sickbed.

"Leave the girl alone," he warned, trying to struggle to his feet. "Don't touch her again!" He swayed with each movement, his face drawn and pale, but his eyes were hot.

Elaina rushed to the injured man's side. "Please, Mr. Morgan, it's all right. You'll open your wounds again." She forced the gunman to lie back down. "Besides, I . . . I probably deserved it."

Tawny eyes gazed into sky-blue as she silently thanked him for trying to help.

Morgan, if that was his name, was trying desperately to understand his actions. Feeling a fierce urge to protect the girl, he'd been unable to stop himself. If he could have risen, he'd have beaten the man senseless for hurting her, yet he didn't even recall who she was. The effort hurt him a great deal, so he closed his eyes and allowed himself to sink back onto the thin mattress.

He was so tired he found it hard to concentrate, but brief snatches of conversation led him to believe the woman had been at least partly responsible for his injuries. Why, then, did he feel such a powerful need to protect her? She acted as if they'd known each other only briefly, probably no more than a day or two. Why should he feel such concern? Why should he risk his life for her? Still a little unnerved, he shrugged the feeling off.

He liked her looks, that much was certain. She was tall, but not too tall, and gracefully built, yet with a full bosom and rounded hips. In that moment he decided that if the girl was responsible for his injuries — and he certainly intended to find out — he'd be happy to pay her back the best way he knew how, by making sure she ended up flat on her back servicing his needs. The thought both amused and disturbed him. He felt the quick tug of a smile. The challenge should make for an interesting recuperation.

With thoughts of the pleasures to come, and niggling glimpses of what might have been his past, he drifted into a fitful sleep.

Before leaving the room, Chuck Dawson continued his tirade, laying the blame for Morgan's injuries squarely on Elaina's shoulders, and Elaina felt he was probably right. It made her all the more determined to ensure the gunman's recovery. She paid little attention to Dawson's abuse, feeling it was a small price to pay for the privilege of voicing the feelings and opinions she'd hidden all these years. Putting the ugly scene behind her, she rechecked her patient and, as soon as Chuck was gone, left to fetch Doc Willowford.

Morgan was awake when she and the doctor returned, and the doctor made a second careful examination of the head injury.

"Looks like you got yourself a pretty bad concussion, mister. That knot on the back of your head's as big as a hen's egg." He peered through a pair of spectacles suspended from a long gold chain. "Can't remember a thing, you say?"

"Not a thing, Doc. Had a few interesting images in my sleep that seem to fit the day I was shot, but nothing more."

"A little loss of memory's not unusual under the circumstances," the doctor said. "Happens sometimes with a blow to the head. Doesn't look bad enough to be permanent." He rubbed his pudgy chin. " 'Course, I could be wrong, but I don't think so."

The doctor pulled his stethoscope from around his short neck and stuffed it into his medical bag. "Laina, you got any information on this man's background? Anything at all that might jog his memory?"

"I don't, but I know Chuck does, He and Dolph got a lot of newspaper articles together before they decided to hire him. I read a few of them. I'm certain they're still around somewhere. I'll get them together for him."

"That's fine. That should be a big help." He turned to the man on the bed. "You just rest quietly. Elaina's near a doctor herself. Read those articles and see if they don't jog your mind some. If that doesn't work, time will probably take care of things."

"How long a time, Doc?" Morgan's concern clouded his light blue eyes.

"Anywhere from a day to a few weeks. Sometimes folks never remember, but as I said, I don't think that'll be the case with you." He closed his black medical bag and let the spectacles fall back to their place on the end of the chain. "You just get some rest."

Elaina spent the next few hours scouring up any information she could locate on the gunman, Dan Morgan. Chuck had a file on him, and the local newspaper had carried several stories of his escapades. Elaina read them all carefully. Some of the stories made the man sound like a sort of western Robin Hood; others made him out to be just a step lower than a cold-blooded killer. Elaina didn't know which to believe, but she hoped for the miners' sake the former was true.

When she took the newspaper articles in to Morgan, he perused them carefully, drinking in every word. Elaina got the distinct impression that Morgan, after reading the articles, also felt ambiva-

44

lent about his true nature. She left him alone with the papers for several hours, then returned to check on him.

"Well, Mr. Morgan, what do you think of yourself? Do you recall any of those events?" She watched uncertainty creep across the hard planes of his face.

"No, Miss McAllister, I don't." He smiled at her ruefully. "You apparently know me better than I know myself right now. What do you think?"

Elaina pulled a chair up next to the bed, pondering the problem. "You speak well, so you must have some education. I know you threatened the miners at the town meeting hall, but I also know you tried to help me when Chuck . . ." She glanced away, no longer willing to look at him. A sense of foreboding filled her as she remembered the anger in Chuck Dawson's brooding eyes.

"Yes," he agreed, "I tried to help. Didn't do you a whole lot of good, as I recall." A muscle bunched in his jaw while his eyes said he well remembered Chuck Dawson's actions and didn't take kindly to a man hitting a woman.

He smiled again, this time wryly. "I guess if I'm a gunman, I'm a chivalrous one."

Elaina smiled back. When he smiled like that he reminded her so much of Ren. It bothered her somehow. It was hard to keep a clear head with such a disturbing man around, especially one who dredged up all her girlhood fantasies. Every time she looked at him, she found herself fascinated by the dark hair curling across his chest, the way his muscles rippled when he moved. When she reached out to pull up the sheet in an effort to stop her disturbing thoughts, her hand touched his flesh and a surge of heat spread through her.

She jerked her hand away as if she'd been scalded, then, feeling slightly foolish, noticed his grin.

"What's the matter, Miss McAllister? You think those articles may be right? Maybe I'm some kind of killer, and you're all alone up here with me."

Somehow the way he kept trying to convince her — as well as himself — made her begin to believe the Robin Hood stories. "Don't forget, Mr. Morgan, you're an injured man. I don't think you'd be a match for me right now."

He reached out and caught her hand, bringing it gently to his lips. "Don't be too sure."

Elaina snatched her hand away and turned to leave the room, but not before tiny goose bumps raced up her arm. Damn him! Damn him to hell! Why did he have to look so much like Ren?

The next four days passed uneventfully. Morgan improved each day and was now able to move about his room and down the hall. He had almost memorized the newspaper articles, and he had to admit some of the stories were beginning to bring back sharp impressions of the past.

He'd gone over every article of his clothing, his weapons. He found plenty of money in his wallet, more than enough to get him through the next few months if necessary, and an envelope stuffed with bills, which he assumed was Redmond and Dawson's down payment on his services. The two men assured him his room and board were being taken care of, so he had no worries there.

His main task, as he saw it, was to heal himself — and maybe even the score with the sable-haired woman. Both Dolph Redmond and Henry Dawson had related the story of the shooting and the events leading up to it. Morgan was convinced the woman's interference had been at least partly to blame, and that suited him just fine. He found himself more and more attracted to her; any excuse he could find to justify seducing her was a welcome one. He wondered if his sexual appetites had always run this high, then chuckled to himself. There were some things about a man even his loss of memory couldn't alter. When it came to women, he was obviously one healthy man.

"Mr. Morgan?" Elaina's melodic voice interrupted his reverie. "Are you awake?"

Grinning up at her, he noted the high curves of her breasts beneath her light green dress. "You need me to defend your honor again?" he teased.

"No, I just figured it was about time you got out of this room and breathed a little fresh air. I'm headed over to the Colsons'. It's out near the patch town, an hour's ride from here. If you feel up to it, the buggy's hitched up out front."

He saw the way her golden eyes watched him a bit suspiciously.

46

"Sure you can trust me out there alone?"

She lifted her chin. "I told you, until your shoulder's healed you're no match for me — and you'd do well to remember that."

Morgan chuckled softly. He liked her spirit. He hoped she'd be that spirited when he had her on her back. His shoulder and leg were healing rapidly and the idea of bedding her was fast becoming an obsession. He knew she was spoken for by Chuck Dawson, but she obviously felt nothing for the sallow-faced man. Morgan felt he owed Dawson nothing, and liked him even less, and he wanted the girl more every day. He was Dan Morgan, a gunman, a man who often took risks, and bedding this woman was a risk well worth taking.

"It would be my pleasure to accompany you on your journey, Miss McAllister," he said with a bit of mockery and watched her bristle. Then he groaned a little as he sat up, and she took pity on him.

"Can you dress yourself? Or do you need me to . . ." She blushed crimson, though he knew she tried not to, and glanced away.

Morgan seized the opportunity for a little close contact. "I'll do my best, but I may need some help."

The girl turned her back as he slipped into his breeches, stumbling on purpose just as he pulled them up over his hips.

She gasped and rushed to his side. "Here, let me help you. You've got to be careful of your stitches."

Draping an arm around her neck, he fastened his breeches with one hand. She helped him struggle into his shirt, brushing a soft breast against his palm as she did so. The contact was jolting. Morgan felt beads of perspiration pop out on his forehead and a sudden stiffening in his breeches.

He smiled inwardly as the girl glanced down and realized what was happening, and her face flamed crimson again. It was obvious she was having doubts about the outing, but she seemed determined to go through with it.

Morgan finished dressing and pulled on his boots. The effort was costing him, but he was determined to get back on his feet as fast as possible. Besides, as he remembered the feel of her soft breast against his hand, his anticipation grew, along with his desire, at the

47

thought of being alone with her.

Doc Willowford had left a crutch for Morgan, and Elaina brought it to the injured man's bedside. She was already sorry she'd suggested the outing, but it was too late to rescind the invitation. Besides, the man did need to get out into the fresh air.

She helped him navigate the two flights of stairs to the lobby, then walk out the mahogany doors of the hotel. Elaina could see the effort had exhausted him. His face looked pale, and tiny beads of perspiration dotted his brow. Again she regretted her impulsiveness. But if he sat quietly, the hour-long ride should renew his strength, and overall, the exercise would be good for him.

Elaina ignored the stares of passersby, the mangy dog barking and nipping at Morgan's boots, and the towheaded youth watching with menace from the alley, his slingshot poised at the ready. Allowing Morgan to use her shoulder to steady himself, she helped him climb into the buggy.

As she climbed into the driver's seat, she looked briefly at the man beside her. Beneath his broad-brimmed hat, his light eyes watched her, and she felt her heartbeat quicken. The heat rushed to her cheeks for the third time since noon. Until she met Morgan, Elaina had rarely succumbed to the feminine urge to blush. She'd been serving meals to the miners for six years, and she was used to their hungry stares. What was there about this particular man that made her feel different? Older, somehow. Womanly.

The bay single-stepped the buggy at a brisk pace out of town. With Dan Morgan beside her, Elaina made her way into the mountainous Pennsylvania countryside. At first Morgan was quiet, introspective, allowing his strength to return. They passed through a covered bridge, and chimney swifts darted from their nests among the eaves. The birds skimmed the surface of the stream, scooping up the tiniest insects. Then the darkness inside the bridge gave way to a bright green meadow, and sheep laurel formed a thick hedge along the road. Elaina was lost in the beauty of the countryside and the scent of wildflowers when Morgan touched a hand to her knee.

"Don't you dare —" she started, but he put a finger to his lips to quiet her. When he signaled her to stop, she pulled the mare to a halt. Morgan pointed to a spot behind a stand of dogwood forty yards across the meadow where a doe stood alert, her brown ears erect.

"She's beautiful," Elaina whispered.

"Do you see the fawn?"

"Where?"

"Just to the left, lying in that patch of arrowhead."

She scanned the meadow. "I still can't see it."

He put two fingers in his mouth and whistled shrilly.

Both Elaina and the fawn jumped at the same time. "There it is!" Pointing excitedly, she watched until doe and fawn were well out of sight. Then she turned and smiled at Morgan, seeing him in a little different light. "You may have lost your memory, but your eyesight is just fine." She clucked a few times, and the mare started up.

They rode along in comfortable silence. By the time Elaina had driven half the distance to the Colsons', Morgan had begun to banter lightly with her.

"You didn't tell me why you're going to see the . . . Colsons, is it?"

"Yes. Little Johnny Colson has a fever, and Doc Willowford's over in Hazleton helping Dr. Montgomery deal with a catastrophe of some sort."

"Maybe they found somebody else to shoot," he teased, half serious.

She felt a stab of guilt. "There's no one else around as unpopular as you . . . unless it's Redmond and Dawson. It wasn't a shooting. Firedamp, I think. That's methane gas. Just a minor explosion this time. Killed a couple of men and injured a few others. Just doesn't seem right somehow, the way those poor miners are treated. Somebody's always getting killed in those damned mines." She flushed at her use of the swearword. Just talking about the problems in the mines sent her into a fury.

"I'm sorry. I didn't mean to get so wound up." She glanced away, keeping her eyes toward the edge of the road until she felt his hand gently turn her face toward his.

"I like a woman with spirit. You care about people. That's nice. Don't ever apologize for caring." His fingers felt warm and strong against her cheek. He looked at her with what might have passed

49

for admiration, his gaze steady, and she felt the heat in her cheeks begin to move through her body.

The wagon seat was narrow. Try as she might, she was forced to sit with her leg pressed firmly against his, feeling the corded muscles of his thighs, the heat radiating from where their legs touched to her private, woman's place. No man had ever affected her so.

Elaina swallowed hard, trying to control her turbulent emotions. "That's an odd remark," she said, needing desperately to put some distance between them, "coming from a man who kills people for a living." When Morgan stiffened, she wished she could call back the words. Or had she imagined that tiny stab of pain she had seen in his eyes?

The girl was right, he thought. Why would a gunman care about what happened to anyone else? According to the newspapers, he hired himself out to the highest bidder. A gunman wouldn't give a whit for who was right or wrong, just who paid the most. So why had the girl's burst of feeling for the miners touched him so deeply? And why did this coal country seem so familiar? As they passed between wooded hills and crossed meandering streams, he had the strangest feeling he'd been here before.

According to Redmond and Dawson, he'd been to Blue Mountain once; maybe that was it, but somehow he didn't think so. He could almost imagine what lay at the end of a path or what town might lie just around a bend in the hills.

"You're right," he said, setting his jaw. "Why would a gunman care about anyone but himself?" Reaching over, he grabbed the horse's reins and pulled the buggy to a halt. He noticed the girl's bewildered expression as he tipped her chin up to capture her lips.

As his arms went around her to pull her close, her slim hands pushed against his chest. She struggled for a moment, but the rise and fall of her breasts and the tautness of her nipples straining against the fabric of her dress betrayed more than mere interest. He felt the familiar tightness in his breeches, and his resolve strengthened. Why indeed? He wanted this woman, and one way or another he was going to have her.

Elaina's surprise turned to fury. How dare he! She renewed her efforts to struggle free and heard his husky gasp of pain as she struck his shoulder, but he didn't release her. Instead, he pinned her hands behind her back and began to gentle his assault. His lips felt warm and firm as they nibbled the corner of her mouth, then claimed her lips again. Slowly her rage ebbed to little more than a distant memory, replaced by a heated languor she didn't quite understand.

He used his tongue deliciously, probing, searching, gently finding entrance, then touching, savoring the inside of her mouth. She could feel his body pressing against her, solid and powerful. His hands moved down her back to the curve of her hip, and he held her close. No longer warmed by fires of indignation, she felt a different warmth heating her blood, melting her resolve. Dear God, was he never going to stop kissing her?

Morgan released her wrists, and her arms slid helplessly around his neck, her fingers slipping into the dark hair curling above his collar. As he pulled her closer, the soft strands felt silky between her fingers, and she suddenly realized she didn't want the kiss to end.

"Please," she whispered and wondered if she meant stop — or continue. His lips moved along the line of her neck seeking the place behind her ear, nibbling the lobe and maddening her with the feel of it. Then his mouth returned to hers with practiced patience, and she felt a moment's anger at his control. Her body was responding to his every touch, leaving her breathless and weak, shivery and warm all over.

Her only consolation came from the small womanly part of her that knew she was disturbing him as much as he was her. It's only a kiss, she told herself and gave herself up to the delicious sensations.

Slowly Morgan released her, picked up the reins, and lightly slapped them against the horse's rump, heading the buggy off the road toward a stand of tall hickory and elm. Elaina straightened in her seat, her trembling fingers tucking a loose strand of hair behind one ear. Then her hand flew to her throat. Taking the liberty of kissing her was one thing. What he intended now was something altogether different.

"Don't you dare!" she raged indignantly. "I know I should have made you stop, but I . . . well, I'd never quite experienced anything so . . ." With exaggerated care, she kept her eyes averted from the bulge in Morgan's breeches. "I mean, I only wanted to see what it felt like." Snatching the reins from his hands, she watched as he glowered down at her, the muscles in his jaw flexing as he strained for control.

"You wanted to see what it felt like?" he repeated. He seemed incredulous.

For a moment she thought he might grab the reins again and continue with his plan. Then he took a deep, ragged breath and shook his head.

"Well, now we both know one thing for sure about me, Miss McAllister. I must be at least a little crazy for letting you stop me. Any other man would have pulled you out of this buggy and off into the weeds for acting like that."

Elaina blushed hotly, acutely aware of the truth of his words.

His gaze turned serious, and his light eyes issued a warning. "Don't try that on another man unless you're ready to pay the consequences."

Elaina worried her lower lip, still tender from his kiss. The gunman was right! What could possibly have gotten into her to make her respond like that? After all, he was only a man, no different from the rest; he was just like Chuck Dawson. The thought sobered her. She closed her eyes and swallowed hard. If that was true, why didn't she respond to Chuck's kisses as she did to Dan Morgan's? Unfortunately, she knew the answer. She felt nothing for her future husband, but Morgan attracted her as no man ever had. Without a sideways glance, her face still on fire, she clucked the horse into a trot, turned the buggy back toward the road, and headed for the Colsons'.

Morgan just leaned back against the seat, pulled his broad-brimmed hat over his eyes, and appeared to doze. His nonchalance infuriated her. Though she'd thoroughly enjoyed the kiss, she regretted her actions. Morgan was not the kind of man to encourage. His arrogance and self-confidence annoyed her, and he was dangerous and calculating. Heaven only knew what might have happened if he'd pressed his advantage. And in less than two weeks she'd be officially engaged to Chuck. The thought made her feel just slightly ill.

Her mind replayed the scene with Morgan. Her body still felt hot and languid from the power of his kiss. She wished she could take back her careless remark about him being a killer. She'd seen a gentleness in Morgan's eyes that had now disappeared. She knew he could feel her presence next to him as strongly as she felt his, and she got the decided impression he was enjoying her discomfort. She sagged with relief as they rounded the final bend in the road where blue skies gave way to gray. Green forested mountains became scarred barren hills, and the mine patch came into view.

It was a dismal stretch of land dominated by a colliery — a coal processing plant and the surrounding metal buildings. Several row houses, each sheltering at least four miners' families, lined one side of town. Sagging clotheslines, heavy with blue overalls and work shirts, cluttered the yards, and small children played tag beneath the dangling garments. Across the way, a railroad track for transporting coal divided the patch town in half.

Elaina headed straight for the Colsons' — a board structure that, compared to the ugly two-story row houses occupied by the less fortunate miners and their families, seemed almost homey. She could see men working at the entrance to the Blue Mountain Mine, their gray, dirt-smudged faces a reflection of the patch itself. Their unrest had been, as usual, short-lived, as hungry children and distraught mothers encouraged the men to return to work.

And the Morgan shooting had shaken everyone up and at least delayed further hostilities. Since Morgan was a gunman, the assailant could have been someone other than a miner, but chances were good the man was a friend or husband of someone they knew. In lieu of costing a fellow worker his freedom, the men were willing to let their grievances go — at least for a while.

# Chapter 5

"You'd better stay in the buggy. I'll go in and let them know we're here." Elaina really meant she was taking no chances. Dan Morgan's welcome might not be a pleasant one.

As she lightly stepped down from the buggy and headed toward the small clapboard home, Johnny Colson's spotted mutt wagged its tail and panted a greeting.

Mary Colson met her at the door, brushing flour from her apron and smelling of fresh baked bread. "Thank ye fer comin', Miss Elaina. I know how busy ye be and — Who's that?" Mary's eyes focused on the man in the buggy. "Man looks pale. He all right?" She wiped her rough red hands on her apron and peered hard toward the buggy.

"I might as well tell you. That's Dan Morgan." Elaina searched the woman's eyes for understanding and saw the light of comprehension dawn. Everyone in Carbon County knew about Black Dan. "He's been hurt pretty bad," Elaina continued. "I figured he needed the fresh air so . . ." She left the sentence unfinished, waiting for Mary Colson's reaction.

"I got no love for bushwhackers. Man who shot Black Dan is no friend of mine." Mary glanced again toward Morgan. "Long as the man behaves himself, he's welcome here. Ye best bring him in. He looks a little peaked."

Elaina smiled gratefully. That was what she liked about the mine patch families. They were good, hardworking people. Mary's family had come from Cornwall. Many of the others were German, some Irish, some from the mines in Tennessee.

"Thanks, Mary. He really doesn't seem to be as bad as they say. I'll go get him." She gathered her skirts and hurried toward the waiting man.

"You decide they aren't going to finish me off?" Morgan teased. Elaina ignored him. "Come on. I'll help you down. You can rest a little inside." Gingerly she helped him out of the wagon, then handed him his crutch. He smiled down at her, and the smile lightened his already pale eyes.

"You're a pretty handy lady to have around," he said. This time his eyes were alight with mischief. It was clear his mind still lingered on their kiss, and Elaina fought to keep from blushing again. She reached behind him, searched beneath the seat, and grabbed her small medicine satchel, which had ridden next to the .45 caliber revolver Morgan insisted on bringing.

As they walked toward the house, Elaina noticed the carefully tended flower beds where lovely daffodils bloomed in startling contrast to their barren surroundings. Morgan propped the crutch beneath his uninjured arm and kept his weight on his one good leg.

Once inside, Mary Colson fetched Morgan a cup of hot coffee. She grinned broadly as he took his first sip, noting the grimace he tried to hide. "Most o' ye city folk don't much like the taste o' chicory, but it makes a bit o' coffee go a lot farther."

"It's fine, Mrs. Colson. Thank you. I think I've dug my share of chicory root in the forest, though I can't remember where."

Elaina supposed anything was possible. Shrugging her shoulders, she went to look after little Johnny. The boy's face was blotchy, his skin hot and damp, but he recognized her and smiled broadly. It was hard to tell where his freckles left off and the blotches began.

"How are you feeling?" she asked.

"I'm awful hot and kinda dizzylike."

Elaina pulled back the covers and looked at the boy's narrow chest. The boy's skin looked pale and his neck a little flushed.

"Mary, has he taken any bad chills lately? This looks like a simple fever of some sort. Nothing dangerous, I don't think, but it's always best to take no chances." She glanced down and began to fish through her medicine bag.

"Well, he did take a tumble into the mill pond. Slipped on a rock, or some such cock-and-bull story. Ye know how boys are." She tried to look at her son sternly, but it was easy to see the love she felt for the redheaded boy. "Come home soaked to the skin, he did. S'pose that could be what done it?"

"More than likely." Elaina handed a small glass vial to Mary Colson. "This is birch oil. Good for quieting the fever. The dosage is a teaspoonful in a cup of boiling water. Just keep him warm and let him get some rest. I'll stop by again in a couple of days. If he isn't better, we'll have Doc Willowford take a look at him." Elaina wrote down the dosage and directions and gave them to Mary Colson.

Mary seemed relieved. "We can't afford to pay Doc's fees. Can't really afford for Johnny here to be off work, but gettin' 'im well is the most important thing. We surely thank ye for comin' all this way.

"Will I be well next week, Miss McAllister?" Johnny's eyes took on an excited glow. "Pa says if I git well quick he'll take me to the circus. There's one comin' to Hazleton. You ever been to a circus?"

Elaina smiled, remembering a time when she'd begged her mother to let her go, but her mother said the circus was dirty and smelly and not the kind of place for a young lady of her upbringing.

"No, I'm afraid I haven't," Elaina told him, "but I've read all about them, and I've always wanted to go. You take your medicine like your mama says, and I'll bet you'll be fine in just a few days." She ran her fingers through his silky red hair and Johnny grinned up at her.

"Thanks for comin'," he said. "I was awfully worried 'bout missin' that circus."

"It was my pleasure." She turned her attention to Mary. "Now, how about a cup of that coffee?"

Dan Morgan watched the two women move from the boy's bedside to the small table in the area that served as the kitchen. He reclined in a thumb-backed rocker, since the boy was stretched out on the settee. There appeared to be only one other room in the house besides the front room–kitchen area, and he assumed that was the bedroom. The women sat at a handmade wooden table covered with a dainty white embroidered tablecloth, probably just for the occasion of Elaina's visit.

Morgan had enjoyed watching the girl as she worked with the child. She had a way with people; she really cared, and they could sense it. He figured most of her cures were probably a result of her concern as much as her grandma's herbs.

He wondered if he had a woman, maybe even a child of his own somewhere. He didn't think so, but his mind kept receiving fuzzy images of another redheaded boy, and he was unable to sort out just who it might be. He continued to feel a sense of familiarity with everything he saw; the feeling even more intense since he'd entered the patch town.

He observed Elaina covertly. From where he sat he could admire the way her dark hair glinted beneath the sun peeking through the open kitchen window. She was a real beauty all right. Mary Colson was filling her in on the local gossip, and her laughter at some outrageous story revealed sparkling teeth between ruby lips that were just a little pouty.

He remembered the warmth of her kiss. It had affected him more than he'd expected. It had been hard to control his urge to open her dress and fill his hands with her high, lush breasts. But his strength had not returned completely, and he didn't want to frighten her. He saw her laugh again and absently twist a mahogany curl around one long, slim finger. A surge of blood to his loins reminded him of the plans he had for the girl. He wanted her in his bed, but he wanted her there willingly.

On Thursday Morgan sat in the straight-backed chair in his hotel room, his feet propped up on the bureau, his gaze following the milling shoppers on the street below. After their return from the patch town, Elaina had tended him faithfully but had been careful to keep her distance.

Chuck and Henry Dawson had been in and out of his room several times, and Dolph Redmond had come to express his fervent wish to see Morgan back on his feet. There were paybacks due the miners who'd had a hand in Morgan's injuries, Dolph said. Morgan guessed that was probably the reason Chuck Dawson had allowed Elaina to spend so much time in his company. The three men were hoping he'd get well enough to take revenge on whoever had shot him. Then they'd be able to use the miner's death as a deterrent to future unrest.

Morgan intended to oblige them, only not quite in the manner the men expected. He was more and more convinced that Elaina had played a role in his injuries, and that suited his conscience just fine. His obsession with bedding the tawny-eyed girl was becoming almost tangible.

It seemed crystal clear to Morgan that Chuck Dawson's only interest in Elaina McAllister was carnal — just as Morgan's was. Marrying the girl, Morgan guessed, seemed to Dawson the only way he could satisfy his prurient urges. For all Morgan's own desire to have the girl in his bed, he knew marriage was out of the question. There was still too much he didn't know about himself. Besides, a gunman had no place in his life for a woman, much less a wife.

On Friday Elaina stuck her head into his room and announced she'd be returning to the patch town to check on Johnny Colson, and Morgan was welcome to accompany her again — if he promised to behave himself.

Morgan welcomed the occasion.

As it turned out, Johnny Colson was much improved, and Mrs. Colson thanked Elaina by packing a picnic lunch for her and Morgan to enjoy on their way back to town. It seemed a perfect opportunity for what he had in mind.

"Any chance I could talk you into stopping long enough to enjoy this lunch?" He lifted the red checked cloth that covered the wicker basket and sniffed. "The food smells delicious. I don't know about you, but I'm starved." He unfastened the top buttons on his shirt and rolled up his sleeves, enjoying the day. The sunshine felt warm against his chest and the back of his neck.

"I'm not sure that's a good idea, Mr. Morgan."

"Please, my name's Dan — or at least that's what you told me." The mare clip-clopped along the rural lane, the swaying movement of the buggy almost hypnotic. Purple lupine, gay yellow mustard, and tiny white snowballs rippled in the gentle April breeze.

Elaina smiled. "I'm not sure that stopping is a good idea, *Dan.*"

"You're not sure. That means you're not sure it's a bad idea, either. You're not still afraid of me, are you?"

"Afraid! Why of all the — I was never *afraid* of you, Mr. Morgan." Elaina stiffened her spine and clucked the horse into a trot.

"Dan," he reminded her.

She smiled in spite of herself. "Dan . . . All right. I guess stopping for a little while couldn't hurt anything. There's a lovely place up ahead. I used to go there when I was a little girl. I haven't been back in years. It might be kind of fun."

"Up around that bend?" he asked, pointing to an opening through the dogwoods.

"Why, yes. How did you know?" She eyed him suspiciously.

"Just a lucky guess," he lied. In truth he had no idea how he knew. He just did.

The buggy jounced along the dirt road until Elaina turned down a narrow path heavily overgrown with honeysuckle. Tiny bees worked the white blossoms that filled the air with their sweet fragrance. She knew she shouldn't be going alone with a man to such a secluded place, but her life had been so dull these past few years, and the challenge had clearly been laid down. Besides, she'd been able to handle Morgan before. This time would be no different. She might even let him kiss her again. After all, she wasn't *officially* engaged yet.

Morgan's wounds appeared to be healing nicely. He was able to climb down from the buggy on his own, though he tore his white shirt in the process. The gaping hole revealed taut muscle over rib and conjured unladylike thoughts in Elaina's mind.

She spread the blanket near a small stream, remembering all the times she'd come to the spot as a child. She and Tommy Daniels had discovered it, and except for showing Ren, they'd kept it their secret.

"There's a cave over there." She knelt on the blanket and pointed through the trees. "It's got Indian writing on the wall."

"Great. Let's go take a look." He extended a hand to her.

"No!" she answered too quickly. "I mean . . . we haven't got that much time." She glanced away. "Besides, I don't like dark places."

He looked at her oddly, then shrugged his shoulders. "Suit yourself." Lowering himself onto the blanket, he stretched out his long legs and made himself comfortable.

"So you sneaked up here without your mother knowing," he teased, and Elaina was glad he'd forgotten about the cave. "Pretty far from home for a little girl, weren't you?"

Elaina glowered. "You men. Why is it all right for boys to have adventures but not for girls?" She picked up his black hat, which he'd set on a corner of the blanket, and threw it at him in mock anger.

Morgan smiled ruefully, catching the hat easily and setting it aside. "Such a spitfire. I like a woman with fire." His blue eyes danced mischievously as he shifted his weight on the blanket, moving a little closer at the same time.

They broke into the lunch and ate heartily, licking the chicken from their fingers, childlike, then ate apple pie for dessert.

"That was delicious." Morgan wiped his hands on the delicately embroidered napkin Mary had provided. "Mary Colson's quite a cook." Again he moved closer.

"Yes, she is," Elaina agreed. For the first time she realized just how close he was.

"Are you?"

"Better than most," she said honestly, beginning to feel more than a little uncomfortable at his nearness. His open shirt revealed the black hair curling against his smooth dark skin, and her heart began to pound.

"I'll just bet you are." Morgan ran a finger down the line of her jaw, evoking a tiny tremor. She was finding it extremely difficult to ignore the man with the fascinating sky-blue eyes.

"I think I must like good food and good wine," he said, continuing his lazy perusal.

And probably bad women, Elaina added to herself. "I believe whatever else you turn out to be, Mr. Morgan — Dan — you're a man of good taste."

"And you're a very beautiful woman."

His hand played absently with her arm, creating several new tremors. She forced her attention toward a bushy-tailed squirrel who whistled his displeasure at the intruders, then scampered to the far side of a massive hickory trunk.

"Tell me why you're marrying a man like Dawson," Morgan said gently.

Seeing what appeared to be genuine concern, Elaina felt compelled to answer. "I owe him. My family and I owe him. My father used to own the Blue Mountain Mine. There were several accidents, fires, unforeseeable disasters. The mine kept losing money, so my father took on Redmond and Dawson as partners. Eventually he gave them complete control. Conditions became unsafe; people were killed, and my father felt responsible. He began to drink heavily, and the debts mounted. When he couldn't stand the pressure anymore, he killed himself." Elaina felt a lump in her throat. "My mother died not long after."

She didn't know she was crying until Morgan reached over and gently brushed a tear from beneath her lashes with the tip of his finger.

"That must have been a terrible time for you."

"It was. I had no place to go. No relatives." She looked down. "Henry Dawson provided for me. Helped me when no one else would. Now it's time to pay him back. He wants me to marry his son, and that's what I intend to do."

Morgan felt the strangest need to comfort her. It was all he could do to keep from pulling her into his arms and kissing away her tears. Again he felt the urge to protect her at all costs. The thought both startled and confused him. He was a gunman. He was not allowed to indulge in those kinds of feelings.

"Maybe you won't have to marry him," he said, uncertain why he'd said it. He cupped her chin with his hand and covered her lips with a gentle kiss. She didn't fight him, and her tender response made him harden with desire. He deepened the kiss and felt her melt against him, parting her lips to allow him entrance. He tasted the sweetness of apples and smelled her lavender scent, and the feel of her supple body sent a fresh surge of blood to his loins.

It's only a kiss, she told herself, as she had before. I have just this one chance to know the kiss of a man I desire before my life belongs forever to a man I can barely abide. She reveled in the touch of Morgan's warm lips and gave herself up willingly to the excitement he stirred.

Shivers ran down the length of her. His lips were firm, full, and insistent, his tongue hot, moist, and searching, probing the inside of her mouth. She entwined her fingers in his thick dark hair and slid her arms around his neck. He nibbled her ear, then moved down her neck to her shoulders. She could feel her nipples harden against the soft material of her dress. She felt hot and languid and at the same time tense and shivery. It was more than she'd bargained for.

Morgan kissed her thoroughly, deeply, his hand sliding down her back to the curve of her hip, then up to tease her nipple. She could feel the heat of his wide palm, even through the fabric. She knew she should stop him. She had to stop him. She felt a button at her back pop free, and still she could not tear herself away. He was kissing her passionately, insistently, using his hands and his tongue and his mouth. As if by magic, the buttons of her dress were popping free.

Now. Now. She had to stop him now! She felt the cool breeze against her skin and knew her dress was open. She felt the straps of her chemise slide down, baring her breasts to his gaze. He paused a moment to look at her, his hands cupping, kneading the fullness, his light eyes darker than before. She'd seen that look in Chuck Dawson's eyes, but in him it had repulsed her. Now it excited her beyond all reason. She pushed meekly against Morgan's broad chest, moaning with the heat, the power he held. Dear God, please let him stop.

He kissed her again while he used his body to press her gently but firmly down on the blanket. She could feel the hard muscles of his back beneath her hands, the corded muscles of his thighs against her legs, and the stiffness of his manhood. When his lips touched the crest of her nipple, she knew there was no turning back. Elaina moaned softly. The heat of her desire was beyond any reckoning, any reason. She had played a game of fire and lost. Now Morgan fanned the flames with his every movement. He kissed each breast, circled the peak with his tongue, then surrounded it with his lips, tugging on it gently. She heard his husky groan of anticipation as he shoved her dress up over her thighs, and she felt weak, powerless to stop him.

Suddenly he tensed, his ragged breath held against the sound he had heard. Elaina strained to listen, but heard only her labored breathing and her heart pounding against her ribs. Morgan rolled away from her and glanced around, searching the wooded hillsides for the source of the sound. After helping her sit up, his hands a little shaky, he pulled her chemise back over her breasts and the bodice of her dress up a bit impatiently; then he buttoned the closure. In a daze, she watched him straighten his own clothes and, after lifting a gentle hand to her cheek, moved into the cover of the surrounding bushes.

Elaina felt numb, disoriented, devastated by the intensity of her emotions. She tried to rearrange her garments, but her fingers trembled so badly she had little success. How could she have let this happen? She'd only meant to kiss him, just wanted a tiny taste of passion before succumbing to a lifetime of duty. She'd had no idea what being with a man like Morgan could do to a woman. The power he could wield, the all-out control. She shuddered to think how close she'd come to losing her virtue.

Until Morgan arrived, she'd spent most of her time working in the hotel, doctoring, and trying to figure a way of putting her family's name aright. Two years ago, she'd agreed to Henry Dawson's proposition. From that time forward she'd been considered Chuck Dawson's girl. She'd never been exposed to the passions other girls her age had experienced. She hadn't had time.

She watched Morgan speaking with two small boys across the clearing on the other side of the stream, and silently thanked him for his gunman's instinct for survival. He'd headed off what could have been a nightmare of embarrassment. As it was, her only embarrassment was how she would face the tall man again. She rolled her eyes skyward and said a silent prayer of thanks to God for saving her from herself, then asked Him to give her the courage to face the handsome stranger.

Her prayer was answered as Morgan strolled nonchalantly back to where she sat disheveled on the blanket, still a little shaky. As he ran a hand through his wavy dark hair, his blue eyes assessed her.

Elaina felt mortified by what she'd done, torn between demanding an apology and begging his forgiveness. Instead she took a deep breath, faced him squarely, and willed him to understand. "I don't know what to say to you." She swallowed hard. "I've never done anything like that. It seemed so innocent at first. . . ." Her voice trailed off and she glanced away.

Morgan looked down at the girl on the blanket and breathed a sigh of disappointment and relief. Still feeling more than a little unsettled, he helped her to her feet. Thank God he'd spotted the boys before they'd spotted him. The whole of Carbon County would

63

have been talking about him and the McAllister girl by noon tomorrow. He hadn't meant to push her — at least not yet. But she had seemed so innocent — and so willing — he'd been unable to control himself.

"I told you once before, Miss McAllister, what would happen if you tried that again. I won't apologize for my actions, but I won't hold you responsible for yours, either."

Elaina didn't know whether to be mad at the man or grateful for his candor. As she thought of what had happened, her face burned crimson. He'd seen parts of her no man had, touched her as no man had. It couldn't be right, yet somehow it seemed so.

As they headed back toward town, Elaina worked up her courage, curiosity outweighing her better judgment. "I know I shouldn't ask this. I mean it isn't a proper thing for a lady to ask a gentleman, but —"

"So far, Miss McAllister, nothing you've done has been quite the proper thing for a lady, but that hasn't stopped you yet. Go ahead and ask." He sounded a little gruff, and she wondered if he was angry with her. He'd taken the reins, and she admired the way he controlled the mare with the same strong hands he'd used on her. The thought made her blush again. It seemed her cheeks had been burning ever since Morgan's arrival.

"Well, Miss McAllister, I'm waiting."

"I think it's time you called me Elaina." That brought a grin and a shake of his head. Elaina thought how handsome he looked when he relaxed.

"What's your question, Elaina?"

She squared her shoulders. "What happened out there today . . . is it always that exciting? What I mean is, I never feel like that when Chuck kisses me." Maybe there was hope for her and Chuck Dawson yet. Maybe she just hadn't let him go far enough. Somehow she didn't think so.

Morgan took a long time answering. "Well . . . Elaina, sometimes, with certain people, it just happens that way. I can't exactly explain it, but thank you for the compliment. Apparently you and your intended have experimented very little."

The conversation was taking a decidedly embarrassing turn, but Elaina persisted. "I've never felt much of anything for Chuck. I

64

never encouraged him, and I think he was a little worried about his father. Henry would be furious if Chuck took liberties with me before the wedding."

"Why did you encourage me and not him?" he asked.

It was Elaina's turn to pause. "Just once," she finally told him, "I wanted to see what it was like to experience passion. Besides, I didn't intend to do more than kiss you, Mr. — Dan, but somehow I couldn't help myself." She faced him squarely. "That's the way a man seduces a woman, isn't it?"

Morgan shook his head in disbelief. God, what had he gotten himself into? Still, he admired her honesty. It was rare that a woman had the courage to experience life to the fullest. It made him want her all the more.

"Yes, Elaina, that's how a man seduces a woman. If those two boys hadn't come along when they did, you wouldn't have to ask any of these questions. You'd know the answers."

Elaina turned crimson from head to toe and sat quietly for the rest of the trip home. A blue jay swooped down from a passing sycamore screeching his anger at their intrusion, and the mare shied, throwing Elaina against Morgan's muscular shoulder. His arm went around her instinctively, steadying her. He held her a little longer than necessary, then let her go.

There were still questions she wished to ask, things she wished to know, but she knew it would be Chuck Dawson, not Dan Morgan, who would teach her. The thought saddened her more than a little.

## Chapter 6

It was time to check Morgan's wounds again.

Elaina had put it off as long as she dared. Burning with embarrassment, she'd avoided him, stayed away from him as much as possible, but she knew sooner or later she'd have to face him.

All business, she knocked on the door, opened it at his command, and strode briskly into the room. Pale eyes, mocking and amused, swept her from head to toe. She could feel the blush creeping up her neck and cursed herself for being powerless to control it. She wished she could summon Doc Willowford to finish her task, but it might arouse the doctor's suspicion — and maybe Chuck's, too.

"I came to check your wounds," she told him, her voice even, her eyes meeting his unwaveringly in spite of her fluttering heart. She held her head high as he rose from his chair by the window.

"I wondered if you were just going to let me lie up here and wither away."

"Mr. Morgan. I had no intention of letting you wither away. I'm certain your wounds are healing just fine. You had no need for my services before now."

His voice, as mocking as his eyes, teased her mercilessly. "How can you be so certain! I've missed you these past few days. I'd gotten used to you being around."

She smiled, pleased at his words in spite of her efforts not to be charmed. "Sit down on the edge of the bed and let me take a look."

He did as she instructed, removing his shirt on the way. Forcing her gaze away from his curly black chest hair to the spot where the jagged scar marked the smooth bronze skin beneath his collarbone, Elaina tested the wound with gentle fingers and felt the corded muscles bunch. "It's mending beautifully," she said, hoping he

66

wouldn't notice the tremor in her hand. "You had an excellent doctor."

"I'm sure of that," he agreed a little too easily.

She ignored the gentle caress in his voice. "Now let me look at your leg."

"This is the best part."

Her blush returned to destroy her control. "You're such a damnable rake, Dan Morgan!"

Grinning broadly, he started to unbutton his pants. "You sure you're up to this? You never know what can happen with a hired killer like me — especially with my breeches off."

She clamped her teeth together and turned around. "I'll wait till you get out of them and pull the sheet up." She heard the rustle of cloth, the clank of his broad belt buckle as it hit the floor, and suddenly wished she'd called for Doc Willowford after all.

"You can turn around now," he told her.

Morgan lay propped up in bed, the sheet pulled to his waist, one long, sinewy leg and a wide, muscular chest bared to her view.

"Oh, God," she whispered, not realizing how it must sound.

He chuckled softly. "You are a gem, Miss McAllister, an absolute gem."

Ignoring his laughter, she checked the leg as dispassionately as possible, found it healing ahead of schedule, then turned to leave.

"If you'll give me a minute to get dressed, there's something I want to give you."

She paused at the door, careful to keep her back to him. At the sound of breeches sliding over tough, muscular legs, she twisted the folds of her skirt. His hand on her shoulder turned her to face him.

"What is it you have for me?" She asked, swallowed hard and tried to ignore the light eyes watching her.

"These." He held up two stiff squares of paper in one long-fingered hand.

"What are they?"

He pressed them into her palm. "Two tickets to the circus. You said you'd never been there, remember?"

"The circus!" She held the tickets up to the light and smiled. "I've always wanted to go. Mama said it was too dirty. And Papa

67

never went against Mama. I sneaked out of the house to go once, but Mama caught me and locked me in my room." She laughed again, her voice melodic, and clutched the tickets to her breast as if they were the dearest present she'd ever received.

"I thought maybe you'd let me take you." Morgan had never seen her react so spontaneously, with such utter joy, and the sight disarmed him completely. She looked like a little girl, her big eyes sparking and cherubic in their delight. Suddenly his grand scheme to get her alone and finish the seduction he'd started on their last outing dissolved into nothing more than a wish to take a young lady to the circus.

"You could consider it my way of making amends."

Her look of joy dissolved as quickly as it had appeared, and she handed the tickets back to him, dropping her hands to her sides. "That's very kind of you, Dan, but . . ."

"But after the other day you don't trust me."

She sighed resignedly. "I guess you could say that — or maybe I don't trust myself."

Her candor always amazed him. Her sable hair shone in the morning's rays, and the pink of her excitement still brightened her cheeks. Looking at her, he was suddenly willing to pay any price to get her to accept his invitation.

"I'll make you a promise. If you'll let me take you to the circus, I won't let either of us do anything we might regret."

She eyed Morgan suspiciously.

"Have I ever lied to you?" He avoided touching her cheek as he ached to do. She looked as skittish as a colt, and he knew that any sudden movement might scare her away.

"I don't know. Have you?"

He smiled wryly. "Not that I know of, but then, I don't remember everything I've said."

His honest answer surprised her. Lord, how she'd love to go to the circus. And Morgan had never really forced her to do anything. Surely she could trust herself, if not him. She just wouldn't let him get her alone.

"Chuck would be furious if he found out."

"Then we won't tell him. Hazleton's far enough away so that no one will recognize either of us. I'll give you money to hire a buggy, and you can pick me up at the edge of town. We'll be back before dark."

She licked her lips and twisted the folds of her skirt.

He held up the tickets. "They have tigers and elephants. Have you ever seen an elephant, Elaina?"

"You'll give me your word you won't try anything?"

"My word of honor."

"Do gunmen *have* honor?"

"This one does."

She grinned broadly and snatched the tickets from his hand. "Then, Dan Morgan, I accept your most gracious offer." Holding up the tickets, she whirled around, her lightheartedness contagious.

"You won't be sorry, I promise you." His voice sounded husky.

Elaina sobered at his words. "I hope you're right, Dan Morgan. Truly I do."

At the edge of town, Morgan climbed aboard the rented buggy. As he settled his lanky frame beside her and took the reins from her hands, Elaina smoothed her pink cotton frock out of his way. The day was lovely. Sunny and warm, with gentle breezes that lifted locks of her heavy hair from the nape of her neck.

Morgan looked ruggedly handsome in his usual crisp white shirt above snug black breeches. His black hat covered most of his dark hair, but the wind caught several strands above his collar. His smile looked so genuine that Elaina managed to push thoughts of their last day together to the back of her mind, but it was difficult to keep them there.

A light slap of the reins on the horse's rump and the mare swung into a gentle trot. Morgan's gaze seemed playful, sparkling with mischief. "From the looks of your smile," he teased, "I think someone has been neglecting you far too long. I don't think Dawson properly appreciates you."

"I'm afraid neither of us has much time for this sort of thing." Hearing Chuck's name brought the hint of a frown, but she quickly subdued it. Today she was going to the circus. Nothing could keep her buoyant spirits down.

"That's too bad. A beautiful woman like you deserves to enjoy lots of days like this."

69

She smiled impishly. "Well, I'm certainly looking forward to this one."

Morgan kept the buggy moving at a brisk pace all the way to Hazleton. He questioned himself only briefly as to why he was escorting Elaina McAllister to the circus. He was just thanking her for tending his wounds, he rationalized. After all, he'd probably be dead if it weren't for her. Besides, this outing would bring him one step closer to bedding her. Whatever the reason, today was a beautiful day, and the girl in his company was even more beautiful. He, too, deserved a day of pleasure once in a while.

When the buggy rounded a bend in the lane and the big top came into view, Elaina sucked in a breath. The massive tent was awesome: Flags waved from each of four pinnacles, and myriad people swarmed over the grounds outside the tent. She could hear the music of the calliope, a whimsical melody familiar from a ride she'd taken on a steamship once, and the sound matched her lighthearted mood. Morgan helped her down solicitously, careful not to catch her pretty pink dress in the wooden spokes of the wheels. The usual deep lines of worry were gone from his handsome face.

As they walked through the ankle-deep grass to the entrance, gaily dressed clowns with white faces and bright-colored costumes cavorted and danced. Elaina sniffed the pungent, earthy smell of fresh-mown hay and sawdust. With each glimpse of something new she felt a shiver of delight.

"There's an elephant!" she gasped, hugging Morgan's arm as he escorted her through the crowd and pointing to a great gray beast with two tails. "But what on earth is that?" A giant cow, taller than a man, with two humps on its back, padded by on huge cloven hooves.

Morgan laughed heartily, totally charmed by his lovely companion. "You really have led a sheltered life, pretty lady." He squeezed her hand, enchanted by her naïveté. "You can remove a bullet from an injured man, but you've never seen an elephant or a dromedary."

"That's a camel?"

"Wait till you see a unicorn."

"Now you're teasing me," she said as they passed beneath the flap of the high-ceilinged tent.

70

He grinned broadly. "Yes, but only because you're so much fun to tease."

They took their seats — dead center in front of the middle ring. Morgan could feel the girl's excitement, her curiosity, her utter joy at being there, and he didn't regret for a moment his decision to bring her, even though he'd promised to stay in line — a promise that would be sorely tested on the long ride home.

He insisted she try a candied apple, and the sweet cinnamon flavor seemed to please her as she ran her tongue over the hard smooth surface. The sight conjured delicious memories he'd been fighting to suppress.

She ate popcorn, fed peanuts to a monkey riding high on a clown's shoulder, even accepted a small hand-painted wooden circus horse he insisted on giving her to help her remember the day.

"I'll have to hide it," she told him. "If Chuck were to see it, he'd probably be madder than my mother."

Morgan laughed. "I'm afraid if he tried to lock you in his room, I might be tempted to shoot him." The thought wasn't far from wrong, and the fact disturbed Morgan more than he cared to admit.

Elaina fought a blush. "Don't tell me you're jealous, Mr. Morgan." She was seeing a different side of him today, a man without worries to keep him on guard. He seemed caring, gentle, and solicitous. She was sure it wasn't an act. Today he reminded her of Ren, or at least the way she'd always imagined Ren would be. She hadn't really known him well enough to be certain. She decided Ren Daniels was nothing more than a fantasy, and for the first time she didn't really care. Dan Morgan was the man who haunted her dreams now.

One incredible performance followed another, each one more stupendous than the last. There was a lion tamer with long blond hair falling to his waist, massive metal-studded black leather belts at his hips and wrists, and a twenty-foot bullwhip in his hand, who looked as wild as the beasts he controlled. Another favorite was the aerial act, which kept Elaina's heart securely wedged in her throat throughout the performance. Morgan kept reassuring her the men and women above had years of practice walking the thin wire and dangling from the trapeze, but his words were little comfort. Only when the none-to-modestly dressed sequin-clad performers were

71

safely on the ground could she release her sigh of relief and clap loudly for their death-defying skills.

Morgan held her hand off and on throughout the afternoon and she found its gentle warmth reassuring. It seemed to add just that extra touch of pleasure the wonderful day demanded.

When the show came to a close, Elaina felt almost as exhausted as the entertainers. She'd walked through a cage of wild beasts, been slung from a trapeze, been nearly crushed between the giant pad of an elephant's foot, stood bareback on a beautiful dapple gray steed as it circled the ring, and been shot from a cannon. Other than that, it had been just a typical sunny spring day.

"You look pleasantly exhausted," Morgan told her as he helped her aboard the buggy.

"I had the most wonderful time. I'll always remember this day, no matter how old I get."

"And I'll never forget the pretty lady I took to the circus for her very first time." He pinned her tawny eyes with his light ones. Then, as if needing to break the spell, added, "Or the look on your face when that clown tossed his bucket of confetti at you. You were sure you were about to be drenched."

She poked him in the ribs, and he grunted and hugged her against him playfully. Forgetting his promise, he dipped his head and captured her lips, feeling them warm and pliant beneath his mouth. He felt them part and tasted the sweetness of her breath. When his tongue slid between her teeth, the contact sobered them both.

"You promised!" she exclaimed, tearing herself away.

He could feel her pulse racing, matching his own, and sighed resignedly. "I guess I did, but somehow I didn't think, surrounded by a pasture full of people, one little kiss would put you in danger."

She glanced around, saw all the people leaving the circus just as they were, and rolled her golden eyes skyward. "I'm sorry. I guess I'm a little keyed up from all the excitement. I didn't mean to cause a scene."

"And I didn't mean to kiss you." He grinned and clucked the mare into a brisk trot. "You're even harder to resist than I thought." They moved onto the dusty road behind other wagons departing the grounds. "I apologize for forgetting myself, even for a moment." He hoped his eyes didn't betray the fact that he wasn't sorry at all.

He only wished he could have explored her sweet mouth further.

She seemed to forgive him and nestled her head on his shoulder, the heat of the day and all the excitement beginning to take their toll. The gentle sway of the buggy and the clip-clop of the mare's hooves against the dusty road lulled her, and she drifted to sleep.

Morgan looked down at her trusting face as she slept peacefully against his shoulder. Protectively, he eased his arm around her, hoping she wouldn't awaken till their arrival outside of town. He couldn't have seduced her today, even if he'd had the chance. Not when she'd trusted him so completely, not after the hours they'd spent together — not unless she'd wanted him to. Pressing against him, her shining hair spilling across his chest, she stirred feelings in him he hadn't known he had.

Again his past rose up to haunt him. Was he always this way with a woman he desired? He hardly thought so. This one seemed different, special somehow. A nagging suspicion he'd known her at some other time haunted him, but that possibility didn't fit into the past he was beginning to remember.

It was all a tangled web, but one he hoped to untangle soon.

"It's time to wake up, pretty lady. We're getting close to town. I think you'd better take the buggy the rest of the way alone."

Elaina roused herself, yawned, and smiled. "I wasn't much company, was I?"

"Better than you might think," he assured her gallantly. He drew the buggy to the side of the road and pulled up on the reins.

Elaina eyed him with a bit of melancholy, hating to see the lovely day end. "I had a wonderful time, Dan."

"So did I." He touched her cheek with a sun-browned hand. "Do you suppose a good-bye kiss would be breaking my promise?"

She knew she should say yes. That any contact with the handsome gunman might lead to disaster, but the day had been so perfect she just couldn't. She shook her head and heard his deep, throaty groan as his lips claimed hers. They felt warm, firm, and gentle at the same time, teasing and delighting her with their touch. When his hands cupped her face, the kiss deepened, and she heard her own tiny mew of desire. His tongue touched the inside of her mouth, and warm shivers surged through her veins. The kiss, no longer gentle, threatened to destroy her control. With shaky hands she pressed against his chest, hoping he would stop, but not really wanting him to.

He surprised her by pulling away.

"You see," he said in a husky whisper. "Even a gunman can be honorable. Your virtue remains intact, my promise unbroken."

Unconsciously she pressed her fingers against her kiss-swollen lips, trying to recapture the wonderful tingling he'd aroused.

"Will I see you back at the hotel?" he asked. Unwinding his tall frame from the buggy seat, he jumped lightly to the ground.

"Not tonight." She struggled to find her voice. "I have to help Mrs. Lowery, and I think . . . Chuck is going to stop by." She could barely choke out the name.

"Then this is good-bye until I see you again."

She nodded numbly, wishing he didn't have to go. Urging the mare into a trot, she headed down the dusty lane toward home. Unable to resist a glance back over her shoulder, she spotted his departing figure as his long-legged stride carried him swiftly from her view.

As she moved through the late day sunshine, she felt an uncommon emptiness without him.

"All right, Mr. Redmond, then our company will plan on taking control of all outstanding shares in the Blue Mountain Mine within ninety days." Philip Gilmore of the Anthracite Mining and Colliery Company addressed Dolph Redmond, who sat across from Henry and Chuck Dawson, late in the afternoon at Blue Mountain headquarters. A clean-cut young man in a well-tailored navy blue suit, Gilmore glanced up from his paperwork, removed his spectacles, and turned toward Chuck and Henry. "Does that meet with your approval, gentlemen?"

"Sounds fine to me," Henry Dawson agreed. Rising from his chair, he clapped the young man on the back. "You men are makin' a fine investment. Times have been tough fer mining what with the slump and all, but this year is the start of an upswing that could make you boys rich. Why, if it weren't for these tired old bones of mine, you couldn't pry the Blue Mountain away from me!"

"I agree wholeheartedly, Mr. Gilmore," Dolph Redmond added,

rising from behind his wide mahogany desk. "My other interests are beginning to take up far too much of my time, but it is with mixed feelings I sell such a fine holding." Redmond glided from behind his desk and extended a thin hand. Chuck Dawson rose from his chair, and his father followed suit. The young man accepted Redmond's handshake along with Chuck's and Henry's.

Chuck ushered the younger man to the door. "Then we'll expect to see you, with the capital, here in this office on the tenth of July," Chuck confirmed.

"That is correct, Mr. Dawson. And we'll expect to receive the shares in return at that time. We'll assume full control within the following thirty days."

"Understood," Chuck said. He walked Gilmore as far as his buggy, then watched from the porch as the man whipped up the bay and waved a good-bye. Gilmore headed toward Keyserville where the Lehigh Valley train would return him to Scranton.

Dawson closed the door and leaned nonchalantly against the jamb, allowing himself a satisfied smile. "Free of the damned, miserable mining business at last," he said, voicing the thoughts of the others.

His father grinned broadly. "Yeah, and the price they're payin' us makes the deal even sweeter. Whaddaya say, Dolph? Makes all the dirty work worth it, eh?"

Redmond smiled thinly. "Let's don't be counting our chickens too soon, men. Chuck, you just make sure you get the McAllister girl to the altar. I'm sure I needn't remind you two she still controls fifty percent of the shares in the mine, even if she doesn't know it. Once you're her husband, Chuck, the stock will be yours. We can all rest a little easier after that."

Chuck frowned. "We should have forced the marriage long ago, when she was younger, more biddable. If anything goes wrong"— he scowled toward his father — "it's going to be on your head."

"Weren't no need to force the girl afore now," Henry Dawson defended. "You had yer lady friends to warm yer bed. Girl needed a little time to git used to the idea of marriage, that's all. She's agreed. She'll stand by her word. If there's one thing them McAllisters is, it's prideful."

"You'd better be right," Chuck said.

"Don't worry," Redmond soothed, "there'll be a wedding — one way or another." Moving back to his desk, he opened the bottom drawer and lifted out three crystal snifters and a fine decanter filled with brandy. Chuck and his father moved back to their tufted burgundy chairs. The office wasn't large, but Chuck could see Redmond's excellent taste throughout. In addition to the desk and chairs, there was a small settee, and the floor was covered by a wide Persian rug depicting a bloody scene from the Crusades. An Oriental vase adorned a carved rosewood stand.

"This calls for a drink to celebrate our good fortune," Redmond said. He poured two fingers of the rich amber liquid into each of the glasses and handed them around. "And Chuck's forthcoming marriage." The glasses clinked together and all three men smiled.

# Chapter 7

Dan Morgan looked through the open window at the bustling streets below his room. His shoulder was nearly healed. It was time he found the men who had shot him.

Morgan buckled the heavy strap of his gun belt around his hips and secured the leather thong to his thigh. Instinctively his hand reached for the butt of the weapon, and as always, it slid with precision into his palm. His slim fingers curled around the trigger. Then he checked the load, feeling the comforting metal cold against his skin, eased the hammer back down, and replaced the gun in his holster.

Plucking his wide-brimmed hat from the iron headboard of his bed, he pulled open the door, descended the two flights of stairs to the first floor, and walked briskly through the lobby.

"Dan?" Elaina's gentle voice drifted from the parlor. She leaned against her broom, a questioning look on her face, her hair tied back in a kerchief that matched her blue gingham dress. "You aren't going out there again are you?"

He walked into the parlor, not wanting to upset her, but determined to get on with his task. "I'm headed to the marshal's office. I want to see if he or the sheriff have turned up any new leads. I told you, I'm going to find out who shot me, with or without the law."

"It's too dangerous, Dan. You're making a target of yourself. Nobody knew about the trips we made out of town. This is different. Whoever shot you nearly killed you before; he might succeed this time." She tossed him a defiant glance. "If you get yourself shot again, I'll be damned if I'll waste any more time keeping you alive!"

Morgan grinned broadly and ran a finger along her cheek. "You're beautiful when you're angry, but you're wrong about my getting shot. I'm ready for him this time. If anybody winds up carrying a bullet, it'll be him."

"What makes you think he'll come after you?"

"Oh, he'll come, all right. A back shooter doesn't like to leave his job unfinished."

Elaina grabbed his arm and felt his muscles tighten instinctively against her touch. Even with his attempt at a smile, his features looked drawn and hard. Gone was any trace of the handsome, carefree man who had taken her to the circus. This was the gunman, Black Dan, a man she barely knew. She felt a shiver of apprehension and let go of his arm. "There's a law against wearing sidearms in town," she said, determined to appear as unruffled as he.

"There's also a law against shooting people, but that doesn't seem to impress your sheriff."

"I'll come with you," Elaina ventured, resting her broom against the wall.

"Not on your life. Being anywhere near me right now is dangerous. You're staying here."

"But, Dan, I —"

"I'll see you this afternoon." He touched the brim of his hat in a gesture of farewell and backed out of the parlor. Even from a distance, she could read the grim set of his features, the determination in his stride as he pushed open the etched-glass doors.

After only a moment's hesitation, Elaina untied her apron, pulled off her kerchief, and walked to the kitchen.

"I'll be back in just a few minutes," she called to Ada. "I have an errand to run."

Ada smiled and nodded, then immersed herself once more in the bread-making lesson she was giving the new kitchen girl.

Elaina wasted no time. She walked out onto the boardwalk and headed toward the marshal's office. So far, little had been done about the shooting, and Elaina was sure Redmond and Dawson must have encouraged the authorities to ignore the incident. The partners wanted the gunman to take matters into his own hands. The knowledge that Morgan was armed and searching for a target would keep the miners in line.

Shading her eyes from the bright sunlight, Elaina marched purposefully across the street, avoiding a wagonload of hay as she passed. It was a warm day, but a cool May breeze ruffled the hem of her skirt. The surrounding mountains looked green, the few fluffy clouds overhead adding to what should have been a more than pleasant day.

Elaina usually enjoyed every minute she spent out-of-doors, but today she barely noticed. As she stepped onto the walk in front of the marshal's office, she heard voices coming from inside.

"No, Mr. Morgan, in answer to your question, we don't have any definite proof, only circumstantial evidence, but our sources say Josh Colson is the man who shot you."

"Circumstantial?" Morgan asked. "Just how circumstantial?"

"Well, we know Colson's the head of the miners' grievance committee. He had a motive. He was at the town meeting hall the day you were there, and he has no alibi for his whereabouts at the time of the shooting. On top of that, a couple of miners said they beard him bragging about it afterward."

Elaina shoved open the heavy wooden door, her temper barely under control. "That's a damn lie, Frank Stratton, and you know it! Josh Colson never hurt anyone in his life! You'd like nothing better than to see Morgan shoot Josh. That'd make your friend Dolph happy, wouldn't it?"

She whirled to face Morgan. "You don't believe him, do you? You've seen Josh. Does he look like a killer to you?"

"Relax, Elaina. I'm not going to shoot anybody — not without a lot more proof than the marshal seems to have." He turned his attention to Stratton, whose eyebrows had shot up at Morgan's unintentional use of Elaina's given name.

"I'll check back with you, Marshal," Morgan said. "Maybe you can come up with something a little more solid than town gossip." He tipped his hat, grabbed Elaina's arm, and with a thin, tight smile escorted her none too gently out of the office, closing the door behind him.

"I thought I told you to stay at the hotel." His words, spoken through clenched teeth, stiffened her spine.

"You don't have the authority to order me to do anything, Mr. Morgan. I want to know just what you plan to do to Josh Colson."

He tugged her firmly down the walk, his hand gripping the top of her arm. "I told you before, Miss McAllister, I don't intend to do anything to Josh Colson, unless the marshal comes up with proof. I don't believe Colson shot me any more than you do."

She stopped short. "You don't?"

"No, I don't. Now will you please go back to the hotel and stay there?"

She smiled up at him, feeling a sweep of relief. She'd begun to worry she'd misread the gunman after all. She was just about to tell him she'd be happy to do just that when a blast of gunfire interrupted her, shattering a pane of glass beside her and a crock of pickles in Walzheimer's General Store.

"Get down!" Morgan pulled her down on the wooden walk behind several barrels in front of the store. Women shrieked, and men pulled them hurriedly to safety inside the shops. Elaina heard the sound of shutters being slammed behind her and rued her foolishness in not heeding Morgan's orders.

"Damn!" he swore softly beneath his breath. "This is exactly why I wanted you safe at the hotel." Morgan glanced around. "You'll have to stay here. If you try to move, it might draw his fire. Looks like he's on the roof of the bank. I'm going to circle around and come up behind him."

"Please, Dan. Can't we just let the marshal handle this?"

He didn't bother to answer. "Promise me you'll stay here." When she didn't answer quick enough he shook her, his eyes boring into her. "Promise me!"

She could only nod. "I promise." He started to rise, but she grabbed his shirtsleeve and pulled him back down. "Promise me you'll be careful."

His hard look gentled. "I promise." He touched her cheek. "Now, you stay here. I'll be back when this is over."

Morgan rolled from behind the barrel, dodging a chorus of bullets that followed him on his dash to a water trough near the alley. Another loud report, and water sprayed from the trough. He glanced back toward Elaina and was relieved to see her well under cover behind the barrel. Then he made a second dodging run, followed by the echo of gunfire. Wood splintered from the sides of buildings as he ran. Once out of sight, he hurried along behind the buildings, careful to stay low and against the walls for cover.

As he rounded the end of the block, he took a deep breath and sprinted across the open roadway. To his surprise, he crossed the street without hearing a shot. He'd hoped the shooter would stay in position atop the bank. Now he was beginning to worry that the man had already moved to a different location.

Flattened against the livery, Morgan heard only a lone horse's whinny as he looked down the street toward the marshal's office. Just as he expected, the marshal remained safely inside. The streets had emptied. Several horses stood at hitching rails in front of the stores, but most had been led to safety by their worried owners.

Morgan held his .45 pointed upward, his wrist supported by his other hand as he skirted the staircase at the rear of the bank. He climbed the stairs to the building next door, holstered his weapon, and swung himself up to the roof. Reaching the top, he crouched, moving carefully to the edge of the building for a clear view of the bank roof. No one. With a steadying breath, he retraced his steps. As he feared, the man had changed position. Now finding him would be more dangerous than ever.

Once on the ground, Morgan headed down the alley, his Colt again in his hand. As he neared the street, a raspy male voice sliced the silence.

"Morgan! I got something of yers. You want to see she keeps breathin', you'd better git out here."

Removing his broad-brimmed hat, Morgan peered around the corner. For the first time, he felt his control slip. The shooter had Elaina's back pinned against his chest, his arm circling her waist just beneath her full breasts. Her labored breathing set them pulsing against the man's arms, and Morgan's chest tightened.

"Let her go! Whatever you want is between you and me. Let her go, and I'll step into the open."

"Not a chance, Morgan. I've waited too long for this. You come out now, or the girl gets it."

Morgan could see the glint of sunlight on metal as the man pressed his gun to Elaina's temple. A tight knot curled in the pit of his stomach.

"Don't do it, Dan!" Elaina's usually soft voice grated as she strained against the shooter's arm. "He'll kill you for sure."

"Who are you?" Morgan asked, stalling for time.

"Lars Kirby. Billy Kirby's older brother. You remember Billy,

81

don't you? The boy you shot down like a dog in the street!"

While the man spoke, Morgan changed positions, moving around the building to a location as near the general store as he dared.

"Sorry," Morgan said. The sound of his voice coming from a closer spot startled the thickset man, but he didn't move away. "Your first bullet cost me my memory. You'll have to fill me in if you want me to know who he was."

"You're a liar, Morgan!"

"Please," Elaina pleaded, "he's telling you the truth."

The big man tightened his hold, nearly choking off her breath.

"You seem to know a lot about him, little lady. You know he's a killer? My brother was only nineteen years old. Morgan shot him down and never looked back."

Elaina could smell the burly man's sour breath. His brown hair, rumpled by the wind, was long and unkempt. He was dressed in canvas trousers and a red plaid shirt, a workingman's clothes, yet she'd never seen him before, and he didn't talk like a miner. Though she couldn't justify her feelings, she didn't believe a word of what the man said about Morgan.

"I'm tired of talkin'," Kirby said. "Come out now or I'll kill her."

The gun pressed harder against her temple, and Elaina felt tiny rivulets of perspiration running between her breasts.

"She means nothing to me," Morgan answered, and the words cut like a knife. "I don't care if you kill her or not, so you might as well let her go."

Elaina felt a wave of nausea, more from Morgan's words than from the heavy man's hold on her.

"You're lying, Morgan. She means plenty to you, all right. I saw it in yer eyes as you was walkin' down the street."

Elaina straightened, her courage restored a little by Kirby's words. Did Morgan really care for her? Had he looked at her in some special way she hadn't noticed? She had no time to ponder the questions.

Morgan stepped into the open, his gun pointed in Lars Kirby's direction. With slow, determined steps he moved toward the spot where the shooter held Elaina. Kirby's name conjured no memory, but the notion that he might have killed the man's brother, as Kirby claimed, weakened Morgan's resolve. If only he could remember.

"That's far enough, Morgan."

Morgan had moved to within easy shooting range, but any shot he took could be deadly for Elaina. He'd been practicing with his Colt for three days. He knew his aim was far better than that of the average man, but the wound to his shoulder had taken a toll. How much of a toll he couldn't be sure.

"You may not remember Billy," the man was saying, "but you know this girl. And she means a whole lot more to you than you're willin' to admit. So before I kill you I want you to know exactly what I intend to do. I'm gonna pleasure myself with her in every way I know how. Then I'm gonna take her the way they do them pretty boys. You got that, Morgan?"

Morgan's control snapped. If he'd had doubts before, he had none now. Working on blind instinct, he pulled his gun, drew back the hammer, aimed, and fired in one fluid motion, the echo of the blast resounding in unison with Elaina's high-pitched scream.

The bullet took the shooter right between the eyes.

His heavy, thickset body crumpled on top of Elaina, the blood oozing onto her skirt as Morgan raced to her side.

Unmindful of the consequences, Elaina wrapped her arms around Morgan's neck and let him lift her into his arms while tears blurred her vision. She barely heard the sound of voices, the scrape of doors and windows being opened, or the sound of running feet as the townspeople surrounded her.

"Thank God you're safe," she whispered against Morgan's cheek. He seemed not to hear her. Instead he handed her carefully into the waiting arms of her intended.

"What in hell is going on here, Elaina?" Chuck asked. He glanced from Elaina's tear-streaked face and bloody skirt to the dead man on the ground, then to Morgan, who had holstered his weapon and backed away.

"I'm all right, Chuck. You can put me down now," Elaina told him, knowing that if Morgan's arms were still around her, she'd have been happy to stay where she was. Chuck complied, helping her to stand on unsteady legs and watching her uncertainly.

Elaina sniffed back tears, determined to be strong. "By the way, Chuck." She lifted her gaze to Chuck's wary, brooding one. "Where were you during all the commotion?"

"I — I just got here. I guess I missed most of the excitement. Long as you're safe, that's all that matters. I'll have to remember to thank Morgan with a little bonus."

"Is that all you ever think about, Chuck? Money?"

"Of course not, dear. I'm just glad you're all right."

Elaina took a deep, steadying breath, her eyes searching for Morgan. Seeing only his broad shoulders retreating toward the marshal's office, feeling dazed and disoriented, and sickened by the sight of the blood on her skirt, she let Chuck lead her back to the hotel.

"Well, Marshal Stratton, looks like you can call off your investigation — that is, if there ever was one." Morgan closed the office door with a bit too much effort, the resounding thump ringing off the walls of the narrow room.

Frank Stratton smiled crookedly. He set his mug of coffee down on his desk and lowered his feet to the floor in one motion. "Do tell. I'll see to the body, Morgan. City'll even pick up the funeral bill so there won't be any hard feelings." He scratched the fringe of graying hair surrounding the bald spot on the top of his head. "Miss McAllister all right?"

"No thanks to you, she's fine. But there is one thing I want from you, Marshal."

"Oh? And what might that be?"

"I want you to get any information you can find on the Kirby brothers, Lars and Billy. Particularly how Billy Kirby died." Morgan flexed his knuckles. "Think you can handle that?"

"I can tell you about the Kirby boys right now," Stratton said, moving from behind his desk to a stack of papers, advertisements, and old Wanted posters. "Lars Kirby's wanted for murder in three states. There's a sizable reward out for him." Stratton handed him the poster. "I'll see you get it. His brother died three years ago in Kansas. You killed him, Morgan, but I guess you don't remember that, do you? Far as I know, it was a fair light. Billy was trying to make a name for himself. He drew down on you. You killed him in self-defense."

Morgan released a long, relieved breath. "How is it you know

84

so much about all this, Stratton?"

"I did a little research for Dolph and Henry before they hired you. They wanted to be sure to get their money's worth." Another crooked smile. "So far, you've been more trouble than you're worth, but after today, those miners oughta be good and scared. My guess is they'll behave themselves as long as you're around."

Morgan clenched his jaw, not liking the marshal or the self-satisfied tone of his words. "Thanks, Stratton, for all your . . . assistance."

"Any time, Morgan. Any time at all."

Morgan let himself out, aware of the burden that had been lifted from his conscience and feeling a whole lot safer as he walked down Broad Street toward his room. Without conscious effort, he let his thoughts drift to Elaina, how brave she'd been, how worried for his safety, even though her own life was in peril. He hoped she'd never know how close she had come to dying. The thought wrenched his guts like a slug of rotten whiskey.

Morgan crossed the street wondering at the intensity of his emotions. Though his memories were limited, more of them were returning each day. He was sure he'd never felt the gut-wrenching, heart-stopping fear he'd encountered seeing Elaina McAllister with a loaded gun at her head. He damned himself for allowing himself to become attached to the girl. If he'd bedded her as he set out to, he was sure he'd be feeling none of these things. That's what happened to a man, he told himself, when he let his loins do his thinking for him.

As he approached the etched-glass doors of the hotel, he resolved again to bring the girl to his bed and get it over with. He needed to get back to being himself instead of some love-struck fool.

# Chapter 8

"Well, tomorrow's the big day." Ada Lowery broached the subject Elaina had been dreading.

"I know, Ada." She glanced across the kitchen to the buxom gray-haired woman expertly slicing thin pieces from a slab of salt pork that rested on the butcher block. She'd met Ada seven years ago. Henry Dawson had moved Elaina into the hotel after her mother died so Ada could look after her, but she was more of a friend than a second mother. Ada had helped Elaina survive the loss of her family, had shown her how to earn her room and board, and taught her to depend on no one but herself.

"Still haven't changed yer mind?" Ada asked, lifting the lid off a kettle of boiling beans. The steamy aroma billowed up in a hazy cloud as she added the salt pork.

"You know very well I haven't changed my mind," Elaina answered. Though she'd worked for her board and room, Henry Dawson had paid for Elaina's schooling, her clothing, and the necessities of life. Elaina had insisted from the beginning that Henry keep accurate records of what she owed him, and Henry had done as she'd asked. A little over two years ago, he'd told her how much she owed, and the sum seemed incredible. Then he told her what he really wanted in return — her promise to marry his son.

"I've given my word, and I intend to keep it," she said as they seated themselves at a wide pine table beside tall stacks of home-made bread. They would need dozens of tiny finger sandwiches for the engagement party tomorrow night. With the expertise of women all too familiar with kitchen work, they began slicing the loaves. "Besides, it's too late now even if I wanted to back out."

"'Well, you sure seem edgy lately." Ada flashed a knowing smile. "Couldn't be that Morgan fella, could it? I seen the way he watches you — and the way you look at him. Can't say as I blame you none, neither. He is one handsome man."

Elaina stiffened. Was she that transparent? She'd tried to stay away from Morgan, been determined not to let him insinuate himself any deeper into her affections than he already had, but her thoughts remained with him, and her unruly eyes watched him covertly whenever she had the chance.

He'd checked on her that day after the shooting, been solicitous, and apologized for getting her involved, but Chuck had been there, so the conversation was formal and remote. Which was probably just as well.

"Doesn't matter one way or another," Elaina replied. "It's too late now. Anyway, why would I want to get involved with a man like Morgan?" Careful to keep her eyes averted, she nervously straightened the bodice of her scoop-necked pink muslin dress.

"Oh, I don't know. He don't seem such a bad sort to me. Hand me that other knife, yonder." Ada leaned across the table, took the knife from Elaina's grasp, and sat back down. "Man's always been right polite and helpful. Never seen him step outta line." She looked up from her cutting, and her eyes danced with mischief. "If'n I was twenty years younger, I might give him a tumble myself."

Elaina grinned at the older woman and shook her head in disbelief. "Sometimes, Ada, you amaze me."

The women worked hard all day preparing for the engagement party the following night. By late afternoon it was time for the balance of the kitchen help to return and begin preparations for the hotel's evening meal. Elaina and Ada had done most of the cooking for the party, and with the foodstuffs other ladies in the community were sure to bring, there was certain to be plenty.

Chuck had promised to send a couple of boys from the mine over in the morning to help hang streamers in the dining room and do the heavy work of rearranging chairs and tables, so all was pretty well in order. Elaina sighed as she covered the last platter of food, glad to be finished and determined to have some time to herself.

"Think I'll go out back and check on my garden," she said as she hung her apron on a peg beside the door. Ada nodded and went back to her chores. With a light step, Elaina closed the kitchen door and headed into the late afternoon sunlight and off toward her tiny garden.

Digging in the rich dark earth, watching life spring forth at the touch of her hand had always brought Elaina pleasure. She particularly enjoyed growing the herbs she used in her healing work. With careful scrutiny, she noticed the few tiny weeds that had crept among the plants in just these past few days.

Glad for a chance to feel the sun's warming rays, she gathered her skirts and headed toward the potting shed at the back of the garden. She couldn't wait to begin working in the warm, dark soil.

"Mrs. Lowery?"

Ada glanced up from her work and took in the tall, rangy man standing just inside the kitchen door. The dark circles were gone from beneath his eyes and his cheeks had taken on a healthy glow, but his gaze remained wary and reflective. He'd seen plenty of trouble in his day — she'd bet on that. But a lot of men had. Somehow she just couldn't believe he was as bad as folks made him out. Everyone in Keyserville had heard about the gunfight and the way he'd saved Elaina. 'Course he coulda got her killed just as easy.

"Why, Mr. Morgan, don't you look fine today. What can I do for you?" She wondered about the thin scar running along his neck, and, as if reading her thoughts, he reached a bronzed hand up to absently finger the mark.

"I'm looking for Elain . . . Miss McAllister. Have you seen her? I wanted to thank her for mending my shirt."

She remembered Elaina had stitched up the white shirt Morgan claimed was his favorite, torn on his outing to the Colsons'. Done a fine job of it, too.

"Last time I seen her, she was headed out back to her garden. You might look there." Ada grinned knowingly, recognizing the words for the excuse they were and returned to her work.

Morgan walked out of the kitchen, down the hall, and out into the paling sunlight. The afternoon was dying, but it was still faintly warm and sunny.

Starting with the garden, he searched the grounds, but saw no sign of Elaina. She'd been dodging him, he knew, but he couldn't really blame her. There was a warm current between them that even

Chuck Dawson couldn't miss. And tomorrow was the engagement party. For reasons Morgan didn't completely understand, the thought sliced his heart like a blade.

Beginning to worry a little and wondering if he could somehow have missed her in the hotel, he had started back toward the porch when an idea struck him and he returned instead to the garden. A small potting shed stood alone in one corner of the patch. There were no windows, only a door, which appeared to be tightly shut. Dainty footprints in the soft earth led up to the door.

As he got closer, he realized a board had fallen in front of the door and jammed itself between two barrels, effectively blocking the entrance.

He tapped on the door. "Elaina?"

After removing the board from behind the barrels, he lifted the wooden latch and opened the door. Elaina McAllister, knees drawn up beneath her chin, arms wrapped protectively around them, huddled on the cold dirt floor. In her left hand she clutched a metal trowel so tightly her knuckles looked pale. Rocking herself back and forth, she stared straight ahead, her eyes bleak and vacant.

"Elaina?" Morgan called to her softly as he knelt beside her.

She didn't answer, made no effort to respond.

"It's Dan," he whispered, prying the trowel from her fingers. "Are you hurt?" Fear gnawed at his insides. What could have happened to leave her so devastated? So completely helpless?

Elaina had retreated into a world of her own, a dark world filled with mine rats and decay. There was no escape from this world, no way to elude the darkness. Her body felt brittle and damp and ached from the cold. She couldn't move, could barely force herself to take the next painful, jagged breath. Time held no meaning; there was no time in this dark hell in which she lived. Deeper and deeper she sank, devoured by her all-consuming fear of the blackness that held her with icy talons like those of some unseen predatory beast.

She was in the mine, searching for Ren and Tommy. She could feel the cold seeping through her clothes, even through her shoes. The kerosene lamp she'd brought cast its glow only a few feet into the passage she traveled. It seemed she walked in a tiny island of light in a vast sea of darkness. The tunnel walls took on frightening shapes and faces, like grotesque characters out of a nightmare. She'd never felt more alone in her life. With small, shaky steps, she headed farther into the depths of the mountain.

Terrifying sounds, unearthly sounds, stopped her. With trembling fingers, she held the lamp down near her feet, trying to locate the source of the slithering noises she'd heard, desperately afraid of what she'd see. She heard it again in the rocks to her left, and her heart beat frantically, the pulsing rhythm echoing in her ears as loud as her own footfalls on the rocky tunnel floor. She wanted to run from the darkness and the terror, but she couldn't. Her trembling legs refused to obey her command.

More noises echoed in the stillness behind her. Her palms were sweating; her lips felt cold and dry. Barely able to control her trembling limbs, she inched slowly forward. Please, God, please help me. Suddenly a movement in the dark drew her attention. A scurrying sound this time, then something heavy touched her foot. Mine rats!

She screamed hysterically, the sound echoing demonically against the walls of the narrow tunnel, and lost her hold on the lamp. Terrified, she ran toward the safety of the entrance only to discover an even greater terror as she fled the circle of light. She was breathing hard again, clutching the wall for support. The tears she'd been holding back fell freely now, dampening her clothes. She was so afraid. She could taste the bile in her throat at the mere thought of remaining in the mine. Fighting her fears as if it were a conquering demon, she used the wall to brace herself, to steady her shaking arms and legs. She couldn't let Ren and Tommy die. She would try one last time.

A voice, a flicker of recognition penetrated the depths of the darkness. Ren? Where are you, Ren? She glimpsed the sunlight streaming through the open door of the shed, began to whimper, and shiver uncontrollably.

Ignoring the pain in his shoulder, Dan Morgan scooped the girl into his arms and carried her out of the shack. As his long strides moved them toward a grassy knoll, she sobbed softly against his chest. What in God's name had happened to her? Gently he lowered her to the ground, then sank down beside her, gathering her protectively against him.

"Tell me what happened, Lainey," he whispered. It tortured him to look at her, to see such anguish on her face. She blinked as the name registered, and her trembling receded, but her arms slipped around his neck and she clung to him as if he were her only chance of escape. As she fought for control, he held her a moment more, stroking her dark hair and whispering soothing words. "You're all right, Elaina. It's Dan. Just hang on to me. You're going to be fine." When she lifted her eyes to his, several large tears rolled down her cheeks.

He smoothed them away with his fingers and offered his handkerchief. "Are you ready to tell me what happened?"

She shook her head.

"Please, Elaina, you must tell me."

She sniffed and dabbed at her eyes, unwilling to look at him.

"Please," he coaxed.

"I'm so embarrassed." Another tear rolled down her cheek.

"Would you please stop crying and tell me what the hell happened!" he demanded, a little more harshly than he intended.

"That's just it. Nothing happened. I went into the potting shed to get a trowel, and the breeze blew the door shut behind me. Then the board fell down and I . . . I couldn't get out." She swallowed hard and glanced away. "It's being shut in . . . in the darkness.

"When I was a little girl, there was a cave-in at Blue Mountain. My friends were trapped. I figured a way to get them out — something I knew that apparently everyone else had forgotten — but I couldn't find my father, and my mother wouldn't listen. In the middle of the night, I sneaked out of the house and went into the mine alone. I guess that's what caused my . . . problem."

"I'd like to hear about it, if you'd tell me." For some strange reason the girl's story struck some chord of remembrance. Why, he could not fathom.

Elaina took a deep, calming breath and related the events leading up to the mine cave-in. Since Morgan worked for Redmond and Dawson, she didn't mention their part in the tragedy.

"My plan was simple," she told him, sniffing again. "The boys were trapped on A level. That meant they weren't in deep, but they were far back. The younger boy and I had built a fort inside an abandoned tunnel on the opposite side of the mountain. I guess the passage was so old nobody remembered it was there, but the boys said they could reach almost any tunnel in the mine through those old shafts.

"My parents used to own the big Victorian house Henry Dawson lives in out at the edge of the mine patch. It wasn't far from there to the mine. In the daytime I could see the main entrance from my bedroom upstairs. I climbed out the window and down the trellis about midnight. I remember seeing crews working at the main tunnel as I passed, trying to remove enough debris to reach the boys, but I was terrified no one would listen, or worse yet, send me home. So I went around to the backside and entered through the fort. I'd sneaked in there often, but I'd never gone far into the mine until that night.

"When I got into the tunnel, I was so terrified I was sick, but I finally found the cave-in and heard the boys tapping. Luckily the dirt and debris weren't too deep in that spot, but of course the boys didn't know that. They dug. I dug. Just before dawn we broke through." She dabbed at a fresh trickle of tears.

"After we reached safety, everything seemed all right. It wasn't until later" — her voice dropped to a whisper — "after my father shot himself in the cellar that I began to have nightmares about the rats and the darkness. Once I accidentally locked myself in a closet at the hotel. Ada found me in the same condition you did."

Morgan exhaled slowly. He did indeed know the story, at least the part about the cave-in. And for some unknown reason he felt guilty about Elaina's condition. He clenched his jaw, wishing he could understand.

"Does Dawson know about your fears?" he asked, suddenly worried about the power Dawson could wield if he discovered Elaina's weakness.

"Only Ada . . . and now you."

"Do me a favor?" he asked, careful to keep his tone light.

"Yes?"

"Keep it that way. And don't worry. Your secret's safe with me." He touched her cheek with the back of his hand.

"I feel like such a coward."

"Don't be silly. You saved your friends' lives, and I watched you at the town meeting hall. It took a lot of courage for you to give that speech. And remember how brave you were when Lars

92

Kirby held his gun at your head." She blanched, and he regretted having brought up the incident. "This is something completely different. A lot of people have fears they can't understand. With some people its snakes or spiders. With you it's being trapped in the dark. It's nothing to be ashamed of."

"You remember the miners' meeting?" she suddenly asked, eyes wide.

He smiled. "Yes, I guess I do at that."

She smiled up at him. "I'm glad for you." Sunlight, red-gold now with the coming dusk, tinged her thick dark hair with the same shade of crimson while casting a warmth over her features. She looks so vulnerable, he thought. Beautiful, yes. Womanly, yes. But, oh, so vulnerable. Moving his hand from the tiny circle of her waist to the thick hair curling down her back, he felt a wave of protectiveness, followed by a surge of desire.

Cupping her chin in his hand, he covered her lips in a gentle kiss, lightly molding his mouth to hers. Her lips were soft and full, her breath warm and flavored with the salty taste of her tears. When his tongue found its way between her teeth, her arms went around his neck, sending a jolt of desire the length of him. With a soft groan, he forced himself to pull away. The hotel was too close, even for a man with his reckless nature.

Elaina let Morgan help her up and brushed the dirt and grass from her pink muslin dress. His kiss had been tender, a promise of gentleness she still had trouble accepting in a tough man like him. She was glad he'd pulled away because she had little desire to break the contact. Memories of their day at the circus and his light, teasing smile crowded her mind.

Then came the forbidden memories — the feel of his muscular body, his practiced hands, his mouth tasting her breasts. Suddenly she wished she were miles away, still wrapped in his strong arms. He might be a hard man, but there was something good and caring about him. She could sense it. She regretted more than ever her engagement to Chuck Dawson, which would be official on the morrow. If it weren't for the debt she owed and her need to restore the McAllister name to its rightful status, she'd tell them all to go hang, and find out just what being a woman was all about.

Accepting Morgan's arm, she let him guide her back to the hotel.

\* \* \* \* \*

After supper, Dan Morgan reclined on his iron bed, feet propped up, hands behind his head, pondering the events of the afternoon. Clouded images of his past, fleeting thoughts, and unclear remnants had played havoc with his mind all evening. Like fireflies, they danced brightly just outside his grasp. His tender response to the girl this afternoon seemed out of character. He was supposed to be seducing her, doing whatever was necessary to bring her to his bed. Yet he'd been seized by those same deep feelings of protectiveness he'd experienced before.

Elaina desired him, of that he was certain. She wouldn't be married to Dawson for weeks, and he was sure at some point during that time he'd find the opportunity he was seeking. Why, then, did his conscience prickle him so? He was a gunman, a hired, paid enforcer. His memory had confirmed the truth of the newspaper stories and his presence at the meeting hall. And he could conjure vague remembrances of other women, other nights of passion, with no regrets, no pangs of conscience, so why not this woman? Besides, he'd probably be doing her a favor. She certainly wasn't attracted to Dawson, and every woman deserved to experience a little passion at least once in her life.

He crossed his booted feet atop the covers. His conscience be hanged! He'd played the gentleman far too long already. He would take the girl to his bed the first chance he got. He wanted her and she wanted him. That was all that mattered.

Hearing a knock at the door, he pulled his Colt .45 from its holster slung over the chair beside the bed. Holding it behind him, he opened the door a crack. A small, pale tow-headed youth looked up at him with wide green eyes.

"Telegram here for a Mr. Dan Morgan. That you?"

Morgan holstered the gun. "It's me." He accepted the envelope, tipped the boy, and got a missing-tooth grin for his trouble; then he closed the door. Breaking the seal, he unfolded the thin ivory paper: "Dan, Have not heard from you in three weeks. Beginning to worry. Please send word of your safety. Your brother, Tommy."

So he had a brother named Tommy. The name brought memories of the same red-haired boy he'd glimpsed before. Not a son but a brother. Now he could clearly see the boy as a man, or at least close to a man — freckle-faced, tall and lean, his shock of red hair tousled by the breeze. Just one more clue to his rapidly returning identity. The telegram had been sent from California. A town called Napa. The word brought images of a lovely valley nestled between fertile rolling hills.

He pondered the telegram and made a decision, one that had been nudging the back of his mind almost daily: He would end his employment with Redmond and Dawson, at least until his memory returned in full. His mind, and now this wire, had given him enough clues to begin a search.

Pulling a shirt over his bare chest, he left his room and headed toward the telegraph office. He would leave for California the day after tomorrow. He could be in San Francisco in less than two weeks. He'd wire his brother to meet him. His brother could fill in the gaping holes in his past. After that, he would decide what course of action to take. Maybe he'd come back to Keyserville and get the girl. There was a good possibility she'd go with him if he pressed her hard enough.

For reasons he refused to acknowledge, the thought comforted him as he headed into the darkness with long, purposeful strides.

# Chapter 9

As usual, Ada's big toe was right — a storm was on its way.

Dark clouds with flat gray bottoms rolled and curled in thick columns against the sky while thunder beckoned in the distance. It could turn into quite a gale, Elaina decided, but maybe if they were lucky it would wait another day.

As Chuck Dawson had promised, two boys from the mine came to string colored paper and tack a large glittery sign on one wall that read "Congratulations, Elaina and Chuck." Lace tablecloths were laid over long wooden tables, and crisp starched napkins were placed in delicate rows. The tiny finger sandwiches, as well as delicate cakes, nuts, and candies were set out, and the punch bowl was filled with a delicious lemonade concoction. A separate punch awaited the menfolk on another table across the room. Elaina could smell the savory aroma of meats and spices as she made a final check and left for her room on the third floor.

She bathed carefully, enjoying the luxury of the lavender scent in her tub. Then she pulled her dark hair to one side, where it curled in long shiny ringlets, and captured it with a lavender ribbon that matched her gown. Ada dashed in just long enough to pull the laces on her corset so snug she could barely breathe, but her waist was a mere handspan, so she thought maybe the discomfort was worth it. She stepped into her petticoats, and secured the soft embroidered material around her waist, then pulled her dress carefully over her head so as not to disturb her curls.

The latest styles were definitely flattering to the feminine figure, she decided as she glanced in the mirror. Her lavender silk dress outlined her hips then fell softly to the floor. A top skirt of an even lighter shade of purple draped across the skirt in front, then swept into soft folds at the back. It was a lovely gown. Henry Dawson had brought it to her all the way from New York as an engagement present, and though she hated to become any more indebted to him than she already was, she could hardly have refused to accept the gift.

Running her fingers over the delicate fabric, she felt utterly feminine. Tonight she would relish the daringly low neckline. She couldn't wait to see the effect the dress would have on Dan Morgan.

Elaina instantly felt guilty for the thought. Damn her unruly mind! She should be thinking of her fiancé, of how proud he would be of her. She knew he would boast to every man in the room that he'd finally made her his. And many of the women would be envious of her position. The Dawson family wielded considerable wealth and power, and most women found Chuck attractive. She wished for the hundredth time he could arouse the feelings Morgan could.

The thought steeled her resolve.

She would learn to care for him, make him come to care for her. She knew he desired her; the hungry look never left his eyes. Maybe if their marriage started with passion, even if only on his part, she could build it into something more, help them make a life together. She certainly hoped so. Tonight, she vowed, would be her first attempt at really being Chuck Dawson's girl. Nothing Morgan could do or say would make her feel a thing. She would banish forever any feelings she might once have had for him. After all, he was nothing more than a hired killer. She certainly should be able to resist the charms of a man like that!

Elaina was dabbing a final dot of lilac cologne behind her ear when she heard the knock at her door. Time to go. She felt a small knot of dread as she opened the door, but seeing the satisfied look on Chuck's face as he appraised her forced the feelings from her mind. She had to admit he looked handsome in his navy blue tailcoat, matching trousers, and crisp white shirt. His usually sallow complexion had taken on a slightly ruddy hue from his work in the strengthening spring sun, giving him a more masculine appearance than usual. His powerful shoulders were outlined by the coat, and she had to tip her head back to meet his dark eyes. A look of triumph seemed reflected in their brooding depths, and she felt her unease surface again.

"You look lovely, my dear," Chuck said.

"Why, thank you, Chuck." She accepted his arm, and they swept into the hall. With long, graceful strides, they descended the two flights of stairs to the rooms below.

At the bottom of the staircase Chuck paused. "For you, my dear." He handed her a tiny blue velvet box, his fingers cool as they brushed against her skin. She popped open the lid. Nestled on a bed of ivory satin, a single large diamond surrounded by blood-red rubies sparkled up at her. The ring was lovely but garish. When Chuck slipped it on her finger, it dwarfed her slim hand.

"Thank you, Chuck. It's lovely." She kissed him on the cheek, and he led her into the dining room. The room was filled with guests; everyone, it seemed, who was anyone from miles around was in attendance. She smiled warmly at the people she knew, many of whom had been friends of her father's, and Chuck introduced her to the others. Henry Dawson joined them, smiling broadly and clapping his son on the back.

" 'Bout time you two got together. I was beginnin' to worry." Dawson gave Elaina a smile that clearly spoke of the debt she owed him. She still wasn't certain why he'd been so adamant about her marriage to his son or, for that matter, why Chuck was so determined to go along with his father's wishes, but that was their business. She had her own reasons for agreeing to the marriage, and she would abide by her word.

"May I offer you some refreshment?" Chuck smiled inanely.

"Why, yes, I'd like that." She watched him head toward the men's punch table at the back of the room, then made use of his absence to survey the remaining guests. She was searching for Morgan, but he was nowhere to be found. She felt a wave of relief, followed by a surge of disappointment, then another bout of anger at herself. She sighed. At least Morgan was one problem she wouldn't have to deal with tonight.

"Well, daughter," Henry Dawson was saying, having ended his conversation with Samuel Smythe, a mine owner from Hazleton. "We Dawsons will be proud to have you in the family."

"Thank you, Henry." She couldn't bring herself to call him Father. They chatted a bit more, and he introduced her to several important industrialists from Wilkes-Barre, who had just arrived. The five-piece orchestra began to play just as Chuck arrived with her punch. Thirsty from her nervousness, she took a big sip, choked, and nearly sprayed it on the man beside her. Tears came to her eyes, and she coughed several times behind her hand.

Chuck patted her on the back. "Are you all right, my dear?"

"Chuck, this is . . . the men's punch!"

He hushed her. "I won't tell if you won't. Come on, drink up. It'll be fun." He smiled and pushed the cup firmly back toward her lips.

Elaina quietly fumed. She had nothing against drinking. She enjoyed an occasional glass of sherry as much as anyone else, but to be pushed into it against her wishes, that was something different. After pretending to take another sip, she set the cup down on a table and pretended to accidentally tip it over.

"Now look what you've done!" Chuck snapped. He pointed a finger at a nearby servant. "You there. Clean this mess up!"

"Why don't we dance?" Elaina interceded smoothly. Chuck glowered at her but led her onto the floor. He refused to look at her, and Elaina smiled to herself. A tiny victory, but a victory just the same.

Chuck was a good dancer. She followed him easily and began to relax a little. And he appeared to be regaining his congenial mood, smiling down at her indulgently. Other couples made way for them as they whirled about the floor to the strains of "The Blue Danube Waltz." Chuck held her so tightly she could feel his sweaty palm through the thin fabric of the lavender silk dress. She focused her attention on the other dancers who dipped and swayed around them, twirling and gliding to the rhythm of the waltz. When the music ended, Chuck gave her up to one of the many men waiting in line to dance with her on the couple's special night.

As dance after dance ended and a new one began, the evening blurred. Chuck danced with her again, and then a tall, auburn-haired man from Scranton — or was it Allentown? — whisked her around the floor just a beat ahead of the music. She was feeling like a wilted rose by the time they finished and another man stepped into position in front of her. His hand felt warm and sure as he lifted hers and guided her steps in time to the music.

Sky-blue eyes touched her face, and her fatigue melted away. Elaina followed him breathlessly, mesmerized by his gentle yet forceful gaze, her heart pounding in her ears. She knew she should speak, but didn't trust her voice. Instead she whirled silently around the floor in the arms of the tall, handsome man.

Following his lead, she let herself go, her feet carrying her unerringly, gliding, matching his long-legged stride step for step. As the firm pressure of his strong hands guided her, she thought of the way he'd handled the mare that day in the country and against her will remembered the feel of those hands on her bare breasts. Fighting to control her fevered emotions, she felt a surge of heat rush to her cheeks. When Morgan smiled down at her, his gaze more than warm, she wondered for a moment if he was remembering, too.

"You look lovely tonight, Miss McAllister." As if in answer to her unspoken question, his eyes drifted to the swell of her breasts.

"Thank you, Mr. Morgan," she replied with equal formality and was thankful her voice sounded even. She no longer heard the strains of the music, just the pounding of her heart. Were there others still on the floor?

"I've been watching you from the porch. There's not a woman who compares."

"Thank you" was all she could manage. He smelled faintly of some musky cologne that lingered on the lapel of his immaculate black coat. Dressed as he was, he looked the part of the gentleman, but unlike Chuck Dawson's classic, almost delicate attractiveness, the sharp angles and planes of Morgan's face gave him a ruthless quality, an agedness that spoke of some past suffering. There was power in the tiny lines that creased his brow, crinkled at the corners of his eyes. Power and strength and a maleness most men lacked. It fascinated her, drew her to him like a river to a turbulent sea. She missed a step, and he paused.

"You're tiring. Would you like a breath of air?"

It would be unseemly to walk outside with him, and she knew it. "Yes, maybe just for a moment." He escorted her out through tall glass-paned doors that opened onto the wide porch at the rear of the hotel.

Outside, the heat of the hall was replaced by a pervasive chill, and the sky had clouded even more. Dense layers rolled and threatened ominously. A flash of lightning, miles away, drew her attention. The rumble was distant, but the storm was moving in their direction.

It would mean many of the guests would be departing early and Elaina suddenly felt grateful.

"So you're going through with it." Morgan's deep voice raised the subject she most dreaded.

"Yes," she whispered, drawn to the tender look in his eyes. How could he affect her so? Why was just being near him such a heady experience? She should go back inside, find Chuck, stay away from this man at all costs.

"You don't love him."

"No. I don't love him." How could she say that? And to a stranger! Then she thought of the time they'd spent together, his hands on her body, and was glad for the shadows on the porch.

"But you owe him." Morgan ran a finger along the line of her jaw, and suddenly her knees felt weak.

"I owe his family. That's the same thing."

The door opened. She heard a few strains of music as a streak of bright light lit the porch.

"There you are. I've been looking for you," Chuck Dawson's gruff voice boomed from the doorway. He took in the scene at a glance. "I see you're in the capable hands of the infamous Mr. Morgan."

"Miss McAllister was feeling a little light-headed," Morgan covered smoothly as Dawson approached.

"Yes," Elaina confirmed. "I didn't see you, so I asked Mr. Morgan to escort me outside for some air."

"Then may I extend a thank-you for rescuing my fiancée a second time." Dawson said the words with a hint of sarcasm, pulling her none too gently beside him. "Now, if you'll excuse us, we have other guests to attend to." With a moist hand at her waist, he guided her back into the dining room and over to a corner.

"Don't make me have to look for you again," he warned as he leaned close. "Stay away from Morgan. Do you understand me?"

Elaina nodded. The expression in his eyes had turned brooding again. It brooked no argument. "Yes," she whispered.

He smiled mechanically. "Shall we dance?"

The last of the guests departed, hurrying to get home before the storm broke. Some were staying in the hotel and would leave in the morning, but most had elected to return to their own beds. Elaina sighed wearily. Other than the hired help, she and Chuck were the last to leave the hall. He'd been drinking heavily all evening, refusing to allow her escape from the party until every guest had left. Now he insisted on walking her up the two flights of stairs to her room. Elaina was too tired to argue. Eager to be rid of Chuck, undress, and slide beneath the covers, she climbed the stairs and opened the door.

"Good night, Chuck," she said, pursing her lips to receive his kiss. His mouth came down full force, and he pulled her hard against him. There was nothing tender in the embrace, just a possessiveness that claimed her as his. She broke away and, thanking him for the evening, tried to escape into the privacy of her room. Chuck blocked the way.

"Not tonight, Elaina. I've waited long enough."

An icy dread froze in the pit of her stomach. "We aren't married yet, Chuck."

"I'm sick of your excuses. It's time I made certain you know just whose property you are." He pushed her into the room and closed the door, then turned the key in the lock.

"Property? Property! I'm not your property or anyone else's. Get out of here, Chuck, before I scream."

Chuck just smiled. "Go ahead. Who's going to hear you? The only ones up here are Morgan and old man Farley. Farley's hard of hearing. Morgan's our man. He's no fool. He's not about to get involved in a family matter."

Elaina swallowed hard. A thousand uncertainties flashed through her mind. She could scream. Maybe Morgan would come — maybe not. Or she could let Dawson make love to her. She'd have to let him when the time came anyway. If she gave in now, maybe she could forget Morgan, begin to think of Chuck as the man she would marry.

He was moving toward her.

In an instant she decided — it was worth a try.

Morgan felt exhausted. The evening had been a trying one, though he couldn't fully comprehend why. Just being around Elaina McAllister, watching her with Dawson, had caused him endless

102

consternation. He'd come to his room to escape the whole affair, try to get some rest, but so far sleep had eluded him. He'd stripped off his coat, vest, and shirt and sprawled on the bed in just his boots and breeches. He had read for a while and was just beginning to feel drowsy when noises in the room next door drew his attention. From years of caution, he poised, listening for signs of trouble.

Determined to respond to Chuck's romantic assault, Elaina steeled herself. With little concern for her feelings, Chuck pulled her roughly into his arms and covered her lips in a wet, sticky kiss. She could taste stale whiskey and the bitter taste of cigars. Moving his palm to her breasts, he kneaded them coarsely through the light silk fabric of her gown. Elaina felt the bile rise in her throat. Sickened, she swayed against him and a small whimper escaped. Chuck mistook it for passion.

"I knew you wanted it, you bitch," he slurred in her ear. "Underneath those fancy petticoats, you women are all alike." The words destroyed the last of her resolve. Panicky, she struggled, her hands pressing futilely against his chest.

Chuck held her fast.

"So now you want to play games?" he taunted. Grinning wolfishly, he exhaled a rush of sour breath. "Nothing I'd like better!"

Roughly he pinned her arms behind her back, and Elaina suffered the wrenching pain.

"Please, Chuck, I can't," she pleaded. "Let me go."

Chuck answered by grabbing the neckline of her lavender gown as well as her chemise and ripping the cloth from her bosom to her navel. Elaina's full breasts spilled forward above her corset, and a sob caught in her throat. In desperation, she tore her hands free of his grasp and flailed wildly against his chest.

Chuck laughed demonically. "And I was worried you wouldn't show me enough spirit!" He grabbed her hands again, but she twisted free.

Planting her feet firmly, she balled her slender hand into a fist and hit Chuck hard in the face. Then she ran for the door. Chuck intercepted her. His smile had faded. Blood oozed from a long, thin gash on his cheek where her diamond engagement ring had sliced through flesh.

103

"That's the second mistake you've made tonight. The first was making eyes at Morgan." Chuck grabbed her wrist with one hand and slapped her hard across the face with the other. A second slap brought tears to her eyes and the salty taste of blood. Seeing the wild-eyed expression on Chuck's face, she finally did scream.

And scream and scream and scream.

Morgan seized his Colt and was on his feet in a second, out the door, and into the hall. He cocked the hammer of the big .45, pointing the barrel upward as he cautiously approached the room next to his. Elaina's door was locked, and the screaming had ceased, but he raised a booted foot and splintered the latch just the same. The door swung wide, slamming solidly against the wall. The sound of heavy breathing filled the silence.

"Get out of here, Morgan. This is none of your affair."

Only the light streaming in from the hall lit the room, but Morgan recognized Dawson's shrill voice. As his eyes adjusted to the darkness, Morgan took in the scene at a glance. Dawson had Elaina pinned beneath him across her narrow bed. Her gown was ripped to her waist, and her skirt was shoved up, exposing her long, slim legs. Her red-brown hair had tumbled loose, leaving damp tendrils clinging to her throat and breasts. Dawson's hand covered a nipple, and he kneaded it possessively, almost casually, in front of Morgan.

When lightening flashed outside the window, Morgan saw an ugly purple bruise beginning to darken near Elaina's eye and blood trickling from a corner of her mouth. Tears glistened on her cheeks. Her tawny eyes held the look of a frightened doe.

It took every ounce of Morgan's will to control his raging temper. "Let her go, Dawson. She's not your wife yet."

"You're making a big mistake, Morgan. You work for us, remember?"

Elaina trembled, fighting Chuck's heavy, suffocating weight. She could feel his thin fingers biting into the smooth flesh of her shoulders. His other hand fondled her breast, and she burned with humiliation.

"Put that gun away, Morgan," Chuck demanded.

"Let her go," Morgan warned, moving a little to the left and out of the bright light of the doorway.

"Brave man, aren't you? Long as you've got a gun in your hand."

Dawson's words seemed to test Morgan's control. He slowly placed the .45 on the seat of a chair.

"All right, Dawson. Now it's just you and me."

"I'm through telling you," Dawson said. "She's mine. I'll see to her any way I want." To prove his point, he slid his hand along her thigh and squeezed her buttocks.

Elaina felt a fresh wave of embarrassment, and a tiny whimper escaped. Through her blurred and spinning vision, she saw Morgan's cold-eyed expression. Then all hell broke loose.

Morgan dived across the room, the movement so quick Chuck's hands released their hold. Elaina sucked in sweet breaths of air as Morgan hoisted him off her.

He punched Chuck hard in the face, the muscles of his bare chest rippling with the effort. Elaina muffled a scream as Chuck toppled to the floor, knocking the blue porcelain pitcher from the bedside table. It shattered as it landed. Snatching up a jagged shard, Chuck waved it menacingly. Morgan kicked the glass away and hauled Chuck to his feet, punching him again and again, but he only swayed and took a few steps back.

Chuck recovered quickly, dealt a solid blow to Morgan's middle, and another to his jaw. Morgan went over backwards, landing heavily on his injured shoulder. He groaned, gritted his teeth against the pain, and struggled to his feet, pausing to regain his balance. Then he swung a right-handed punch that caught Chuck full on the chin and followed it with a left-right combination to the stomach, doubling him over. A hard right fist to Dawson's face sent him sprawling. He crashed across a chair, splintering the wood, then pitched solidly onto the shard-covered floor. Blood spattered the wall and oozed from his nose, and his lip was cut and swollen.

When he hauled himself to his feet, he stared murderously at Elaina, then wiped at the blood on his face with the back of his hand. Tiny splinters of porcelain had left nicks and cuts on his arms and neck. Retreating toward the door, he pointed a shaky finger at Morgan.

"You'll pay for this, Morgan." His eyes bored into Elaina. "You'll both pay." His voice sounded brittle and ragged.

Self-consciously, Elaina pulled at her torn dress, wanting to hide her body from Chuck's ugly gaze. As he slammed the door, she began to shiver uncontrollably, but relief that the danger had passed calmed her ragged spirit. After taking a steadying breath, she turned her attention to the man still poised for danger in the center of the room. He was breathing hard, his hands balled into fists.

Morgan ran his fingers through his dark, wavy hair, shoving several stray locks out of the way. He picked up his .45, reached behind him, and stuffed the weapon into the top of his breeches, but his eyes remained fixed on Elaina. Sitting down beside her, he smoothed several wild strands of hair from her bruised and battered face.

"Are you all right?" he asked gently.

She closed her eyes and leaned against him, reaching up to entwine her arms around his neck. It broke the dam of his resolve. He lifted her and with long strides carried her away from the painful memories in the room.

After nudging open the door to his own room with a booted foot, he strode to the bed, set her down carefully, then went back and locked his door. As he sat down on the bed beside her, he reached into his boot and slid a narrow-bladed knife from its hiding place. Her eyes widened, and he sensed her new alarm. Ignoring her tightening grip on his wrist, he sliced through the strings of her corset. With a sigh of relief, she sucked in deep breaths of air while he pulled the remnants of her torn dress up to its former position. Though it did little to hide her charms, she attempted a grateful smile.

He left her for a moment to pour some water into the basin from a pitcher on the washstand. After dipping a corner of a towel into the water, he gently wiped away the trickle of blood at the corner of her mouth, then placed the damp cloth on the bruise beside her eye. Though he tried to keep his attentions businesslike, a tremor shook his hand.

"Chuck said you wouldn't help me," she told him, fighting to hold back her tears. "He said you were too smart to interfere." She noticed the bruise on his jaw, reached toward it, and touched him tenderly. "I should have known you would come."

"God, Lainey." He gathered her to him and held her close, burying his face in her thick hair, his cheek pressed against hers until her trembling subsided. When he pulled away to look at her, thankful to God for her safety, the crest of one rosy nipple escaped from the torn bodice of her gown.

It was more than he could stand.

With a groan of defeat, he laced his fingers in her hair and tilted her head back. Tenderly, aware of her battered condition, he covered her lips with his.

# Chapter 10

Elaina would have sworn she'd been through too much to respond. But at the touch of his kiss, her body stirred.

He nibbled gently at first, afraid of hurting her. But she felt no pain, only a fierce joy at being beside him, held in his strong arms. As if reading her thoughts, he deepened the kiss, and she opened her mouth to allow him entrance. His tongue tasted sweet and warm, and its probing created tingling sensations that surged and ebbed and surged again. He gathered her against him, kissed her brow, her cheeks, her nose. His masculine, musky scent inflamed her. His palms roamed across the bare flesh of her back, now exposed through the tears in her dress, and she gasped at the heat of his hands. Warm lips touched her shoulder, traveled with aching tenderness along her skin to the curve of her breast. She laced her fingers in his wavy dark hair.

She was beyond caring about promises. Chuck had made it all too clear it could never work between them. Still, she had given her word. Tomorrow. She'd think about broken promises and family honor tomorrow. For tonight her life was her own. Her passion, her love, was hers alone to give. She'd take tonight for herself — and God help her tomorrow.

Morgan had intended only to comfort her, care for her, but his desire, his wanting, was too strong. He'd promised himself he'd take her, seduce her at the first opportunity. Now was the chance he'd been seeking, and yet —

With a shaky hand, he freed himself from her tender embrace. "I leave on the morning train. I've received a wire from my brother. I have to find him." He searched her tawny eyes. "Stop me now," he whispered, his voice rough, "or it will be too late."

She placed gentle fingers over his lips to silence him. "Who

108

knows what the morrow will bring? If tonight is all we have, then let us not waste it."

Morgan groaned. Hungrily he captured her lips, claiming her, possessing her. The fire in his loins burned bright. He pulled the shredded lavender silk from between them, and her breasts felt hot against the prickly hairs of his chest.

Her mouth felt warm and pliant beneath his, her lips delectably curved.

Lightning flashed, followed by the roar of thunder.

Elaina felt Morgan's hand travel along her flesh to cup the fullness of her breast, but unlike the cruelty of Dawson's touch, the warmth of his gentle fingers brought a tiny moan of pleasure. Her nipple hardened, and she heard his breathing quicken. Her own breath was coming in ragged gasps, an ache building in her secret, womanly place. Caught up in a flood of swirling sensations that matched the fury of the storm outside, she felt her heart beating crazily, fluttering against his touch like an injured bird. His lips left her mouth to trace a line of fire from her ear down the side of her neck to her shoulders. He paused, lifted his head as if in silent debate, then began to strip off the rest of her torn garments.

First the gown and then the corset fell away, then her petticoats and pantalets. Bare to his gaze and feeling suddenly shy, she turned away. Cupping her chin with his hand, he turned her face toward his.

"Don't," he whispered. "You're breathtaking." He claimed her lips in a long, deep kiss that sent a gush of warmth to the place between her legs. Then he broke the contact to pull off his boots and shed his breeches. Lightning flashed, providing a glimpse of his hard male torso. As he sat back down, she ran a hand along the rippling muscles of his stomach, fascinated by his taut, feral beauty.

The storm raging outside matched her emotions, and the down-pour began in earnest. For a moment, before his body covered hers, she could hear the thunderous pounding of the rain on the rooftop; then the pounding of her heart blocked out all other sounds. She could feel his male hardness pressing intimately between her legs, seeking entrance, as if seeking shelter from the storm. He parted her thighs a little more with his knee and positioned himself above her.

"Only a moment of pain, pretty lady, then pleasure like nothing you've dreamed."

She tensed, afraid for the first time. He stroked her breasts, kissed each peak, then ran his hands lightly over her quaking flesh to the triangle of darkness that marked her womanhood. When his finger slid inside, he found her moist and ready, but he didn't stop his ministrations until she writhed against his hand and he knew she wanted more. He kissed her passionately, forcefully, thrusting his tongue into her mouth while his shaft found entrance and slid inside her. Meeting the last barrier of resistance, he surged gently — once, twice. Then he plunged against her. Pain seared the place between her legs. She struggled, pushing her hands against the hard muscles of his chest, her eyes brimming with tears, but he held her fast.

"It's all right, Lainey," he soothed. "Trust me." He kissed away a tear from beneath her lashes, holding himself in check, waiting for the pain to subside. She could see the hunger — and concern — in his eyes, and relaxed a little, her faith in him restored.

When he moved this time, there was no pain, only a pulsing, warm, filling sensation like nothing she'd known. As he glided in and out rhythmically, she felt a momentum building, a craving for more and still more of something mysterious, something that lured her, yet lingered just beyond her reach. He thrust faster, deeper, harder, and her body arched to meet each thrust. Her hands roamed the length of his taut, hard body, feeling the sinewy muscles ripple and bunch.

Wrapping her slender legs around his long corded ones, she pulled him closer, wanting to absorb every inch of him, wanting to possess him in a way she hadn't before. Torrents of emotion swirled around her. Lightning flashed, thunder rolled. She could no longer separate the fury outside from the storm within.

He stroked her breasts, spoke jumbled words of passion, all the while driving himself wildly inside her. Just when she felt unable to endure the exquisite torture a moment more, limitless waves of pleasure washed over her. Tiny pinpricks of light like miniature stars burst, blinding her, filling her with such rapture she cried out Morgan's name. Consumed by the power of her pleasure, she shuddered uncontrollably, the taste and feel of Morgan blotting out all other thought. As she gave herself up to the surging delights, she heard

Morgan call out to her. Then he reached his own release.

In the minutes that followed, she felt a glowing happiness unlike anything she'd known. A closeness, a oneness. For the first time she understood about the wolves and the eagles, animals who mated for life. She felt as if she'd discovered the other half of her soul. And yet, how could that be? He was a gunman. A man on the move. Doubts crept in. Uncertainties.

Tomorrow. Tomorrow. She'd think about her feelings tomorrow.

He enclosed her within the circle of his arms and pulled her against him, fitting their bodies together perfectly. His breathing leveled off, and she thought he must be sleeping. She ran her hand lightly along the corded muscles of his side, his narrow, muscular buttocks, appreciating his taut, masculine grace. How could such a hard man be so tender, so gentle?

As she thought of him leaving on the morrow a hard lump swelled in her throat. She brushed the thought aside and lingered instead on the tender feelings he stirred. Feelings she thought she would never know. The warm embrace of a man she desired, the gentle touch of his lips. She gasped as she felt a demanding stiffness that pushed her thoughts in another direction.

Turning toward the tall man beside her, she found his blue eyes dark and smoldering again. He slipped a bronzed hand behind her neck and pulled her mouth toward his. As she tasted the warm fullness of his lips, her doubts lifted on the winds of the raging storm outside. Returning his kiss, she gave herself up to his passionate ministrations.

# Chapter 11

Faint gray light, a milk wagon rumbling, bottles clanking together, the horses whinnying, their hooves plodding against the dirt streets below.

Morgan shook his head to clear what little sleep he'd had and slid from beneath the covers. The floor felt cold against his bare feet. Elaina was still sleeping. The bruise near her eye had darkened even further, and he cursed Chuck Dawson for the hundredth time.

After pulling on his breeches and boots, he drew a clean white shirt over his naked chest and fastened the buttons. This morning his mind was a maze of fuzzy images: delicious memories of the last few hours, of the woman with the red-brown hair and the warm, sensuous body. Other thoughts were not so clear: golden fields and rolling hills, crowded buildings overlooking a broad blue ocean, stiff breezes, and sunny days. And darker images: deep, dank mine shafts, fistfights, guns, bullets.

None of the memories seemed to fit together.

Not even the name that now came sharply to mind. Daniels. Ren Daniels. Somehow it felt right to him, unlike the name he'd been using. But if his real name was Daniels, why was he in Keyserville calling himself Dan Morgan? For that matter, why was he in Keyserville at all? The answers lay in California. And he intended to have those answers by the end of next week.

He glanced at the woman still sleeping in his bed. Her glossy sable hair spilled softly around her face and onto her creamy shoulders. The crest of one pink nipple peeked from beneath the sheets. He felt himself harden and smiled to himself. She was some woman, all right.

The thought gave him a sudden twinge of conscience. It seemed

112

every time he thought of making love to her, he felt rotten, as if he'd taken someone's special gift, all brightly wrapped in colored paper and glittering bows, and smashed it into a thousand pieces. He couldn't understand the feeling. If he was Dan Morgan, he was a hired gun. The kind of man who took what he wanted. He was certain even Daniels, if that was his name, was not the kind of man to stand on principle where bedding a woman was concerned.

The face of a petite blonde came to mind. Melissa. Yes, that was her name. Was she a wife? A girlfriend? Was she the reason for his guilt? Somehow he didn't think being faithful to a woman had caused him much concern before.

He moved toward the bedside to awaken the girl, but found her golden eyes open and watching him. He stroked the smooth skin of her cheek. "Morning, pretty lady."

Elaina smiled, liking the husky sound of his voice, then winced at the pain in her split and swollen lip. Every muscle ached, and she knew how she must look. She touched the bruise beside her eye. It had to be purple and ugly. Her lip was puffy, and she felt a dull throbbing between her legs. But Morgan seemed not to notice her less than perfect appearance. His tanned features glowed with the pleasure of their lovemaking; his eyes held a tender caress. The appreciative way he looked at her lifted her spirits, and she made a second attempt to smile.

"Good morning," she said.

Morgan kissed the nape of her neck; then, feather-soft, his lips touched the bruise beside her eye.

"How are you feeling?" Concern softened the hard planes of his face.

"I've felt better, but I guess I'll live."

He smiled down at her, running his hand through her hair. "You'd better get back to your room and dress. We've got enough trouble on our hands already." He winked, and his train of thought was apparent in his eyes.

She glanced around, remembering her circumstances, snatched up the shirt he offered, and donned it quickly. The shirt reached just inches below her bottom.

"You're a mighty fetching picture in that shirt, Lainey." He smiled at her teasingly, his blue eyes alight with mischief. "If you

113

aren't careful, you'll wind up back in my bed, and I'll have to fight Dawson all over again."

She smiled, but the thought sobered her. With a sigh of resignation, she nodded her agreement. She glanced at Morgan. Suddenly all the doubts she'd felt the night before surfaced to weigh her down. Morgan was leaving on the morning train. As she watched him emptying drawers and folding shirts, she knew his plans hadn't changed. At least he'd been truthful. He'd promised her nothing — now "nothing" seemed a high price to pay.

She swallowed hard. "I guess this is good-bye, then."

He looked up from his packing.

"Good-bye? You don't think I'm leaving you here with Dawson? Pack whatever you can carry, and we'll make that morning train."

Her heart swelled at his words. He wanted her to leave with him. He cared about her after all.

"I can't take you with me," he was saying, "at least not all the way. But I'll take you far enough so Dawson won't find you. I'll leave you some money. You can get another job. Make a fresh start."

She was barely listening. Run away? To where? To what? He was going to leave her alone in some distant town. Some distant world. No. She wasn't about to run. Keyserville was her home. Chuck had been disgustingly drunk last night, too far gone to worry about where she'd spent the rest of the evening. Odds were, he'd never find out. She remembered the way he acted and shuddered. He'd been out of his mind, and maybe she'd been a little crazy herself.

She looked hard at the tall man strapping his Colt to a sinewy thigh. "I'm not going."

"We can make it as far as — You're not what?" Morgan sounded incredulous.

"I said I'm not going."

He grabbed her arm and jerked her roughly against him, his blue eyes no longer tender, but dark and angry. "Are you out of your mind?" He tugged her over to the minor. "Take a look at yourself. A good, long look. Next time Dawson might kill you."

Elaina felt the sting of tears. She looked even worse than she'd imagined. "That's my business, not yours." She tried to break his grip, but he held her firmly. She could feel the heat of his hands through the thin fabric of the shirt, and against her will her nipples hardened in response. Her face flamed red, but she didn't turn away.

He lessened his hold, his eyes riveted to the twin peaks beneath the shirt. He took a ragged breath, trying to maintain his control.

"Listen to me, Elaina, you can't stay here. Sooner or later Dawson will hurt you again. Next time I won't be around to stop him. Now please go pack your things. The train will be here in less than an hour."

Elaina looked up at him. He was so masculine, so handsome in his own rugged way. She wanted to memorize each line of his face, etch the look in his light eyes so deep in her heart she could never forget him. She wasn't going with him. Wasn't going to let him discard her in some unknown town on his way back to whatever life he'd had before. If she decided to leave Keyserville, it would be in her own time, on her own terms.

She remembered their night together, the feel of his body, the gentleness of his touch. The thought of never seeing him again tore at her heart, but she swallowed the lump in her throat and denied the tears that threatened to betray her. Running her fingertips over the taut, bronzed skin of his cheeks, she rose on tiptoe to gently cover his warm lips with a kiss. She could feel his heartbeat quicken, feel him stiffen with desire where his body pressed against hers.

He broke the contact. "Damn you, Lainey! There isn't time for this — at least not right now. Go get your things. I'll meet you out behind the hotel in twenty minutes." He spun her around. "Now scoot." He smacked her bottom, bare beneath the shirt, and she smiled at him over her shoulder as she hurried through the door.

She paused only for a moment. "Good-bye, Dan Morgan."

"Hurry," he murmured behind her retreating figure.

As she walked down the hall, she added the rich timbre of his deep voice to the many memories she would treasure, then quietly shoved open the door to her room.

Morgan checked his watch for the tenth time. Where could she be? He heard the train coming, its engine bellowing, black smoke darkening the sky in small puffs that drifted toward the station. He couldn't wait much longer. Deciding to see if she was still in her room, he headed toward the back porch of the hotel. Before he reached it, a window on the third floor opened and Elaina stuck her head out.

"Don't miss your train, Dan Morgan," she called down to him.

"Damn!" He cursed her and all crazy females from here to hell and gone. Clenching his jaw, he looked up at her. Golden rays of sunlight shone on her hair, turning it to molten umber. Her ruby lips were parted in a smile of triumph, but her tawny eyes hinted at sadness. He wished he could hold her one last time.

"You won't change your mind?"

She shook her head.

"I may not be back."

"I know." She pulled a lavender ribbon from her hair. It floated on the gentle breeze, hung suspended a moment above him, then drifted to his feet. He stooped to pick it up, feeling the softness of the velvet crushed against his palm. He pushed his broad-brimmed black hat back on his head to look up at her more carefully. Even with the bruises on her face, she looked lovely. He could still see the blush of his kisses on her tempting ruby lips. Her eyes seemed wistful, as if there was something more she wanted to say, something of herself she still wished to give. He thought he caught the glint of a tear.

"You'd better go," she said. "You'll miss your train."

He nodded and stuffed the ribbon carefully into his pocket. Turning to leave, he took a last glance over his shoulder. A tightness gripped his chest till he could barely breathe.

"Take care of yourself," he called a little too gruffly. He pulled his hat back to its usual place across his brow.

"Don't forget me." Her voice floated melodiously on the cool morning air.

He didn't answer. He knew he would never forget.

# Chapter 12

*"I may not be back."*

The words echoed through Elaina's mind the remainder of that day and into the next.

Another woman might have been saddened by the words, but it was Elaina's nature to look to the good side of things. He could have said "I won't be back" or "I can't come back." Instead he'd said "I may not be back." To Elaina that meant he just might return.

She'd decided to speak with Henry Dawson about her engagement to Chuck. Surely, when Henry saw the ugly bruise on her face, he would reprimand Chuck and release her from her promise. She'd just have to find some other way to repay her family's debts.

Both Chuck and Henry had been conspicuously absent from the hotel ever since the party. She was certain Chuck must be feeling terribly guilty for the way he'd acted. Henry, she was sure, if he knew about the incident, was giving her time to cool down. Well, sooner or later, they'd have to face her again, and when they did, she'd tell them the marriage was off.

Just having made the decision gave Elaina a whole new outlook on life. She hummed as she worked this morning. Until her bruises healed, Ada had allowed her to work upstairs, do a little cleaning away from the hustle of activity in the dining room. Elaina welcomed the opportunity.

Wearing a faded gingham dress, her hair tied back with a pale blue kerchief, Elaina immersed herself in her work. She cleaned and swept Morgan's now empty room and tried not to remember the warmth she'd felt in his arms just nights before. As she stripped the sheets from the paint-chipped iron bed, she flushed at the dark red stain that gave testimony to her lost virtue. Instead of the remorse she knew she should feel, she felt only loneliness and a desire to be back in Morgan's arms.

She pushed the thought away and knelt beside the bed to sweep beneath. A knock at the door interrupted her. Ada peeked in, a look of consternation lining her usually smiling face.

"I got somethin' to show ya," Ada said. "I was cleanin' a room downstairs. The room your friend Morgan slept in the night before he was shot. When I lifted the mattress, these fell through the slats. I'll be hanged if I know what to make of 'em, but I figured you would." She handed Elaina a small leather address book and several bits of paper.

Elaina stood up, accepting the papers, her interest aroused by the tiny leather-bound book in her hand. A faded yellow newspaper clipping, worn from being folded and carried between the pages of the book, protruded from the edges. Several calling cards with the name Reynold Lee Daniels engraved in plain black letters with an address in San Francisco made up the balance of the information.

She swallowed, hard. What would Ren's calling cards be doing in Morgan's room? Surely he couldn't have known him. Could they be related? Half brothers? Or cousins? Even as she asked the questions, her mind knew the answer. Dear God, please tell me he didn't lie. With a trembling hand, Elaina pulled the newspaper article from among the pages of the tiny book and began to read.

As the words formed pictures in her mind, her hand crept to the base of her throat. She didn't realize she was crying until a teardrop darkened a tiny spot on the paper. She could feel the erratic beating of her heart as she scanned the article a second time. It was dated February 10, 1878, and had been published in the *Daily Alta California*, San Francisco.

Jacob Stanhope of San Francisco has announced the engagement of his daughter, Melissa, to Reynold Lee Daniels of that same city. The wedding is scheduled for May 23 at Saint Jude's Church. The ceremony will be followed by a gala reception in the gardens of the Stanhope estate on Nob Hill. All of San Francisco society is expected to attend.

"You better sit down, honey," Ada cautioned. "You look kinda pale."

Elaina could only nod. The lump in her throat threatened to squeeze off her breath as Ada guided her to a seat on the bed. Why had she listened to him? Believed him? She'd known he was Ren Daniels from the very first day, but he'd lied to her, denied he ever knew her. Her vision blurred, and fresh tears slipped down her cheeks. The wedding was set for May 23. Morgan — no, Ren Daniels — would be returning to San Francisco just in time.

"What's it mean?" Ada asked, reaching gently for Elaina's trembling hand.

"Oh, Ada, I'm such a fool." Her voice caught in her throat as she looked at the gray-haired woman who was always there when she needed her. "He wasn't Dan Morgan after all. He was Ren. Ren Daniels, the boy — I mean the man I told you about."

"Well, what if he is this Ren fella? That don't make him any less a man, now, does it?" Ada had rarely seen her friend in such a state and, wily old fox that she was, had a pretty good notion as to the cause. A glance at the dark stain on Morgan's sheets, carelessly tossed into a pile on the floor, confirmed her suspicions.

"Did you read the clipping?" Elaina whispered.

Ada took a deep breath. "Yes, I did, and, honey, I still think Mr. Morgan — Mr. Daniels is a good man. I don't think he'da done you wrong on purpose. He didn't know any more than you did who he was."

"He knew the first day, Ada. He knew, but he lied to me." Elaina glanced away, but not before Ada had seen the misery in her friend's golden eyes.

"Life's never easy, Laina honey. Sometimes things just ain't meant to be."

"Would you mind leaving me alone for a while?" Elaina said softly.

"Sure, honey. Try not to fret yerself. Few men are worth it." Shaking her head, Ada pulled the door closed.

Elaina read the newspaper clipping a third time: "All of San Francisco Society is expected to attend." God, what a laughingstock she'd made of herself. She'd prayed he wouldn't forget her. Now he was sure to remember the girl he'd made a fool of back in Carbon

County. She clung to the edge of the bed and tried to control her breathing. If only he'd told her the truth in the first place, none of this would have happened. She could have told him who he was, helped him to remember.

But would knowing he was Ren have changed things? Would she have cared that he was betrothed to another? Remembering his kiss and the touch of his hand, she wasn't so sure.

Elaina clutched the article to her breast and crumpled across the bed. Dear God, how could this have happened? Deep racking sobs shook her. Why had he come back? Why couldn't he have stayed out of her life? Her chest constricted, and her heart ached as though she'd been stabbed. She remembered the way he'd defended her, comforted her, the regret she'd seen in his eyes when they parted, the sadness in his husky voice. How could they all have been lies? The Ren she'd loved as a child would never have lied to her.

Maybe it was just as Ada said. Some things were never meant to be.

*"I may not be back."*

Now she saw his words for the good-bye they really were. He couldn't come back, even if he wanted to. In a little over two weeks, he'd be married to Melissa Stanhope, married into one of the wealthiest families in San Francisco. She wondered if he'd think of her, wondered if he'd even remember her name. How many other women had there been in his life? How many more would there be? He'd have money, power, position. Women would dance at his command. Ren Daniels had come a long way in the last nine years.

Allowing the cleansing tears to fall, Elaina sobbed into the pillow until she finally fell asleep, all the crying and the events of the days before having finally taken their toll. She rested fitfully for several hours, until another of Ada's gentle knocks awoke her.

Sitting up on the old iron bed, she pulled the kerchief from her head, ran her hands through her tangled hair, and as she remembered the newspaper clipping, felt again the searing pain in her heart.

Without waiting for permission, Ada bustled into the room. "I let you sleep as long as I dared," she said, patting Elaina's cheek.

Elaina sighed resignedly and straightened the bodice of her dress. She knew she should finish her cleaning, but had little desire to do more than wallow in her misery.

120

"Truth is," Ada continued, "I'm afraid I got somethin' else unpleasant to tell you, so we might as well git to it."

"God, Ada, what now?" Elaina twisted the folds of her skirt, wondering what could be worse than the news she'd already received.

"Curse blasted men wherever they are," Ada mumbled. "You're gonna have to leave Keyserville."

"Leave! But why, Ada? Where would I go?"

"Henry Dawson ain't about to let you outta that weddin'. I heard him talkin' to Chuck in the office while you was up here workin'. He's plannin' on bringin' the preacher over tomorrow. Chuck musta told him what happened between you two. Henry says it just seals the bargain. Says he shouldn't have let you put Chuck off this long, what with a man's needs and all."

Elaina felt stunned. She closed her eyes and sagged against the old iron headboard. Henry couldn't be serious! How could he possibly expect her to go through with the wedding after what Chuck had done to her? Surely he couldn't force her to go through with it. But knowing the power the Dawsons wielded, the outlandish gossip he could spread, she wasn't so certain. Ada was right. She'd have to leave town.

But where would she go? What would she do? As usual, Ada read her thoughts. She handed Elaina a small velvet pouch, heavy with coins.

"I've got a sister, Isabelle Chesterfield, out in San Francisco. She'll take you in till you git yerself settled. I'll send a wire tellin' her to expect you. She's a good woman. You can trust her."

San Francisco. Just the name twisted her heart. Ren would be there — with his wife. She couldn't bear it.

"I can't go there," she whispered. "That's where Ren is."

"You got no choice, honey. Ain't neither of us got kin anyplace else. At least you'll be far enough away so's Dawson won't find you. Somethin's beginnin' to smell fishy about this whole marriage business."

Elaina barely registered Ada's words. She would be leaving Keyserville, doing the very thing she'd tried to avoid. But what did she really have to lose? And what would happen to her if she stayed? A marriage to Chuck Dawson was out of the question.

Ada was right. She had no choice.

The older woman helped her to her feet. "There's a train west-bound this afternoon. You best be on it, honey."

Elaina hefted the pouch. "How can I take your money, Ada? You've worked for years to save this much." Elaina remembered the debts she already owed and for a moment thought maybe marrying Chuck was still the best solution for all concerned.

"You'll pay me back when you get out west. There's lots of opportunity there. I'm content right here, and who knows? Maybe I'll visit you both someday."

Elaina choked back tears and hugged the older woman. "You're the best friend I'll ever have."

Ada hugged her back. "Come on, now. We got a heap to do if we're gonna git you outta here this afternoon."

Elaina slipped Chuck's garish engagement ring from her finger with a trembling hand. "I was planning on returning this in person; now you'll have to do it for me. I don't want to be any more indebted to the Dawsons than I already am."

Ada only nodded.

The wheels chanted their monotonous, melodic song as the train rumbled inexorably across the plains. The steady rhythm lulled Ren Daniels, scattering the last of the cobwebs from his mind. The first-class car wasn't crowded, though the coach class down the way was filled to capacity. He'd been resting in the plush velvet seats of the Pullman Sleeping Car by day; the seats were converted into comfortable berths at night.

He'd kept to himself for seven days, willing himself to remember, recalling more about his past with every passing hour. In the last few days, he'd been blinded by the deluge of bits and pieces. When he finally fit the puzzle together, he almost wished he hadn't.

He was struck by the enormity of his guilt. He'd left Elaina McAllister, the woman who had saved his life, alone in Keyserville to face the wrath of the very men he'd vowed to destroy. On top of that, he'd seduced her — played up to her sympathies, conned her into his bed, and taken her virginity. Ren was never easy on himself, but this time his self-disgust was almost more than he could bear.

He stared out the window of the train. Barren tracts of land broken only by sagebrush and an occasional yucca or century plant were all he'd seen for the last twelve hours. The steam engine roared past an Indian wickiup, and two scrawny brown-skinned children ran smiling from the hut to watch the massive black locomotive chug by.

Memories of Elaina, their days in the sunshine, the feel of her skin beneath his hand, flooded his mind. He remembered their night together, the sweet taste of her lips, the feel of her hard-tipped, upturned breasts pressing against him. Shifting in his chair, he fought to cast his thoughts in another direction and ease the swelling in his breeches.

He damned himself for wanting her again. He was engaged to be married, and Elaina was not the kind of woman to trifle with a married man. A fresh wave of guilt swept over him as he remembered the way he'd plotted to seduce her. He drew some comfort from the knowledge that Elaina had wanted him just as much as he'd wanted her, but it wasn't enough.

Settling himself deeper against the seat, he dozed fitfully, his mind tormented by thoughts of his marriage to Melissa Stanhope just a little less than two weeks away, and again his conscience pricked him. He had betrayed not only Elaina but the woman he was engaged to as well.

He had to admit Melissa's feelings seemed of lesser importance. Theirs was a marriage of convenience, arranged by Jacob Stanhope to "bring new blood into the Stanhope family." Fidelity was not a condition of the marriage. Considering Melissa's fragile constitution, Ren was certain he'd be forced to keep a mistress to satisfy his lusty needs.

That wouldn't have been the case with Elaina. His stomach tightened. If only things could have worked out differently. But there was Jacob Stanhope to consider. Jacob had been like a father to Ren from the first day they'd met, over five years ago.

Ren glanced back out the window. The squalor of a squatter's shack, the sun-baked skin of the woman washing clothes in front of the house as the train roared by, sent his thoughts tumbling into the past. Ren was not a stranger to poverty. After he left Keyserville nine years ago, he and Tommy had wandered aimlessly from town to town. Just finding enough scraps of garbage for food had been an all-day chore. There were few odd jobs in the East; the area was moving toward a depression. Since Ren was determined to leave the mines forever, he and Tommy headed west.

Ren remembered all too well mucking out the livery stable, sweeping the floors of the saloon, emptying spittoons — whatever it took to earn enough money so he and Tommy could eat. Ren had been gone from Keyserville six months when he landed a job sweeping floors at McClintock's Saloon in Hays, Kansas. It was the best job he'd had since he left Pennsylvania.

"Hey, kid! You there, with the broom!" Si Wilkins, the new saloon manager, had begun giving orders like an army sergeant the minute he'd walked through the door. Pete Simmons, the man who'd hired him, had been a decent sort to work for, but Wilkins was a bully and a fool. Ren had worked long, hard hours in the mines of Carbon County, but the other miners had respected him. Here things were different.

Ren could barely control his temper. "My name's Daniels, Mr. Wilkins. Ren Daniels."

"Yeah? Well, who cares? Just git over there and clean up that mess!" Wilkins pointed to the floor with a meaty hand.

Clenching his teeth, Ren did as he was told. A drunken cowhand had littered the boards with hard-boiled egg shells. Ren finished sweeping them up just as a slapping sound pulled his gaze to the saloon's double doors. Sunlight streamed in from behind the tall, well-dressed man who entered. The bar quieted, something just short of awe settling over the saloon. As the newcomer moved farther into the room, Ren could make out a powerfully built man with shoulder-length brown hair. He was immaculately dressed in an expensive black suit. Two Colt revolvers, worn butt forward, hung a little below his waist.

"Hello, Mr. Hickok. What can we get for you today?" Wilkins's manner was simpering as he rushed behind the bar to tend Hickok's needs.

"A whiskey. And bring me a glass of water while you're at it. Getting warm outside already."

Wilkins couldn't move fast enough. As Ren worked, he heard two men whispering beside him.

"That's Bill Hickok, fastest gun this side of the Missouri. Man's greased lightning. Heard tell he drawed one gun on a man in front of him, while he fired the other over his shoulder at a man behind. Kilt 'em both. Ain't many men 'round these parts don't give plenty of respect to Marshal Hickok."

Wild Bill Hickok. Ren had read stories about him in discarded day-old papers. A write-up a little over a year ago in *Harper's New Monthly Magazine* by Colonel George Nichols particularly came to mind.

"Hey, Hickok!" A burly man at the back of the bar shoved his chair aside. "You as fast as you claim?"

The piano player ended his tune abruptly, and people quietly stepped from between the two men.

Hickok looked unruffled. "Friend, I'd advise you to sit back down if you're plannin' on seeing the sun set."

"I think you're all talk, Hickok." He flipped his coattail out of the way and rested a hand on the butt of his Remington .44.

Hickok just smiled. The burly man went for his weapon, but it never cleared his holster. Hickok's hand, faster than the eye, pulled a revolver, thumbed the single-action hammer, and fired. The man flew back against the wall and slid to the floor, smearing a trail of blood from the exit wound in his back. Blood erupted from the wound in his chest. Hickok holstered his weapon, leaving a patch of acrid blue powder smoke to hover in the air. Ignoring the dead man on the floor, he moved back to the bar and casually finished his drink.

"Some folks never learn how to be friendly," the marshal said to no one in particular.

"Hey, kid," Wilkins called over to Ren. "Git that slime outta here."

With the help of another onlooker, Ren dragged the man's body into the alley behind the saloon. Word traveled fast in a town like Hays. Hickok had added another notch to his gun. The undertaker had already been summoned.

As Ren walked back inside, he'd known, for the first time, how he would make his way. A gun could win him the respect he so badly wanted from the men around him and earn him a good living to boot.

The whoosh of steam and the clanking of metal against metal

jarred his thoughts back to the present. The train braked for a flock of sheep crossing the tracks ahead. A shepherd, floppy-brimmed hat pulled low, worked beside two collies to keep the herd from straying.

In minutes the train was past the flock and roaring full tilt across the barren landscape. Ren glanced down at his suntanned hands: fingers long and fine but not delicate, grip solid and sure. Firm hands, capable hands. Even as a boy he'd been good with his hands.

After he became a gunman, money was no longer a problem. He and Tommy were able to live in grand style: good food, good clothes, and for Ren, good women. But he was no fool. He could see where the violent path was leading. Though he took only those jobs he believed in, helped only those whose interests were within the law, he vowed to save enough money to abandon Dan Morgan — the identity he'd adopted — at the first opportunity.

Seven years later, with the ongoing help of Jacob Stanhope, he succeeded. He became Ren Daniels again. A wealthy, respected businessman. Dan Morgan had quietly disappeared — or so Ren thought — until he received the letter from Redmond and Dawson seeking Morgan's services to quell the unrest at the Blue Mountain Mine. It was a coincidence — and an opportunity — he had been unwilling to pass up.

Now, riding back to his own comfortable identity in San Francisco, he wished for the hundredth time he had.

"She's gone!" Chuck Dawson threw open the heavy plank door to the quiet interior of Blue Mountain Mining Company headquarters.

"What do you mean, gone? Gone where?" Dolph Redmond swiveled his chair in Chuck's direction, apparently unwilling to acknowledge the distressing turn of events.

Henry followed Chuck into the room, and the two men proceeded to tell Redmond all they knew of Elaina's disappearance.

"We'll git her back, Dolph. Don't you worry," Henry Dawson soothed as he leaned across Redmond's desk.

"You'd better, my friends, you'd better."

Chuck recognized the threat in Dolph's words. He looked broodingly toward his father. "If you had forced the marriage two years ago, like I told you, this would never have happened."

126

"Yeah, and if you hadn't been trying to put yer pecker where it weren't s'posed to be, it wouldn'a happened!"

"Gentlemen, gentlemen. Fighting among ourselves is no way to solve the problem. Sooner or later we'll find out where she's gone. When we do, we'll bring her back."

"How we gonna force her to marry Chuck?" Henry wanted to know.

"You let me worry about that. You just find out where she is."

"We'll find out, all right." Chuck clenched his fist, thinking of Morgan's interference and wondering if the girl had run off to meet the gunman somewhere.

He hoped so. Even though Morgan had left the money they'd paid him in an envelope at the bank, along with extra for his hotel bill, it wasn't enough. Chuck still carried the cuts and bruises Morgan had inflicted, and his nose would never be quite as perfect as it once was. No, Chuck had a score to settle with Morgan. He had a score to settle with them both.

Leaving the office, he stormed toward his horse. The first person he wanted to talk to was Ada Lowery. She was Elaina's closest friend and a woman who knew just about everything that went on in Keyserville.

Mounting his sorrel gelding, he headed purposefully toward town, his mind fixed on the buxom woman working at the hotel. Ada always made him think of his mother, though they looked nothing alike. Mabel Dawson was a woman with style. Though Henry Dawson was a strong man, he could never dominate Mabel. She just let him think he could.

She had doted on Chuck from the day he was born. "You're not like the others," she would say. "You're special. Don't ever forget that." And Chuck never had. His mother always told him he had the most beautiful eyes in the world, and his nose was patrician, not plebeian like Henry's.

Chuck always thought of Henry Dawson as Henry not Father, though he humored the old man by calling him that. In a moment of contempt, his mother had told Chuck the truth: Henry wasn't his real father. She had never loved Henry; Chuck knew that. But Henry had plenty of money and, though crude and overbearing, provided his mother with security — and a home for the son she adored.

Chuck smiled mirthlessly. The truth of his heritage was a secret he would carry to his grave. Henry Dawson was powerful and wealthy, and though Chuck would be a wealthy man in his own right after the sale of the mine, he had every intention of claiming Henry Dawson's estate as well.

Chuck's thoughts turned to Elaina, to the last time he'd seen her, the night of the party. She'd wanted him that night. He had sensed it. She was only playing a game with him. If Morgan hadn't interfered, he'd have won the game and they'd both have gotten what they wanted. Chuck touched his broken nose and cursed the gunman. Morgan was probably off someplace with Elaina right now, the little bitch. Well, he'd find them sooner or later, it was just a matter of time.

# Chapter 13

Ren spotted his red-haired brother standing outside the station even before the train rumbled to a halt.

For over a month he hadn't been able to remember whether or not he had a brother. Now, standing tall and proud, his bright hair ruffled by the wind, Tommy Daniels was a mighty pleasant sight.

Ren rose from his seat as the train braked to a stop. He retrieved his satchel, slung it over his shoulder, and headed up the aisle. He was descending the stairs when Tommy spotted him, smiled, and waved him over.

"Mighty good to see you, little brother," Ren said, draping an arm across the younger man's shoulders.

Tommy grinned broadly. "Good to see you, too. You sure had us worried for a while. You must have had some trip."

"That, Tommy, is an understatement." They elbowed their way through the arriving and departing throngs, then escaped through the glass-paned station doors into the bustling streets of San Francisco. "This is one story you may have trouble believing."

Ren hailed a passing hack, and the two men climbed aboard. Once inside, Ren spent the better part of the ride telling his brother about his accident, about Keyserville, Dawson and Redmond, and the Blue Mountain Mine. He filled Tommy in on everything that had happened on his trip — except Elaina McAllister.

Finally Tommy could stand the suspense no longer. "What about Elaina?" he asked. "Did you see her? Does she still live in Keyserville?" At seventeen, he had grown into a tall, slenderly built man of intelligence and integrity, but his patience had increased very little.

The hack's arrival at their Pacific Heights town house gave Ren a moment's reprieve. They departed the carriage and entered the small but stately residence. The brothers' business interests — mostly shipping, trading, and real estate — necessitated spending a lot of time in the city. Though their ranch in Napa was home, overnight visits to the city had become such a common occurrence that buying a residence was the only practical solution.

"Well?" Tommy persisted as they dropped into comfortable overstuffed chairs. The narrow wood-frame structure stood three stories high, had wide bay windows that looked out over the blue Pacific, and was elegantly furnished with Oriental carpets and classic mahogany furniture richly upholstered in forest green and brown.

"Well, what?"

"You know very well what: What about Elaina?"

Just the sound of her name twisted Ren's heart. "Yes, she's still there, and yes, I saw her."

"How did she look? Did you talk to her?"

Ren looked hard at his brother. They'd been through too much together to keep secrets, but his relationship with Elaina McAllister was far too intimate a subject to discuss even with Tommy.

"She's beautiful," he said, meaning it more than ever before in his life. "She has thick reddish-brown hair, and her eyes are golden, kind of like a she-lion's. She has skin as smooth as silk and pink cheeks. She blushes, but only if you hit a sensitive subject. She's tall, but not gangly like she used to be. She has beautiful full breasts and —" Ren stopped short. He'd already gone too far, but once he started talking about her, he couldn't seem to stop himself. He refused to meet his brother's questioning look.

"Anyway, she's engaged to Chuck Dawson, and that son of a bitch —" He clenched his teeth, biting the words off. "So I have to go back as soon as I get things cleared up here. I just hope it isn't too late."

Tommy had never seen his brother in such a state. He'd been fine as long as he was discussing Blue Mountain, the Dawsons, and even the two bullet wounds he'd received. But the subject of Elaina McAllister had him talking in riddles, speaking in disjointed sentences, and circling the matter entirely. Something was definitely wrong.

"Slow down, big brother. I'm getting a little confused. You're going back to Keyserville?"

"Yes."

"But you just got here."

"I've got to see Jacob first, get the wedding postponed. I've got to get back to Keyserville before Dawson hurts Elaina again."

Tommy bristled. "What the hell did he do to her?" Tommy seldom swore, but Elaina McAllister was a lady dear to both men's hearts. She had saved their lives. Neither Tommy nor Ren would ever forget that.

Ren explained about the engagement party, being careful to leave out the heated lovemaking that had followed. Tommy eyed him speculatively, as if sensing there was more to the story than Ren was willing to admit.

"Well, you can stop worrying about the wedding, at least for the time being. When Jacob didn't hear from you, he got worried. He was just getting some men together to go after you when I got your wire. He'd already postponed the wedding by then. Melissa's been under the weather again, so it all worked out for the best." Tommy grinned broadly. "You got a reprieve, Ren, at least for a while."

Ren felt such a wave of relief at Tommy's words he was almost dizzy. But the fact was, nothing had changed. He was going to marry Melissa Stanhope sooner or later. He owed it to Jacob, and more importantly, marrying into the Stanhope family would fulfill his lifetime dream of respectability and status.

Somehow the dream seemed a little tarnished now.

Elaina had been riding in the crowded coach compartment of the Pacific Express with dozens of other weary passengers for five days when the train pulled into Cheyenne, Wyoming. Trying to save as much as she could on her fare, she'd elected to travel coach class, and the crowded, uncomfortable seat had taken its toll. Most of the journey she'd spent trying to forget Ren Daniels. Determined to hate him, she'd conjured images of him in Melissa Stanhope's arms — even though she didn't know what the Stanhope girl looked like.

She'd tried to tell herself he tricked her into his bed, tried to convince herself he lied to her, took her virginity just to satisfy his lust. But she knew it just wasn't so. She'd gone to his bed willingly, and if she could have waved a magic wand, she'd be there again. She missed him terribly. Where was he now? What was he doing? She could see his light blue eyes as clearly as if he were next to her on the uncomfortable seat. She yearned to reach out and touch the long, thin scar along his neck, comfort him, ask him how he'd been hurt, then soothe away his pain.

No, she couldn't hate him. Not ever, no matter how hard she tried. In her heart she knew he'd done no more than she'd allowed, and truthfully she didn't regret one moment of their time together. She only regretted she couldn't spend the rest of her life with him — as Melissa Stanhope would, after their wedding next week. The thought tore at Elaina's heart. She had to guard constantly against crying; whenever she wasn't careful, she felt hot tears on her cheeks.

Someday, she told herself, she would forget him. But that would be a hard task to accomplish. She'd dreamed about Ren Daniels for the last nine years. Now it looked as though she might dream about him forever.

The stop in Cheyenne was scheduled for twenty minutes, just long enough to allow for arriving and departing passengers, to take on water, and to feed the passengers not wealthy enough to travel first class. Elaina had found the food in the depots along the way less than memorable: beefsteak, fried eggs, fried potatoes — usually worse.

According to the conductor, however, their stop in Cheyenne would be extended at least an hour, possibly longer. A stretch of track near Laramie had washed out in a flash flood. Elaina was actually glad for the delay. She intended to stretch her legs and buy herself a decent meal. Riding coach class, she had slept sitting up, so every joint, bone, and muscle screamed for a brisk walk.

Clutching her reticule, she tried to brush the fine powdery soot from her gray traveling suit as she stepped from the train. She was glad she'd listened to Ada, who'd insisted she wear something that would blend with the dirt. Even the decorative black frogs that closed the front of the suit and the heavy black braid on the bottom of the jacket and around the hem of the skirt were gray now. She would never have believed the soot could filter over every inch of her body. She could even taste the grittiness in her mouth.

Cheyenne was a city like none Elaina had seen. It was truly a wild West fantasy. As tired and dirty as she was, the variety of interesting people in the streets piqued her curiosity and sent excitement pumping through her veins. False-fronted buildings, built of tar paper and old wooden boxes, lined the dirt streets. Flattened tin cans had been used for roofing. She passed the Cheyenne *Leader*, which appeared to be the local newspaper office, and the First National Bank. There was an impressive courthouse building up the street and a fine-looking city hall.

It seemed every third building housed a saloon: McDaniel's Place, the Old Greenback Rooms — "Largest Saloon in the Western Country." Young's Bathhouse advertised "Creek water bathing — hot and cold."

As she walked farther away from the station, she noticed men dressed in fringed buckskins and women in calico skirts and practical sunbonnets that covered most of the face as well as the head. Dark-skinned Indian men, women, and children walked through the dusty streets wearing a hodgepodge of garments, from soldiers' blue uniforms to soft white-fringed leather dresses. Tiny infants wore no clothes at all. Hogs and cows had the run of the streets, and dogs roamed everywhere.

As Elaina strolled briskly along the board planks near the buildings, a heavyset, broad-faced Indian a few paces ahead of her made the error of bumping into a skinny blond youth and his pudgy friend.

"Stay outta my way, you redskin trash!" The blond boy shoved the Indian against a buckboard stopped in front of McCloskey's General Store.

The Indian bristled, grunted, but did nothing to defend himself. Then the chubby, stringy-haired boy pushed him, this time into the dirt. Again the Indian did nothing. Elaina glanced around, wishing she could help, but there were throngs of milling people watching just as she was, and none seemed willing to interfere. She didn't know the customs of the West, but if this was an example of western hospitality, she was not impressed.

The Indian rose as if nothing had happened, brushed himself off, and with a grunt of resignation, widely skirted the two young men. The boys, apparently content with their mischief, allowed the Indian to continue on his way. The whole scene made Elaina feel slightly ill. Like all easterners, she knew the stories of the Indian Wars and of the hostilities between the white man and the Indian the wars had created. Like all prejudice, she decided as she continued on her way, only time could cure ill will.

Continuing several blocks farther and with plenty of time to spare, Elaina headed toward the sign up ahead that marked the Delmonico House. A quick peek in the window assured her the place was clean, and as she walked through the door, her nose assured her the food would be good. She seated herself at a small table, wishing she could have done a more thorough job of cleansing the dust from her face and hair before leaving the train. As it was, she was glad for the narrow-brimmed straw hat that covered most of her red-brown hair. The rest she wore pulled into a tight bun at the back of her head.

A buxom young woman took her order of fried chicken, mashed potatoes and gravy, biscuits on the side. When the steaming plate arrived, Elaina breathed deeply of the delicious aroma, then ate every bite on her plate, savoring each mouthful. She was still nearly three days from her destination and guessed this might be the last good food she'd eat till she arrived.

She paid her bill at the counter and pushed the door open, the bell above signaling her departure. A tall, gangling youth and two younger boys accompanied by a broad-shouldered, bearded man pushed her roughly aside. Her hat tumbled to the wooden walk as she was jostled among the four people.

" 'Scuse me, ma'am," the bearded, graying man said as he steadied her. Without waiting for a reply, he tipped his hat and followed the others out of sight.

Elaina retrieved her own hat, a little unsettled at the rough encounter, and started walking back toward the train.

She'd gone more than a block when she felt the color drain from her face. For the first time, she realized her reticule was gone. Panicky, she glanced around, madly searching the dirt at her feet. Her gaze scanning every inch of the ground along the way, she dashed back to the boardwalk. When she reached the restaurant, she rushed inside, checked her seat and the counter, but in her heart she knew she'd been robbed. The four men had run into her on purpose and had stolen her purse while she was distracted.

Dear God, now what would she do? All her money — all Ada's

money — was in her reticule. And her train ticket! Oh, God, her ticket! Now she couldn't even get to California. She slumped down on the wooden bench beneath the restaurant window, feeling light-headed and slightly sick to her stomach. Of all the rotten luck! It seemed her whole life had been nothing but a string of bad luck. The loss of her family and the mine, believing Ren Daniels was Dan Morgan, Chuck Dawson forcing her to leave Keyserville — now this! Was nothing ever going to turn out right for her?

Refusing to give in to despair, Elaina stood up and squared her shoulders. It was silly to feel sorry for herself. She was a grown woman. She could take care of herself. She'd been doing it for years.

"Excuse me." She approached the first respectably dressed person who passed. "Could you direct me to the sheriff's office?" She would simply go to the sheriff, tell him what happened. Surely he could help her.

The blond man tipped his broad-brimmed fawn-colored hat. "Be happy to, ma'am," he said with a soft southern drawl. "But it's the marshal, not the sheriff. Marshal Taylor's office is down the street 'bout two blocks on your left. You all right, ma'am? You look kinda pale."

"I — I'm afraid I've been robbed."

The tall man frowned. "Cheyenne's a tough town for a woman alone. You are alone, aren't you?"

"I'm traveling west to California on the train. At least I was until some men stole my purse."

"If you don't mind my sayin' so, ma'am, you may have a problem. Did anyone see them do it? Have you got any proof?"

Elaina swallowed hard. She sank back down on the bench, wringing her hands. The man was right. What proof did she have? Maybe she had just lost her purse. There was no real evidence to suggest the men had taken it. Tears welled in her eyes.

"What am I going to do?" she whispered, mostly to herself.

A smile lit the well-dressed man's warm hazel eyes. "Nothin's ever that bad. Surely there's someone you can wire for money. Someone you can ask for help."

Elaina shook her head. She'd taken every cent Ada had, and there was no one else to ask. "Thank you for your trouble. I'm sure

I'll think of something." She rose and started past him, but he caught her arm.

"Here, take this." He handed her his card. "If things don't work out, come and see me. Maybe I can help."

Elaina accepted the card. "Thank you, Mr." — she glanced down — "Cameron. Thank you very much."

"Pleasure meetin' you, Miss . . . ?" His warm-honey accent seemed to echo the warmth in his eyes.

"McAllister. Elaina McAllister."

"Pleasure meetin' you, Miss McAllister." He tipped his hat again and walked off down the boardwalk.

Elaina sat back down, trying to compose herself, trying to decide what to do. She thought again of Ren and tried to blame her current troubles on him. If he hadn't come to Keyserville in the first place, none of this would have happened. If he hadn't come to Keyserville . . . If he hadn't come to Keyserville, she would never have known the passion he'd aroused, never felt the warmth of his kiss. As always, she had to admit, even in her dire circumstances, she wouldn't have missed one moment of their time together for anything in the world.

Tears welled at the thought, and self-pity threatened to swamp her. Was this her punishment for falling in love? The thought sobered her. She refused to call what she and Ren had "love." Desire, yes. Passion, yes. But love? Love was something two people shared. It was built on honesty and trust. Their relationship had been based on lies.

Elaina wiped the tears from beneath her eyes, sniffed, and pulled herself together. She would have to get a job. Earn the money for her passage the rest of the way to San Francisco. Worse things had happened to lots of people. She was more than halfway there. She was lucky to have made it this far. She stood, squared her shoulders, and marched determinedly off down the street. Only the lonesome whistle of the train as it pulled out of the station dampened her spirits.

By nightfall more than her spirits were damp. When the train pulled out of the station, it had left Elaina behind, but unfortunately it had not left her clothes. She'd been so upset, so unnerved by the whole ugly mess, that she hadn't been thinking straight. She'd forgotten to collect her satchel before the train departed. Now she not only had no money but she had nothing to wear except the clothes on her back, and they were dirty, damp with perspiration, and wrinkled. Her feet ached miserably. She'd been to every merchant, every shopkeeper, anyone and everyone who might be able to offer her a job. The story was always the same. There were ten people waiting in line for every job in Cheyenne.

Returning to the bench in front of the Delmonico House, Elaina sat down, fighting back tears. It was rapidly getting dark, and she had no place to go, no one she could turn to. She didn't even have money for a room. The delicious aroma of beef stew wafted through the door of the restaurant as a customer entered. Even though she'd had a big lunch, her stomach rumbled. Walking for hours had given her an appetite. If only she had the money for a bowl of that stew.

Beginning to feel desperate, she fished in her pocket and came up with Chase Cameron's card, wanting to read the man's address before it got too dark. All it gave below his name was Cameron Enterprises and an address on Main Street. She probably should have gone to Cameron's office in the first place, but she'd been so upset, and he'd already been so helpful, she didn't want to take advantage of his generosity.

Now she had no choice.

Taking a deep breath, she straightened the bodice of her traveling suit and tucked a few stray tendrils of her hair into the bun at the back of her head. Resolutely, she marched down the street toward Cameron Enterprises.

# Chapter 14

Chase Cameron glanced up from his card game just in time to see Elaina McAllister's tawny eyes peeking over the swinging doors of the saloon.

The fine features of her oval face registered shock and dismay. He smiled to himself and shoved his chair back. He'd known she would come sooner or later. The defeated look on her face earlier today had told him she had nowhere else to turn. And there were no jobs in Cheyenne — at least not the kind of jobs a girl like Elaina McAllister would consider. Chase had expected her long before now.

As he walked toward the door of the White Elephant, he watched indecision play across her face. She couldn't believe this was Cameron Enterprises. She wanted to turn and walk away, but couldn't. She wasn't the first woman to face the same dilemma. Being in the saloon business, Chase had seen scores of them. Pretty girls, desperate for money, who finally ended up making a living flat on their backs. Chase wondered if Elaina McAllister would be another of life's casualties.

"Hello, Miss McAllister. Won't you step into my office?"

Her mouth moved, but no words came. Finally, she swallowed and found her voice. "This is your . . . office?"

"Yes, ma'am, I'm afraid it is. This is my saloon. Cameron Enterprises owns saloons all over the West . . . even in California," he teased.

"I — I see."

But she didn't really see at all. He was sure this was hardly what she'd expected. His elegant clothing had given her the impression he was a gentleman of means — and he was. To a certain extent.

Chase took the girl's arm and escorted her through the men's boisterous laughter and lusty remarks and into his inner office. Dazed and confused, she let him lead her. When he closed the door she jumped as if a gun had been fired. She seemed disoriented and a little shaky. He was sure she'd never seen the inside of a saloon before.

"I was hope— hoping," she stuttered, "to take you up on your offer of assistance. I thought maybe you could offer me a job, but —"

"But that's exactly what I can do, Miss McAllister."

She eyed him uncertainly. "Where?" she asked, and he read the hopeful expression in her eyes.

"Why, right here, of course."

She sank down on the deep red leather chair he offered, her face pale, her eyes bleak. "But I couldn't possibly . . ."

"What other choices do you have, ma'am?"

She didn't answer.

"I know how scarce jobs are in Cheyenne. Unless there's someone you could wire for money, I'd suggest you hear me out."

"But what . . . what would I be doing?"

"Stand up."

"What?"

"I said stand up."

She did as Cameron directed.

"Now lift up your skirt and show me your legs."

"I most certainly will not! How dare you! I thought you were a gentleman!" She tried to brush past him, but he caught her arm.

"Please, Miss McAllister, I assure you this is strictly business. I'm only tryin' to help. If you're goin' to work here, you'll have to show me your legs. I want my customers to like what they see."

She sat back down. "Please, Mr. Cameron, isn't there anything else I could do?"

Chase heard the quiver in her voice. His eyes raked her. Though she looked dirty and tired, he couldn't miss her fine cheekbones, slim straight nose, and delicate arching brows. She stood tall and graceful. He had little doubt her legs would please his most discerning customer — he had an eye for the ladies.

He liked the girl's style. She was desperate but still unwilling to

139

put her integrity aside, at least for the time being. He'd have to move slowly with this one.

"Can you sing?"

Elaina looked at him suspiciously. "A little. Why?"

"I've got a singin' job open at the Black Garter in Central City. You'd still have to show your legs, but you wouldn't have to mix with the customers."

"Central City?"

"Yes. It's in Colorado, about a four-hour train ride from here. A minin' town in the Rockies. I'll be goin' there myself. The company will pay your fare, and I'll escort you personally. For tonight you can stay in one of the rooms upstairs."

Elaina felt sick. How could she possibly accept this man's proposal? And spending the night in a saloon — it was unthinkable! But where would she go if she didn't accept? What would she do? She couldn't roam the streets of Cheyenne all night. Look what had happened to her in only an hour. She slumped resignedly in her chair.

"You're certain all I have to do is sing?"

"All you have to do is sing. Your virtue will be safe, I promise you." He grinned broadly.

Elaina watched his hazel eyes for some sign of the truth. He was a handsome man, one who inspired trust, even though she knew better than to rely on the word of a stranger.

She straightened. "I accept your generous offer, Mr. Cameron. And thank you. Now, if you will show me to my room . . ."

"Don't you want to know how much the job pays?"

"As you said, I have no choice. Now if you'll be kind enough —"

"The evenin's young yet, Miss McAllister. Why don't I have a bath sent to your room? You can freshen up and join me for dinner. You *are* hungry, aren't you?"

She was starved. It was a more than tempting offer. "Thank you, Mr. Cameron. That would be nice."

"Chase. Please. May I call you Elaina?"

She wanted to say no. To keep their arrangement as businesslike as possible, but it would be far too rude. "Certainly, Mr. — I mean, Chase."

He led her from the office and up the stairs to her room. It was

140

small but comfortably furnished with a wide bed, a nightstand with a yellow-flowered basin and pitcher, and a small three-drawer bureau. The bath arrived shortly, and Elaina had seldom beheld a more pleasant sight. The copper tub roiled with steam as she undressed and slipped into the water. The creamy suds and warmth of the water conspired to relax her aching muscles. She lathered her hair and scrubbed herself with the rose-scented soap Chase had sent along with towels and a sponge. Just to be completely clean again after five days of spot baths felt wonderful.

After a good long soak, she rose from the tub and dried herself. A knock at the door, interrupting the completion of her toilette, signaled the entrance of a dark-complexioned woman carrying an elegant blue silk gown.

"Mr. Chase send this for you," the girl told her with a bit of a Spanish accent. "I take your others and clean."

"Thank you." Elaina didn't ask the woman how Chase Cameron happened to have a gown that would fit her. She was too happy not to have to put her dirty gray suit back on. Though the décolletage was daringly low, Elaina felt civilized and beautiful in the light blue gown.

Over dinner, an elegant affair in the lobby of the Inter-Ocean Hotel, she questioned him about the dress.

He answered with a devilish smile. "When you travel as much as I do, Elaina, you make a lot of friends. Some are close friends, some are not, but all of them are useful at one time or another. This particular friend owns a dress shop here in Cheyenne."

Elaina was beginning to get a clear picture of Mr. Chase Cameron. From the looks he'd been receiving all evening from the ladies, she was certain he had more than a few women friends. The bold way he watched her made her wonder if part of his helpfulness was due to an intention to add her to his list.

"Well, your friend certainly has good taste," she told him with just a hint of sarcasm. "The dress is lovely."

"It's yours, Elaina. We'll call it a bonus to sweeten our deal."

"Why, I couldn't possibly . . . It's far too expensive and I — I . . ."

"Please, I insist. The gown wouldn't look nearly as lovely on someone else." Chase allowed his gaze to assess the slender woman seated across from him. Even with his eye for beauty, the girl had surprised him. Her hair was the color of rich dark coffee sprinkled generously with ruby highlights. Her lips were full and her cheeks pink. As slender as she was, she had a more than ample bosom, and the dress did little to disguise the fact. Her breasts seemed ready to spill over into Chase's eagerly waiting hands. He felt an itch to have her stronger than he had felt in some time.

Most women fell into his bed without the slightest effort. This one seemed impervious to his charms. She was polite, a good conversationalist, and certainly pleasant to look at, but he sensed she did not desire him, and it piqued his interest. There was nothing Chase liked better than a challenge.

On the pretense of a headache, Elaina retired to her room a little early. She had enjoyed the meal and Chase Cameron's company, but the events of the day had worn her out. As she crawled under the covers in a fresh cotton nightdress she'd found waiting on the bed, her thoughts began to wander.

Though her escort for the evening was certainly a handsome man, with fine features, curly blond hair, and smiling eyes, she thought of a man whose eyes were pale, the color of the sky on a too-hot day. Hard eyes, vague and distant, until they lighted with warmth and passion. Where was Ren now? What was he doing? Had his memory returned? Was he laughing at her, thinking what a fool she'd made of herself, or was he missing her as she missed him? An ache wrapped itself around her heart, and a hard lump closed her throat.

How she missed him. How she loved him. It was foolish to deny it. She'd been in love with Ren Daniels since she was ten years old. There might be other men in her life — who knew what life held in store? — but there would never be another love. Not for her. She'd given him her heart the night she'd given him her body.

Hot tears rolled down her cheeks. She had to stop crying every time she thought of him. Had to forget him. But how? A sob escaped as she thought of his marriage, only a week away. If she really loved him she would wish him happiness with Melissa Stanhope, but she could not. Maybe she didn't love him at all. She tried unsuccessfully to convince herself as she drifted into a fitful sleep.

The morning train for Denver and on to Central City left right on schedule. Chase Cameron, charming as usual, escorted her to a seat in the first class section. It certainly beat the accommodations she'd had on her trip from Keyserville. Plush velvet seats, brass lamps, heavy draperies over the windows and elegantly garbed men and women who conversed pleasantly while sipping refreshments: lemonade, fruit juice, or something stronger for the gentlemen. She was dressed once more in her now clean and pressed, gray traveling suit, but her hair she'd left loose, to curl down her back. Chase told her it sparkled with rubies when she wore it like that.

The train ride through the Rockies was spectacular. Shear walls of granite thousands of feet above a raging river had been blasted away, leaving a narrow ledge just wide enough for the train to pass. There were tunnels through solid rock, and snow bridges — covered tunnels in areas of heavy snowfall to keep the tracks clear in winter. Chase had answered all her questions and explained about the town they were going to.

Central City was a center for gold mining — just the word "mining" sent a shiver of dread down her spine. But Central City, he assured her, had all the modern conveniences. It was just a little rowdy, he said.

"I hope you really can sing," he teased lightly, and she grimaced at the thought. She was no songbird, but she could carry a tune better than most. She'd do her best — at least until she could save enough money to make her way west again. As soon as she reached Central City, she would wire Ada Lowery of her whereabouts. She knew her friend would be worried when Elaina didn't arrive at her destination.

"Well, Elaina, here we are." The noise from the Black Garter echoed through the open windows out into the street. They'd stopped only once on the way from the train station, to send Ada a wire.

Chase pushed open the swinging doors and the plinkety-plink of a cheap piano tinkled above the din of voices. Elaina's heart pounded. Through the haze of smoke hovering above the tables, she could barely make out the wide, curtained stage at the far end of the room. Women in brightly colored dresses — purple, red, orange, and canary yellow — well above their knees, smiled at drunken miners. One man slapped a blond woman's bottom, and she giggled delightedly. Another cupped the full breast of a dark-skinned, raven-haired girl. Elaina's heart sank. How could she have let Chase Cameron talk her into this? The place was even worse than the White Elephant! Sensing her nervousness, Chase extended his arm.

"You don't have to be afraid, Elaina. You're with me."

She clung to him as if he were saving her life and let him lead her across the room.

A tall, buxom red-haired woman wearing a yellow and black lace dress and a long black feather in her hair turned as they walked up. Chase smiled at her warmly. Elaina wondered if the woman was another of Chase's friends.

"Delsey," he began, "I'd like you to meet a frienda mine."

Elaina cringed at his use of the word "friend." From the corner of her eye she glimpsed a sign near the stage: "We're looking for a star. Apply Delsey Stevens."

"This is Miss —"

"Starr," Elaina interrupted, daring Chase Cameron to contradict her. "Lainey Starr." If she was going to act the part of a saloon girl, she might as well sound like one.

He smiled indulgently. "This is Miss Starr."

"Pleased to meet you, Miss Starr," Delsey said.

"Why don't you show Miss Starr up to her room?" Again he smiled. "Delsey will see you're settled. You can stay here at the saloon until you find more suitable lodgings — unless you'd prefer to stay here permanently?"

"No! No, thank you. I'll find a place as soon as I'm able."

"You can start workin' with Mike, the piano player, this afternoon. I'll expect to hear a song from you tomorrow night."

"Tomorrow night? But that's too soon!" She looked at him pleadingly.

He grinned wryly. "I've got great faith in you, Miss Starr. Besides, I'm dyin' to see your legs."

She laughed in spite of herself. "All right, Mr. Cameron, at least one song by tomorrow night."

Delsey escorted her upstairs and down a long, narrow hall. Unlike the White Elephant, the Black Garter had more going on than just drinking. A rotund middle-aged man, foul-smelling with whiskey, pushed open one of the narrow crib doors. A slender young woman no more than fifteen sprawled naked on the rumpled bed.

"Bye, Howie," she called after the fat man. "See ya next week." The man buttoned his shirt and smoothed his hair as he passed Elaina in the hall. His glance took in her out-of-place clothing, and Elaina wished she could crawl in a hole. Her cheeks burned furiously, and she wanted to strangle Chase Cameron with her bare hands. How could he have brought her to work in a house of ill repute?

Elaina's room was far more spacious than the ones she'd passed in the hall. She glanced at the wide bed and swallowed hard. Delsey seemed to read her thoughts.

"Where you from, Miss Starr?"

"I — I'm from Pennsylvania."

"You ever sang in a place like this?"

"No . . . no, I haven't. Someone stole my purse, and I left my clothes on the train and . . . It's a long story. I'm sure you wouldn't want to hear my hard luck tale."

Delsey surprised her. "Don't you worry, Miss Starr. Mr. Cameron won't force you to do nothin' you don't want to. He's basically a fair man. A bit of a rounder, always an eye for a pretty woman, but not a mean man. This is just a business to him. Long as he's here, ain't nothin' gonna happen to you — leastwise not unless you want it to. Can't say for sure 'bout what'll happen after he leaves. Central City's a rough town. Most of us girls who don't turn tricks got us a protector. Big Willie Jenkins is mine, I'm proud to say. You'd do well to find a man a yer own."

Elaina smiled a little uncertainly. "Thanks, Delsey. I hope we get to be friends." She didn't know if the woman's words were a comfort or a warning, but she liked her honesty.

Delsey smiled, too. "I think yer gonna be all right, Miss Starr."

"Please, call me . . . Lainey."

"Lainey. I like that. If there's anything you need, just holler. I'm right down the hall."

Elaina nodded as Delsey left the room. She wondered what had possessed her to change her name. It was probably just as well. She didn't plan to be here long, but it certainly wouldn't do her reputation

145

any good if this little episode should be discovered. She allowed herself a small smile as she imagined the look on Ren Daniel's face if he ever found out. After all, he would soon belong to one of San Francisco's most prominent families. She wondered how his dear Melissa would take to discovering she was sharing her life with a man who'd bedded a common saloon girl.

She sighed at the thought. Who was she kidding? Elaina McAllister wasn't the first girl Ren Daniels had taken to his bed. He'd had plenty of practice, of that she was sure. She wondered if she'd chosen the name "Lainey" because that was what Ren always called her. Probably not. But she wasn't really sure.

Ren Daniels had been in San Francisco less than a week when he wired Keyserville. He sent the wire to Ada Lowery, just in case Chuck Dawson was reading Elaina's mail. There was little he'd put past the man. Ren told Ada to tell Elaina he was coming back to talk to her. He'd be there in two weeks.

He was going back to explain about his engagement, try to make her understand and forgive him for what had happened, but mostly he was going back to take her away from Keyserville — one way or another. He had lots of friends in San Francisco. He'd make certain she had a good job, a nice place to live, a fresh start. She could take Ada Lowery with her if that was what she wanted. He told himself he'd just help her get settled; then he'd leave her alone. He wouldn't go near her once he was married. He'd make contact only occasionally, as a friend, just to be sure there was nothing she needed.

It was the only part of his plan he wasn't sure of.

When it came to Elaina McAllister, he wasn't certain just how much willpower he had.

He received an answer to his wire the next day. He was in his front parlor with Jacob and Melissa Stanhope when the telegram arrived. He paid the slim-faced messenger and tore open the envelope: "Elaina not here. Dawson tried to force marriage. Had some trouble. Working in Central City, Colorado. Good luck, Ada."

Ren read and reread the wire, wondering what the ominous words "had some trouble" could mean — and what in God's name Elaina was doing in Central City.

"Something wrong, son?" No matter how old Ren got, Jacob still thought of him as a boy.

"Yes, I'm afraid there is. I've been meaning to discuss this with you, Jacob, but somehow the time just hasn't been right." He looked at Melissa's pale face and knew this was not the right time either, but he had no choice.

"A friend of mine is in trouble. Someone who once saved my life." He looked at Tommy, who eyed him intently. "Both our lives," he corrected. "Tommy's once and mine twice." He met Jacob's unwavering gray-eyed gaze. Jacob was a big man, tall, with shoulders well-muscled from years of hard work. Only a slight paunch and a receding hairline betrayed his advancing age.

"We've never repaid that debt," Ren told him. "Now this person needs help. I have no choice but to do all I can."

"But what about our wedding, Ren? Papa's already postponed it once. How long will you be gone this time?" Her golden hair glistened, and her wide blue eyes looked at him anxiously.

He wished she stirred his blood as Elaina did. Her words spoke concern, but the relief on her face made him wonder at her thoughts.

"I'll be back before the wedding." He smiled at her and touched her cheek. "This time I promise I won't forget."

She pulled away with a slight tremor. As always when they were together, he sensed her fear of him and wondered at the wisdom of their union. What would happen on their wedding night? How could someone so delicate possibly appease his lusty appetite? He could well understand Jacob's desire to see some sturdier stock in the family.

"Is there anything we can do to help?" Jacob wanted to know. Ren had told both Jacob and Melissa about the shooting incident in Keyserville, but little else. He'd never discussed his reason for going east in the first place, and Jacob hadn't pressed him. Melissa didn't really care.

"No, thank you, Jacob," Ren said. "This is something I have to do alone."

"Wait just a minute," Tommy broke in. "I'm going with you. I owe Ela . . . this person, too."

"Sorry, little brother. Someone's got to mind the business — and

147

the ranch. I've been away far too long as it is."

"But, Ren —"

"Tommy, you know I'm right. You've got to stay here. I'll wire you as soon as I get to . . . wherever I end up. This time I'll keep in touch."

"You're certain there is no way I can help?" Jacob pressed.

Ren knew Jacob would put any amount of money, any amount of manpower, at his disposal. Jacob had absolute faith and unwavering trust in him, and that was one of the reasons Ren Daniels would go through with a wedding neither he nor Melissa really wanted. "Thanks, Jacob. I appreciate the offer, but no. There's nothing you can do."

Tommy Daniels studied the hard planes of his brother's face, the blue eyes dark with repressed anger. Pulling the telegram from Ren's hand, he read the words "had some trouble . . . Central City." It made no sense at all.

Tommy watched the careful control Ren exerted, his expression a taut mask. Melissa Stanhope recoiled from his touch as he escorted her to the door.

Tommy wished he could talk his brother out of this senseless marriage. Ren deserved more than a woman who would only tolerate him in her bed out of a sense of duty. It wasn't that Melissa didn't like Ren, or that she wasn't a sweet girl. It was just that she was shy and afraid and too frail to handle a forceful, demanding man like Ren. Melissa needed a gentle lover, someone who would hold her hand and coo sweet nothings in her ear. A man who would lie beside her for days before exercising his husbandly rights.

Ren would take her on their wedding night and every night thereafter until he was sure he'd given Jacob an heir. Then, as sickly as she was, Melissa would probably be confined to her bed to ensure a safe delivery.

Tommy sighed. At least Carolina Williams would be happy. Ren would probably be forced back into the woman's ready and waiting arms. She'd been Ren's mistress for the past two years, until Ren ended the arrangement for Jacob's sake. Ren wanted the Stanhopes to suffer no scandal. Carolina had been furious. She'd been certain that sooner or later she could persuade Ren to marry her. Tommy knew it was a futile hope. The only thing Ren wanted from Carolina was passion, and she knew just how to give it, though she offered little else. Ren would go back to her, all right. No man with his brother's appetite could survive on the skimpy rations of love Melissa was sure to dole out.

Tommy thanked God for Carrie Salzburg, his own lady fair. They were engaged to be married, and Tommy loved her more than life itself. She was fair-haired, soft, and delicate, but not a weakling like Melissa. More than anything in the world, Tommy wished his brother could find someone to love as he loved Carrie. Damn! Why did things always turn out so tough for Ren?

# Chapter 15

Elaina had been singing at the Black Garter for ten days.

Chase Cameron had left a few days after her debut, but returned again yesterday. He seemed pleased with her work. The miners loved her, though she knew her singing wasn't the best, and she had to admit she'd had little trouble with the men so far. Unfortunately, she was afraid that was because the miners believed she was one of Chase Cameron's "friends."

"Gittin' near show time." Delsey stuck her head through the door and smiled. She and Delsey were already becoming fast friends.

"Thanks, Delsey. I don't know what I'd do without you and Willie." A big, tough miner who held women in the highest regard, Willie Jenkins had, at Delsey's urging, taken Elaina under his protective wing along with Delsey.

"I got a feeling you'd make out just fine."

Elaina smiled and Delsey closed the door. Elaina was still living in the saloon — Chase had neglected to mention that every square inch of Central City was overflowing with humanity. It had taken her days to find the tiny room above Herman Hoffman's General Mercantile she would move into in the morning. Elaina could hardly wait. It was tough getting to sleep with the racket and commotion downstairs, to say nothing of the embarrassing grunts, groans, and sighs from the men rutting in the rooms next to hers.

She took a last quick glance in the mirror above the bureau, and a smile curved her lips. If Constance McAllister could only see her daughter now. The costume she wore was scandalous — a dress of red and black vertical-striped satin trimmed in black lace and, beneath it, black net stockings. The bodice was cut so low it barely covered her nipples, and when she bent over, black ruffled under-

"What?" Elaina shrieked. The prospectors laughed uproariously. She smiled at the crowd, but refused to budge. "Get away from me," she said through clenched teeth.

"Don't make a scene, Elaina," he warned softly, smiling all the while. "These miners can get pretty rough." He gripped her arm and tugged her toward the wings.

"Let me go," she said, jerking free of his hold. "Just go away and leave me alone." The men in the audience were beginning to mumble among themselves. It wouldn't be long before the whole place exploded around them.

"Damn you, Lainey." Ren set his jaw. She'd left him no choice. "You're going with me one way or another." Bending down, he seized her firmly around the waist and threw her over his shoulder.

"I'll scream, Ren, I swear it. Put me down!" she demanded, wriggling and squirming and pounding his broad back.

He slapped her bottom hard with the palm of his hand, and heard her astonished gasp just before she started squirming again.

"Put me down!"

The miners howled with laughter, sure it was part of the show. Ren smiled and waved at them and headed into the wings.

Angry tears filled Elaina's eyes. How could he! She pummeled his back and kicked her legs, but he kept on walking. With long, purposeful strides he carried her off the stage, down the stairs, and out the back door.

When they got outside, he set her on her feet, his light eyes dark with fury, his temper barely under control.

"Just what do you think you're doing?" she demanded, tilting her chin defiantly, her dark hair tumbled around her shoulders. How dare he humiliate her in front of half the men in Central City!

"I intended to ask you the same question."

"I don't see where that's any of your business, Mr. Daniels. That is your name, isn't it? *Ren* Daniels?"

Chase Cameron stepped through the door and looked at her questioningly. "Are you all right?"

Ren sliced him a look that would have melted steel. "That depends on what you mean by all right," he said.

"I'm fine," Elaina told Chase, not wanting any more trouble than she already had. After an uncertain pause, Chase closed the door.

"So you know," Ren said, releasing his hold as he stepped away. His expression remained a study in taut control. "I was hoping to explain it myself."

Elaina felt a hard lump swell in her throat. It was true! Every terrible word. Feeling suddenly cold, she wrapped her arms around herself and forced a note of calm into her voice she didn't feel. "You needn't bother explaining. I'm perfectly aware that you lied to me. I know everything."

He didn't try to deny it. God, how she wished he would.

"I never wanted to hurt you, Elaina. If I'd known who I was, none of this would have happened. I came here to explain, to try to make you understand."

"Understand?" she repeated. "What is there to understand? You told me your name was Morgan. It isn't. In fact, you aren't any of the things I believed." A glimpse of concern flashed across his features and tore at her heart. Why in God's name had he come here?

"I wish there was some way to change things," he said. "All I can say is that if I had it to do again, I wouldn't do anything to hurt you."

Elaina sagged in defeat. As much as she wanted to hate him, she couldn't. "I guess in my heart I know you're telling the truth. Now, please, let's just leave it at that. I've got a life of my own now and —"

Ren grabbed her arms and hauled her up short. "You call singing in Chase Cameron's whorehouse a life? I want you to come back to San Francisco. I have friends there. I'll find you a decent job, a nice place to live, make sure you have everything you need. You saved my life, Elaina. It's the least I can do."

There it was again. His sense of duty. Just the same as when he'd left Keyserville. He always wanted to do what was right for her — but always for the wrong reasons.

"I don't want your charity, Ren. Please, just go away and leave me alone." They were standing outside the saloon, and moonlight reflected on the sprinkling of silver at his temples. Where her hands pressed against the fabric of his shirt, she could feel the hard bands of muscle beneath. As he held her immobile, the warmth of his hands heated her flesh and a tremor raced up her spine.

"I'm not leaving you here, Elaina. Not this time."

"I'm not going with you. And if you try to force me, I'll call Chase. He'll stop you."

Ren bristled. So Chase Cameron was behind all this. Chase always had an eye for a beautiful woman. Somehow he'd met Elaina, and if Ren knew Chase, he was scheming right now how to land her in his bed — or maybe he already had. A hard knot curled in Ren's stomach.

"If I decide you're going with me," he said, "there is nothing Chase Cameron can do to stop me." He looked into Elaina's tawny eyes. They betrayed nothing. Her bosom heaved beneath the low-cut dress, conjuring memories of rose-colored nipples and skin as smooth as satin. His blood pounded in his ears, and his body stirred with desire. It was all he could do to keep from pulling her into his arms. He ran his tongue across his lips, fighting the urge to kiss her. If it weren't for Jacob Stanhope and the promises he'd made . . .

"This isn't over, Elaina. Not yet." He looked at her hard. "I'll be back."

Elaina watched as he turned and walked away, his broad back and narrow hips receding into the darkness. Hot tears welled in her eyes as she ran back inside and up to her room. Why couldn't he have left her alone? Now that she'd seen him again, she felt worse than ever. Sinking down on her bed, she steeped in her misery until a knock at the door interrupted her. Drying her eyes with the hem of her dress, she opened the door.

"Is there anything I can do?" Chase Cameron's lazy drawl and warm smile only made her feel worse.

"No, Chase, but thank you for asking. If you don't mind, I'd like some time alone."

"Whatever you say, but if your friend Daniels gives you any trouble, you just call me."

So the two men knew each other. She nodded. "Thanks, Chase, I will."

"Promise?"

She smiled in spite of herself. Chase had a way of doing that to her. "I promise. Thanks."

She closed the door behind him and tried not to think of Ren.

Ren checked into the Central City Hotel, knowing he was lucky to have found a room at all. He removed his boots and shirt and stretched out on the narrow bed. So far he'd made a mess of everything. Elaina practically hated him, and now Chase Cameron, with his southern-gentleman drawl, was smack in the middle of things. Not that Chase wasn't a decent man, in a cunning sort of way. Ren actually liked him — up to a point. But Chase was certainly not the man for Elaina. When it came to women, Chase had the morals of a gutter rat. Surely Elaina was smart enough not to fall for a guy like Chase?

Ren pulled a small gold pocket watch from his breeches and snapped open the cover. He'd been lying on his bed trying to fall asleep for almost two hours. Pressing the cover closed, he sat up and slid the watch back into his pocket. Why the hell fight it? Maybe if he had a couple of drinks, he'd be tired enough to sleep. He pulled on his boots, shrugged into his shirt, tucking the hem into his breeches, and headed into the night.

Though a warning voice told him it was a bad idea, he walked toward the Black Garter, pushed his way through the swinging doors, and melded into the surging crowd.

From where he stood near the back of the bar, Ren had a clear view of the staircase leading to the rooms above the saloon and could even see a few doors. A procession of prospectors and cow-hands beat a never-ending path up those stairs, and it was all Ren could do to resist the urge to pound on every door up there until he found Elaina. The thought that someone might be in her room right now caused his stomach to churn.

Elaina awoke to a light tap at her door. Exhausted from her jumbled emotions, she had fallen asleep without even removing her red and black dress.

"Give me just a minute," she called out. Walking to the basin, she poured in some water and washed her face. With a rough towel, she patted the water away as she walked to the door.

"Hello, Miss Lainey."

"Hello, Willie. What can I do for you?"

Willie Jenkins stood in the hallway, hat in hand, a decided droop to his mouth. "Could I speak to you for just a second? It's about Delsey."

Though the hour was late, Elaina was usually up much later. Knowing he wouldn't have bothered her unless it was important and seeing his forlorn expression, she invited him in. After all, nobody else worried about propriety. "What is it, Willie?"

He towered above her, tugging the lobe of one coffee-cup ear. "It's just that . . . well, I was wonderin' if you might speak to Delsey for me."

"I'd be happy to, Willie. What about?"

Willie cleared his throat. "Well, me and Delsey been seeing each other regular now for nigh on two years. My gold claim is paying off steady, and I want Delsey to marry me."

"Why, Willie, that's wonderful. So what on earth do you need me for? Just ask her."

"It ain't that simple, Miss Lainey. Where Delsey comes from, down Tennessee way, a woman who's . . . who's, well, a might less than pure, she don't marry. Delsey thinks she ain't good enough for me. I told her it's all a bunch of hooey, but she won't listen. I want to provide for her, take her away from here. Please talk to her, Miss Lainey. She'll listen to you."

Elaina clutched Willie's hand. "Of course I'll talk to her. Delsey's a good woman. She's true to you, and there's no reason you two shouldn't marry."

For the first time Willie smiled. He slapped his floppy-brimmed hat against his thigh, then set it back on his head, pulling it low. "Thanks, Miss Lainey. That's mighty fine of you." Jerking open her door, he stepped out into the hall.

"Oh, by the way," he said, "Delsey loaned me some money the other night when I forgot my pocketbook. I meant to give it back to her earlier. Ed Drake and some of his boys is waitin' for me in the alley. We's headin' over to Ed's place to play a little poker. Could you give it to her for me?"

He handed Elaina a wad of money and, from habit, she stuffed it down the front of her dress. The men often threw money to her while she sang, and she'd learned quickly there was only one safe place to stash it.

"If I don't see her tonight, I'll give it to her first thing in the

159

morning. Good night, Willie."

"Good night, Miss Lainey, and thanks for everything."

Elaina smiled at him and closed the door. Well, it looked as though her friend Delsey had a chance for happiness. She wished she could say the same for herself.

Standing at the end of the bar looking up at Elaina's door, Ren Daniels gripped his whiskey glass until his knuckles turned white. So that was the way of it. Elaina was more than a singer at the Black Garter — she was a whore.

Damn! Surely this couldn't be his fault, too? He watched the burly miner descend the stairs with a wide grin on his face. Elaina must have performed well. A picture of her slender, full-breasted body writhing beneath the big miner set his blood to pounding. He was torn between sadness at the lot she had chosen in life and rage that he was not the man who had just left her room. How like a woman to turn him away, then fall into a stranger's arms without a second thought.

He'd seen the miner hand Elaina a wad of money. He hoped she hadn't priced herself too cheap.

"Barkeep!" he called to the graying man who stood polishing glasses just a few feet away. "Bring me another drink. Make it a double." He clenched his fist and set his jaw. Damn her! Damn her to hell for making him feel so bad.

The third whiskey bolstered his courage and brought him an idea. Why should he be any different from the others? She was a whore now. She sold her favors to the highest bidder, and Ren had a pocketful of money. He wasn't married yet, and even if he were, Melissa would never expect fidelity. She would probably encourage him to have affairs — it would mean less obligation for her. He downed the whiskey, paid the barkeep for a couple of tokens, and headed toward the stairs. No one else had entered Elaina's room, so he knew she was alone. Alone and hungry for another customer. Well, that was just fine with him.

Elaina slipped out of her dress and donned a light silk wrapper. Seated in front of her mirror, she began to brush her hair. A hundred strokes a night. That's what her mother always said. For the third

160

time that evening, she heard a knock at her door. Maybe Delsey had come to say good night, and she and Elaina could have their talk, though the subject of marriage was not one she relished discussing. It always brought thoughts of Ren to mind.

Elaina sighed in defeat. No matter how hard she tried, she couldn't blot out the image of his handsome face. When she opened the door, it seemed as though some magic genie had read her mind and brought him to her.

"Ren?" she whispered, not quite sure he was real.

He meant to keep things businesslike. Make love to her, pay her fee, and leave. But she stood there looking so lost, so vulnerable, so beautiful, all he could do was pull her into his arms and bury his face in her hair.

"Lainey, God, I've missed you."

He felt her sway against him, lace her fingers through his hair. Pulling her inside the room, he closed the door behind them, cupping her face in his hands, needing to touch her, wanting to feel the warmth of her body pressed against him. When he kissed her, he smelled the scent of jasmine, and hardened with desire.

Elaina meant to deny him, meant to send him away, but the pain in his voice when he whispered her name banished the last of her will. She kissed his lips, his cheeks, his eyes. Feeling his hands beneath her knees as he carried her to the bed, she clung to him as if she would never let him go. It was wrong what they were doing, wrong, but it seemed so right. He kissed her thoroughly, passion-ately, his lips seeking, searching every part of her mouth. His breath was hot and moist, sweet with the taste of his desire. His tongue thrust into her mouth possessively, branding her, telling her she was his and his alone. He left her lips to nibble the spot behind her ear; then he trailed fiery kisses along her throat. She was gasping for breath, battling the heat of desire that spread through her body.

"I want you," he whispered thickly. Pulling the silk wrapper from between them, he lowered his lips to her breast. His tongue circled the hardened peak just before he surrounded the bud with his mouth. Mindlessly she moaned and arched against him.

He left her only long enough to shed his clothes and remove her robe, then he was beside her again. She could feel the corded muscles of his body, his sinewy thighs. She ran her fingers through the stiff black hair curling on his chest, and the muscles beneath rippled beneath her hand. With a soft groan, he called her name. His mouth claimed hers again — fiercely, passionately. Dear God, she wanted him. She ached with wanting him.

Sensing her need, he began to stroke her thighs, moving upward until he parted the soft flesh at the juncture of her legs and slid his fingers inside. Hot flames flicked across her skin as she moaned and writhed against his hand. Feeling her readiness, he positioned himself above her, spreading her thighs with his knee.

"I need you, Lainey," he whispered, so softly she almost didn't hear him. The words filled her with joy. Nothing mattered but the feel of him, the touch of his hand. Nothing mattered but the two of them. Nothing mattered but loving him.

She clung to him as he entered, filling her and making her whole. Just as before, she felt complete, as if her soul had found its mate.

He held himself in check a moment, letting her feel the strength and power of his body. Then he began to move rhythmically inside her, each thrust stronger than the last. He plunged against her, his muscles tensed as he drove himself, carrying her along with him to the heights he was seeking. She met each thrust with one of her own and soon their bodies were covered with a fine sheen of perspiration.

She breathed in his virile male scent and felt the corded muscles of his buttocks beneath her hands. Then her mind emptied of all but the sensations of pleasure he was giving — timeless, endless, mindless pleasure. Pleasure so vivid she could taste it. Only when she moaned and cried his name, felt the tingling joy of climax, did he permit his own release.

As they spiraled down, he stayed within her, not wanting the delicious sensations to end. She felt warm lips against her neck, then a feather-soft kiss on her mouth. Even as he rolled away, he pulled her against him, as if he were afraid to let her go.

For the first time since her nightmare began, Elaina felt safe and protected. She almost dozed, so content was she, but soon she felt Ren's warm palm move along her skin. She stirred as he cupped her bottom, felt his hardness and knew he was ready for her again.

Turning to face him, she let him begin his magic.

162

# Chapter 16

Elaina smiled contentedly.

Rays of sunlight peeped through the faded muslin curtains that hung at her window. Stifling a yawn, she rolled over, her hand groping the place beside her for Ren's warm, solid torso. Instead she felt only the cold roughness of the muslin sheet. Bolting upright, she searched the empty room, her heart beginning to pound. Dear God, he hadn't even said good-bye.

Elaina took a steadying breath and calmed her racing heart. Maybe she was upsetting herself for nothing. Maybe he'd just gone downstairs. Picking up her thin silk wrapper, which had fallen carelessly to the floor, she slipped it on and glanced at the bed. Her breath caught in her throat as memories of their desperate lovemaking filled her mind.

*Desperate.* There was no other word. Each had known it would be the last. Each had needed the other desperately. Surely Ren would be back — at least to say good-bye. Her eyes teared at the thought of his leaving. This time would be even harder than before.

Elaina straightened the sheets, pulled up the quilt, and fluffed Ren's pillow, inhaling the musky, manly smell that clung to the rough muslin case. What they'd shared last night was special. Ren would be back. As she picked up the second pillow, a round brass token beside a wad of bills caught her eye. Her hand trembled as she picked them up. Who could have left them there? Who had been in her room?

A wave of nausea hit her like a blow. Only Ren. Only Ren could have put them there and only for one reason. She'd worked in a house of ill fame long enough to know how a whore got paid: in brass tokens that were later redeemed for money. Unable to breathe, she clutched the cold piece of metal against her breast and sank down on the bed, her heart thundering in bitter spasms. *Dear God, don't let this be!* Her chest felt leaden. Ren Daniels, a married man, had slept with her because he thought she'd become a whore.

She curled up on the bed and sobbed uncontrollably. What should she have expected? She knew he was married, yet she'd given herself to him, let him make love to her as no one else could.

It took more than an hour for her tears to turn to anger. Twice she'd trusted him. Twice he'd wounded her to the depths of her soul. How dare he! How dare he believe her capable of something so low? In that moment Elaina McAllister swore her revenge. She'd pay him back if it took the rest of her life.

Marching to the door, her newfound hatred giving her strength, she leaned into the hall and called out for Benny Thompson, the houseboy, to send up a bath. When the tub arrived, she bathed and dressed, careful to keep her mind a dull blank. Ren Daniels did not exist for her, would never exist for her again. This time she would blot memories of their nights together forever from her mind. This time she would erase his image from her heart and soul. This time things would be different.

With a toss of the thick dark hair she'd left loose at her back, she straightened her sturdy brown muslin dress and stiffened her spine. She had better things to do than grieve over Ren Daniels. Today was moving day.

Packing what few possessions she had into a worn leather satchel Chase had loaned her, she walked down the stairs. When she reached the bottom, Chase Cameron stood waiting. He studied her face carefully, and she wondered what secrets it betrayed.

"You look as though you could use a friend," he said softly, lightly caressing her cheek. "Would you care to join me for break-fast?" There was little privacy in the Black Garter. By now she was certain Chase knew exactly who had spent the night in her room. Her cheeks flamed at the conclusions he would draw — conclusions that were more than correct.

"Thank you, Chase. You're right, I could use a friend." Though part of her wanted to slip away and continue to feel sorry for herself, the other part told her to face up to her problems, solve them, forget Ren Daniels. As always, her resilient nature won out.

"You look lovely this mornin'," Chase said. "A little tired, perhaps. But lovely just the same." Elaina blushed, but Chase merely smiled and offered his arm. They headed through the swinging doors and off down the boardwalk lining the dirt street.

"How about the Central City Café?" he suggested. "Best sausage and biscuits in town."

She nodded, but her stomach rolled at the thought. She knew she looked wan and pale, and her hand shook slightly as she held his arm.

"Want to tell me about it?" he asked.

She started to say no. "Ren was just a mistake I made," she told him instead. "Unfortunately, last night I made the same mistake again."

"Where'd you two meet?"

She took a breath to steady herself. Since he seemed genuinely concerned, she told him the story, going into as little detail as possible.

"Are you in love with him?"

She pondered the question, knowing in her heart the answer was yes. "Does it matter?" she finally replied.

He patted her hand where it rested on his arm. "No, I guess it doesn't. Not really." They walked a little farther, then stopped in front of the café.

"Elaina, you know how fond I am of you." He lifted her chin so her eyes would meet his. "If there's anything I can do to help, don't hesitate to ask."

She smiled at him tremulously. "Thank you, Chase. I appreciate everything you've done, really I do. I don't know how I'll ever be able to repay you."

As he held open the door, her skirts brushed against his brown serge trousers. "I'm sure I'll think of somethin'," he teased.

As always, he made her smile.

Ren stuffed his wrinkled shirt into his satchel and buttoned the cuffs on the clean white shirt he'd just put on. His mind seemed fuzzy, distracted. He'd replayed the scene with Elaina over and over and each time felt the same gut-wrenching pain he'd felt earlier this morning, when he'd closed the door to her room.

165

For the first time in years, Ren was unsure what course of action to take.

Should he leave Elaina with Chase Cameron, to continue a life that was worse than degrading? Or should he drag her back to San Francisco and force her to lead a respectable life? What was best for Elaina? Surely being a whore in Central City held the least possibilities for happiness.

Ren released an uncertain sigh and tucked his shirttail into his breeches. He regretted, not for the first time, leaving the brass token beneath her pillow. But some jealous demon had wanted her to suffer just as he did. Wanted her to feel the hurt and pain he felt every time he thought of her with another man.

Striding purposefully, he headed for the door, his satchel slung over his shoulder. Deciding to put some food in his stomach while he took some time to think, he headed down the stairs and along the street to the Central City Café.

He found the place bulging at the seams with prospectors, merchants, and cowhands, all clamoring noisily, banging tin coffee cups, and clanking metal flatware against thick white porcelain plates. If booming business was any indication of the quality of the food, the café's reputation was well deserved.

Seating himself at a small table near the back of the café, Ren hung his black hat on the back of his chair, then ordered coffee, biscuits, and gravy from a skinny, flat-chested girl who looked no more than fifteen. She smiled brightly, and he decided the smile made her look almost pretty.

As he sipped the coffee she brought him, he glanced around the room. It took only an instant to spot Chase Cameron's blond head. Then he caught sight of Elaina's tawny eyes, glittering with anger and locked with his. Her jaw was set stubbornly, her cheeks flushed with rage. Beneath her simple high-necked dress, her bosom heaved with the force of a bellows, and all he could think of was kissing her again.

Leaving her plate half full, she shoved back her chair and marched toward him, her shoulders straight and proud, her eyes snapping fire. He thought she'd never looked more beautiful. Out of the corner of his eye he caught sight of Chase Cameron leaning back in his chair, his mouth curved in a lazy, amused smile.

"You!" Elaina choked out, as she stood before him. "You're the most vile, the most despicable —"

"Surely you can do better than that," he said.

"Get out of Central City." Her slender hands rested on her hips; her chin jutted defiantly. "Leave me alone. Don't ever come near me again."

Ren came to his feet. He'd known she'd be upset about the money, but he'd expected her to be contrite, not angry.

"It's a free country, Elaina. I'll go where I want, when I want. You ought to know that by now." His eyes ran the length of her, taking in the swell of her breasts, the tiny waist he could span with his hands.

Elaina felt her anger seethe to overwhelming proportions. Through the blur of miners surrounding her, her vision narrowed till she saw no other person in the room. Ren stood over her, regarding her like some distant acquaintance rather than the woman he'd made love to for most of the night.

Clenching her teeth, Elaina drew back her hand and slapped him hard across the face, the resounding crack muffled by the din in the room. But the rosy imprint of her hand left notice of the deed.

Ren's pale eyes narrowed into slits, and a muscle bunched in his jaw. He grabbed her arm and pulled her against him.

"I probably deserved that," he told her. "But don't ever try it again."

She could feel the strength of his hand circling her wrist. "You don t scare me. You're nothing but a cheap, womanizing —"

"Don't push your luck, Elaina." His grip tightened on her wrist.

"Bastard!" she finished. "If it hadn't been for me, you'd be dead!" Instantly she regretted the words. Just the thought of his dying left her with a sickening knot in the pit of her stomach. "I'm sorry," she whispered. "I shouldn't have said that."

Ren released his hold, and his look softened. "Why not? It's true, isn't it? I haven't forgotten, Elaina, I promise you. I'll be leaving on the afternoon train. My offer is still open if you want to make a new life for yourself in San Francisco." He glanced toward Chase Cameron who watched them both with amusement, and Elaina a bit protectively, it seemed. "But if this is what you really want, I won't make any more trouble for you."

She swallowed hard, a little ashamed of the dark red welt she'd left across his cheek. "I wish things were different," she told him softly, thinking of the wife he'd left behind and feeling the sting of tears, "but they aren't." She steeled herself. "Good-bye, Ren."

Ren watched the gentle sway of her hips as she walked back toward her table and Chase Cameron. The skinny serving girl arrived with his biscuits and gravy, but the sight of the food only sickened him. He left a coin on the table, settled his hat back on, and walked out the door.

"Feel better?" Chase pulled out her chair and guided her into her seat.

Tears threatened, but she held them at bay. Looking down at her half-full plate, she felt the bile rise in her throat.

"Come on," he said, reading her pale expression. "I think you've had enough fun for one day." He stood up, tossed a coin on the table, and helped her from her chair.

"I just want to be alone for a while."

"Not a chance. Today's moving day. We're going to turn that little room of yours into a palace."

She smiled up at him, shaking her head. "I don't need a palace, Chase. Just a little place I can call my own. But you're right. Moving will keep my mind off . . . other things."

"Good girl." He patted her hand. They moved along the streets of Central City, threading their way through the throng of men, horses, and wagons. Some of the wagons were filled with ore, some with brightly colored cloth, sacks of flour, tins of coffee, and others with building materials — brick and mortar, smooth round stones for chimneys.

Breathing the fresh, high mountain air revived her lagging spirits. The day was warm and bright. Just a few wispy clouds made patterns above the towering mountains that surrounded the city. Grateful for the distractions, Elaina barely noticed the gentle tug at her sleeve.

"Miss McAllister? Is that you?" A scruffy prospector, bearded, his overalls torn and dirty, hands gnarled and callused, looked at her from beneath his shaggy brown hair. She watched his sad brown eyes and wondered how the man knew her real name.

"What is it you want?"

Chase Cameron stiffened protectively. "Here, take this," he

168

handed the miner a coin, "and leave the lady alone."

The man handed the money back, ignoring Chase and speaking instead to her. "I don't want a handout. I'm looking for a grubstake, Miss McAllister. I'm Richard Marley. I used to work for your father."

Elaina sucked in a breath. "Mr. Marley, of course. I'm sorry, I didn't recognize you."

"I don't look much like I used to, but times have been tough for me lately. I left Pennsylvania about a year ago, determined to get my wife and sons away before the damned coal dust killed them." He dropped his gaze to the dirt street.

"I lost Elizabeth about six months ago. Some kind of fever. The boys are still with me, Peter and Benjamin, but our money's run out. When I saw you, I thought maybe my prayers had been answered." He straightened, some of his former pride returning to remind her of the man he used to be — proud, determined, loyal. One of the smartest, hardest-working men in the mine, he'd been made foreman before he was twenty-five All the other miners had respected him, but he always vowed someday he'd go west and make his own way.

"Mr. Marley, if I could do anything to help you, I'd be more than willing, but you see —"

"I've found it this time, Miss McAllister. I'm so close I can smell it. I wouldn't be asking you to stake me if I wasn't sure I'd be able to pay you back. You stake me for six months, and we'll be partners, fifty-fifty, in anything I find in the mine."

Elaina closed her eyes, wanting to help an old friend, but knowing the price she would pay — more long nights of singing in the Black Garter. More lewd remarks, more bruises on her bottom from the men's rough pinches as she made her way through the saloon. More loneliness in a town where she knew almost no one. And more weeks of Chase Cameron's kind but purposeful advances.

"There's no use discussing this further, Mr. Marley," Chase was saying. "Miss McAllister is not in a position to help you. I am, but if I helped every miner who asked me for a grubstake, I wouldn't be for long. We wish you the best of luck, Mr. Marley. Now if you'll excuse us . . . ." He tugged at Elaina's arm to lead her away.

169

"Just a minute," she heard herself saying. She knew she was being a fool, but was somehow unable to stop herself. Reaching into her reticule, she pulled out the wad of bills Ren had left as well as the small amount she'd been able to save so far. She always carried it with her, unsure where else it would be safe. But she'd learned a lesson in Cheyenne and watched her bag carefully. "Mr. Marley, if there's anyone who can find gold in those mountains it's you."

"Elaina," Chase interceded, "this is an everyday occurrence here. Think what you're doing."

She placed her fingers over his lips. "I know what I'm doing." She turned back to the short, disheveled prospector. "Take this and good luck. Give Peter and Benjamin a hug for me."

"We'll never forget you for this, Miss McAllister, never." His eyes misted, and he looked away.

She squeezed his arm and turned to leave with Chase.

"Wait a minute!" he called out. "Where will I find you to give you your share?"

She felt the tug of a smile. "I'm living above Hoffman's General Mercantile — or you can catch my show at the Black Garter six nights a week. Good luck, Richard." She caught his stunned expression as she turned to walk away.

Ren strode into the Golden Saddle Saloon and ordered a beer. Maybe the alcohol would numb his senses and settle his stomach. He took several long, slow draws, then set the mug back on the bar. He had hours to wait before the train arrived.

Another long draw and he glanced at the man beside him, a tall, barrel-chested miner with too-large ears. He wore clean coveralls, and his large hands were callused from years of hard work.

Ren cursed his luck. It was the man he'd seen coming from Elaina's room.

"Excuse me," the man said, trying to be friendly. "Didn't I see you over to the Black Garter last night?"

"Yeah, you saw me," Ren snapped. Thoughts of the big man lying in Elaina's warm arms nearly blinded him.

"Name's Willie Jenkins." The man stuck out a meaty hand.

"Look, Jenkins, I've got nothing against you personally. It's just that Elaina McAll . . . Miss Starr is a friend of mine, and it's damn

170

hard for me to stand here and drink with a man who spent time in her bed."

The meaty hand grabbed the front of Ren's shirt, the huge hairy knuckles turning white with rage. "What did you say about Miss Starr?"

"Get your hands off me, mister," Ren warned, his temper barely under control.

Jenkins released his grip, but stood his ground. Taller than Ren and outweighing him by thirty or forty pounds, the big man glowered down at him.

"Miss Lainey's one of the finest ladies I know. She's kind and decent — and ain't no man in Central City spent time in her bed, least of all me."

Ren eyed the big man warily. "There's no call to lie, Mr. Jenkins. I saw you leave her room last night."

Jenkins stiffened again and looked as though he might hit Ren just for drill. "I don't lie, Mr. Whoever-you-are, and if I didn't think you had some reason for mentioning Miss Lainey, I'd knock you through that wall. I went to see Miss Starr last night because I wanted to ask a favor. She and my gal, Delsey, is friends, and I knew Delsey would listen to Miss Lainey. I want Delsey to marry me. Miss Lainey was gonna put in a good word for me."

"But the money —"

"That was Delsey's money. Miss Lainey was just givin' it back to her for me."

Ren slumped against the bar, lowering his head into his hands. With a long, ragged breath, he closed his eyes, seeing again the scene at the café, the hurt and angry expression on Elaina's face. Then he straightened. "I owe you an apology, Mr. Jenkins. I hope you'll accept it." He extended a hand.

Jenkins shook it, grinning broadly. "Call me Willie, Mr. —"

"Daniels. Ren Daniels."

Willie eyed the red handprint still glowing on Ren's cheek. "Don't suppose that mark on yer face come from our mutual friend, by any chance?"

Ren glanced away. "I wish she'd hit me harder." He smiled slightly as he thought of the slap, then touched the side of his face. "But she does pack a helluva wallop."

171

Willie shook his head, then took a long pull on his beer. "Miss Lainey's got the day off. She's movin' outta the saloon today, gettin' her own place above Hoffman's General Mercantile. I probably shouldn't be tellin' you this, but there's somethin' in yer eyes tells me you care. I don't think you want anything to happen to her any more'n I do." He drew himself up to his full height. "And if'n you do cause her any trouble, you'll be answerin' to me. Do I make myself clear?"

Ren smiled, glad Elaina had someone like Willie to look out for her. "Very clear, my friend. Very clear." He turned back to the bar. "Barkeep, bring my friend here and me another beer." He might as well make himself comfortable. He had plenty of time. The train would be leaving without him.

# Chapter 17

"Well, I guess that just about does it." Chase Cameron rolled his shirtsleeves back down and buttoned the cuffs.

"It's wonderful, Chase. I couldn't be more pleased if it were the President's suite at the Palace Hotel." She flashed him an appreciative smile, surveying with wonder the tiny rooms above the store that Chase had transformed into a homey retreat.

One corner of his mouth tilted up. "I don't see how two rooms furnished with hooked rugs, old oak furniture, and a couple of overstuffed chairs could ever equal the Palace," he teased, "but if you like it, that's all that counts."

Lovingly, she ran her hand over the smooth grain of the small oak table in front of the settee, fingering the delicate white lace doily on top. Several of the girls had given her gifts as she left the saloon, each wishing her well. Their longing for the respectability she represented was unmistakable, but the women had long ago given up hope of living any other sort of life.

Delsey had given her the doily, along with several embroidered pillowcases and a set of sheets for the iron bed in the other room. She said they'd been meant for her hope chest. Elaina had taken the opportunity to mention Willie's proposal, giving Delsey gentle reassurances that Willie's love would overcome any obstacles that might stand in the way of their happiness. Though she hadn't persuaded Delsey to marry Willie, she'd made a start in the right direction.

"It's the first home of my own I've ever had," Elaina told Chase, with a look of gratitude. The look he returned spoke of far more than friendship.

"It hardly does you justice." He stepped closer, turning her face with his hand. Before she could stop him, he covered her lips in a gentle kiss.

173

Elaina broke away. "I'm sorry, Chase. I don't think I can handle this right now."

"You don't have to," he said. "Take your time, Elaina. I'll be here when you're ready."

She nodded, wondering if she would ever be ready for Chase Cameron — or any other man, for that matter.

"Thank you, Chase. Now if you don't mind, I'm awfully tired. It's been a long day."

"Of course." He drew her hand to his lips. "Enjoy your evening." Picking up his fawn-colored hat, he settled it over his curly blond hair and headed for the door, closing it softly behind him.

Elaina sighed and sank down on the settee. Chase Cameron was a handsome man. Dashing, courteous, a man of some means. Why was it his kiss sparked none of the excitement one look from Ren could stir? She knew Chase was holding himself in check, disguising the hunger he felt for her behind a kiss of compassion.

In truth, Chase wanted the same thing from her Ren Daniels had taken. Though she'd given herself to Ren, she felt no desire for Chase and probably never would. Even his loan of a few odd pieces of furniture made her uneasy. She knew what it felt like to be indebted to a man she didn't love.

Hoping to refresh herself, Elaina poured water from the pitcher on the bureau in the bedroom into the basin and washed her face. Two boys from the saloon had done most of the work of moving her in, but she still felt bone-tired. She knew it was partly the strain of seeing Ren in the café. For a moment after she slapped him, she'd regretted it. Now she wished she could hit him again. How could she have been so wrong about him?

It doesn't matter, she told herself firmly. He's gone by now, and you'll never see him again. The thought constricted her throat and brought the hot sting of tears. Damn it all, why did just thinking about him always make her cry?

After washing and drying her face, she returned to her tiny parlor. There were still a few personal items to be unpacked and placed in drawers. Now that she'd given Richard Marley her savings, she would be here longer than she'd expected, so she decided to make herself comfortable.

A knock at the door interrupted her. Wondering who it could be, she opened the door a crack and found Oscar Whittington, one of the boys who'd helped her move in, standing at the top of the stairs. A big strapping youth of seventeen with a wide mouth and curly brown hair, Oscar was a bully and a braggart, but a good worker. Chase used him whenever he needed someone with a brawny back.

"May I come in, Miss Starr? I think I left my pocketknife here."

Elaina opened the door. "I haven't seen it, Oscar. Are you sure?" He brushed past her with a smile, then pushed the door closed from the inside, leaning his heavy frame nonchalantly against it.

"Only thing I left up here is the prettiest gal west of Denver."

God, not another one, Elaina thought with a sigh. "Oscar, I don't know what you think you're doing, but you'd better leave." She reached for the door, but he stepped in front of her.

"You ain't bein' very friendly, Miss Starr."

"And you aren't acting like a gentleman. In fact, you're acting very much like a spoiled little boy."

Grabbing her wrist, Oscar pulled her against his chest. "I'm no boy, Miss Starr. I'm as good as any other man in this town, maybe better. You'd see that if you'd just give me a chance."

Furious at his audacity, Elaina jerked away. "Get out of here, Oscar. Get out before I tell Chase what you've been up to."

"Please, Miss Starr, couldn't we at least talk about it?" He ran his thick fingers along her cheek, and for the first time Elaina felt a tiny prickle of alarm. Oscar might be a boy, but he was a very *big* boy.

"Oscar —" Another knock at the door stopped her in midsentence. Ignoring Oscar, who had set his jaw in a possessive manner, she reached for the door.

She felt his hand on her shoulder. "Go ahead and open it, but get rid of 'em. You and me got some talkin' to do."

Biting back an angry retort, she turned the knob and opened the heavy wooden door. The last person she would have expected stood in the frame.

She'd rehearsed a dozen clever phrases just in case she ever saw him again, but not a single one came to mind. Instead, she just stared at the compelling lines of his face.

"Hello, Elaina," he said. "We need to talk."

"Just like that. 'Hello, Elaina, we need to talk'?"

"Yes. Exactly like that." He pushed open the door, and though she could have used his assistance with the brawny youth, she slammed it against him. Ren blocked it with his boot and stepped inside.

"Need some help, Miss Starr?" Oscar asked.

"I see you have company," Ren said.

Knowing what he thought of her, she found the words more than she could bear. She would deal with Oscar Whittington somehow — without any help from Ren! "Yes," she told him, with a saucy toss of her head. "I'm with a customer. A girl's got to earn a living somehow. Now, would you mind leaving?"

Ren smiled, but the smile never touched his eyes. He looked at the brawny youth, feet spread in the middle of the room. He didn't know what Elaina's game was, but he would play along, at least for a while.

"Whatever you say, Miss Starr." Ren tipped his hat and backed out the door, closing it softly behind him.

Elaina heard his steps receding, and her fury threatened to swallow her whole. *How little he must think of me. How easy it is for him to believe the worst.* She'd almost forgotten Oscar Whittington when she felt his arms close around her waist and draw her back against his chest.

"I knew you liked me, Miss Starr. I could tell by the way you been so nice to me and all." He nibbled her neck, careful to keep her arms pinned, then turned her to face him.

All the fury she felt toward Ren, all the anger she was feeling against men in general, Elaina unleashed on Oscar Whittington, lashing out with her slender fists, pummeling his chest, and kicking his shins. If she'd had a gun, she probably would have shot him.

From where Ren stood in the shadows at the bottom of the stairs he could see Elaina clearly through the window. He could see the brawny youth manhandling her — and her wild struggles to ward the young man off. Whatever the boy was doing up there, it was clear to Ren that he was obviously not invited. He cursed Elaina's pride in not asking for his help. It would serve her right if he let the boy maul her a little before he went back in. Then he thought of the youth's hands on Elaina's full breasts and put the idea quickly to rest. Taking the stairs two at a time, he turned the knob and kicked the door open.

Oscar had Elaina pinned against his chest, his head buried in her hair. He held both wrists so easily her efforts to resist him were nearly nonexistent. Drugged with the feel of her, he looked up to see the tall man who had come earlier, his face a mask of quiet rage, standing once more in the room. Oscar released Elaina so abruptly, she lost her balance and nearly toppled to the floor.

Watching Ren's purposeful approach as if he weren't quite sure he was real, Oscar never saw the punch that landed on his jaw or the left-right combination that doubled him over. Ren grabbed him by the back of the neck and the seat of his pants and ran him headlong out the door. The crash of his massive body thundering down the stairs, then the groan that followed his landing brought Elaina to the door, a trembling hand to her throat.

Ren walked up beside her. "Don't worry, he'll be all right. He's too damn big to hurt." His legs outstretched in front of him, Oscar sat at the bottom of the stairs, rubbing his jaw. With a wary glance at Ren, he shook his head, stood up, and stumbled off into the darkness.

Elaina sagged against the doorjamb, feeling a wave of relief. When she turned around, she saw Ren watching her, his light eyes filled with concern. Why, in God's name, was he looking at her like that?

"You didn't really think I'd be that easy to get rid of, did you?" he said softly.

As glad as she was to be free of Oscar Whittington, the seductive tone of Ren's voice renewed her fury. "Don't think you can saunter in here the way you did last night. You're just a paying customer," she taunted. "You can wait your turn like the rest of them."

One corner of his mouth curved into an indulgent smile. "So I have to wait in line, do I? What, no special treatment, even for the man who broke you to the saddle?"

Elaina's fury threatened to boil. Grabbing a dainty flowered vase, intent on ending his mocking smile, she suddenly remembered the look in Sadie Anderson's eyes when she'd given her the pretty piece of glass. With a trembling hand, she set it back on the table.

"Now that you've driven off a paying customer," she said, "I'd appreciate it if you'd leave."

"I'm not leaving until we've had a chance to talk."

"Then make yourself comfortable, because I'm not talking to you, now or ever. I think you're vile and despicable. You don't care about me. You think I'm a . . . a" — her voice broke — "whore," she whispered and blinked against an unwelcome blur of tears.

Ren moved closer and, though she tried to hold him away — gathered her against him. "Elaina, please, listen to me."

She twisted free, her voice ragged. "Get away from me. You'll only hurt me. You shouldn't have come here. You should have let things be."

Ren set his jaw, his eyes dark as his own ire began to build. "You're going to listen to me if I have to tie you to the bed," he threatened, feeling a familiar twinge in his loins as he conjured the image. "Maybe that's the best idea I've had so far." He took one ominous step in her direction, and Elaina backed away.

"All right," she agreed a little nervously, "I'll listen to what you have to say. But only because you leave me no choice."

"No choice at all," he confirmed, his look traveling over her from head to foot. In her tussle with the youth, the combs had slipped from her hair, leaving it a tumbled mass around her shoulders. Her cheeks were flushed, her lips just a little bit pouty. Under any other circumstance, he would pull her into his arms and kiss her senseless, forcing her to respond as she had the night before.

Instead, he laced her stiff fingers through his warmer ones and led her to the settee. "Sit down," he ordered. She lifted her chin, but did as she was told.

"First of all, I know you're not a whore."

"No you don't. You're just saying that to . . . to take advantage of me. One night wasn't enough for you. You're just —"

"Damn you, Lainey, will you be quiet?" His grip tightened on her fingers. "I'd like nothing more than to bed you again," he told her, "but not because I think you're a whore. Last night I saw Willie Jenkins leaving your room, saw him give you a wad of money. I know what goes on upstairs in Chase Cameron's place." He paused, steeling himself to tell her the truth. "I guess I let my imagination run away with me." And my jealousy, he added to himself. She watched him intently, trying to read his expression. "I guess I was also looking for an excuse to make love to you. I wanted you badly." He cleared his throat, adding a little gruffly, "I still do."

For the first time that night her look softened.

"Today I met Willie Jenkins," he continued. "He told me the truth about what happened in your room last night. I'm sorry, Elaina. So sorry. I should have had more faith in you. I should have trusted you."

His words seemed to crumble her resistance. "Oh, Ren," she whispered, and he heard the catch in her voice.

Burying his face in her hair, he kissed her neck, her cheeks, then covered her lips with his. As his tongue slid inside her mouth to taste the warmth within, she swayed against him, her soft breasts pressing against his chest. With a groan of resignation, he forced himself to pull away.

Elaina stiffened. "I'm sorry. I . . . we shouldn't have done that. I know you're a married man and I —"

"I'm not married, Elaina."

Her heartbeat quickened. "Not married? But I thought the wedding was May twenty-third." A date she would never forget.

"Jacob Stanhope postponed it when I didn't return from Keyserville on time."

Tears of happiness filled her eyes. Throwing her arms around his neck, she pressed her cheek against his and heard him groan. Gentle fingers freed him from her embrace as he drew away.

"The wedding's only been postponed. That's what I came here to tell you." Light blue eyes, piercing in their intensity, pleaded for understanding, but Elaina felt none.

"You're going through with it?" she asked, her voice brittle, her mind refusing to grasp the meaning of his words. He was free. He had made love to her, been with her as no man ever had, no man ever could, and yet he planned to marry another. Dear God, she prayed, don't let it be true.

"I have to marry her, Elaina. I have no choice."

Tears coursed down her cheeks, but her fury, now uncontained, blotted all but the words he was saying.

She came to her feet, slender hands balled at her sides. "You . . . you callous, deceitful bastard! How dare you come back here! How

179

dare you use me like some harlot!" She backed away from him. This time when she picked up Sadie Anderson's pretty flowered vase she saw only the sky-blue eyes and hard lines of Ren Daniels's handsome face, and she wanted to destroy him. Fingers trembling against the smooth surface of the glass, she hurled the vase at him with all her might. "Get out of here!"

Ren ducked and the vase crashed to the floor, shattering into a thousand tiny pieces.

"Get out!" she repeated. "If you ever come back here, I'll shoot you!" She searched the room for something else to throw, but in two long strides he caught her wrists and hauled her against him.

"Listen to me, Elaina. I didn't come here to take advantage of you. I came to help, but when I saw you again I . . ." He glanced away. "In the beginning, I agreed to marry Melissa Stanhope because I wanted the power and position the Stanhope alliance would bring. I wanted respectability, acceptance into society. Since then, I've achieved my own success, and I've discovered the rest is unimportant." With the tip of his finger, he lifted an angry tear from beneath her lashes. "I just didn't realize *how* unimportant until I met you."

Tawny eyes met his, obviously not convinced. "Then why are you going through with the marriage?"

"I have an obligation to Jacob, a commitment. You more than anyone ought to know why I have to keep my word." He looked at her hard, his own ire building again. Why couldn't she understand? She'd said those same things about her engagement to Chuck Dawson, and if Dawson hadn't treated her so badly, Ren had no doubt she would have gone through with her plans.

"An obligation?" she repeated. "Does your obligation to Melissa include spending hours in another woman's bed?" Elaina jerked away. Just hearing the Stanhope woman's name on Ren's lips had set the blood pounding in her ears. She wanted to punish him, hurt him as he hurt her. Clenching her teeth, she drew back her hand and swung with all her strength. Ren caught her wrist.

"I warned you, Elaina, never to try that again." He pulled her close, fitting her body perfectly to the length of him. With his mouth set in a grim line, he looked as though he wanted to murder her.

"Damn you!" she cursed, struggling futilely to free herself. "Damn you to hell!" She could feel his anger as he held her with little effort. His eyes raked her, his gaze drawn to the curve of her bosom, rising and falling beneath her high-necked dress. Even through the thick folds of her skirt, she could feel his manhood pressing against her.

Lacing his fingers through her hair, he pulled her head back punishingly. With an anguished groan, he claimed her mouth, his kiss fierce, possessive, as if he would never let her go.

Elaina's knees went weak. She sagged against him, and only his arms wrapped tightly around her kept her from falling. She felt his hands beneath her knees; then he lifted her and in long strides carried her to the iron bed in the other room. He fumbled with the buttons on her dress, then gave up and ripped the cloth down the back.

"I'll buy you another," he mumbled in her ear.

The heat of his hands seared her flesh. Though she wanted to resist, her efforts were feeble, useless. He pulled the dress from her shoulders, baring her skin to his hands and eyes. The cotton straps of her chemise fell away; then, as if by magic, the dress lay in a heap at her feet. She felt his burning lips on her shoulders, the side of her neck, the place beneath her ear. His possession of her was complete; there was no way to deny it. He owned her, body and soul.

His embrace was exhilarating, intoxicating, filling each of her senses. When his hands stroked her breasts, her nipples hardened, begging him to continue. A sob caught in her throat as his head dipped and his mouth covered the throbbing peak. Thick strands of his wavy hair brushed against her skin and she laced her fingers in the silken mass.

Though Ren had promised himself a thousand times he wouldn't weaken again, wouldn't take her as he wanted, as they both wanted, he was a man whose reason had fled. A captive of the beautiful woman whose flesh quivered beneath him, he stroked her heated skin, tasted her honeyed lips, and wanted nothing less than to lose himself forever in the warmth of her body.

His desire more intense with every agonizing second, he laved her breasts with his tongue as he stroked her thighs, wanting the pleasure to be right for both of them. No matter how he wished things could be different, this night would be their last.

A flash of despair nearly blinded him. How cruel life's jests could be. He moved above her, his shaft hard against the triangle of her womanhood. Easing himself between her ivory thighs, he fought to blot out the pain, filled his mind with thoughts of the heated flesh beneath him — images of golden eyes, upturned breasts, the slim waist and thrusting hips meeting his own heated skin — thoughts of the woman he loved and would leave on the morrow.

He felt another flash of pain as the cold realization hit him. *Love.* He would leave his love forever in this desolate mining town. Give her up to the care of a man like Chase Cameron. He drove into her like a madman, claiming her with every thrust, wanting her to know she belonged only to him. Wishing things could be different. Wishing he could claim her forever. Holding her tightly, he unleashed the fury of his anguish, let the fierceness of their passion swirl him into its stormy depths.

Elaina could feel the heat rising, the ache in her loins building to a crescendo. Ren had never loved her like this, never filled her with such reckless abandon, such driving need. It sent her senses spinning. She felt possessed, controlled, desired, and loved all at the same time. Her body burned and ached and pounded and thrust. On fire, she tensed, consumed by the flames. As she burst upon the glittering embers of their passion, she cried out his name, and he whispered hers as he followed her to release.

Mindless swirling pleasure gave way to calm. She let him pull her against him, curl her protectively in the circle of his arms. There were no words of comfort. There was nothing left to say. She prayed he wouldn't leave; she couldn't face the empty night without him. Tomorrow would be soon enough. Tomorrow, with the sunlight at her back, she could say good-bye.

She entwined her fingers in his thick black hair and pulled his head down to receive her kiss. She would steal his heart this night, leave him nothing of himself to share with his bride. Tonight he was hers and hers alone. Tonight she would live and love and pray that the morning would never come. She wondered what price her own heart would pay, wondered who the real victor would be and, as she felt his gentle touch, felt his lips caressing hers, knew it would not be she.

"It's time, pretty lady."

The words, gently spoken, wrenched her heart.

"So soon?" Her voice sounded hollow, empty, just like her soul.

"The longer I stay, the harder this will be on both of us."

She nodded. "I know." She kept her back to him as they stood in the parlor. They had freshened up. She wore a simple lavender batiste dress with a scoop neckline, and her hair hung loose almost to her waist. She could hear his muffled footsteps on the calico hooked rug as he approached, but she hadn't the strength to face him.

"I'll never be able to see lavender without thinking of you," he told her, his voice husky. She felt his long, firm fingers on her shoulders; then he was lifting her hair and kissing the back of her neck.

"Please," she pleaded, her careful control ready to crack.

"Let me lend you some money. You can pay me back whenever —"

"No, Ren, you know that's not what I want."

"Last night . . . your dress. At least let me —"

"The dress can be mended. Please, Ren, don't say any more."

"How can I leave you here, Lainey? Do you know what it does to me to think of you here alone?"

"I'm not alone," she whispered. "I have friends here."

His fingers bit into her shoulders. "Friends like Chase Cameron?"

She stiffened and pulled away, turning to face him at last. She needed her anger now, needed it to keep her sane. "Yes, friends like Chase. He's been good to me — and he never treated me like a whore."

The words stung like a slap. He reached for the black hat hanging on a peg beside the door, ran a hand through his wavy hair, then pulled the hat low across his forehead. Maybe it was better to leave her this way, with her tawny eyes flashing in anger, her shoulders proud. If she looked at him just once with love in her eyes and asked him to stay, he would. He would stay no matter how he hated himself for it later. No matter how much he'd regret breaking his faith with Jacob.

"Good-bye, Elaina." As he opened the door, he allowed himself the luxury of one last glance. Elaina stood in the middle of the room almost regally, her head held high. A few thick, dark curls cascaded over her shoulder. Her tawny eyes were dry; no sadness showed in their golden depths. Her bosom heaved slightly as if her effort to maintain her control was strained to the limits of her endurance. He felt his own control slipping badly. His hand shook as he pulled open the heavy door. He could feel the brisk morning air, the sunlight against his tanned skin, but they couldn't ease the tightness in his chest or the lump that swelled in his throat.

Then he heard her footsteps, caught the single soft sob in her throat. He turned in time to catch her against him, to wrap his arms around her and feel her arms go around his neck. When she pressed her face against his, he felt the wetness of her tears on his cheek, mingled with his own. He kissed her fiercely, passionately, a last kiss that was all of himself he had to give. Then, as if by agreement, they pulled away. She turned, shoulders straight, and walked to her bedroom.

And he closed the door behind him.

# Chapter 18

Chuck Dawson pushed open the door to Blue Mountain Mining Company headquarters.

"Well, we've found her." He smiled at Dolph Redmond who sat behind his mahogany desk, smoking a thin cigar.

"Where is she?" Redmond leaned forward. "Time's running a little too short to suit me."

"We think she's in San Francisco."

"*Think?*" he shouted. "By this time, you damn well better know!"

"We're doing the best we can, Dolph. The woman just disappeared."

"What about Morgan? Couldn't you get a line on him?"

"Well, that's just it. When we hired Morgan, we wrote to him at a post office box in San Francisco. Ada Lowery has a sister there named Isabelle Chesterfield, and the stationmaster here in Keyserville says he's pretty sure that was the destination on Elaina's ticket. Damned fool couldn't remember the first time we asked him."

"Have you talked to Ada again?" Dolph asked.

"Yeah, I've talked to her till I'm blue in the face. The old lady refuses to confirm or deny anything. Says she didn't know a thing about Elaina's plans. I've threatened to fire her — and worse, but she still won't talk."

"Well, be careful. Ada Lowery does a damn good job over there. We'd be hard pressed to find anybody more capable. The woman makes us money. We'll find the McAllister girl with or without Ada's help."

Chuck smiled. "I'm leaving for San Francisco in the morning. I'll find the Chesterfield woman, or Morgan. One of them will lead us to the girl."

185

"They'd better, or money or no money, we'll have to make the old lady talk."

Chuck nodded. "I'll wire you as soon as I reach the coast. I'm takin' Andy Johnson and Bill Sharp with me. We'll find Elaina and bring her back."

"I have every confidence in you, Chuck." Dolph sat back in his tufted leather chair and propped his fine-grained boots on the desk.

"I'll keep you posted." Chuck closed the door softly behind him. He clenched his fists as he strode toward his horse. San Francisco. He should have known the little bitch would head straight for her lover. Well, she and Morgan made an error when they underestimated Chuck Dawson. Elaina McAllister had promised to be his wife, and one way or another, she'd keep her word. The final paperwork on the sale of the mine was to take place July 10. By then Chuck planned to be a happily married man — and the proud owner of half the Blue Mountain Mine.

"Well, my boy, did you get your friend's problem resolved to your satisfaction?" Jacob Stanhope sat in the parlor of Ren's town house overlooking the blue waters of the San Francisco Bay.

Ren had been back for over a week, but had avoided any contact with Jacob. Even now he had trouble meeting the older man's eyes. "I'm afraid there was little I could do to help after all."

"I'm sorry to hear that. Is there anything I can do?"

Ren smiled. "You're always there for me, aren't you, Jacob? You know, I haven't forgotten the way you helped me get started."

"You had your own money, son. I just helped you make it grow." He scratched the graying hair at his temple.

"You did a lot more than that. I'd probably have lost most of it if I hadn't met you. I had no idea how to invest. I'd have been an easy mark for just about anybody."

Jacob Stanhope laughed heartily, his deep voice resonating across the room. "You, my boy, were never an easy mark. You'd have educated yourself about investing just as you did everything else. You once told me you had very little formal education till you were well into your teens. After you left the East, you spent every spare minute learning, schooling your brother as well as yourself. That's what I admire about you, son. Your determination to make something of yourself, better yourself. You've got character, Ren. You're a man of action and forcefulness. Qualities I see dying off in my family.

"Melissa is the sweetest child alive," he continued, "but she's got no stamina. I need grandsons who'll take over for me. Strong men. The kind of men your young loins could produce."

Ren grinned broadly at Jacob's uncharacteristically long speech. "Somehow I don't think Melissa would appreciate our discussing her as if she were a brood mare."

Jacob frowned. "No, I don't suppose she would. That's the one thing that worries me about this marriage."

Ren uncrossed his legs and looked at Jacob, his hopes beginning to rise. "What's that, Jacob?"

"You two are so different. I just pray you'll be able to make each other happy. I'd hate to think the two of you were just going through with this for my sake."

Ren's chest tightened. Now was his chance, the moment he'd been waiting for. He could tell Jacob what was in his heart: that the woman he loved was not a sweet, fair-skinned child but a woman with rich dark hair and passions that matched his own.

"But I suppose that's a foolish thought," Jacob was saying. "A man takes a woman to wife because he needs the alliances she creates. You and Melissa. Your drive and ambition, my power and name. The two of us will be unstoppable."

Ren stood up and moved to the sideboard to pour himself a drink and give himself time to find the right words. "Brandy?"

"Maybe I'd better," Jacob said. "I've got something else to tell you."

Ren poured a small amount of golden Napoleon brandy into each of two small crystal snifters, giving his friend a chance to speak, but eager to resolve the matter of his marriage. He'd been planning since his arrival to find a way to dissolve his engagement. He handed a snifter to Jacob, who inhaled the rich aroma as he warmed the glass between his palms.

"Sit down, son."

Ren sat back down in the dark green overstuffed chair.

"There's no easy way to say this, Ren, so I'll just come out with it. I'm afraid my heart's in worse condition than I thought."

Ren leaned forward. "What do you mean? Just how bad is it, Jacob?"

"The doctor says if I'm careful, don't exert myself too much, don't drink too much of this stuff" — he lifted his glass — "I may live a couple more years."

"Surely it can't be that bad. You look so healthy."

"I'm afraid it is." He pulled from his coat pocket a small glass bottle filled with tiny pills. "Glycerin tablets. I carry them with me at all times, just in case. . . ."

Ren tried unsuccessfully to hide the stricken look on his face.

"Don't feel so bad, son," Jacob was saying. "I've lived my life to the fullest. I have no regrets."

Ren had trouble finding his voice. He swallowed the lump in his throat. "Doctors can be wrong, Jacob. We'll get a second opinion. We'll —"

"Don't talk nonsense, boy. We both know the doctor's right. My heart condition has been getting worse for years. That's one reason this marriage is so important to me. I want my little girl looked after; I want her safe and secure. I know you'll take care of her."

Ren turned away. He closed his eyes and gripped the brandy glass so hard he feared it might shatter. Then he opened his eyes and downed half the fiery liquid in a single gulp.

"You know I'll do my best for her," he promised, pushing thoughts of his own happiness aside.

"I know you will, son. Now we'll speak no more unpleasantries. I've got to be going. Melissa and I will expect you for dinner on my birthday. I've got some out-of-town business. Won't be back much before then. Be sure to remind Tommy and Carrie that they're invited."

"I will." Ren struggled to keep his voice even.

"It should be an interesting evening," Jacob said. "I've invited some friends from the old days. I get damned sick and tired of San Francisco society. Thank God I have enough money so that I can tell them to go hang once in a while."

Ren felt the tug of a smile and realized again why he thought so highly of Jacob Stanhope. "Sounds like my kind of evening."

"Let's hope Melissa finds it as amusing as we do." He winked and slapped Ren on the back. They started toward the door.

"Don't bother, my boy, I know the way. I look forward to seeing you at the party."

Jacob let himself out, and Ren tossed down the rest of his brandy, stilling the slight tremor in his hand. After refilling the crystal snifter, he carried it over to the settee and tried unsuccessfully to force thoughts of Jacob's illness — and images of Elaina McAllister — from his mind. He'd come so close. So very close. But with Jacob's illness to consider, there was no way out now. He wondered where Elaina was. What was she doing. Was she trying to forget him in Chase Cameron's more than eager arms? Even after Ren's marriage, he knew he wouldn't be able to stop thinking about her.

Work. Good, honest, hard work was what he needed. He would spend some time out at the ranch. With grim determination, he downed the second brandy and headed for the stairs.

Elaina endured the endless nights of singing, the crowds of drunken miners with their crude, lusty gibes, the days that seemed more endless than the nights. It was the loneliest, most miserable time of her life. With Ren gone, she tried to bury herself in her job, tried to keep some of her goals in mind, even allowed Chase Cameron to play a larger and larger role in her life.

Nothing worked. All she thought about was Ren. Where was he? What was he doing? Did he ever think of her? No matter how hard she fought it, he was always there.

Curled up on the settee, she opened an issue of *Harper's Bazaar* that Delsey had given her. Delsey had finally agreed to marry Willie Jenkins, and Elaina was thrilled. She felt, if nothing else, she'd accomplished something while she'd been in Central City. At least she'd been able to help two people she cared about find happiness. She wished she could find a little of her own.

She thumbed through the magazine, glad for the distraction. She had two hours before she would be forced to make her way backstage to begin her nightly routine. She wondered why the miners never tired of her singing. She knew she wasn't that good. But they applauded louder and filled the room a little fuller at each performance. Chase was pleased to no end. He'd been gone for over a week, inspecting other saloons he owned in other towns. But he was due back today or tomorrow. Elaina found herself looking forward to his return, if only for a break in the monotony.

A gentle tap at the door drew her attention. With a weary sigh, she opened it, though now it was secured by a thick chain that allowed her to see her caller before she let him in.

"Richard!" She recognized Richard Marley in an instant even though he now stood before her clean-shaven, wearing a well-pressed brown-striped suit and holding a small bouquet of ox-eye daisies. She unhooked the chain. "Won't you come in?"

"Thank you," he replied a little shyly, handing her the flowers.

"You look more like your old self, Richard. Are things going better for you?" His hair was freshly washed, cut short, and neatly combed, and he wore shiny new brown shoes.

"*Us,* Miss McAllister. Things are going better for *us.*"

Elaina smiled indulgently. "Please, Richard, call me Elaina."

"I'd be proud to call one of the wealthiest women in the state of Colorado by her first name." He grinned at the confusion on her face.

"Richard, what are you talking about? Are you feeling all right?"

"I assure you, Miss . . . Elaina, I've never felt better in my life. Hold out your hand."

She did as she was told, still bewildered by Richard Marley's strange behavior. He pulled a brown leather pouch from his inside coat pocket and poured a heap of bright yellow gold dust into her palm. Her hand trembled slightly. "Richard?"

"Yes, ma'am, we struck it rich!"

"You found gold?" she asked, still incredulous.

"Lots of gold. More gold than you and I will ever need."

"But how? When? Where?"

"The Golden Duchess Mine. That's what I named her — golden for all the gold she'll produce and duchess for you. That's what you seemed like to me when you handed me that money. She's the same mine I told you about, the one I've been workin' all along — partner." He seemed to be enjoying her confusion.

"Partner? But I couldn't take . . . I mean, I wasn't the one who did all the work." She ran her fingers through the gold in her palm. It felt heavy and cold, yet her palm fairly burned with the heat of her excitement.

190

"If it hadn't been for you, Elaina, there wouldn't have been any strike. I couldn't have lasted two more days. My boys were hungry, my mules broken down. Elaina, this strike is half yours, and I mean to see that you take it."

"Oh, Richard!" She threw her arms around his neck, taking care not to let go of the gold in her hand, and hugged him tightly. Tears of happiness gathered in her eyes. "What do we do now?"

"Well, we've got several alternatives."

As he talked, she poured the gold back into the pouch and led him to the settee.

"We can either sell the mine outright," he said, "and take our money and run, or you can sell just your share, or we can continue to work the mine ourselves."

"It's up to you, Richard. I'm just a partner — a silent partner."

He grinned, liking her confidence in him. "We'll make the most if we operate the mine ourselves. I've already mined enough gold to keep us in high style for the next year or so, and I've only been at it a few weeks."

He caught her smile, then noticed the tiny crinkle of a frown. "What's that frown for?"

"Nothing," she lied, forcing a smile.

"We're partners, Elaina. Partners tell each other the truth."

She felt a little guilty. "Well, it's just that . . . I was hoping to leave Central City, go on to San Francisco, as I'd planned." Though God knows I may suffer for it, she added to herself.

"Is that all?" He sounded relieved. "I never expected you to stay and work the mine. We'll settle on a fair compensation for the boys and me, since we'll be taking on the majority of the responsibilities, but that'll still leave more than enough for you to go anywhere in the world you want. The gold in that sack belongs to you."

He looked down at her sternly, a fatherly expression on his face. "I've seen you singing over at the saloon. There's enough gold in that one pouch so you don't ever need to go back. And, I might add, your daddy'd skin me alive if I let you go back in there when you didn't have to."

Elaina felt giddy with happiness. "I'm through with saloons forever!"

"What kind of talk is that, coming from the star of our show?"

Chase Cameron removed his fawn-colored hat as he stuck his blond head through the door.

"Chase!" Elaina leapt to her feet and rushed to him as he stepped through the doorway. She hugged him excitedly. "Chase, the most wonderful thing has happened. Richard and I struck it rich!"

Chase cocked a brow, his gaze unreadable. He glanced at Marley. "That true, Marley?"

"Darned right, it's true. This little lady's one of the richest women in the state."

Chase smiled lazily. "Well, I guess this calls for a celebration. I'll buy you both the best steak dinner in Central City. Then tomorrow I'll accompany Miss McAllister to San Francisco. That is where you were headed, isn't it, Elaina?"

Elaina wasn't certain, but she thought she caught a hint of sarcasm in his voice. "Yes, Chase, it is. I wasn't planning on leaving quite so soon, but if you're willing to escort me, then I'm certainly going to take advantage of your generosity."

"I have some business on the Coast. But it would be my pleasure to escort you, even if I didn't. Now, about that dinner. I'll stop by the Washoe Club and reserve a table. Would half an hour be too soon?"

"Fine," Richard Marley said.

"Perfect," Elaina agreed, her enthusiasm bubbling to the surface again. She'd wear the daringly low-cut gown Chase had given her that first night in Cheyenne. Richard might think it a bit unseemly, but she had little else that was suitable. Besides, she was a woman of wealth now. She could do exactly as she pleased.

"I'll see you tonight, Duchess," Richard Marley teased.

Chase eyed the little man oddly, but said nothing.

"I can hardly wait!" Elaina told them. After closing the door behind the two men, she dashed to her tiny bedroom. A narrow oak chest held what few dresses she'd been able to purchase since her arrival. When she reached San Francisco she would order dresses by the score.

If the mine was as rich in gold as Richard Marley said, she'd be accepted into San Francisco society without so much as a qualm. She'd attend parties, socials, do all the things every girl dreamed of. For the first time, she purposely thought of Ren. Though she loved him with all her heart, he hadn't loved her enough to marry her. No, he was too concerned with his ambitions, his social position — and Melissa Stanhope's fortune. Well, now she had her own fortune. She couldn't wait to see the look on Ren's face when he found out.

# Chapter 19

San Francisco was all Elaina expected. Soft ocean breezes, grand vistas, blue water, and skies that were bluer still.

They'd arrived five days ago amid a hoopla of newspaper head-lines and speeches of welcome. A brass band had played at the train station to honor San Francisco's newest celebrity. To Elaina, it was like something out of a dream.

As Chase's insistence, she had taken an elegant suite of rooms at the Palace Hotel. He'd been, as usual, solicitous, helping her get settled and escorting her through myriad stores to order the latest in fashions and accessories. It was obvious Chase knew his way around the finer ladies' apparel shops.

Elaina spent money shamelessly, immersing herself in her new-found wealth, enjoying all the luxuries she'd never experienced, and trying desperately to keep her mind off Ren Daniels.

It was a losing battle.

From the moment the train pulled into the station, she'd thought of little else. Even while she clung to Chase's arm as he showed her the sights, she thought of Ren and wondered if she'd made the right decision in coming to San Francisco.

Tonight Chase was escorting her to her first real ball. She'd received countless invitations since she arrived, her reputation as a woman of wealth and the story of the fabulous Golden Duchess Mine having preceded her to town.

Through a light drizzle, Chase's carriage rolled up before an impressive two-story brick building, and the driver jumped from his perch to open the door. Chase climbed out ahead of her, circled her waist with his hands, and lifted her down. They entered the foyer of the Lick House, a prestigious establishment famous for its fabu-lous parties, and stood beneath gilded sconces that bathed the guests in candlelight. Every San Franciscan cherished an invitation to a Lick House ball.

Chase squeezed her hand reassuringly and excused himself for a moment to check their cloaks.

Elaina fidgeted nervously, watching several couples eye her with speculation. She wondered what secrets they whispered behind their hands.

"Hello, Duchess." The deep, familiar voice, speaking softly from a few feet away, spun her around.

A hand went to her throat at the mere sight of him. In a single sweeping glance, she took in his dark skin, his broad shoulders and narrow hips, the familiar lines and angles of his face, and her heart began to pound. She had never seen him dressed in such finery, and the dashing picture he presented set her blood on fire.

"Ren," she said a little breathlessly. "I — I didn't expect you to be here."

"Why not? Did you consider Dan Morgan too merciless a fellow for such frivolous pastimes?"

She smiled a bit nervously. "Something like that, I guess."

"I came to see you." His light eyes caressed her, spoke volumes without words.

When he stepped toward her, it was all she could do not to rush into his arms.

"You're looking lovely," he said, his voice a little husky, "but then, you always do." He lifted her hand in his long brown fingers and brushed it gently against his lips. "Your new status suits you perfectly. You look as though you were born to royalty."

She felt the warmth of his lips, and a tiny tremor shook her hand. "Thank you," she whispered softly, barely able to make her voice work.

"Where's . . . your escort?"

"Chase? He went to check our wraps. And your fiancée? Or is it 'wife'?"

"My fiancée isn't feeling well. I was forced to attend without her. I heard you'd be here. I thought it might give us a chance to talk."

Elaina allowed herself a moment to assess him, giving her heart a chance to slow. She felt a tiny rivulet of perspiration trickle

195

between her breasts. Ren was dressed elegantly in a black cutaway coat and breeches. Only the toes of his fine-grained black leather shoes, polished to a mirror sheen, flashed beneath the bottoms of his beautifully tailored trousers. She had never seen him in formal attire and wouldn't have expected him to look quite so at ease in the clothes. But then, how could it have been otherwise? A man like Jacob Stanhope would wish only the best for his daughter.

"What is there to talk about? I'm here to start a new life — just as you once suggested. You already have a life here, and it doesn't include me."

"Well," Chase Cameron drawled, "I see you've discovered the duchess." Strolling up beside her, he captured her hand possessively. "It seems all of San Francisco's at her feet. You'll have to stand in line, Daniels."

Ren stiffened. "Where do you stand, Chase? I've never known you to wait long for a lady."

"I assure you, our mutual friend is worth it — but then, you know that already."

"Chase, please," Elaina broke in.

"That's quite all right, Miss McAllister," Ren said formally. "I'm used to your friend's lack of charm. I hope you two enjoy yourselves; I know I'm going to." Excusing himself with a curt nod, he turned and walked away.

Barely able to still her trembling hands, Elaina watched until his broad-shouldered frame disappeared through the doorway into the ballroom. She hadn't expected to see him. He'd been right in his assessment: She did have trouble imagining the handsome gunman she'd known as Dan Morgan attending a formal ball. She wished she'd been better prepared and vowed not to let it happen again.

"Shall we go, Duchess?" Chase extended a black-coated arm. He looked exceedingly handsome this evening with his blond hair curling above his stiff white collar and his hazel eyes dancing with mischief.

"Must you persist in calling me that, Chase? It makes me feel ridiculous."

"Why not? Everyone in the city is calling you that, though not always to your face." Chase glanced at the beautiful woman on his arm. In a gown of beaded gold satin, with her thick coffee-brown hair piled in charming ringlets atop her head, she was easily the most beautiful woman in the room. The gown dipped low, baring her creamy shoulders and slender, arching neck. She looked elegant, regal. And indeed she was.

The story of the fabulous Golden Duchess had spread like wildfire throughout the city. Even before Elaina arrived, she was being touted as "the duchess." So far, none of the newspapers had mentioned her singing career as Lainey Starr or made any reference to the Black Garter Saloon, but Chase was sure sooner or later they would. He didn't really think it would matter. Her wealth ensured her position in society, and her aura of mystery would only be enhanced by rumors of her slightly shady past.

Amid appraising looks and speculative glances, Chase ushered her into the ballroom. A ten-piece orchestra, dressed formally in black, was seated at one end of the room. The dance floor, of black and white marble tiles, was already crowded with couples whirling to the strains of a waltz.

Without hesitation, Chase led her onto the floor. Elaina could feel his hand at her waist and appreciated his quiet assurance as they dipped and swayed to the music. Though she tried to immerse herself in the rhythm, her gaze kept straying to Ren. With an air of nonchalance she found infuriating, he leaned against the wall, a buxom redhead clinging to his arm. The heated way the woman's startling green eyes looked up at him made Elaina's own eyes green with jealousy. Just how many women did he have? Was the city full of women he'd bedded? This one certainly eyed him as if she knew him well — intimately, in fact.

"Do I detect the green-eyed monster?" Chase teased, and she forced her gaze to his face.

"Why, whatever do you mean, Chase?" she replied, her voice dripping with false sincerity.

He grinned broadly. "Just so you won't be at a disadvantage, the lady you keep eyein' with such daggers is Ren's mistress, Carolina Williams. At least she was. I'm not quite certain of the lady's current status."

"Mistress! He has a fiancée *and* a mistress?" The whole thing seemed incredible. How could he? And how could she have been foolish enough to believe he felt anything more than lust for her —

and perhaps a sense of obligation. Suddenly she wanted to cry.

"Dozens of admirers are waiting to dance with you," Chase said. "Are you ready to face them?"

She tossed her head and squared her shoulders. "I'm the duchess, am I not? Of course I'm ready."

Chase whirled her toward the edge of the dance floor and lightly kissed her cheek. "That's my girl."

His girl. Dear God how she wished she were! Exceedingly thoughtful and considerate, Chase was always there when she needed a friend. She wondered why he put up with her when he knew how she felt about Ren, knew what had transpired between them. Feeling a slight blush creep up her cheeks, she looked up just in time to find Ren's light blue eyes looking back at her.

"May I have the pleasure of this dance?"

"I'm afraid I need a breath of —"

Before she could finish, he clutched her waist, gripped her wrist, and whirled her onto the floor. "Damn you, Lainey. I just want to talk to you."

"Mr. Daniels," she said, feeling her anger flare. "There is nothing left to say between us. You have more than your share of ladies. Must you keep half the women in the city in your bed in order to satisfy your brutish appetites?" She missed a step in her fury, and on pretense of steadying her, he pulled her closer — too close to be proper, especially for a man who would soon be marrying.

"Just exactly what is that supposed to mean?" he said.

"I'm sure you wouldn't know. Now please return me to my escort."

"I'll return you when I'm damn good and ready. You ought to know that by now, Elaina."

She clenched her teeth. "You, sir, are *not* a gentleman."

That brought the flash of a grin. "I never told you I was."

"You are the most infuriating —"

"And you, my dear duchess, are beautiful, even when you're angry."

The heat of his hand warmed her waist while his gaze drifted to the swell of her breast above the low neckline of her gown. In spite of herself, she began to warm to his charm.

"I suppose you *did* warn me about not being a gentleman," she finally admitted, doing her best to look angelic. "But there were times I could have sworn one lurked in there somewhere."

This time he laughed aloud, the rich timbre of his voice sending a tremor across her flesh. He sidestepped deftly, missing a gangly youth dancing with a matronly gray-haired woman, and both dancers turned to look at them.

"How does it feel to be the queen of the ball?"

"Not the queen," she replied, "merely a duchess."

Another quick smile. "Yes, a duchess. The Duchess of Carbon County. I wonder what the folks in Keyserville will say about you now?"

"God only knows. But at least I'll be able to repay my debts."

"Yes. You'll be able to set the McAllister name right. Isn't that what you've always wanted?"

His eyes raked her again, and she felt the heat of the room growing to immense proportions. "It's what my mother always wanted. Somehow it doesn't seem all that important to me anymore."

He whirled her unerringly, the feeling heady as the music of the waltz filled the magnificent ballroom. She wished they could dance forever. Biting her lip as her gaze fixed on the fullness of his mouth, she wished she could taste those lips, feel their masculine firmness just one more time. Then she glanced toward the buxom redhead who stood pouting at the far end of the room. She watched Ren possessively, and Elaina felt a surge of temper.

"I believe, Mr. Daniels," she said stiffly as the dance came to a close, "I'm beginning to tire. Again I ask you to return me to my escort."

Ren set his jaw. What in the hell was wrong with her? When he'd parted from her in Central City, she'd been sobbing against him, holding him as if she would never let him go. What had happened in the few short weeks since then? When he waltzed her from the floor, Chase Cameron was waiting. This time, the look in Elaina's eyes as she smiled seductively at Chase said they were more than just good friends.

"I'm sorry for keeping you two lovebirds apart," he told Chase sarcastically. "I can see that every moment you're separated is an eternity. With a mocking bow, he handed Elaina to Chase and backed away.

"Damn him! Damn him to hell!"

"Your subjects are watching, your ladyship," Chase said with his usual amused smile, but his message was clear. With all the gossip about her, she had captured the attention of the entire room. She needn't stir up anything more for the city's wagging tongues.

Elaina fought to control her temper. She accepted the hand of a young auburn-haired man who looked to be no older than she and let him lead her, with an awkward rhythm all his own, around the dance floor. Next came an older, graying gentleman whom Chase introduced as Asbury Harpending, a man with a powerful presence and a wide, flashing smile. He was a good dancer as well as an interesting conversationalist. They discussed the banking business, and Mr. Harpending recommended a man he believed could help with her financial decisions. He returned her to Chase a little less bedraggled than before.

"Mr. Harpending," Chase told her as the man danced with a pudgy woman with faded brown hair, "once raised millions of dollars to invest in a diamond field in the Wyoming Territory. 'Diamonds on the ground for the taking,' Harpending said. And they were there all right. Unfortunately for Mr. Harpending, they came from the diamond mines in South Africa, not Wyoming. Made a laughingstock of the poor man. He left for London shortly after it became known the field was salted. This is the first time he's been back in San Francisco in years."

Elaina smiled, grateful for Chase's story and the relief from the tension. She was just beginning to enjoy herself when Carolina Williams approached.

"Well, Miss Williams," Chase said in that lilting southern way of his. "How beautiful you're lookin' this evenin'." Dressed in a blue-green silk chiffon gown that heightened the color of her eyes and dipped daringly low, Carolina accepted the compliment as if it were her due, and Chase made the introductions.

Elaina smiled a little too brightly. "Pleased to meet you, I'm sure."

"So you're the famous duchess. I was hoping I'd get to meet you. It seems we have a mutual friend."

Her sugary voice didn't fool Elaina for a moment. The woman's claws were showing, and Elaina knew exactly why. She felt like doing a little scratching herself.

"Oh, really? And who might that be?"

"Why, Ren, of course. Chase, be a darling and excuse us for a moment, won't you?"

Chase smiled, his hazel eyes laughing.

"Why, certainly." He bowed. "Ladies." Backing away, he left the two women alone. Several young men hovered nearby, and Elaina was certain she and Carolina would soon be swooped upon like helpless prey.

"Just what is it you'd like to talk about?" Elaina asked, smiling sweetly.

"I'd just like to inform you that Mr. Daniels is already spoken for."

"Yes. I'd heard of his engagement. Mr. Daniels is a very lucky man." Two could play the game just as surely as one. Elaina could see the woman's flawless skin flush with anger above the low-cut neckline of her gown.

"That's not what I meant. Everyone knows that's only a *mariage de convenance*. I was speaking more from the heart. You see Ren and I . . . well, let's just say we care about each other a great deal. It wouldn't be wise of you to try to interfere in our friendship."

"Far be it from me, Miss Williams, to interfere in anything Mr. Daniels does. The idea is quite absurd. Now if you'll excuse me, I believe Chase has brought me some refreshment." Elaina brushed past the woman with scarcely a backward glance, wanting to murder Ren Daniels and already regretting her decision to come to San Francisco.

She accepted a glass of punch from Chase, took a deep cooling sip, then turned to face him, her nerves a little steadier. "Chase, I hope it won't spoil your evening, but I'd really like to go home."

"I'd rather have you all to myself anyway," Chase soothed. "I'll get our cloaks."

They made their way through the crowd of elegantly dressed ladies and gentlemen and out onto the street. The fog had rolled in, blotting out the stars, and the drizzle made the air heavy and cold. Chase signaled for a hansom cab, and Elaina pulled her *paletot* closer around her.

"*Help!*" A high-pitched woman's scream shattered the quiet night.

"Somebody get a doctor!" a deep male voice chimed in.

"Stay here!" Chase ordered. "I'll find out what's going on." He turned and rushed in the direction of the disturbance. Ignoring his command, Elaina followed close at his heels. They rounded the corner to see what appeared to be a youth, one of the carriage drivers, sprawled on the grass beside the horses, clutching a bloody wound in his side.

"Someone tried to steal my pocketbook," a heavyset gentleman explained. "The boy chased the man down and got a knife in his belly for his trouble." He glanced at Elaina, who was kneeling beside the boy. "Begging your pardon, miss."

Chase knelt to check the boy's pulse. "Go get a doctor," he told the well-dressed man. "Maybe there's one inside Lick House. I'll stay with him till you get back." The woman who had screamed was sitting on the ground some distance away, the sight of so much blood apparently having made her ill.

Elaina whipped off her cloak and Chase did the same. He laid his on the wet grass, settled the boy over it, then covered him with her *paletot,* tucking it around him for warmth. Elaina began tearing strips of cloth from the lace petticoat she wore beneath her satin skirt.

"Does anybody know who he is?" she asked.

Several other drivers had gathered around and were listening sympathetically as the boy moaned. Tears gathered beneath the youth's dark lashes.

"He's Jimmy Lundstrom, Mr. Daniels's driver," a young man said.

"Go get Daniels, son," Chase instructed, and the boy raced toward the front of the hotel. "And somebody get blankets — and a tarpaulin, if you can find one."

"He's losing a lot of blood, Chase. We've got to stop the bleeding." Elaina finished making a thick pad of bandages from her torn petticoats and, lifting her *paletot* and the boy's bloody shirt, stuffed the cloth against the wound. "Keep pressing against it as hard as you can."

Chase complied, watching her with an admiring light in his eyes.

One of the drivers ran up with a woolen blanket and a small canvas cover. At least they could keep the boy warm and dry.

"Am I going to die, miss?" The youth swallowed hard and wet his dry lips.

She was glad he was still conscious, though he'd have suffered less pain if he'd blacked out. "We're not going to let you die. Who'd drive Mr. Daniels's carriage for him? He probably can't get along without you." Jimmy Lundstrom clutched her hand. Ignoring the soggy ground and the blood that soaked her beautiful golden gown, she sat down on the grass beside him and cradled his head in her lap, brushing several blond strands from his pale face.

"That's right, Jimmy," Ren's deep voice confirmed. "Everything's going to be fine. I can tell you from experience that Miss McAllister's just about the best doctor you could have."

Jimmy tried to smile, then trembled slightly as he felt another wave of pain. "She's . . . sure the . . . prettiest," he whispered between breaths.

Elaina gave him an encouraging smile. When she looked up at Ren, his light eyes shone with gratitude and something that might have been pride. She was basking in the warmth of his look when Carolina Williams walked up behind him and, seeing the blood, clutched Ren's arm.

"Oh, my God! Please, Ren, take me inside. I think I'm going to faint."

"Charlie!" Ren called to another of the carriage boys. "Take Miss Williams back inside."

"But, Ren," she pleaded, "he's only your driver. Surely someone else can handle this?"

"Go with Charlie, Carolina." Ren's blue eyes had darkened. "Now!"

Elaina watched the exchange and felt smugly satisfied to know the woman was exactly what she appeared to be — a self-centered, heartless bit of baggage. She wondered what Ren could possibly see in the woman, and the thought brought a stab of pain.

Ignoring the haughty swirls of Carolina's skirts as she walked away, Ren knelt beside the boy. "Don't worry, Jimmy. You're gonna be just fine." He glanced at Elaina. Thick dark strands of her hair had fallen loose from the pins, the heavy drizzle leaving everything wet and soggy. Though her gown was soaked with blood, she seemed not to notice. Her attention rested on the boy as if she might absorb some of his pain. He wished he could hold her, tell her how he admired her, tell her how much he cared.

"How is he?" Ren asked her instead.

"I'm not sure. He's lost a lot of blood." She glanced at him only briefly. "Isn't there a doctor inside? Surely there's someone?"

"I'm afraid not. We aren't blessed with many physicians, and those we do have often work long hours. I've sent someone to fetch Dr. Jameson. He's the closest. Until then we'll just have to make do."

"I'd better check Jimmy's wound," she said. "Let's see if the bleeding has slowed any."

Chase lifted the canvas and raised his hand away from the bandage. The white petticoat material was now dark red, soaked clear through with blood. Elaina eased herself from beneath the boy's head, lifted her skirt and began to tear more long strips of cloth. By now the group of observers had increased to quite a number, but Elaina was too engrossed in the boy's injury to notice. Ren felt the pull of a smile as he watched her display a goodly portion of shapely leg to the men surrounding the boy. He heard a gasp from one of the ladies, and several men cleared their throats. He noticed none of them turned away.

He'd come here tonight to find her. To try to get something settled between them. He wasn't sure exactly what, but he knew they would meet sooner or later and he wanted the encounter to be as painless as possible for both of them. Watching her now, he realized it would never be painless. Because it would never be possible for him to be near her and not want her. Never be possible not to love her.

Elaina applied the fresh bandage herself. She wanted to feel the wound, she told him, check its proximity to the vital organs in that part of the boy's body.

The drizzle increased, driving the onlookers back inside. Even the other drivers sought the protective cover of their carriages. Elaina's gown was no longer golden, but merely a soggy tan. Her wet hair clung to her neck and shoulders.

"Unless the knife went in at an odd angle, I don't think it hit

204

anything vital. Dear God, where is that doctor?"

"Maybe we should try to get him to the hospital," Chase suggested.

"I don't think so, Chase," Elaina replied. "We've got the bleeding pretty well under control. If we move him, it's sure to start again. Let's wait till the doctor comes. Then, when he's properly bandaged, we can get him down the hill in relative safety."

Ren watched Elaina closely. Covered with blood, wet to the skin, she'd never looked more beautiful. She was all woman, and he had never wanted her more. He watched her with Chase and wondered about their relationship. Now that his temper had cooled, he refused to believe Chase had bedded her. Chase was far too solicitous. Besides, Ren didn't want to believe Elaina could forget him so quickly.

The doctor finally arrived. He examined Jimmy carefully, bandaged his wound, and loaded him aboard Ren's carriage. Ren thanked Elaina for all she'd done, though he knew his words weren't nearly enough. He admired her concern for another human being and wished he could show her just how grateful he was.

He wondered how he'd be able to stay away from her now that she lived in the city, then chided himself for his selfish thoughts. By the time he'd reached his town house, well past midnight, after leaving the boy and the doctor at the hospital, he had convinced himself Elaina would never have the bad taste to involve herself in his world, so he, most certainly, could never involve himself in hers.

By morning, after he'd endured a long, cold night alone, he wasn't so sure.

# Chapter 20

"Still think your rooms above Hoffman's General Mercantile are equal to these?" Chase Cameron teased.

"I have to admit, *this* Palace Hotel really is a palace." They stood in the main salon of the elegant suite of rooms Elaina had rented on her arrival — the presidential suite, the finest rooms in San Francisco. Rich coral draperies hung beside the floor-to-ceiling windows overlooking the bay, and the white and gold Louis XIV furniture was elegant. Delicate crystal vases filled with roses the same shade of coral sat on marble-topped tables.

"You know, Chase, sometimes I feel as if I'm dreaming. As if I'm going to wake up in the middle of a song at the Black Garter Saloon."

"You're not dreaming, Elaina. I can assure you of that. And I'm happy for you, at least in some ways."

Elaina turned, straightening a red-brown curl that rested on her shoulder. Her hair was once again coiffed in thick ringlets at the crown of her head, a few carefully arranged curls gathered at the side of her neck.

"But not in all ways?"

"Part of me enjoyed your dependency. I liked taking care of you, Elaina, even just a little. I'd like to continue."

"Chase, that's sweet of you, but —"

"But you're in love with Ren Daniels."

"That's not what I was going to say, and you know it!"

He touched her cheek. "Have I told you how pretty you are when you pout like that?"

She glanced up at him, feeling the pull of a smile at the back-handed compliment. "No, that's one you've missed."

He stepped closer, taking her hand. "There are lots of things I'd

206

like to say to you, Elaina, if I thought you were ready to listen. Maybe after tonight you will be."

Elaina stiffened at his reference to the Stanhope dinner party. They'd been in San Francisco only a short time, but word of the mine and her ownership of half a fortune in gold had earned her carte blanche in society — and an invitation to dinner from Jacob Stanhope. Jacob had invited Chase and "the intriguing lady who owns the mine," and Elaina was going one way or another.

"You look beautiful," he soothed. His hazel eyes sparkled with mischief, but his hands felt warm, and she knew he meant the compliment. The forest green silk gown she wore, the loveliest she'd ever owned, was trimmed in gold to match her eyes. Its square-cut neckline showed a daring amount of cleavage, while the waist fit snugly and the skirt, narrow over the hips, swept up in back to drape in soft folds to the floor. Gold embroidered poppy leaves lay next to her skin on the bodice and glittered in golden rows on the skirt.

"You'll steal the heart of every man in the room — even your friend, Daniels, though I have no doubt you've already done that, even if he won't admit it."

"Chase, you are incorrigible," she teased, but her smile was sad. She wished his words were true, wished she could hear Ren say them. Then, thinking of Carolina Williams, she wondered if they'd be true if he did.

"Are you sure you want to go through with this?" Chase asked.

"I wouldn't miss it for the world." Though she lifted her chin convincingly, inside she wasn't so sure.

Chase drew Elaina's fingers to his lips and kissed them softly. He knew Jacob Stanhope intimately, had been his friend for years. The older man had earned his fortune the hard way — working the docks. Chase had met him on the Barbary Coast when he was a younger man and Jacob was a rounder who spent many an hour and many a dollar at Chase's Silver Ingot Saloon. Chase always ran the prettiest women in the city, and Jacob appreciated a comely wench.

Both men's wealth had grown — Jacob's beyond all bounds. But he never forgot his early years, never forgot his friends. Tonight was no exception. It was Jacob's birthday. He would only admit to being sixty, but Chase figured him for at least sixty-five. When Jacob heard Chase was in town, escorting the wealthy young woman who was already the talk of the city, he'd insisted they come. Chase knew Elaina well enough to know she wouldn't refuse the invitation.

He offered her his arm, and her slim fingers tightened over the sleeve of his black cutaway coat.

"You know, Chase, I believe I've neglected to tell you how handsome you look this evening."

He was formally dressed, with a crisp white shirt beneath his black cutaway. He knew the suit fit perfectly; he used only the finest tailors. The cut flattered his wide shoulders and lean waist, and he wondered how Elaina McAllister found it so easy to resist his usually overpowering charms. Most of the women he knew, including those who took care of his needs when he finished squiring Elaina around, were more than eager to fill his bed. Maybe her aloofness was what attracted him to her.

"Why, thank you, ma'am," he teased, accepting her compliment and hoping she meant it. He intended to lure her to his bed sooner or later, but he wanted her willing. Tonight she'd see Daniels, escorting his fiancée, Melissa Stanhope. After Elaina's run-in with Carolina Williams, the sight of Ren with Melissa ought to make Elaina good and mad. Maybe it would be just the shove she needed to wind up beneath him. Chase relished the thought.

The Stanhope Mansion on Nob Hill overlooked the city like a great walled fortress. Its three-story brick and mortar facade was softened only by the white wooden columns that supported the roof of the massive veranda. Chase's sleek black open carriage rolled up the gravel drive, the hooves of his matched black horses crunching on the pebbles. They reined up beneath the covered veranda, and a young valet opened the carriage door. Elaina's hand trembled slightly as she accepted the young man's assistance from the carriage.

Clinging to Chase's arm, she took the four steps up to the huge white front door. The beveled-glass window, as if hinting at the gaiety inside, sparkled in dazzling colors, illuminated by the crystal chandelier in the foyer. Elaina enjoyed the soft tinkle of the prisms as the breeze followed her inside.

"Chase, my boy! Welcome. Welcome." Jacob Stanhope greeted them.

"Happy birthday, Jacob," Chase replied, handing Jacob a bottle of fine old scotch.

Jacob accepted the bottle, winked, and slapped Chase on the back. "And this must be the lovely Miss McAllister." He held up the scotch while his glance flicked over Elaina. "Chase, you always were a man of exceptionally good taste."

He bent to brush her hand with his lips, lingering for just a moment. Elaina could feel the strength of his hands and for an instant was taken aback. She hadn't expected him to be a man of such presence. Dressed formally in black, his masculine figure left no doubt as to his once overwhelming magnetism. She still felt its pull, though he looked to be well past his sixtieth year.

"I'm pleased to meet you, Mr. Stanhope. Chase has told me a great deal about you."

"Call me Jacob, my dear. And don't you dare believe a word this rogue says."

She smiled up at him, beginning to understand why Ren felt so close to him, and wishing she didn't. He had an easy, likable manner that captured her attention completely. It was not until their conversation ended that she had trouble controlling her gaze, wanting desperately to catch a glimpse of the tall blue-eyed man who was certain to be near.

Just then a lanky red-haired young man with a small, brightly smiling woman in tow swept into the foyer.

"Chase Cameron, Elaina McAllister," Jacob said, "may I present Tommy Daniels and his fiancée, Carrie Salzburg."

Elaina knew her stunned expression matched Tommy's perfectly. Forgetting everything but her joy at seeing him after all these years, she took a step forward and felt his arms go around her in the same instant.

"Is it really you, Lainey?" he whispered, ignoring the stares of those around them.

She stepped away, tears shimmering in her eyes. "Oh, Tommy, you look wonderful."

"And you, Lainey, you're beautiful, just as Ren said."

She blushed a little, her heartbeat quickening at Tommy's words

— Ren's words. "And this is your fiancée?" she asked, changing the subject. She wondered just how much Ren had told Tommy and felt her cheeks flame.

Tommy reached proudly for Carrie's hand. "Yes. Carrie and I will marry in the fall." He smiled at the small girl lovingly. Her copper-blond hair was swept off her shoulders revealing a slender, graceful neck. Her round green eyes watched Tommy with obvious adoration.

"Elaina was my best friend when we were young," he explained to Jacob. "She saved my life and Ren's, too. Dug us out of a coal mine when she was just ten years old."

Jacob Stanhope looked at her oddly, but said nothing.

"Tommy, please," Elaina said, "that was a long time ago. I'm sure Jacob and Carrie aren't interested in our recollections."

"Oh, but that's not true," Carrie said. "Tommy's been telling me about you for years. I'm so glad I finally got to meet you."

"Why don't we go into the salon for some refreshments?" Jacob instructed, and the group moved away from the door.

Elaina was happy for the chance to head the conversation in another direction, away from any reference to her association with Ren. She already liked Carrie Salzburg. She could see how much the couple loved each other and was happy for them.

A gentlemen's bar had been set up in the salon, and a black-clad waiter was serving fine French champagne.

"So far so good," Chase teased with a lazy smile, "but the moment of truth has yet to arrive."

"Must you always be so infuriating?" Elaina retorted, knowing Chase was not far wrong in his assessment of the situation. Her unruly eyes scanned the room, but so far neither Ren nor Melissa had appeared. Jacob returned to the foyer to continue greeting his guests.

The Stanhope residence was just as impressive inside as out. A huge stained-glass dome rose out of the fifteen-foot ceiling in the salon. The walls were covered in fine rose silk, the massive windows draped with heavy burgundy velvet. Thick Persian carpets covered gleaming hardwood floors parqueted in intricate patterns. The furniture of dark mahogany was upholstered in silks of light and dark rose.

210

No wonder Ren Daniels had been unwilling to marry her, Elaina mused with a flash of jealousy. Here was wealth and position beyond anything she had ever dreamed. Wealth and position Ren would soon be part of. She set her chin determinedly. She had her own money now and soon would occupy her own position in society.

"Just as soon as you're settled," Tommy was saying, "you'll have to join us for supper."

"Thank you, Tommy. That would be lovely." She smiled to herself, imagining just how pleased Ren would be at the news. Of course she would find some reason not to attend, but she'd have loved to see the look on Ren's face when Tommy announced his plans. It was obvious Tommy knew little of his brother's relationship with her, and she was grateful for Ren's discretion.

They talked only a few minutes more, the dinner party having turned into quite an affair. There were at least fifty people in attendance, which gave her some measure of anonymity. Accepting a second glass of champagne from Chase in an attempt to calm her nerves, she turned just in time to find Ren staring at her, his blue eyes wide with surprise. For an instant she thought they warmed with pleasure; then a slow, tight smile curved one corner of his mouth. A tiny, pale, fragile-looking blonde clung to his arm, but she kept her eyes cast downward, unwilling, it seemed, to meet Ren's piercing look.

"Well, fancy meeting you here," Chase Cameron drawled, his lazy smile amused. "I believe you know Miss McAllister."

Ren nodded stiffly. "May I present my fiancée, Melissa Stanhope. Melissa, this is Chase Cameron, an old friend of your father's."

Though he spoke to his fiancée, his gaze remained on Elaina. The tanned skin over his cheekbones looked taut, and Elaina could read cold fury in his eyes.

"And this is Miss McAllister," he added, "an old friend of mine."

"I'm very happy to meet you, Miss McAllister," Melissa said sweetly. "Everyone's been talking about your fabulous gold mine, but Ren didn't tell me you were a friend of his."

"That's right, Miss Stanhope," Chase cut in. "Miss McAllister is a very old friend. It seems she once saved your fiancé's life. Dug him out of a coal mine."

"Please, Chase, I'm sure that's of no interest to Miss Stanhope."

Elaina pinched his arm and felt him flinch, but his grin only broadened.

"Oh, but it is," Melissa said. "I wish I had the courage to do something like that." Her blue eyes shone with such sincerity that Elaina wanted to cry. She'd hoped to hate the girl, hoped she would be spoiled and selfish, like Carolina Williams. She hoped Melissa would make Ren's life miserable. Instead she seemed no more than an innocent child.

"I'm sure you have other attributes, Miss Stanhope," she choked out, wishing she were somewhere far away. Ren was obviously furious with her, and suddenly she was furious with herself. She'd come here to make Ren squirm. Now, she would have to endure the evening without even that small consolation. Why should he be uncomfortable? His fiancée was sweet and lovely, he had a mistress who obviously welcomed him to her bed, and he was marrying into a fortune. What a fool he must think her. How could she ever have believed he'd be interested in marrying her?

As if he could read her jumbled thoughts, Ren's hard look softened. "You're looking well, Miss McAllister. I trust you survived that little ordeal the other night without any further mishaps." He turned to Melissa. "Miss McAllister is also adept at doctoring. She probably saved Jimmy Lundstrom's life the other night."

Melissa's eyes gleamed with admiration. "You really are amazing, Miss McAllister."

"Thank you."

"You'll be happy to know that Jimmy is doing just fine," Ren said. "He'll be out of the hospital in a few days, thanks to you." Ren's voice held a slight caress that hadn't been there before. Feeling a tremor of warmth, she steeled herself and tightened her hold on Chase's arm.

"You're exaggerating my small contribution," she told Ren softly, "but I appreciate the kindness." His gaze held hers, and she had trouble looking away. How did he always manage to seem so sincere?

"Your fiancée is lovely," she added, changing the subject and hoping to put him on the defensive. "I'm sure you'll both be very happy."

Melissa Stanhope paled. "Would you excuse me a moment?" she

asked shyly. "I need to have a word with Papa."

"Of course." Ren released her arm, and she glided away on tiny satin slippers.

"I believe I see someone I know," Chase added. "You two will excuse me, won't you?"

"Chase, please," Elaina pleaded, but he only winked and walked away.

Turning toward Ren, whose face was a mask of control, she swallowed hard. "I — I shouldn't have come," she said, feeling her own control slipping badly. "It was a stupid thing to do, but I . . ." She glanced toward the petite blonde standing next to Jacob Stanhope and lifted her chin. "Is Miss Williams here tonight, too? Last week she seemed reluctant to let you out of her sight."

For the first time Ren's smile looked sincere. "Do I detect a note of jealousy?"

"You flatter yourself, Mr. Daniels."

"Elaina, I ended my relationship with Carolina Williams months ago, long before I met you. There was never anything between us — nothing of any value. She was a woman to care for my needs, that's all. A man does have needs, Elaina."

She eyed him with suspicion. "She's no longer your mistress?"

"No."

"Then you were telling me the truth in Central City."

"Every word."

Elaina felt a wave of relief far greater than she would have wished. She smiled tremulously, then glanced at Melissa and felt a jolt of pain. "You must think me a fool."

Ren answered with careful control. "No, Elaina, never a fool." She looked beautiful tonight. All elegance and grace. Her taller than average height as well as her tawny eyes and ample bosom set her apart from every other woman in the room. He longed to pull her into his arms, whisper words of comfort, words of love.

Instead, he glanced away, unwilling to meet her golden gaze a moment longer. He had to leave her, join Melissa and Jacob, yet he could not force himself to take a step.

"You look lovely tonight, the most beautiful woman in the room," he said. "But to me you looked just as beautiful in your simple lavender dress."

*He hadn't forgotten.* A hard lump swelled in her throat. She should go, find Chase, make him take her home on whatever pretense necessary, but she couldn't tear herself away. Ren looked so handsome, so masculine. The black suit fit perfectly across his broad shoulders, down the line of his narrow hips. All too well Elaina remembered the feel of his hard male body pressing against her. Hot color stained her cheeks at the thought.

"I'd better find Chase," she heard herself say, and watched Ren straighten. The rugged lines of his face became a mask of indifference.

"Yes, I suppose we'd both better go."

She nodded and turned to move away, but Jacob Stanhope, approaching from behind, caught her arm.

"Well, I see you two have discovered each other again after all these years."

"Actually," Ren told him, "we saw each other briefly at the Lick House ball last week."

She smiled tremulously. "Yes" was all she could manage as she noticed Jacob's odd, speculative glance.

"She's quite a treasure," Jacob said. "I'm surprised you never spoke of her before."

"Ah, but I did," Ren corrected. "I told you once about the little girl who dug me out of the coal mine."

Jacob grinned slyly, tugging at his tight white collar. "You did at that, my boy. I take it you were just as surprised as I to find the little girl had grown into a beautiful woman?" He seemed to regard Ren closely, and Elaina wondered at the quizzical look.

"Pleasantly surprised, Jacob. Pleasantly surprised. Now, if you two will excuse me, I'd better find Melissa."

As always, the sound of the girl's name twisted Elaina's heart.

"Of course," Jacob agreed. "You needn't worry. I'll take care of Miss McAllister. Besides, the longer I keep her away from that rogue, Cameron, the safer she'll be."

Ren bristled slightly, nodded, and left.

Relief washed over her, followed closely by sharp jabs of despair. She tried unsuccessfully to listen to Jacob's conversation, but her mind kept wandering, her gaze straying to the handsome dark-haired man who was talking to Asbury Harpending and several other ladies and gentlemen she recognized from the ball last week. As gold eyes met compelling light blue, she was forced to look away.

A soft tinkling dinner bell sounded, and Jacob extended his arm. Chase stepped up behind them, and the three walked into the huge dining room. One long table, set with gold-rimmed china, gilded silver, and golden goblets, sparkled in the center of the room. A massive bouquet of hyacinths, gladiolas, and long-stemmed yellow roses sat in the middle of the table, filling the room with a potpourri of sweet scents.

Long tapered candles flickered above golden candelabra as Chase pulled out the chair Jacob indicated. As she sat down, Elaina glanced at the tall man seated beside her and felt her heartbeat quicken. Ren seemed as surprised as she to find her next to him. Chase took his seat at the opposite end of the table, his smile, as usual, amused.

"Well, I see Jacob hasn't lost his sense of the dramatic," Ren said, a sardonic curve to his mouth. "I'm beginning to wonder at his game."

Elaina lifted her chin. "And just what game might that be, Mr. Daniels?"

"I'm not quite certain, Miss McAllister, but I intend to find out." He pulled his crisp linen napkin from the ring beside his plate and laid it across his lap.

"Whatever reasons Mr. Stanhope may have had for these seating arrangements," Elaina said with conviction, "I'm sure were quite innocent, and we'll just have to make the best of it. Jacob Stanhope appears to be a fine man."

"A fine man with a canny way of finding out whatever he wants to know. But I'm not complaining, Miss McAllister. There's no one I'd rather dine with this evening." He lowered his gaze to the curve of her breast above the glittering golden poppies. "No one."

"Might I introduce myself?" the gentleman to her right politely inquired, and she was grateful for the intrusion. "I'm Joshua A. Norton, emperor of these United States and protector of Mexico."

Elaina smiled brightly. So this was the famous Emperor Norton, San Francisco's own self-appointed royalty. She'd been fascinated by the man all evening. Dressed in a navy blue regimental uniform with slightly tarnished epaulets, he seemed to be one of the most popular people at the party.

"I'm so very pleased to meet you, Your Highness," she said with a tinge of humor. "I should have recognized you immediately. I humbly beg your pardon."

The emperor smiled indulgently. "That's quite all right, my dear. Quite all right. You're new to the city, aren't you?"

"Why, yes." She'd already decided to keep her story as simple as possible, leaving out the part about her singing as Lainey Starr. "I'm from Pennsylvania originally."

"Wasn't there something about a gold mine?" he questioned.

"The Golden Duchess Mine near Central City, Colorado. I staked an old friend, and he struck it rich. We're partners now."

He patted her hand solicitously. "Why, that's wonderful, my dear, wonderful. Quite a place, Colorado. I just accepted it as a state, you know. Had to prove itself worthy at first. But I'm glad to have it in my domain."

She stifled a grin at his sincerity, but enjoyed the emperor's wit. He'd proclaimed himself emperor almost twenty years ago, and Chase had explained how the city had grown to love him. Though he had no money and lived in a six-by-ten-foot room, reporters had written stories about him in every newspaper in the country, from the San Francisco *Bulletin* to the famous Virginia City *Territorial Enterprise*, where Mark Twain immortalized the old eccentric, along with his dog, Bummer.

A raven-haired woman on the emperor's right seemed disturbed by his lack of attention. "Joshua, would you please explain to me again why you've dissolved the State Supreme Court?" The woman simpered on the graying man's arm, so he excused himself and turned his attention in her direction.

Elaina took a sip of light Sancerre from her golden goblet and allowed herself a glance at Ren. His light blue eyes met hers, unreadable, yet unwilling to look away. Elaina swallowed hard.

A thin-faced waiter brought the first course, tiny quail eggs in aspic. Elaina feigned interest in the meal, but her stomach felt queasy, and she had trouble swallowing even the tiny bites she forced herself to take.

"How do you like our emperor?" Ren asked with forced lightness.

She brightened a little, enjoying the husky timbre of his voice. "He seems a most interesting man."

216

"The people here love him. They provide his clothes; he attends the theater and the ballet, eats anywhere he pleases — and pays nothing. He's quite a character."

"So it would seem."

The second course, cream of watercress soup laced with shallots and sherry, arrived at the table. Again Elaina ate only a few spoonfuls. She could see Melissa Stanhope seated near the opposite end of the table chatting pleasantly with a fair-haired man of about her same age. She seemed less tense than when Elaina first met her, more relaxed as she spoke animatedly with the young man beside her. She was lovely indeed, though delicate and a bit pale. Watching her now, Elaina noticed her cheeks seemed a bit pinker, her blue eyes a little brighter than before.

Ren broke off his conversation with the woman to his left. When he spoke to Elaina again, his voice sounded strained; the lines of his face seemed taut.

"Do you have any idea how difficult this is for me," he whispered through clenched teeth, "sitting here beside you, wanting you, not being able to touch you?" In the din of laughter and gaiety surrounding them, the words carried only as far as her ears. He was becoming angry with her again.

This time her own anger flared in return. "San Francisco is going to be my home. You're going to have to get used to my presence, because I most certainly don't intend to stay home while you and your fiancée are out enjoying yourselves I'm my own person now. I can do whatever I want, whenever I want, wherever I want."

"Damn you, Lainey," he warned, his voice gruff. "You're making it harder on both of us."

"Oh, really?" She lifted her chin. "I hadn't noticed. You seem to be doing just fine. You have a lovely fiancée; you'll be marrying into one of the richest families in California — I don t see where that is hard on you at all." She smiled at him, enjoying his discomfort.

A muscle flexed in his jaw. His eyes had narrowed and darkened, and a deep frown creased his brow. Reaching beneath the heavy lace tablecloth, he grabbed her hand and pulled it none to gently against his thigh. Her eyes widened in shock, and a tiny gasp escaped as she felt his hardened manhood.

"Now do you understand?" he ground out.

She jerked her hand away as if she'd been scalded, then glanced around the table, hoping none of them had noticed. Her face flamed red. How dare he! She'd never felt more humiliated in her life!

"You've got plenty of money, Elaina," he was saying in a low, strained voice. "Do us both a favor. Find somewhere else to live — or by God you'll wind up flat on your back beneath me one way or another!"

She shoved back her chair, shaken to the core. Tears welled in her eyes. "I'm afraid I'm not feeling well. Would you gentlemen please excuse me?"

Both Ren and the emperor rose while she left the table. Ren caught Chase Cameron's amused expression as he also excused himself and followed Elaina from the room.

Ren breathed a deep, controlled sigh. Dammit, why did he feel so rotten? He'd done the girl a favor. Told her the truth. There was an undeniable attraction between them, something neither of them was strong enough to resist. If she stayed in San Francisco, she'd wind up being his mistress. He knew it, even if she was too young and blind to see.

Watching Chase Cameron follow Elaina through the door, Ren fought down a sudden vision of the roguish southerner in Elaina's bed. Would she turn to him tonight seeking comfort for the way Ren had treated her? The thought tightened his gut. When the waiter set a plate of delicate smoked salmon dressed with lemon and capers before him, he thought he might be sick. He picked at the food and glanced toward his fiancée. Melissa was engrossed in lively conversation with Stewart Pickman, heir to the Pickman fortune and a bright, well-educated lad just a few years older than she.

Ren had rarely seen Melissa smile so brightly and had never seen such radiance in her cheeks. He wondered what they were discussing so animatedly. He and Melissa rarely spoke to each other at all. Whenever he tried to initiate a conversation, she only became more reticent, fearful, it seemed, he might disapprove of what she had to say. Each of his efforts to encourage their closeness had ended in failure. Tonight was no exception. She'd avoided him at every opportunity, hiding behind her father's protective coattails.

He thought of their wedding, a scant two weeks away. She would never willingly accept him in her bed. He'd have to force himself on her, and though some men were excited by that sort of violence, Ren would much rather have a willing bride beneath him.

He shoved at the food on his plate and made strained conversation with the woman to his left. He was glad when the meal ended. Chairs scraped against the parquet floor as the women retired to the salon for sherry and the men to the drawing room for brandy and cigars.

Melissa was safe from him again tonight. He dreaded their wedding night, when she would be forced to accept his advances, whether she was willing or not.

# Chapter 21

The drive in the open carriage through the streets of San Francisco refreshed her.

The sky was clear, the stars bright, the air brisk and tinged with a salty sea breeze. Chase had said little since they left the mansion but had ordered his driver to take them along the shoreline. Elaina was glad for the distractions beside the bay. Fishing boats bobbed at the docks, and several large silver fish broke the surface of the water, sending shimmering circles to reflect in the light of the moon. Chinese vendors jogged beside the carriage hawking their wares, though the hour was late. One held up a lovely silk wrapper, and Chase told the driver to pull up the horses.

"Do you like it?" he asked.

"It's beautiful. I've never seen such fine workmanship." Embroidered flowers of dark pink and silver covered most of the pale pink wrapper. Chase handed the man a coin and gave the robe to Elaina.

"It's yours."

She smiled at him, accepting the gift graciously. "Thank you."

They drove along the bay a minute more, the clatter of hooves on the cobblestone streets soothing her frayed nerves. Then Chase instructed the driver to head for the hotel. The massive structure on Nob Hill wasn't far from the Stanhope estate. The thought of Ren and Melissa enjoying a laugh at her expense set Elaina's blood to boiling all over again. She felt tense and edgy, and furious at Ren's audacity.

Chase helped her from the carriage, escorted her through the ornate lobby, handsomely furnished in red velvet and gold, and up to her rooms on the top floor.

"May I come in?" he asked.

Noticing his heated look for the first time, Elaina grew pensive. "Why not?" she finally said. It was high time she ended this madness Ren stirred every time he came near. Chase was handsome, wealthy, charming — and he wanted her in his bed. Well, it was high time. High time indeed.

The champagne Chase opened was the best money could buy, but the cold bubbling liquid tasted sour against her tongue. They were sitting on the settee, Elaina desperately trying to enjoy Chase's kiss, the gentle touch of his hand.

His mouth moved along her throat to nuzzle the back of her neck, his lips warm and firm. She felt a slight tremor as his hand unfastened the buttons at the back of her gown, but knew it as fear, not passion. She felt nothing as he pulled the dress down to her waist, nothing as his hands caressed her breasts through the thin fabric of her chemise. When he dipped his head to kiss the rounded swell of her breast, she heard his soft groan of pleasure, felt the hardness of his manhood pressing against the front of his trousers. Tears welled in her eyes and slipped down her cheeks.

He pulled her to her feet, pushed the dress down over her hips, and left her standing in only her chemise and lacy pantalets. When his skillful fingers unstrung her corset, she still did not move. Like a statue, she let him finish undressing her. Only when she was naked to his gaze, her sable hair freed to tumble about her shoulders, did he raise his eyes to her face.

His hand shook and his mouth was set in a grim line as he wiped the tears from her cheeks. She felt his muscular arms lifting her up. Resigned to her fate, unwilling to say no to him, not wanting to hurt him as Ren had hurt her, she let him carry her into the bedroom.

When he reached the bed, he pulled back the quilt, then lowered her gently, covering her lips in a feather-light kiss. Then he pulled the satin comforter over her naked, trembling body.

He watched her a moment in silence then: "Not like this, Elaina. Never like this."

She thought she heard a catch in his voice as he stepped away from the bed. Beneath a wave of guilt, she closed her eyes and sank into her pillow, listening as he closed the door softly behind him. Hearing his heavy footsteps on the thick Tartan carpet, then the click of the door as he left, she broke into deep racking sobs.

* * * * *

It was well past midnight before Ren was able to quietly excuse himself and make his way out of the mansion. He needed some time to himself. What he really needed, he admitted, was a way to salve his conscience for his cruel treatment of Elaina. Tommy had taken the carriage, so he drove through the city in a rented hack. He paid the driver handsomely to haul him aimlessly through the quieting city streets, but his mind kept straying to the woman who again tonight had captured his mind and heart. It seemed they were fated to torture each other, just as he was being tortured now.

He knew where she was staying; the paper had reported that she was residing in the grand manner in the presidential suite at the Palace Hotel. She'd come a long way from the tiny rooms above Hoffman's General Mercantile and an even longer way from her shabby quarters on the third floor of the Hotel Keyserville.

The carriage rounded a corner and headed up California Street before Ren noticed his surroundings. The hotel loomed ahead. On the top floor Elaina McAllister would be resting in a deep feather mattress. Was Chase lying beside her? The thought twisted like a knife. He didn't want to believe it, wouldn't let himself believe it.

The urge to go to her raged strong. Elaina had come to San Francisco to find him, he told himself, and she had gone to the Stanhope mansion in order to see him again. It was obvious she wanted him just as much as he wanted her. Why should he deny himself? Deny her? He wasn't married yet, and even after his wedding he would need someone to care for his needs. He was through with Carolina Williams, had been for some time. In fact he could hardly imagine what he'd seen in the feather-headed woman to begin with.

The horse's hooves drummed a rhythm on the stone streets, carrying him nearer the hotel. Tonight he'd warned Elaina in no uncertain terms what would happen if she stayed in San Francisco, but maybe that was what she really wanted. The thought of having her as his mistress, spending nights in her warm, inviting arms, sent the blood pulsing through his veins.

"Take me to the Palace," he ordered, knowing what he was doing was wrong but unable to stop himself.

He knew the night clerk at the front desk. Timothy O'Banyon

owed him a favor — several, in fact — and tonight he would collect. It took little persuasion to obtain the key to the suite and information that the lady was within, apparently alone: The gentleman who had escorted her to her room had left some time ago.

Ren breathed a sigh of relief. He thanked Timothy and assured him he'd tell no one how he'd obtained the key. His heart raced as he walked purposefully down the wide carpeted hall on the top floor of the hotel to the double mahogany doors at the end. Feeling a moment of indecision, he paused; then, as if he had no choice, he inserted the key in the lock.

A gentle click, a turn of the knob, and he stepped inside the elegant suite. His excitement grew, along with his desire, just at the thought she was near. God, how could a woman hold such power over him? He opened the door to the huge bedroom and spotted Elaina's slim form curled beneath a satin coverlet. As he pulled the door closed, he noticed that the moonlight streaming through the window gave a silver glow to Elaina's skin. He caught his breath at the picture of loveliness she made. Her sable hair glistened on her pillow. Her ruby lips were slightly parted as she slept.

He unbuttoned and loosened his collar, then shed his jacket and boots and shrugged off his shirt.

With a tiny gasp, Elaina bolted upright in the bed. "Chase? Is that you?"

The sound of the man's name sent sparks of fury through Ren's veins. "Sorry to disappoint you. Were you expecting him?" If he'd had doubts before, they were gone with Elaina's words.

"You!" she cried, her eyes adjusting to the dim light in the room. "How did you get in here? Get out this instant or I swear I'll scream for help."

"You'll do nothing of the sort," he warned. "Not unless you want to headline the morning edition of the *Alta California.*"

"What do you want?" Elaina asked, already feeling a little breathless. Muscles rippled across his hard torso, and dark hair curled in a V on his chest. Fighting a wave of desire, she licked her lips. What in God's name was the matter with her? The man was nothing but a cad. He would say or do anything to get what he wanted; he'd proved that again and again. Yet here she was, yearning for his touch, her body already on fire with wanting him. As she watched him casually remove the remainder of his clothing, a tiny moan of anticipation escaped, and she cursed herself for her weakness.

"Get out of here," she whispered, but he only moved closer. She could feel the weight of his body as he made room for himself on the bed.

"I want you, Elaina, more than I've ever wanted another woman. I can't get enough of you." He wound a finger in one of her shiny curls. "All I can think about, dream about, is holding you, making love to you. I need you, Elaina."

She moaned at his words, knowing she was already damp and aching for him. "Please, Ren," she pleaded. "You were right and I was wrong. I shouldn't have come to San Francisco. I'll go someplace else. I'll leave tomorrow."

"It's too late, Elaina. I can't fight it anymore. You're mine. You were mine from the start. You always will be." He stroked her cheek gently.

"Never," she whispered, tearing herself away. "I won't let you use me again. I'll fight you."

He hauled her against him. "It's useless, Elaina. You want me just as much as I want you. Your body betrays you " — he stroked the hard bud of her nipple, already stiff and eager for his touch — "even if your mind says no."

Unwilling to admit the truth of his words, she lashed out at him with her fist, determined to hurt him, determined to prove him wrong. He caught her wrist easily, pressed her into the mattress, and rolled on top of her.

"No," she whispered, her voice barely audible. She felt his hardened shaft and wanted it inside her, though the heat of humiliation raced through her veins.

"Yes, Elaina. You want it, and so do I."

Thrashing against him, she struggled, fighting the heavy, hot burden of his body. This time she wouldn't give in. She wouldn't allow herself to betray everything she'd been taught to honor. She tore her hand free and raked her nails across his chest, wanting to hurt him, wanting to punish him for the things he made her feel.

Again he caught her wrist, then gently but firmly restrained both of her hands above her head.

"Don't fight me, Elaina. It's a battle you can't win." As if to prove his point he lowered his mouth to the peak of her nipple, and she moaned with the jolt of desire.

She could feel his strength, the power he held, but she also sensed his tenderness. You can't give in, she told herself. He'll have to force you. But even as she said the words she recognized them for the lies they were. He kissed her with maddening skill, subdued her with his masterful hands, stroked her, teased her, until her struggles became more a caress than an attempt to keep him away.

How she wanted him. Burying her fingers in his thick black hair, pulling him closer, she clutched him against her breast, begging him to ease the burning ache in her loins. He filled her slowly, with agonizing deliberateness, proving his mastery as no other could. She clawed his back and cried his name as he lifted her hips and drove himself into her. She matched his every pounding thrust. The heat of her desire burned so bright she felt she might turn to ash. The fierce flames ravaged her, devoured her. She called his name over and over, then spoke the words she denied even to herself — "I love you. I love you."

She forgot her sorrow, the pain in her heart, forgot all but the pleasure he gave. The pounding, pulsing rhythm of their coupling lifted her; then a thousand tiny shards of sweetness lanced her with violent, joyous stabs of delight. She was lost in her pleasure, consumed by her bliss. Ren reached his own powerful, shuddering climax. Then he kissed her gently, nuzzling her neck, and holding her against him.

They were quiet for a while. She wondered if he'd heard the words she'd whispered in her passion and wished she could call them back. She couldn't afford to let him know how vulnerable she was, couldn't give him more power over her than he already had. She felt his warm lips against the place below her ear.

"I love you, too, Elaina. I have almost from the start. Sometimes I think I'll die of loving you."

The words sent delicious tremors the length of her. God how she'd yearned to hear them. She turned to face him, unsure what to say. Tears gathered in her eyes, and her heart ached worse than before. "But not enough to marry me."

He rolled away, swung his legs over the edge of the bed, and sat up. "Jacob's dying," he said softly.

"Oh, no."

"His one wish is to see his daughter cared for properly. I can't refuse him."

She could see the anguish in his eyes, though his words sounded brittle. Only tonight she had wished with all her heart she could hear him say he loved her. Now that he had, the words seemed hollow, empty somehow. What did it matter if he loved her, if they had to remain apart?

"Stay with me, Lainey. I'll find us a place . . . along the coast somewhere. A place where we can be together."

"And what of your marriage?" she asked, trying to read the tension in his expression.

"It'll be a marriage in name only. A marriage of convenience."

She remembered those same words spoken by someone else only the week before, and the words twisted her heart. "That's what Carolina Williams said."

"Forget her. She means nothing to me. She never has. You mean everything." He ran a gentle finger down the line of her jaw.

The words swayed her. She loved him so. "But Jacob must want heirs? Someone to carry on the Stanhope name?"

He glanced away, no longer willing to meet her eyes. "Yes," he admitted. "I've promised him that."

"Oh, God, Ren," she whispered, her voice an agony of despair. A sob escaped, and she buried her face in her pillow. He pulled her into his arms and held her as she cried against his chest.

"Please don't cry. I didn't come here to make you cry."

"Don't you see? It could never work. Not for you, not for Melissa, not for me. I can't live that way, sharing you with another woman, eventually sharing you with your family. And what of the children *I* would conceive? They'd be . . . they'd be —"

"Elaina, stop it."

She jerked away. "Bastards, Ren. Our children would be bastards. I won't have it. It wouldn't be fair, don't you see?" He pulled her back into his arms and stroked her hair as she sobbed out her grief.

"You make it sound so dirty, like the worst thing in the world. But it isn't like that between us. It never has been." He tilted her chin up and forced her to look at him. "Lots of people have arrangements. At least we could be together. Promise me you'll think about it."

She knew what her answer would be, but he was here with her now, and she wanted him again already. She wouldn't spoil the short time they had.

"I'll be gone tomorrow," he told her. "I have some business to attend to. I'll be back in the city on Wednesday afternoon. We can talk about it then."

She nodded, unable to trust her voice. He kissed her softly, reassuringly, as if he wanted her to feel his love. Then, as always, the kiss became demanding, and she gave herself up to the burning fire that carried them into the night.

# Chapter 22

Dolph Redmond flipped the towheaded boy a coin, waited for him to close the door behind him, then opened and scanned the wire: "Found the girl. No sign of Morgan. Time running thin. Delay closing. Will get her to Keyserville as soon as possible. Chuck."

Damn! A delay in closing the sale on the mine! That was the last thing he needed. Everything else was going as planned: The Anthracite Mining and Colliery Company still wanted the property and all was in order. The only thing they needed was control of Elaina's shares. Damn! The woman had always been nothing but trouble. He handed the wire to Henry Dawson.

"Looks like your boy's found her all right," he told Henry, "but he's still got to get her here." They were sitting in the inner office of the Hotel Keyserville, Dolph Redmond in his chair, his feet, as usual, propped up on his desk. The sun had just risen, and the day looked cloudy.

"He'll git her here all right. You can always count on Chuck when the chips is down. Jus' like his mama when it comes to that."

"Well, he'd better. This sale will make us all rich. We can't afford to louse it up." He drew on his thin cigar. "Chuck was right about one thing — we should have forced the marriage years ago. You and your damned sentimentality, Henry. You always were a soft touch for a pretty face."

Henry just grunted. "It'll only be a two-week delay. We've waited years fer this. A couple more weeks ain't gonna hurt."

"I suppose not, but I'll feel a lot better after she's married to Chuck."

"I still can't figure that one. If she wouldn't marry Chuck afore, how you gonna git her to now?"

"You let me worry about that. I assure you, Elaina McAllister is going to be your daughter-in-law in the very near future."

Henry just nodded, accepting Dolph's word as if the marriage were already an accomplished feat. Henry trusted him, and in a way Dolph felt the same. Hoisting his heavy frame from the chair, Henry pulled on his narrow-brimmed straw hat and headed for the door. There was still a mine to run, and Henry took his job seriously. It was one of the things Dolph liked about the man. They'd been partners for fifteen years. It was as unlikely a twosome as God had ever dreamed up.

"Keep me posted," Henry called over his shoulder.

Dolph just nodded. Initially, Dolph had needed Henry's money, and though the vulgar man had seemed beneath him at the time, Dolph had come to recognize Henry's strong points. He was good at getting things done. He was steadfast and a hard worker. Since he was also willing to do just about anything to accomplish his purpose — that usually being to earn more money — he and Dolph had gotten along just fine.

Now they were about to make the fortune they'd struggled toward all their lives. They would let nothing stand in their way. And though Dolph didn't relish splitting the money with Henry and Chuck, his share would still amount to a fortune.

He was glad Chuck had taken Bill Sharp to California with him to bring the girl home. Sharp was a strong, capable sort — and incredibly fast with a gun. The kind of man who would get the job done one way or another. The sooner the matter was settled, the better off they'd all be.

"You sure she's alone up there?" Andy Johnson asked.

"She's alone all right," Chuck said. The man he'd discovered to be Chase Cameron had left the Palace before midnight. "I saw the fella take off before I headed back to our hotel." Chuck, Andy Johnson, and Bill Sharp had taken rooms at the Geary House, a small hotel just down the hill from the Palace. Chuck had slept for a few hours, till the sun began to light the window beside his bed. Then he'd summoned Bill and Andy to his room.

Elaina had been easier to find than he'd imagined. Though he'd had no luck in the beginning — even Isabelle Chesterfield knew

229

nothing of Elaina's whereabouts — his persistence had eventually paid off. Well before her arrival in the city, Elaina McAllister had been front-page news.

Chuck smiled mirthlessly. This was going to turn out better than his wildest dreams. Elaina had become a fabulously wealthy woman, and as soon as she married Chuck, he would control every dime. All he had to do was get her back to Keyserville, and he intended to accomplish that task right away.

"You're sure you two can handle this by yourselves?" His sandy brows drew together in an uncertain frown. "I'm afraid if she sees me, it'll only make things worse."

"We can handle her," Bill Sharp assured him. "She's only a woman."

"I warn you," Chuck said, "don't underestimate this particular woman. I did once and wound up with this." He pointed to the jagged scar on his cheek. He looked forward to taming the little hellion once they were married. She'd had far too long an engagement already.

Looking as though he'd never be stupid enough to allow any woman to get the better of him, Sharp merely grunted. They left the hotel and headed up the hill to the Palace. The day was fair, the light of early morning glistening on the waters of the bay.

"I'll wait for you down here," Chuck instructed once they reached their destination. "Use the steam elevator in the back. I'll meet you near the rear entrance."

"Don't worry, boss," Andy Johnson put in. "This'll be a snap."

Chuck remembered the last time he'd thought controlling Elaina McAllister would be a snap — the night he'd tried to ravish her and succeeded only in upsetting their wedding plans and getting his nose broken. At least Morgan was no longer in the picture. Chuck had found no trace of the man in San Francisco. If he'd ever lived in the city, he was long gone now.

Andy Johnson, carrying the small bottle of chloroform they planned to use, moved toward the rear entrance of the Palace. He was a master at picking locks; neither these heavy doors nor the smaller ones leading to Elaina's suite would be a problem. Thin and lithe, Andy had worked for the Redmond-Dawson partnership off and on for years.

Bill Sharp was a recent addition. Tall and well proportioned, with narrow-set eyes and bushy brows, Sharp had been hired to replace Dan Morgan. He'd easily frightened the miners into submission without firing a single shot. Chuck had seen him draw down on a man once — the man's pistol never cleared his holster. Sharp could easily have killed the man, would have, too, if Chuck hadn't stopped him. He was fast with a gun, all right. Faster than any man Chuck had ever seen — probably even faster than Morgan. Too bad Morgan wasn't around so Chuck could find out. He'd have liked nothing better than to see the gunman get his comeuppance.

Ren heard the soft click of the lock and opened his eyes. He'd been awake off and on for an hour, enjoying the soft feather mattress and the luxury of watching Elaina sleep. Warily he eased himself from the bed and pulled on his breeches, mindful of the faint creak as the heavy front door of the suite swung wide. Leaving Elaina undisturbed, he moved quietly toward the bedroom door. The brass knob turned just as he reached it. Unable to get the pearl-handled derringer from the pocket of his coat, he stepped behind the door just as it opened.

"She's a beauty, ain't she, Bill?" whispered a soft male voice.

Ren glanced at Elaina's sleeping figure. She'd pushed the satin sheet down, leaving one full breast exposed to the men's view. Ren felt his stomach tighten. It was all he could do to control his temper. From his place behind the door, he heard footsteps muffled by the carpet as two men moved into the room.

"A figure like that and money, too," the second man agreed. His voice sounded husky, and Ren knew what the man was thinking as he feasted on the sight of Elaina's perfect breast.

Ren's control snapped. He shoved the door into the tall, well-built man and kicked out at another shorter man. Elaina screamed and sat up in bed, clutching the covers around her. The smaller man grunted as he stumbled into a chair, tipping it over, and the tall man punched Ren hard in the jaw, hurling him across the bed, where he almost collided with Elaina. Ren regained his feet quickly, ducked another punch, and delivered a dense blow to the tall man's middle, doubling him over. The little man skirted the two brawling men and headed toward the door.

"Come on, Bill!" he yelled in his high, soft voice. "We didn't count on this!"

The one named Bill punched Ren again and ran through the salon to join his friend. Ren followed at a dead run. Wrapped in the sheet, Elaina raced behind them. Before the bigger man could reach the door, Ren leapt on him and the two of them sprawled on the marble tiles, upending the settee and sending a silk-shaded lamp crashing to the floor. Ren spotted a flash of metal as the tall man pulled a gun, but was unable to avoid the barrel, which cracked against his head with a resounding thump. He sagged to the carpet, fighting to remain conscious. Pulling himself upright, he took another two steps in the men's direction as they escaped through the doorway and disappeared down the hall. Then everything turned black.

"Ren!" Elaina screamed, racing toward him. She knelt beside him, her hands shaking so badly she could barely lift his head onto her lap. "Ren, please be all right."

He groaned as if in answer. Then his eyelids fluttered open, and he raised a hand to the knot on his forehead. He tried to lift himself up, only to sag back against her.

"Seems like we've played this scene before," he joked, but he couldn't suppress a grimace of pain.

"Just lie still. I'll get a damp cloth."

She returned quickly to find him already sitting in a chair, his head tilted against the back. She laid the cloth on his forehead.

"What . . . what do you think those men were after?" she asked with a nervous glance at the now closed door.

"I don't know, but I intend to find out. Probably hoped you had some money up here. Everyone in the city has heard about your gold mine by now. There was something familiar about the one who hit me and about the way he used that gun. . . . I don't know, maybe it was nothing, then again . . . I don't like the idea of your being in danger. Much as I might wish it, I can't be here all the time. You need servants — a butler, a lady's maid, people who'll be around to discourage the likes of men like that."

"I've already spoken with an agency," she told him, though she didn't say she had no intention of hiring anyone now. She would soon be leaving San Francisco for good. "I'm sure whoever they send will be trustworthy."

"We'll have them checked out thoroughly," he said, "just to be on the safe side. In the meantime, I guess I'll just have to keep a closer eye on you." He ran a long brown finger along the line of her jaw, a slow smile curving his mouth. Then he noticed her sheet had come open, and his eyes focused on the shapely hip and slender leg exposed to his view. As his palm moved along her thigh to cup her bottom, the feel of her warm skin against his hand tingled his flesh and sent a surge of blood to his loins.

Playfully she slapped his hand away. "I see you're going to live," she told him. But he didn't miss the relief in her golden eyes.

"I'll be fine," he assured her. "Unfortunately I have important out-of-town business to attend to tonight. I won't be able to take up my bodyguard duties until tomorrow." His hand returned to her bottom, his long fingers fanning out to tease her rapidly heating flesh.

Elaina felt a shiver of the same desire she knew he was feeling, but forced it away, dwelling instead on his words. There was nothing she wanted more — and nothing she wanted less — than for Ren to look after her body.

"You'll be safe enough today," he assured her. "They won't be back soon, and probably not at all. But I'll send my man Herbert Thomas and his wife, Flora, over as soon as I get home."

He grinned devilishly. "Herbert's an excellent shot, and Flora can keep an eye on Chase Cameron — just in case he tries to match his audacity with mine."

Elaina pulled the wet cloth from his forehead and tossed it at him in feigned anger. "Men! You're all incorrigible!"

He pulled her into his lap and kissed her soundly. "Would you have it any other way?"

She kissed him in answer, but when she drew away, his light eyes had darkened.

"Today's the third, isn't it?" he asked.

"Yes, why?"

"I'd forgotten about tomorrow. Tomorrow's the Fourth of July. I promised Jacob I'd accompany him and Melissa to the fireworks celebration. There's a big ox roast and picnic. The earliest I'll be

233

able to get back here will be late afternoon."

Elaina turned away, her eyes threatening to tear. She swallowed hard. Why did it hurt so when she'd known all along what it would feel like to be the other woman? Ren would spend every holiday, every weekend, with his family. She'd see him only when it was convenient. That was why she could never agree to his wild scheme for them to be together; why she was going away. As much as she loved him, she refused to share him, and she would not come between him and the family he would soon be responsible for. She would not lower herself to the level of someone like Carolina Williams.

"I wish I had time to make love to you again," he was saying, "but I want to let the hotel know what happened here this morning. Then I'll speak with the constable."

"What? Ren, you can't!" She pulled away from him. "Don't you see, they'll know you were here. They'll know you spent the night. They'll —"

"Elaina, listen to me." Ren tipped her chin up and willed her to understand. "No matter how discreet we are, people are going to know. It doesn't matter. Lots of people have arrangements of this sort."

He sounded so matter-of-fact. But then why shouldn't he? He'd done this before. She could feel tears burning her eyes, then slipping down her cheeks. "It matters to me," she whispered, and he pulled her against the hard wall of his chest.

"All right," he conceded. "I won't go to the police. I'll hire someone private to look into the matter. In the meantime, I'll send over the Thomases. You stay close to the hotel. Tomorrow I'll be back and we can talk about all this and get a few things settled."

Tomorrow Ren would enjoy Independence Day with his fiancée, she thought. He would laugh with Jacob, plan his family's future. He'd speak of grandchildren, talk about the wedding. Melissa would look at him with her gentle blue eyes, thinking of her honeymoon, the nights she'd spend in his arms. Elaina closed her eyes, trying to blot out the awful images, trying to be strong.

Tomorrow she would be on an eastbound train headed for a lonely destination that only she and God would know. This time she wouldn't tell anyone where she was going, not even Ada Lowery.

She fought back a wave of despair, and pasted on a smile. "Until tomorrow, then."

With a hand beneath her chin, he claimed her mouth in a fiery kiss of possession. She fought hard to keep her lips from trembling beneath his, fought to keep the tears in her eyes from spilling down her cheeks.

"Tomorrow," he repeated, as if it were only a matter of hours until they'd be together again, not the eternity Elaina knew it to be.

She followed him to the door and closed it softly behind him. Only then, as his footsteps echoed down the hall and faded into silence, did she allow the tears she'd held back to fall in warm wet droplets on her breast.


"Of all the rotten luck." Chuck Dawson paced the floor of his hotel room while Bill Sharp and Andy Johnson related the story of their failure. There'd been no time to explain what had happened until now. All three had made a mad dash for their rented carriage and returned as quickly as possible to the safety of their rooms.

"What did the man look like?" Chuck asked.

"Well, he was really tall," Andy said, exaggerating wildly. "Taller than you by at least six inches, with huge arms and a thick neck and —"

"He was about your height," Sharp interrupted. "He had black hair, slightly gray at the temples, and the lightest blue eyes I've ever seen."

"Morgan! You say the son of a bitch was in her bed?"

"Well, not when we went in, but from the looks of things, he damn sure spent the night there."

"That little tramp. I should have known she'd be with Morgan. He was right here under our noses all along. I'm surprised we didn't turn up any trace of him."

"She sure is pretty, boss," Andy put in. "The smoothest, whitest skin I've ever seen. And those breasts, so full and round and —"

"Shut up, you fool!" Chuck clenched and unclenched his fists.

"Sorry, boss," Andy whispered in his high, soft voice.

"So that was Dan Morgan." Bill Sharp seemed amused. "I've been wantin' to run into him for years. He's got quite a reputation. Man who kills Morgan'll add more'n a notch to his gun. I'd like nothin' better'n to draw down on him."

"And I'd like nothing better than to see Morgan dead," Chuck said. "You'll have your chance at him, Sharp. You just better hope you're faster than he is."

"Oh, I'm faster, all right. Morgan goes up against me, he'll be dead, all right." Sharp leaned back in his narrow oak chair, his booted feet stretched out carelessly in front of him.

"Right now," Chuck said, "the important thing is to get the girl back to Keyserville. We'll have to be more careful this time. Morgan's no fool. He'll be ready for us." He stopped pacing and turned to stare out the window. The streets were noisy with early morning traffic. A newsboy hawked the *Alta California*, his voice easily carrying up three stories to the open window of Chuck's room.

"I think I might just have an idea how we can lure her away from Morgan's protection," he continued.

"How we gonna do that, boss?" Andy asked.

"All in due time," Chuck assured him. He smiled and sank down on the narrow iron bed beneath the window. "All in due time."

Elaina strode briskly across the thick fringed rug to the inner office of the prestigious law firm of Douglas, Wright, Wright, and Jones. The younger Mr. Wright represented her, along with Richard Marley and the Golden Duchess Mine.

"You're looking lovely, Miss McAllister," Louis Wright told her. "But then, you always do."

"Thank you." She accepted the chair he offered and leaned back against the tufted brown leather. She could smell its musky scent, though the chair was far from new.

Louis Wright seated himself behind his massive rosewood desk. "Let me begin by handing you another bank draft. This one, I'm pleased to say, is even larger than the last."

Elaina accepted the ivory envelope and carefully tucked the draft into her reticule. The bag matched her rich brown silk faille walking suit. Its overskirt of a lighter brown rustled with her movements. She'd kept a fleet of seamstresses busy since her arrival and been rewarded with an elegant wardrobe of the finest dresses, hats, gloves, parasols, and lacy lingerie.

"I didn't come here about the money. I came to see how our offer to purchase the Blue Mountain Mine is progressing. I know it's only been a few days, but I was hoping you might have some word."

"I'm afraid, Miss McAllister, we've run into a problem on that score." Louis Wright tapped his pencil against the green felt pad on his desk. "It seems the Anthracite Mining and Colliery Company has already made an offer to buy the property. The sale is due to be closed right away."

"I see."

"Now, unless you'd be interested in purchasing the property from the new owners —"

"No, Mr. Wright. At least not yet. I only wanted to buy the mine in order to improve conditions there for the miners. Do you know anything about this new company?"

"Only a little." Louis Wright scratched his balding head. Though still a young man, he was losing his sandy hair rapidly; a few telltale strands rested on the shoulder of his navy blue suit. "But they have an excellent reputation."

"What about their employees? Are they treated fairly?"

"I can't say for certain, but as far as I know, there's no record of unrest at any of their locations."

"That's what matters most to me. Maybe we can keep an eye on things, and if it looks as though conditions aren't getting any better, we'll offer to buy them out."

"Fine," Wright agreed.

Elaina handed him a piece of paper. "I want you to send a draft to Henry Dawson in the amount mentioned on that paper. You can reach him in Keyserville at the address I've written on the bottom."

The attorney looked at her questioningly.

"It's an old debt," she told him. "I've wanted to repay Mr. Dawson for some time."

"I'll see to it personally."

"I'd also like you to handle the purchase of the Hotel Keyserville. Pay whatever's necessary. When you've completed the transaction, I'd like the deed drawn up in the name of Ada Lowery. I want her to receive not only the property but also enough money to restore the hotel to its original condition."

237

"This Ada Lowery, she's a close friend?" he asked.

"More than a friend, Mr. Wright. Much more."

"You needn't worry. I'll begin the negotiations immediately. There'll be paperwork. I'll need your signature. Can I continue to reach you at the Palace?"

"No. I'm checking out tomorrow morning. I'll inform you of my whereabouts just as soon as I arrive at my destination."

"Which is . . . ?"

"I wish I knew, Mr. Wright." She smiled wanly. "But wherever it is, I'll keep in touch. You've done a fine job for me, and I certainly wouldn't want to lose you."

"Why, thank you, Miss McAllister." He started to rise.

"There's one more thing I'd like you to handle."

Louis Wright sat back down. He was beginning to admire this young woman. She knew exactly what she wanted and how to get it. He'd seen few young people — fewer females still — who were as self-assured as she. She sat before him proudly, confidently, as if she'd managed vast amounts of money for years.

"I want to found a hospital in Keyserville. In my father's name. I know it will be expensive, but I believe I can afford it. I'll add to it a little at a time as the money from the Golden Duchess comes in. Will you make contact with people who can get the job done?"

"Certainly." He watched her thoughtfully. "You're an amazing woman, Miss McAllister. I'm sorry to hear you'll be leaving. We were all hoping you'd make San Francisco your home." Before she glanced away, he saw tears shimmering in her golden eyes.

"I was hoping the same thing, Mr. Wright, but some things just aren't meant to be."

"I suppose that's so." He moved from behind the desk, took her hand in a brief gesture of farewell, and noticed a slight tremor in her touch. For the first time, he realized she was maintaining her control by force of will. She'd fooled him for a while. Now he wondered at her sudden decision to leave the city. He hoped there was nothing seriously wrong, but looking at her forlorn expression, he wasn't so certain.

"Thank you, Mr. Wright," she said, her voice stronger again, "for all your help."

"My pleasure, Miss McAllister." He wondered at her tremulous smile, then she walked through the open doorway and out into the hall. He watched the gentle sway of her hips as her graceful strides carried her from his view.

# Chapter 23

"Mr. Daniels surely won't like this, mum." Flora Thomas clucked and fussed as she helped Elaina finish packing.

"Mr. Daniels has nothing to say about where I go or when I go," Elaina told her.

The Thomases had turned out to be a pleasant middle-aged couple who obviously cared a great deal for each other, and there'd been no mishaps or intrusions since their arrival at the Palace. Elaina had started packing the evening before, and this morning, with Flora's help, was just about finished.

"Mr. Daniels was awful worried yesterday," Flora said. " 'E told 'Erbert not to take any chances. If those men came back, 'e was to shoot first and ask questions later. 'E gave 'Erbert strict instructions and a Colt forty-five, and my 'usband knows very well how to use it." A short, gray-haired woman who had once been blond, Flora spoke with a cockney accent that betrayed her English roots.

"How long have you worked for Mr. Daniels?" Elaina asked, placing a lacy chemise on top of the clothes in her steamer trunk.

"Long as 'e's been living in the city. Three, maybe four years. 'E's a fine man, Miss McAllister, and 'e surely does care for you, that's for certain. I never seen 'im act this way about a woman before, not even Miss Stanhope."

Elaina slammed the lid of the trunk down a little harder than necessary. "Well, he's marrying Miss Stanhope, so he d better get used to caring for her instead of me."

"Yes, mum."

Herbert Thomas strode into the room with a skinny, black-haired bellboy in tow. "We be ready whenever you are, miss. But Mr. Daniels is likely gonna skin me alive for lettin' you go without sayin' good-bye."

240

"I really don't have time to wait for Mr. Daniels," Elaina said. "You'll have to say good-bye for me." She tried to keep her tone light. "Now, if you two gentlemen will be so kind as to load these into a carriage, I'll be on my way."

"Oh, miss, I almost forgot to give you this." Herbert handed her a slip of paper. "Front desk said a man came in this morning and dropped it off."

She unfolded it carefully. Inside was a message from Isabelle Chesterfield: She was ill and needed Elaina to come immediately.

"Is it important, miss?" Herbert asked.

"Yes, I'm afraid it is. I may have to delay my departure a bit, but whatever happens, I'm leaving the hotel."

Herbert nodded and proceeded with the job of loading the trunks on the cart. He was a tall gray-haired man, narrowly built but not skinny, with eyes that rarely missed a move. Elaina went down ahead of the Thomases, paid her bill at the front desk, then followed them out to the rented carriage. When the bags were loaded, she turned to face the couple and suddenly felt the sting of tears.

"Thank you for all your help. You've both been very kind."

"We were only following Mr. Daniels's orders," Herbert told her.

"It's been a pleasure, mum," Flora said. "Is there anything you want us to tell Mr. Daniels for you?"

A lump swelled in Elaina's throat. Was there anything she wanted to tell Ren? Only that she loved him, would always love him. That she would miss him every day of her life, that every waking moment and lonely night would be an agony without him. That despite all that had happened between them, she hoped he'd be happy. Hot tears threatened.

"No," she whispered. "Good-bye."

She climbed into the carriage and gave the driver the directions to Isabelle Chesterfield's house on Maiden Lane. She should have gone to see the woman sooner, but she had been so busy that she'd simply sent a message declining the woman's hospitality and thanking her for the offer. She just hoped nothing was seriously wrong.

As the carriage rolled away, she sat with her back to the driver, watching the hotel fade into the distance, and glimpsed the window of her bedroom on the top floor — the room she and Ren so recently

241

shared. She tried to push images of the tall handsome man away, but they only became clearer. The tender look in his light blue eyes, the feel of his hands on her body. Finally her vision blurred, but she blinked back her tears. The window disappeared from sight, and the carriage merged with the noisy city traffic.

Something was wrong. Ren could feel it in his bones. Something had nagged him all night, something Elaina had said, or perhaps it was the way she'd said it. He checked his watch. He was supposed to pick up Melissa and Jacob for the Fourth of July picnic in half an hour, but they would have to wait. He'd send his driver over with a message after he stopped by the hotel.

The carriage rolled up in front of the Palace. "I'll just be a moment," he told his driver. He wanted to see Elaina and still this nagging suspicion he'd been fighting since dawn. With purposeful strides, he crossed the plush red carpet in the lobby, passed the front desk, and headed toward the stairs.

"Mr. Daniels?" came Timothy O'Banyon's cool, slightly arrogant voice.

Ren was surprised to see the thin-faced man. Timothy usually worked the night shift. Ren changed direction, returning to the front desk.

"Are you looking for Miss McAllister?" Timothy asked, his look slightly smug. Ren grimaced as he imagined the way Elaina would handle that look in the future, once he was married to Melissa and Elaina was his mistress. She'd hate those knowing glances, the snickers behind the hands. The thought tugged at his heart.

"Yes," he answered curtly. "Is she upstairs?"

"I'm afraid she's checked out, sir."

"Checked out!"

"Yes, sir. Less than an hour ago."

Ren swore beneath his breath. He should have known something like this would happen. He'd seen it on her face; he just hadn't wanted to believe it. "Do you know where she was heading?"

"No, sir, but she did get a message this morning."

Ren reached inside his light brown suit coat and removed his pocketbook. "Would you happen to remember what was on that message, Timothy?"

Timothy O'Banyon licked his lips. "We aren't supposed to give out that sort of information."

Ren pulled a bill from the brown leather wallet.

Timothy eyed the money greedily. "But I suppose in your case I could make an exception."

Ren pressed the bill into the thin man's palm.

"It was from someone named Isabelle Chesterfield. Said she was ill and needed Miss McAllister to come immediately to an address on Maiden Lane. I'm not sure which house number."

Ren knew the street. It was only a few blocks long. "Thanks. Oh, there's one more thing."

"Yes?"

"Could you send a man to the Stanhope residence on Jones Street to tell Jacob Stanhope to go on to the Fourth of July celebration without me? I'll meet him there later."

"I'll take care of it."

"You've been very helpful."

"My pleasure, Mr. Daniels," Timothy fawned. "Good luck."

Ren walked back through the high-ceilinged lobby and out the massive double doors. He climbed into his carriage, giving instructions to his driver to head for Maiden Lane. The clap of firecrackers, the roar of sirens, and the echo of gunfire could already be heard throughout the city, though it was still early in the day.

San Franciscans took their celebrating seriously. The streets were draped with red, white, and blue bunting, and the Stars and Stripes waved from houses and street corners. Every road was crowded with rowdy patriots, many of them already inebriated. Ren didn't like the look of things one bit.

Damn that woman! Why couldn't she ever do as she was told? It was dangerous for her to be out here alone. The detective he'd hired had turned up no trace of the men who'd entered her room, and until he did, Ren couldn't be certain Elaina wasn't still in danger.

He urged his driver to move faster. The matched sorrels stepped lively, but the crowded streets inhibited their progress. He hoped Elaina had found the streets as difficult to navigate as he did.

Elaina barely noticed the surging, raucous crowds surrounding the rented carriage. All she could think of was the way Ren had

243

looked that last night. The way he had held her, kissed her, the way he'd made love to her. He'd said he loved her, told her she meant everything to him. Maybe she did — or maybe it was just his conscience talking. Either way, he was out of her life for good this time.

A loud crack followed by a string of smaller popping noises spooked the horses and jerked her upright in the back of the open carriage.

"Sorry, ma'am," the driver was saying. "Everybody's celebrating already. Those were firecrackers. Nothing to worry about, but it's slow going."

Elaina nodded and sank back against the leather seat. The Fourth of July. In her haste to leave the hotel, she'd forgotten all about the celebrations today. Now that she remembered, her heart felt even heavier than before. Ren would be with Melissa and Jacob. The family all together, just as it should be.

Family. The word brought a lump to her throat. Would she ever marry? Have a family of her own? The thought nearly sickened her. Without Ren, the word "family" held no meaning. She pulled a lacy white kerchief from her reticule and blotted the tears from beneath her lashes.

A deafening crack nearly unseated her. At first she thought it was just more fireworks; then she saw the driver slump over on his perch. She screamed as the horses, their reins slack, reared and bolted. They had just crested a hill, so the downhill momentum sent the carriage careening forward. She tried to climb into the driver's seat, but the lurching motion of the carriage made it impossible. People lining the street screamed and darted out of the way of the runaway carriage. Then a man raced toward the frightened animals, a man whose face was all too familiar — the tall man who had entered her rooms at the Palace Hotel.

Clutching the seat for support, she screamed for help as the man grabbed the horses' reins. At first it looked as though the carriage was going to slow. Then suddenly the horses swerved to avoid a wagonload of celebrants. The wheels jackknifed, and she felt her world begin to spin. The seat tilted crazily, and the street rushed up to meet her. Her last thoughts were of Ren.

God, how she wished she'd said good-bye.

# *Chapter 24*

The room was blurred and fuzzy, the images indistinct. She felt nauseated, her head throbbed as if it might split apart, and her ribs hurt so fiercely she was forced to breathe in short, uneven gasps.

Her eyes finally began to focus on surroundings that looked strange, unfamiliar. She tried to sit up, but the agony in her side and a firm hand on her forehead pressed her back against the pillow. She heard water splash somewhere near the bed as a damp cloth was removed from her forehead, rinsed and wrung out, then replaced. She turned her head and her eyes locked on dark snug-fitting trousers, lean hips, and a narrow waist.

With a sharp intake of breath and the resulting jolt of pain, she looked up to see Ren standing over her, his blue eyes filled with concern that quickly changed to anger. The fury in the taut lines of his face made her want to cringe.

"Just what in the hell did you think you were doing?" Ren demanded. "Of all the idiotic, insane — You could have been killed out there! Why were you going to Maiden Lane? Did you plan to meet Chase Cameron there and live happily ever after? Didn't you think I deserved at least a good-bye?"

Tears filled her eyes, but she refused to let them fall. She wanted to unleash an angry retort in her own defense, but the pain in her ribs forced her to silence. How dare he act like the injured party when it was she who had suffered, she who hurt in every joint and muscle, she who would spend the rest of her life trying to forget the man who married Melissa Stanhope!

"If you didn't look so damned pitiful," he said, "I swear I'd thrash you myself."

"You have no . . . right to speak to me that way." She raised her head a little, and beads of perspiration popped out on her brow. A tiny whimper escaped her.

Ren was instantly beside her, his face tense, his angry expression gone. Worry lines creased his brow. "Don't," he ordered softly. "I shouldn't have said that." He pressed her gently back down into the soft feather mattress. "I was just so damned worried. . . ." With a steadying breath he looked away. When he spoke again his tone was even. "The doctor says you have a concussion and a few badly bruised ribs. He doesn't think anything's broken, thank God." She noticed the way one lock of his dark hair, a little unkempt, fell across his forehead. His hand trembled slightly where it rested on her shoulder.

"I didn't mean to get angry," he told her, his husky voice sounding tired. "It's just that I feel responsible for what happened. If I'd left you alone in the first place, it would never have come to this."

"It isn't your fault," she said softly. "I should have listened to you. I just wanted what was easiest for both of us."

"I know." He watched her with eyes that were shadowed and haunted, and she sensed the effort it was taking him to maintain his steady control. "You took quite a spill," he said a bit too lightly. "I was just around the corner. I didn't see what happened, only the mob of people surrounding the carriage. A constable was there when I arrived."

"How did you find me?"

"Let's just say I have friends in high places."

When she smiled, a sharp stab made it hard to breathe, and he captured her fingers in his fine dark hand.

"Take shallow breaths, pretty lady. If the pain becomes too great, I have some laudanum powder for you."

His temper fired again. "Damn it, Lainey, don't you know how worried I was? We could have talked things over, worked something out."

"No, Ren," she said. "I left because I can't live the way you want me to. I can't be your —"

He pressed a tanned finger to her lips to stop the hateful word. "I know." He looked so handsome, so troubled.

"I guess I've known that all along," he said. "I just didn't want

246

to believe it. I wanted us to be together no matter what."

He released a long, slow breath. "When you get well, I'll help you find someplace to go. Someplace far from San Francisco. A place where you can make a fresh start."

"I'm leaving, Ren, but I don't want your help. You once said I was only making it harder on both of us. Now I'm saying that to you. Please, Ren. Let me go."

"Not until I know you're safe."

She reached out to touch his cheek, then stopped herself and changed the subject. "They shot the driver. Is he dead?"

"No. Only wounded. He will recover fully. Did you get a look at anyone?"

"Yes. I recognized the tall man who broke into my room at the hotel. He was trying to stop the horses just before the carriage turned over. That's the last thing I remember."

"The police were on the scene almost immediately," Ren said. "The man had no time to carry out his plan."

"Then you really think those same two men were after me?"

"I'm sure of it. That's why I brought you here."

She glanced at her surroundings. The carved oak four-poster bed gave her a view of the bay while a fluffy blue satin comforter kept her warm. For the first time she noticed her clothes had been removed, replaced by a simple cotton nightshirt she recognized as one of her own.

"How . . . how did I get undressed?" she asked, fighting a rosy blush. "Where am I?"

"You're in my town house. As soon as you're well enough, I'll move you out to our ranch in the Napa Valley. As to how your clothes came off, I'll leave that to your vivid imagination, but you can be sure your precious pride is still intact. I may be a cad, but I prefer my women awake when I make love to them."

Elaina blushed hotter, but felt the tug of a smile. A sharp jab in her side reminded her of her injuries. She closed her eyes, calmed her breathing, and began to feel a little better.

A moment later she heard voices in the hall, and Tommy Daniels walked into the room, blue eyes a shade darker than Ren's betraying his concern. He knelt beside the bed. "How are you feeling, Lainey?"

"I've felt better, but I guess I'll live." She took his hand.

247

"Tommy, I don't think I should stay here. What are Jacob and Melissa going to say? And you have Carrie to consider."

"Don't be silly. Both Carrie and Melissa will understand. Carrie's downstairs right now. She's already volunteered to stay with you if need be, and I know Jacob would insist that you stay here. Whether you like it or not, you're part of the family."

*Family*. There it was again. Ren and Tommy were as close to family as she had, and yet her affair with Ren could only hurt them.

Three faces appeared in the doorway as she took a painful breath. Seeing Carrie, Jacob, and Melissa, she felt a terrible wave of guilt. Determined to put up a brave front, she smiled.

Jacob Stanhope moved to her bedside and lifted her hand with thick, gentle fingers. The tender gesture was almost more than she could bear.

"My dear girl, I do hope you're all right."

"I want her to stay here until I can move her out to the ranch," Ren explained.

"Quite right, my boy." He patted Elaina's hand. "You do just as Ren tells you. He always knows what's best. A little country air and you'll be fine." He straightened the white cravat above his dove gray suit.

"Papa's right," Melissa agreed, coming to stand near the bed. Her golden curls bobbed, and her delicate bow-shaped mouth parted in a soft smile. "Ren's ranch is beautiful. You'll love it out there."

"I'll come and stay with you," Carrie Salzburg announced, the skirts of her pink French bunting dress flouncing as she entered the room. "You'll need someone to keep you company."

Tears slipped down Elaina's cheeks. "You're all so thoughtful. I'm lucky you consider me a friend." She felt utterly miserable. Only the night before last Ren had been in her bed. Now here was his family, even the woman he would marry in less than two weeks, being kind and considerate to her. Elaina wanted to die. This was like a nightmare from which she couldn't awaken.

Attempting a smile, she bit her trembling lip. "If you all wouldn't mind," she said, her voice barely audible, "I'm afraid my side is hurting me quite a bit."

"Of course, my dear," Jacob said.

"Is there anything you need?" Melissa asked. Sunlight glinted

248

on her golden curls as her tiny form hovered beside the bed.

Elaina could barely shake her head.

"You'll feel better in the morning," Tommy assured her. He and Carrie left the room.

"I'll be right down," Ren said to Jacob and Melissa, impatient for all of them to leave. He glanced at Elaina, who looked wan and pale. Her thick dark hair fanned out on the pillow, framing her oval face. A darkening bruise marred her cheek and her lip was swollen, but to him she looked beautiful — and he'd never felt so rotten in his life. How could he have let things get so messed up? And how could he ever have believed Elaina could be happy as his mistress? She was too sensitive, too caring, too easily hurt by other people. He had seen the anguish in her eyes when she spoke to Melissa. Now she lay on the bed with her face against the pillow, staring blankly ahead. Tears glistened on her cheeks. Ren knew they were from the ache in her heart rather than the pain in her ribs.

He knelt beside her, pressing her hand against his cheek then kissing her cold, stiff fingers. "Don't, Elaina, please. I can't stand to see you like this."

She turned to face him. "I can't stay here, Ren. I just can't."

"The doctor says you need at least a week of rest, and we still have those men to worry about. Someone's got to protect you."

"I just want to go away. Please, Ren, please let me go." Her soft words and anguished look tore at his heart.

"Get some rest, Elaina," he said softly. "You'll feel better in the morning." He moved to the doorway wondering if he would ever feel better as long as he lived.

At the corner booth in the Cold Day Grill Chuck Dawson sat with Bill Sharp and Andy Johnson.

"I can't believe she slipped away again!" Chuck raged. Sharp sliced through a thick rare steak, and Chuck turned up his nose in disgust at the bloody beef.

"Wasn't much we could do with that constable so close," Sharp said, talking as he chewed. "Damnable bad luck if you ask me."

"I'll say," Andy Johnson broke in. He took a small bite of his fried fish. "And who'd have figured on the carriage turning over?"

"Well, we're running out of time," Dawson said. "We damn well better not botch things up again. We're lucky we didn't kill her. Then we'd really be up a creek."

"At least we know where she is," Andy added. "We'll do some checking on that Morgan fella, keep an eye on the house. As soon as we get the chance, we'll grab her."

Dawson wiped his mouth with a linen napkin, then took a drink of his dark ale. The restaurant was fairly quiet. Most of the regular patrons were at home recovering from yesterday's celebrations. He could even hear the sizzle of the grill when the waiters weren't barking orders. The place smelled of hearty food and was slightly humid from the open, steamy kitchen.

"We'll be ready for her next time," Chuck said. "Ready for Morgan, too, if that's what it takes. Andy, you best eat up and get back over to that house of Morgan's. From now on, we take shifts. We keep an eye on the girl twenty-four hours a day. As soon as I think the time is right, we move in."

Bill Sharp took another bite of bloody steak. "And I move in on Morgan."

As soon as Elaina could get around without too much discomfort, Ren insisted she be taken to the ranch. Carrie and Tommy would accompany her, along with the Thomases, who would act as chaperons. Ren told her he had business in the city, but she knew he was just staying away as a concession to her wishes.

The ranch was everything Melissa had said. The Napa Valley was a lovely hilly basin filled with fertile soil and vineyards heavy with grapes. Some of the fruit had just turned a rosy red. Tommy told her soon the grapes would darken to the rich wine color she expected.

The ranch house was a sprawling one-story redwood affair with wide porches off the front and back. There were hundreds of acres out behind the house, and Tommy was building a home for Carrie and himself in the northwest corner of the property near a grove of live oak trees. Ren and Melissa would settle in the main ranch house.

Elaina had immediately come to love the gracious old home, and she was filled with new despair at the thought of Ren and Melissa sharing it. She wished her concussion would heal so she could leave

Napa, leave San Francisco, and most of all, leave the memories of Ren Daniels behind once and for all.

A knock at the huge rough-hewn front door interrupted her reverie as she lay curled up on the wide leather settee in the parlor in front of a fireplace large enough for a man to stand in. She wished she could see it in winter, with a huge fire blazing, warming the bear rug that covered a portion of the pegged oak floor.

"I'll get it," Carrie told her, and she relaxed against her pillow.

She was propped up reading the morning paper when Chase Cameron strolled lazily into the room. She took in his handsome face, curly blond hair, and lazy smile in an instant. Straightening a little, she self-consciously pulled her robe together.

"Chase, it's good to see you. Carrie, you remember Chase, don't you?"

"Of course I do. It's nice to see you again, Mr Cameron." She smiled. "If you two don't mind, I think I'll go out and find Tommy. That'll give you some time to talk."

Elaina wished the girl wouldn't leave. Images of Chase Cameron's advances, of the way she'd allowed him to touch her, threatened to overwhelm her.

"How are you feeling?" he asked.

"Much better now, thank you. The doctor says I should be up and about in a couple more days."

"I read about your accident in the papers. I wish you'd sent word."

"I — I guess with all the excitement it just slipped my mind."

"You've never been much of a liar, Elaina. There's no reason for you to start now. You've been avoiding me."

She started to deny it, then changed her mind. "I made a fool of myself, Chase. After that I didn't know quite what to say."

"May I?" He indicated the place on the settee beside her.

"Of course."

"You know, Elaina, I remember the first time we met. You had on that dirty gray traveling suit, and I asked you to show me your legs."

She laughed aloud. "I remember."

"You really haven't changed much since then. At least not where your values are concerned."

251

She glanced away. "The other night I showed you a lot more than my legs."

He took her hand, cradling it in between his wide palms. "You were hurt and confused — and desperately in love. Daniels is a fool. He's willing to throw away your happiness as well as his own in order to fill some misguided need for social position and respectability."

"It's more than that, Chase. He feels he owes Jacob Stanhope a debt. He's given Jacob his word; now he'll abide by it no matter what the cost. I understand that, probably better than anyone in the world."

His hazel eyes urged her to continue.

"You see, that's the reason I set out for San Francisco in the first place. I was running away from a debt I owed. The only difference between Ren and me is that I've learned something he hasn't: Our own happiness has to come first. It's the only hope we have of making anyone else happy. So you see, Chase, I have changed. I love Ren, but I can't make him happy unless I'm happy with myself. And I could never be happy as his mistress. That's why I have to leave San Francisco — and the sooner the better."

"If I loved a woman the way he loves you, I'd tell them all to go hang."

"What makes you think he loves me at all?"

"Are you kidding? The man reads like an open book. You'd have to be a fool not to notice the way he watches you. He loves you all right. There's no doubt about that."

Looking at Chase, Elaina suddenly remembered all the times he had comforted her, all the times he'd helped. She felt guilty for not trusting him as she should have. Impulsively she hugged him, and he wrapped his arms around her, being careful of her ribs. "I've thought of you often," she told him honestly. "I'm glad you came."

He held her a moment more. "So am I." Releasing her, he straightened and stood up. "If you ever need a friend — or a job," he teased, "you know how to find me."

As always he made her smile. "Good-bye, Elaina."

"Good-bye, Chase." She watched his tall frame move through the open doorway. Then the massive door slid solidly shut behind him.

He was a good friend, Chase Cameron. And she'd never be ashamed to call him that again.

A few days later Elaina was sitting by the window reading when a loud rap at the door interrupted her. She rose a bit stiffly and opened the door.

Jacob Stanhope stood tall and impressive, filling the massive doorway. A navy coat above light gray trousers outlined his broad shoulders and enhanced the silver in his hair.

"May I come in?"

"Certainly. It's good of you to have come, Jacob."

He took a seat across from her and smiled warmly. "How are you feeling, my dear?"

"Much better, thank you. The doctor says I can go outside tomorrow. I'm itching to get some sunshine and take a look around."

"How do you like the valley so far?"

"It's lovely. One of the prettiest spots I've ever seen. And the house is so inviting it seems almost friendly. Even as big as it is, it doesn't feel empty." She glanced from the massive hand-hewn beams, to the heavy oak furniture to the Navajo blanket slung over the back of the settee. "The place seems so much like Ren. It suits him perfectly."

"You think so, do you?"

"Why, yes," she said a little too softly, hoping she hadn't revealed too much about their relationship.

"How do you think my daughter will suit him?" he asked unexpectedly.

"Melissa's a wonderful girl," she answered, avoiding the question. "Any man would be proud to have her for a wife."

Jacob eyed her solemnly. "Ren's worked hard to get where he is today."

"Yes."

"Marrying my daughter will put him in his rightful place in society. Give him the power and respectability he has earned."

She lifted her chin, wondering just what Jacob was getting at. How much had he guessed about their relationship? Was he angry with her? Angry with Ren?

"If that's what will make him happy, then I'm glad for him."

253

"But you don't think it *will* make him happy."

"I didn't say that."

Jacob smiled and patted her hand. "No, you didn't. And you didn't say whether marrying my daughter would make him happy, either."

She glanced away, unwilling to hold his probing gaze. He was after something, but she wasn't certain what it was.

"So you like the valley," he said, changing the subject and glancing out the window.

"It's lovely. The soil looks so fertile; I imagine just about anything would grow here."

"Do you enjoy growing things?"

"Yes. I had a vegetable garden back in Pennsylvania. I also grew herbs. My grandmother taught me to doctor some." She smiled. "I'm pretty good at it, too."

"You're the girl who took care of Ren after he was shot." It was a flat statement, one she didn't bother to deny.

"Yes. I didn't think he'd told anyone about that."

"He didn't. Tommy mentioned something about it, and I just put two and two together."

"I'll bet you're good at that, Jacob," she parried.

"Very good at it, my dear." He seemed to eye her curiously. "What are your plans for the future? Will you be staying in San Francisco?"

"No. I'll be leaving just as soon as I'm well enough. I would already be gone if it weren't for the accident."

"Oh, really?" He seemed surprised. "I'm sorry to hear that. I was hoping . . . I don't mean to be indelicate, my dear, but I hoped maybe you and Ren might continue your . . . friendship."

She stiffened her spine. "And just what friendship is that?" There it was, that knowing look again.

He watched her closely, then sighed and leaned back in his chair. "You'll have to pardon an old fool, my dear. You see, I was raised to believe a man owed his wife very little loyalty. It was all right for him to make a life for himself in any manner he saw fit." He tugged at his collar nervously.

"What I'm trying to say is that I want Ren to be happy. I thought maybe he could find that happiness with you, even after he was married. I was wrong. I meant no insult. Please forgive me."

"And what about Melissa? Doesn't her happiness count?"

"But of course, my dear. With Ren she'll be cared for. He'll see that she's pampered. And he'll spoil her just as I do. He'll provide her with children and be a good father."

"Yes," she whispered, "I suppose he will." And how could Melissa not love him? she wondered. She could picture the tenderness in his eyes, remember the feel of his body, the touch of his lips. Her hand trembled slightly against the folds of her skirt.

Jacob rose and straightened his navy blue coat, then shook out the legs of his trousers. "Warm today. Too warm for me. I'll stick with the cool ocean breezes in the city. Ren can have his valley."

"Ren and Melissa," she couldn't resist adding.

"Yes. Ren and Melissa." He moved to the door, and she accompanied him slowly, still a little sore.

"You're a good girl, Elaina. The man who marries you will be fortunate indeed."

She smiled. The compliment meant a lot to her, though she couldn't fathom why. Jacob Stanhope was causing her endless misery, yet she couldn't fault him. In his own way, he wanted what he believed was best for his family. Maybe that was what he was trying to tell her.

"Take care of yourself, my dear."

"I will, Jacob. Thank you for coming."

He touched her cheek and closed the door firmly behind him.

# Chapter 25

Puffy clouds, hinting at a summer shower, gave relief from the heat. Tommy was working in the barn. Carrie had returned to her home not far away.

Elaina pulled on a bright lavender batiste dress, soft and simple, a little reminiscent of those she used to wear in Keyserville. Though her wardrobe now comprised every article of feminine apparel a woman could want, it felt good to be free of her corset and wearing something simple again.

For the fourth time this week, she paused in front of the door to the room she knew was Ren's. This time her curiosity wouldn't be denied. Lifting the heavy iron latch, she shoved the door open and peeked inside.

A huge canopied four-poster bed, Spanish in design and covered with a bright quilt, dominated the room. Wide windows overlooked the vineyards, and a cone-shaped fireplace stood ready to warm the corner. Leather-bound books lined one wall, and a massive oak armoire stood partly open to reveal a bounty of expensive clothing.

Elaina eased the wardrobe door farther open. Chambray shirts and denim breeches, a long oilskin raincoat, and several straw hats — a workingman's clothes. This was a side of Ren she hadn't seen. As she moved about the room, a ray of sunlight flashed in her eyes and pulled her gaze to a peg beside the fireplace. The wide-brimmed black felt hat with its stunning silver concha hung atop the leather gun belt draped across the peg. The staghorn-handled Colt .45 Ren had been wearing that first day in Keyserville threatened ominously from its holster.

Memories of their first meeting, the days in the country, the circus, the gentleness he'd shown when he'd found her in the potting shed, all rushed up to swamp her. She picked up the hat; it felt warm and prickly against her hand. The concha shone as brightly as her life had shone whenever she'd been with Ren. She took a last glance around the room. What would it have been like to share the big bed with the tall man who slept there? What would it have been like to live as Ren's wife?

Almost unwilling to give the hat up, she finally replaced it on the peg, left the room, and headed toward the back of the house, determined to turn her thoughts in another direction.

Descending the short flight of stairs from the porch to the grounds behind the house, she saw a cluster of dark-skinned men laboring among the rows of grapevines off to her right. A horse-drawn cart followed them, carrying tools and a crock of drinking water. Elaina wandered toward the corrals behind the barn, her attention drawn by a sleek-necked dapple gray stallion unlike any horse she had ever seen.

She rounded the corner of the barn and collided with a brown-skinned, sweat-covered man whose broad-brimmed straw hat covered most of his face. He carried a shovel and was bare to the waist.

"Excuse me, I was just —" Elaina stopped, staring speechless as the man's brown hand shoved the hat back to reveal the lightest blue eyes she had ever seen.

Ren Daniels grinned broadly. "I see you're feeling better." His eyes, sparkling with devilment and what might have been appreciation, scanned her from head to foot.

"I thought you were in the city," she said, wishing she could force herself to look away.

"I said I had some work to do in the city. I did. But I also told you I wanted you protected. I've been here all week. Out in the bunkhouse. I hadn't planned on letting you know I was here . . . but I can't say I'm sorry you found me out."

Elaina fought to calm her turbulent emotions. She hadn't wanted to see him, but now that she had, she wasn't about to deny herself the pleasure of his company — even though the sight of his half-naked body set her blood on fire.

"What do you think of the ranch so far?" He propped the shovel against the barn, pulled a red plaid kerchief from the pocket of his breeches, and mopped his perspiring brow.

She tried not to notice the way the muscles of his arms and

shoulders rippled as he moved. His skin had darkened even more from his week of working in the sun, and the bronze color of his face made his blue eyes seem even lighter.

"It's lovely, Ren. I've been wanting to take a better look all week, but this is the first day the doctor would let me go out. I was headed toward that beautiful horse in the corral. I've never seen an animal like him."

"That's Sultan," he told her as they walked toward the horse. The animal snorted and blew when they approached, and pranced majestically. "He's a full-blooded Arabian stallion."

"He's exquisite. Such a fine head and almost dainty feet."

"Don't let that fool you. The Arabian is actually one of the hardiest of breeds. His endurance over tough terrain is remarkable, and his stamina's unmatched. I had him brought here by ship. I've got a mare due to arrive next month. I want to start breeding. Sultan will be the sire of a long line of Arabians."

"He's beautiful, Ren."

He watched her as if he wanted to say something, then glanced away. When he turned back, he smiled warmly, but she could sense his control. It matched her own perfectly.

"I'll give you the Cook's tour," he said, "if you can wait long enough for me to clean up a little."

She wanted to tell him he needn't bother, that she loved every sweat-covered inch of him, but instead she just nodded, and he headed toward the bunkhouse.

For a while she leaned against the corral, watching Sultan; then she wandered toward the huge vegetable garden that ran along one side of the barn. The corn was high, and several varieties of squash hung beneath dark, fuzzy leaves on thick vines running along the ground. Hearing the crunch of booted feet against the hard-packed earth, she turned to see Ren walking toward her. He had washed his face, and his black hair, now damp, curled just above his collar.

"You always did look beautiful in lavender," he said softly as he reached her side. His expression spoke of the past, and she glanced away.

"Come on." He grabbed her hand and tugged her along after him, then stopped short. "Are you sure you're all right?"

"I feel fine. Really I do." She started to add "Good enough to leave the ranch," but she didn't want to spoil the mood. "Besides, the doctor said I was supposed to get some exercise."

He grinned again, and his straight white teeth flashed in his tanned face. "Then exercise is what you'll get." For a moment his gaze looked hungry; then his control returned. "We'll walk up under the oaks. From there you can see clear across the valley."

It was obvious he loved the ranch, and it pleased her to discover this new side of him. She only wished she could be with him to share his plans and dreams.

By the time they neared the stand of oaks, Ren could see Elaina was tiring. He paused for a moment to let her catch her breath. "I shouldn't have let you come this far."

"I'm fine. Besides, I want to see the view. It's just a little farther." Her ruby lips turned pouty, just the way he liked them. "Please." The impish note in her voice made him smile.

"All right. I said we were going up to the oaks, and so we shall." Effortlessly he scooped her into his arms. She hooked an arm around his neck to balance herself, her face so close he could feel her warm breath on his cheek. She smelled clean and fresh, and he wanted to hold her forever. He felt a familiar tightening in his loins, the urge to take her, to bury himself within her and forget everything but the two of them.

On a patch of soft, dry grass, he set her down, then seated himself beside her. She didn't speak for a while, and he wondered if the contact had affected her as much as it had him.

"It was worth the walk," she said finally. "You should be proud of all you've accomplished."

"I am." He rested his hands on a large granite boulder, determined not to touch her again. If he did, he knew his careful control would shatter. He should have stayed out of sight, just kept an eye on the house as he'd planned. Now he was testing them both. Still, he couldn't say he was sorry. Just having her beside him seemed to fill some basic need.

She was eyeing him curiously. "You never told me how you got that scar."

Self-consciously, he rubbed the deep gouge along his neck. "Dan Morgan got this scar. In a knife fight down on the Brazos."

"Over a woman?" she asked with a slightly feline smile.

259

He faced her with a roguish smile of his own. "Pretty little Mexican *señorita,*" he teased. "Johnny Langton and I both had a claim on her. Johnny took his a little more seriously."

"So you fought for her?"

"Not exactly. Johnny decided to pay a surprise visit to the lady's room. Unfortunately, she had company."

"You."

"I was younger then. I had more stamina. Like the Arabian. He still needs a whole herd of mares to keep him happy." He glanced at the curve of her breast, watching the perfect mounds rise and fall with her breathing. "All I need now is one fiery little filly."

She laughed, picked up a stone, and tossed it at him playfully. It was the first time he'd heard her laugh in weeks. Maybe it was the resignation they were both feeling that allowed them these last moments of happiness together. Neither had spoken of the future, or of the wedding just two days away. Each seemed to be savoring these final hours, wanting nothing to spoil the treasured memory.

"Tell me about Dan Morgan," she said.

Ren glanced across the valley. Elaina watched his hard, lean profile, though much of his face was hidden by the straw hat he still wore. She admired the curve of his mouth, his high cheekbones and proud chin.

"Dan Morgan was never meant to live as long as he did," he told her. "I always intended to be Ren Daniels. I just wanted Morgan to make Ren's life a little easier."

"And did he?"

"For a while. Then the whole masquerade became a nightmare. Gunfighters started calling Morgan out for no reason, wanting to make a name for themselves by killing Black Dan."

"So you quit."

"After I saved enough money, I let Morgan disappear. That was a few years after I met Jacob. He hired me to help him with some dishonest dockworkers. By the time the job was finished, we'd become friends. He kept me on for a while, but I told him sooner or later Dan Morgan was through. I wanted to take the money I'd earned and make an honest living. Tommy was getting older, and I wanted him to have a decent life."

She watched him closely. He seemed desperate to make her

understand why he owed Jacob so much.

"Jacob understood," Ren said. "He told me he'd been in the same situation. When he first came to this country people treated him badly, called him a foreigner. He worked and scrimped for every dime. He started as a dockworker and ended up owning the company — as well as several others. Only after he became a wealthy man was he given the respect he deserved.

"For some reason, Jacob decided to help me. He introduced me to people who mattered, treated me like a son. With Jacob's connections, success came easy. He even put up his own money to back several of my ventures."

"So you believe Jacob is responsible for your success."

"To a large extent, yes. I can never truly repay his kindness. I can only do the one favor he asks."

"Marry his daughter."

"Yes."

She wondered if she'd imagined the catch in his voice. "I think we'd better be getting back," she said. "I'm feeling a little tired."

"Of course." He helped her up, and she noticed a tremor in his hand.

When they neared the porch, he stopped. "You know how much I wish things could be different."

"I know," she whispered.

He let go of her hand. "Tommy and I will be leaving first thing in the morning. He'll be back here on Sunday."

*After the wedding,* she thought. You'll be gone on your honeymoon, lying with your wife in some soft feather bed.

"He'll help you get wherever you've decided to go. It looks as though we've lost the men who were after you. I don't think you'll have to worry about them anymore."

"Thank you for everything you've done for me." She hoped her voice didn't sound as brittle to him as it did to her.

He swept off his hat, raked his hand through his thick dark hair, then turned the hat nervously in his hand. His pale gaze rested on the brim. When he looked up, his eyes betrayed raw emotion. "Done for you? What have I ever done for you except bring you misery?"

His words made her knees feel weak. She could see the battle he waged with himself, the tension in every line of his face.

"You'd have been better off if you'd never dug me out of that coal mine."

It was all she could do not to throw herself into his arms. He looked so beaten, so vulnerable. How could it seem he was the one who needed comforting? He who suffered more than she? She held her fingers to his lips. "Don't ever say that — not ever."

"I never thought I'd care for a woman the way I do you. I never thought I'd ever love." His voice sounded broken, ragged. "I didn't understand what two people could mean to each other. You mean everything to me, Elaina." His pale eyes searched her face. He caught her hand and kissed her palm. Staring at her as if waging some inner war, he groaned softly and pulled her into his arms. For a moment he held her against him, his arms surrounding her, clutching her against him; then he cupped her face and kissed her, sharing her pain, her heartbreak. Fighting back tears, she clung to him, helpless, while he buried his face in her hair.

Then they moved apart.

"Be happy, Lainey."

She nodded, knowing she'd had more happiness in their short time together than most people have in a lifetime. Maybe it had been selfish of her to hope for more. Feeling the weight of her loneliness, she straightened her shoulders, turned, and slowly climbed the stairs.

## Chapter 26

Saint Jude's church resounded with the hubbub of muffled voices, the swish of petticoats, and the footfalls of society's finest ladies and gentlemen thronging to fill its massive nave.

The huge organ piped softly as guests were escorted to their pews by young men in elegant black swallowtail coats and the stained-glass windows let in a kaleidoscope of colored light.

Tommy Daniels took a last glance around the church and closed the wide oak door to the suite of rooms to the right of the altar. Along with Ren and six close friends who would act as groomsmen, Tommy spent these last crucial minutes readying himself for the wedding ceremony.

Propping his foot on a bench to wipe the dust from his shiny black shoes, he watched his brother covertly. Ren seemed to have aged ten years in the past two weeks. Every line in his face was taut, there were new creases across his brow, and his eyes looked vacant. He moved around the room, checking his suit, helping the others finish dressing, and acting as though he were going to the opera instead of making a commitment that would alter the course of his life.

Ren was calm all right — too calm. His carefully controlled demeanor made Tommy feel slightly sick. Where was the happiness this day was supposed to bring? Where was the joy Tommy knew he would be feeling on his own wedding day three months from now? There was no joy in Ren because he felt no joy.

Ren should be marrying Elaina. It was obvious he was in love with her. And she was in love with him. She'd told Tommy and Carrie she wasn't feeling well enough to make the trip into the city for the wedding, and they had allowed her to keep up her pretense, but both of them had known the truth just from watching the way

Elaina would look at a photograph of Ren or touch something of his. That was the way Tommy felt about Carrie. He could scarcely keep his mind off her. That was the way Ren should be feeling about Melissa. But he didn't.

Tommy hadn't spoken to Ren about the marriage, at least not lately. He knew his brother too well. Once Ren made up his mind, there was no changing it. He felt he owed Jacob — and maybe he did — and he'd go through with the wedding no matter what the consequences to himself or to the woman he loved.

Tommy walked over to where his brother stood straightening his black bow tie. "Are you all right?"

"Why? Don't I look all right?"

"You look *too* all right. That's what worries me."

Ren smiled, but the smile never reached his eyes. "I'm fine, little brother. But thanks for your concern." Ren adjusted the cuffs of his crisp white shirt, then picked at a speck of lint on his tailcoat. He could hear the strains of the organ, even through the thick walls of the room. Pulling his watch from the pocket of his vest, he checked the time. "Won't be long now," he said.

"No. I suppose not," Tommy agreed.

"Did you remember the ring?"

Tommy pulled the velvet box from his pocket and flipped open the lid. A huge diamond cluster, appropriate to the status of the woman Ren was marrying, sparkled from its berth of navy satin.

Ren laid a hand on his brother's shoulder. "Looks like we're all set." He eyed the glittering jewels on the tiny platinum ring. If Elaina were joining him at the altar, he'd have chosen a plain gold band. He would shower her with diamonds — he'd love nothing more than to buy her everything she dreamed of — but the ring would be his way of pledging his love. It would be simple — and meaningful. He knew no matter what he gave her she would love it. She didn't care about pretensions. She never had. Even now that she was a woman of means, she seemed to prefer a simple existence. It was one of the things he loved about her.

*Love*. He had never expected to fall in love. Told himself love was for fools. Marriages were arrangements between families for the benefits each would receive. But he'd fallen in love with Elaina,

264

though he'd fought it from the start. Now he was paying and paying dearly.

He wondered what she was doing. How she was feeling. Was she crying softly as she had that day in Central City? Or being stoic, forcing herself to remain dry-eyed when her heart was breaking just as his was now? He wished he could see her, hold her one last time, but he knew he would never see her again. Couldn't chance seeing her, couldn't chance hurting her again. He would remember her smile and would imagine her laughing as she had that day beneath the oaks. He'd remember the sun lighting her hair with ruby hues that matched her lips. He would remember her golden gaze and the way her mouth always looked just a little pouty, as if she wanted his kiss and would settle for nothing less. He would remember everything. And make those memories last him a lifetime. Elaina McAllister was part of his past. Just as he had let Dan Morgan disappear, he would let her disappear. If only he could make her disappear from his heart.

He forced his mind in another direction. So far, he'd been able to control his thoughts of her. It was imperative he continue to do so.

Jacob Stanhope poked his head through the door. "All set in here?" He looked dashing in his own black suit. As always, he carried himself erect, but there was a slump to his shoulders that hadn't been there before. It strengthened Ren's resolve.

"We're ready whenever you are," he replied, trying to keep his tone light. He waited as Tommy threaded a delicate pink rose into his buttonhole.

Jacob watched him a moment more, a slightly odd look in his eye; then he closed the door. The organ music grew louder, indicating time for their entrance into the church.

"It's now or never," Tommy said, making an attempt at a smile.

Ren nodded solemnly. The men walked into the church in single file and waited to the right of the altar. The crowd quieted. The hush of anticipation strained Ren's nerves as all eyes looked toward the back of the church and the organ music swelled.

The bridesmaids began their slow procession down the long sloping aisle to the strains of the wedding march. They were gowned in delicate pink silk chiffon. Each carried a bouquet of pink roses entwined with lace and wore a broad-brimmed pink satin hat with roses at the base of the crown. Pink satin slippers peeped from beneath their gossamer dresses.

Ren stood calmly, his mind carefully blank. The music lulled him, enabled him to remain within his trancelike state. He watched the last bridesmaid walk down the aisle, followed by Elizabeth Pickman, Melissa's maid of honor. Elizabeth's gown was a darker shade of pink, her bouquet larger and studded with darker pink roses. She wore a smile, but hers seemed a little less genuine than the rest. Ren wondered if it was because she sensed the truth about Melissa's marriage.

The organ increased its volume until loud strains of the wedding march echoed off the walls of the church. It was time for the appearance of the bride. Melissa stepped into the doorway on her father's arm, wearing a high-necked gown made of yards and yards of snowy white lace. The delicate cloth billowed out from her tiny waist, the skirt so full it brushed the pews on both sides of the aisle as she walked. Above the bodice and down each sleeve, only the lace covered her fragile, translucent skin. Her blond hair, gathered in dainty ringlets beside her ears, glistened in the candlelight.

She looks like a china doll, Ren thought. She's beautiful. Sweet and delicate and beautiful. And any man would be happy to take her to wife. Any man except me.

Jacob moved beside her in the step-halt rhythm of the march. He looked every bit the proud father, walking tall and straight, his shoulders squared. When he reached the place before the altar where Ren stood, he gave Ren his daughter's hand, then backed away, taking his place in the pew.

Ren held her dainty fingers between his, wondering at the tiny size of Melissa's hand. It felt as cold as marble. Before turning toward the altar, he glanced at her face. The lace veil couldn't hide the bleakness in her eyes or the stiffness of the smile she kept carefully in place. Her blue eyes stared straight ahead, fixed on the minister who would sentence her to life imprisonment with a man she didn't love.

The minister began to speak in a strong, clear voice: "Dearly beloved. We are gathered together today, in the sight of God and in the presence of these witnesses, to join together Melissa and Reynold in the bonds of holy matrimony.

"Marriage is an honorable and holy estate, instituted by God and sanctioned by Christ's presence at the marriage in Cana of Galilee, and likened by Saint Paul to the mystical union which exists between Christ and his Church."

The minister droned on. Ren lost track of his words. He was trying to remember where he'd seen that tortured look before. Who had worn it? What meaning had it held? Suddenly it hit him like a blow to the stomach. It was the same look he'd seen in Elaina's eyes when she looked at Chuck Dawson. The look of a frightened doe.

"Marriage is therefore not to be entered upon lightly," the minister was saying, "or thoughtlessly, but reverently and fully, and in the eyes of God."

Ren could barely concentrate on the words. The terrible fear he'd seen in Melissa's eyes staggered him. The images in front of him blurred, and his palms felt clammy. If she looked like that here, surrounded by her family and friends, what expression would she wear tonight when he entered her bedchamber to consummate their marriage? How could he force his will on her? What gave him that right? What gave any man that right? The answer was suddenly clear to him: no one. Not him. Not Jacob. Only God had that right.

"Into this holy estate these two persons now desire to enter. Therefore if any man can show just cause why they may not lawfully be joined together, let him speak now or forever hold his peace."

The silence in the church echoed in his ears. He squared his shoulders. "I'm afraid I do," he said, his voice resonant. The minister looked stunned. The guests began to mutter softly among themselves.

"And I," came Jacob Stanhope's booming voice. He rose in his pew, standing tall, the flickering candles lighting the tears in his eyes.

"And I." Stewart Pickman rose from his seat by the aisle, gripping his hat in his hands.

Ren looked down at the tiny blond woman beside him. Tears glistened in her eyes and slipped down her cheeks. She smiled up

267

at him so gratefully he wanted to cry.

"Stewart?" he asked.

"Yes," she whispered.

"Why didn't you tell me?"

"Father loves you so much."

"I know." He kissed her cheek through the veil. Then he took a calming breath and fought to control the tremor in his voice. "He loves you, too."

She nodded.

Pandemonium reined among the crowd. There were loud whispers of shock and outrage. The organist began to play softly, trying to quiet the commotion.

"You stay here," Ren ordered Melissa. "I'll be right back." He moved with long strides up the aisle to where Stewart Pickman stood nervously but proudly.

"If I'm the cause of this," Stewart said, "I don't apologize. You may feel free to demand satisfaction."

Ren just grinned. "Do you love her?"

"Desperately."

"Then the only satisfaction I want is to see you two married. Follow me."

Solemnly Stewart followed him to the foot of the altar. When Ren reached Melissa's side, he lifted her hand and placed it in Stewart's. He could see the tension drain from Pickman's face, replaced by loving warmth as he looked into the eyes of the woman who would be his bride.

How close, Ren thought. How close they had all come to destroying each other's happiness. And for what? Some misplaced sense of loyalty. Thank God he'd finally come to his senses.

"Please be patient," Ren said to the minister. "You'll get to finish in just a moment." He moved up the opposite aisle to where Jacob Stanhope still stood, a wide smile now lighting his face.

"Forgive an old fool?" Jacob said.

"Stewart's a good man."

Jacob nodded. "Go to Elaina, son. She loves you. Tell her . . . tell her we'll all be proud to have her in the family."

Ren shook Jacob's hand, then leaned over and briefly embraced the man he owed so much.

"Thank you, Jacob. For everything."

"Thank you, my boy." Jacob moved toward the wide-eyed minister, intent on reassuring him and seeing his daughter happily married to the man she loved.

Ren waved over his shoulder and moved up the aisle. He could hear the minister intoning the ceremony again, this time with new names. His heart felt near to bursting with happiness. As he moved through the massive doors of the church and into the sunlight, he began to rehearse the words he would say to Elaina. They ranged from "Please forgive me" to a simple "Will you marry me?" It didn't really matter what he said. One way or another he was going to marry Elaina McAllister and never let her leave his side again.

# Chapter 27

Elaina McAllister buttoned the cuffs of her light gray traveling suit, then smoothed the narrow burgundy-trimmed skirt and adjusted the folds of material that fell in soft pleats at the back.

She'd chosen to wear something somber, something that matched her mood. She'd cried herself to sleep last night, though she promised herself a thousand times she was through shedding tears. She knew her face looked haggard and drawn, her hair lackluster. It didn't matter. All that mattered was leaving the ranch, leaving the valley, leaving her memories behind.

"You ready, mum?" Flora Thomas bustled up to her, her expression disapproving. She'd already voiced her opinion of Elaina's unscheduled departure.

"I'm ready. Does Herbert have the wagon loaded?"

" 'E's right out front."

Elaina nodded, pulled on clean white gloves, and moved toward the door.

"You sure you don't want to wait for Mr. Tommy? 'E'll be back tomorrow."

"It'll be easier on everyone this way."

"Mr. Simpson's gonna ride to the train station with ye. Mr. Daniels is paying him to keep an eye on you, and that's what 'e intends to do." They walked across the porch and down the front steps to the gravel roadway where the wagon waited. Simpson, a burly ex-guard Ren had hired to protect her until she left, sat in the back of the wagon, his revolver strapped to his thigh and a .44-40 resting across his lap.

"I don't expect any trouble, Miss McAllister, but you never can be too careful." The big man laid the rifle down and jumped from the wagon to help Elaina up. Herbert Thomas sat in the

270

driver's seat holding the horse's reins.

Elaina started to climb aboard, Simpson's hands at her waist, then stopped short. "Wait just a minute. I forgot my book. I'll be right back." Gathering up her skirts, she headed toward the porch, followed inside by a clucking Flora Thomas.

"I've a bad feeling about this, mum, a bad feeling."

The loud crack of rifle fire and the tingle of shattering glass sent her ducking to the floor.

"Get down, Flora!" she ordered as two more bullets whizzed through the air. The gray-haired housekeeper seemed hesitant until the next shot splintered the vase beside her. Hurling herself onto the thick bear rug, Flora began to say her prayers.

Elaina slid across the floor to the window and raised herself up enough to peek out. The guard lay sprawled, unmoving, beside the wagon. Herbert Thomas crouched beside the seat, unable to reach the rifle in the back. Elaina stayed low, her heart pounding wildly.

" 'Erbert," Flora sobbed. "They're going to kill my 'Erbert."

Elaina glanced back out the window. Two more shots knocked chips of wood from the wagon seat just above Herbert's head. If Elaina didn't do something soon, Flora's husband would be the next victim. Since they were obviously after her, not Herbert or Flora, Elaina couldn't let that happen.

"Hold your fire!" she called though the broken window. "If I'm the one you want, leave them alone."

"Put your hands up and come out on the porch. And bring the housekeeper with you."

So they knew about Flora. They must have been watching the house for some time.

"No, mum," Flora pleaded, raising herself from the rug. "They'll kill you if you go out there."

"I don't think so, Flora. They're after something. I'm not sure what. But whatever it is, I intend to give it to them." Elaina stood up and moved to the door. Flora wrung her hands but fell in behind her. Pushing open the heavy door, Elaina moved out on the porch.

"Hello, Elaina. You're looking well." Chuck Dawson's shrill voice was unmistakable.

"My God, Chuck. You're the one behind all this?"

"You know what they say about a jilted lover." He smiled

mirthlessly, his now slightly crooked nose giving his face a some-what distorted appearance. Walking up beside her, he pointed his revolver ominously. "Get back inside."

As Elaina backed through the doorway into the front room of the house, two other men, both waving guns, appeared from behind the hedge, one tall and well built, the other thin and pale. They ordered Herbert Thomas down from the wagon seat and hustled him and Flora into the house. Simpson lay on the ground in a widening pool of blood and Elaina feared he was dead.

"You two get over there away from the door," Chuck com-manded, pointing to Flora and Herbert as he crossed the room toward Elaina. "Tie 'em up, Andy." The shorter man did as he was told. The other gunman disappeared into the kitchen, and Elaina soon heard the sound of water being poured, followed by the clink of a spoon against crystal.

Elaina stood in the middle of the sitting room, wondering what Chuck could be after. "If it's money you want, Chuck, I've got more than enough. Let us go and I'll make you a rich man."

"Oh, you're going to make me rich, all right. Have no fear of that. But we'll do it my way, not yours. I'm running this show, and you'd better get used to the idea right now." He paused to look at her, his eyes brooding.

"Chuck, please —"

"Shut up!" He stepped toward her, his jaw set; then, controlling himself, he backed away. "You never were any good at taking orders, Elaina." He turned to his companion. "Bill, are you ready?"

The taller gunman returned from the kitchen and approached Elaina. He was carrying a small glass of cloudy liquid. "Drink this," he ordered.

"What do you think you're doing?" she demanded, her fear surfacing again.

"Just making you a little more comfortable for the trip, ma'am."

"You'd better be careful, Chuck. You're not dealing with the same naive little girl who left Keyserville. I'm a wealthy woman. People will be looking for me."

"Let 'em look, Duchess. You won't be hard to find. You'll be in Keyserville with me, just like we planned."

Elaina took a step toward the door.

"Don't even think about it," the tall man said, "unless you want your two friends to wind up in the same condition as that man outside."

Dawson grabbed her chin in a crushing grip. "I wouldn't advise you to make this any more difficult than need be. You've already cost me more trouble than you're worth."

Elaina fought back a shudder of fear. The one called Bill shoved the glass toward her, and she took it with trembling fingers.

"Drink all of it," the man with the low-slung revolver said. His bushy brows rose as he watched her drink.

She swallowed the last of the bitter contents — water mixed with something else — and handed the glass back to him. Almost immediately she began to feel dizzy and disoriented, then the room began to blur. Swaying slightly against the little man who had walked up beside her, she blinked and fought to remain standing, but her vision narrowed till the light was merely a speck. She clutched the short man's arm as a wave of blackness engulfed her.

"Put her in our buggy," Chuck Dawson directed, "and don't forget to load her trunks. She'll need something to wear." The two men picked up the unconscious woman and headed for the door. Chuck walked to where the housekeeper and her husband huddled on the floor, their wrists and ankles carefully bound, gags in their mouths.

"I want you to give a message to Morgan — or Daniels, or whatever his name is. Tell him Elaina's marrying the man she should have married in the first place. Tell him not to worry about her; she'll be well tended. I doubt he'll care anymore, anyway. By now he's married to the Stanhope girl. I'm just solving a little problem for him."

Roughly he nudged the housekeeper's foot. "You listening? Tell him if he's dumb enough to come after her, he'll be going up against Bill Sharp, not me. If he's smart, he'll stay away. This is none of his affair. It wasn't then — it isn't now." He looked at the man tied beside his wife. "You'd best remember that man out there was killed in a fair fight. He drew down on Sharp first."

The bound man nodded.

Dawson went out the door, moved down the porch steps, dragged the dead man's body into some bushes beside the house, and walked

273

to where the other two men waited with a rented buggy. If they hurried, they could make the one o'clock train east, back to Keyserville and the wedding that would make him a wealthy man. Chuck already saw himself sipping Napoleon brandy and smoking Havana cigars.

The hour and a half trip from the city had seemed like an eternity. Ren climbed down from the train and made his way across the platform toward the wagons for hire. Herbert Thomas usually picked him up and drove him to the ranch, but today there'd been no time to make arrangements; Ren was too eager to get to Elaina.

He couldn't wait to see her. Couldn't wait to hold her again. A hundred times he'd rehearsed his speech, but no two times had it come out the same. He would play it by ear when the time came. In the meantime, he'd fidgeted nervously all the way to the ranch.

Even before the wagon approached the long gravel drive, Ren knew something was wrong. He had a sixth sense about trouble that rarely failed him — and he clearly sensed trouble now. His heartbeat quickened as he neared the wagon waiting forlornly in front of the house. The horses snorted and blew and had pawed holes in the soft earth beneath their hooves. They'd been standing for some time.

"Pull up here," Ren instructed the driver while they were still some distance from the house. "Wait for me. But keep the wagon away from the house. There may be trouble."

The man at the reins nodded his understanding, waited till Ren climbed out of the wagon, then turned and headed toward a shady place beneath a distant oak. Ren approached the house cautiously. Everything looked quiet — too quiet. He flattened himself against the side of the house, then, crouching, moved quietly up the front porch steps to a place beneath the parlor window. One pane was shattered, another marred by a neat, circular bullet hole. His instincts had been right.

He raised himself up just enough to see inside. Herbert and Flora Thomas huddled together in one corner of the parlor, their wrists and ankles bound. Elaina was nowhere to be seen. His heart pounded harder.

Cautiously circling the house, he carefully looked through several windows. Finally convinced the men and Elaina were already gone, and sick at heart, he entered the house through the back door. He made a careful search of each room, grabbing his rifle on the way; then he entered the parlor. He knelt beside Herbert Thomas and loosened the gag.

"They got her, Mr. Daniels. Said to tell you Miss Elaina was going to marry the man she should have married in the first place."

"Dawson!" Ren removed Herbert's bonds, then let the older man untie the ropes that bound his wife. Herbert relayed Dawson's message, including the part about Bill Sharp; then the two men went outside to look for the guard.

They found Simpson's body hidden beneath a shrub.

"What're we gonna do, Mr. Daniels? Miss McAllister didn't want to go with those men. They made her drink something, then carried her away unconscious."

Ren clenched his teeth. "You take the team into town and fetch the sheriff. Tell him exactly what you told me. Nothing else. I'll take care of Miss McAllister."

Herbert suddenly looked at him. "Where's Miss Stanhope?"

"Probably getting ready to go on her honeymoon," Ren told him as they moved back up the stairs and into the house.

"Without you?"

Ren felt the tug of a smile. "With her new husband, Stewart Pickman. I, my friend, am going to fetch my future wife — Miss McAllister."

Herbert Thomas grinned so widely his cheeks dimpled. "Bravo, Mr. Daniels, bravo!"

Herbert left the house at a run as Ren moved into his bedroom. Removing his now dusty wedding clothes, he pulled a clean white shirt from his massive armoire and slipped on snug-fitting breeches. Shiny black boots came next. When he finished dressing, he moved toward the peg beside the fireplace. Settling his broad-brimmed hat across his brow, he pulled his .45 Colt from its holster, spinning the cylinder to check the load.

Cold, hard anger worked a muscle in his jaw. What would Dawson do to Elaina? Would he force himself on her as he'd tried to do before? If he had settled his score with the Dawsons and Dolph Redmond as he'd set out to do, none of this would have happened and Elaina would be safe here with him now. He cursed Chuck

Dawson and swore that if he so much as touched Elaina, he'd kill the man this time for sure.

He strapped on the Colt and tied the thong securely around his thigh, then pulled the revolver from its holster, feeling the familiar weight of the weapon in his hand. Though it had been weeks since he'd used the Colt, it slid into his palm with the same practiced ease as always. For the third time in his life he was breaking the promise he'd made to himself. No longer was he the entrepreneur and gentleman farmer, Ren Daniels. For the next few crucial days he was Dan Morgan — Black Dan.

Again the gun slid into his palm with lightning speed. If he had to draw against Sharp, he would be ready. He knew the man's reputation. Sharp was good. One of the best. Though Ren didn't relish the possibility, he knew he might be forced to find out just how good Bill Sharp really was.

Ren pulled his satchel from the armoire and began stuffing it with clothes. The train trip to Keyserville would take more than a week. Chances were Elaina would be safe for at least that long. According to Herbert and Flora, Dawson didn't have much of a head start. When the men arrived in Keyserville, Ren planned to be right behind them.

Elaina woke to a soft, lulling motion. Her mind was foggy. Images rushed by outside the window, but her mind couldn't seem to focus. She could hear men's voices beside her, but couldn't remember who the men were. How long had she been sleeping? Had her ribs begun to hurt? Had the doctor given her something to kill the pain? She felt as if she were floating above the ground. The seat beneath her seemed to sway and vibrate, but the rhythm only lulled her, made her want to sleep some more.

"Wake up!" A rough hand shook her. "Here. Eat this."

"I'm not hungry," she said, her words sounding slurred.

"I don't care if you're hungry or not, I said eat it."

She took the bread and meat, chewed, and forced herself to swallow. Then she took a sip of water from a cup someone held to her lips.

"Take her down the aisle," the voice commanded. "Wait for her to finish, then bring her back here."

"Okay, boss," a soft, high voice answered.

She felt someone lift her arm, and she meekly rose and followed the man to the front of the coach. She was on a train; she could see that now. Rows of seats, most of them empty, stretched out ahead of her on either side of the aisle. She made her way toward the front, assisted by the small man behind her, who deposited her behind a narrow door in a tiny washroom. She ran some water over her hands and splashed some on her face. She relieved herself, washed again, and opened the narrow door. The little man waited patiently outside. Wordlessly he helped her back to her seat. She rode silently for a while, trying to discern the passing landscape, realizing after a while that the man beside her was Chuck Dawson. Then she lapsed back into sleep.

It was a pattern repeated over and over again until she couldn't remember any other time or place. The only break in the daily routine came when she was given her medication. Chuck would bring her a cup of bitter liquid. She would drink it and then drift back into her pleasant, problem-free world.

She assumed Chuck was taking her home. Back to Keyserville. Why had she ever left? She couldn't quite remember. Something about a gunman. Morgan — that was his name. Funny. Whenever she thought of the gunman, she felt a moment's pain. It was the only thing she could really feel anymore. She wondered when she'd be able to stop taking her medicine. But Chuck would take care of that. He'd take care of everything just as soon as they were married. That's what he had told her. And the way he'd been seeing to her needs, why shouldn't she believe him? She hoped they would get home soon. She was tired. So tired. All she wanted to do was sleep.

"What seems to be the trouble?" Ren asked the conductor as the train slowed, the clank and grind of the brakes jarring him as he turned to look through the open window. The engine blew off steam, then came to a shuddering halt.

"Track's washed out up ahead," the conductor told him. The rotund man lifted his stiff black-billed cap and used his elbow to mop the perspiration from his brow. "We'll be delayed at least three or four hours. Might as well make yerself comfortable, though in this damnable heat I don't rightly see how."

Ren leaned back against his seat. They were somewhere near Salt Lake City. The terrain they were crossing was mostly flat wasteland, dry and arid, with temperatures well into the hundreds. The three-day journey so far had been an agony of worry for him. All he could think about was Elaina. Now Dawson would arrive in Keyserville at least a full day ahead of him.

Dawson was traveling on the Atlantic Express, the only train that had left within the men's possible departure times. Ren was riding a less expensive train, the Flyer, the first connecting train he could get after leaving the Napa station. This train carried no dining car, so stops were made along the route to feed the hungry passengers. That would give Dawson a decided edge. Ren just hoped whatever the man had planned, he wouldn't be too late to stop him.

Visions of Dawson with Elaina clouded his mind. He remembered the way Dawson had beaten her; he could still see the bruises the man had left near her eye, her bloodied and swollen lip. Damn him! Damn him to hell for the bastard he was. He hoped Dawson had learned his lesson the first time. If he hadn't, he was a dead man.

# Chapter 28

"You're looking a little peaked, Elaina. Maybe you'd better sit down." Dolph Redmond guided her into a chair in the small, book-lined study of Henry Dawson's mansion, once the McAllister family home.

Beulah Knudsen, Henry's housekeeper, had kindly assisted her in bathing and changing into something appropriate for the wedding. A light silk gown in her favorite shade of lavender.

"There are just these few matters to attend to," Dolph was saying, though his voice seemed indistinct. "Then we'll get on with the ceremony."

She nodded her understanding.

Waiting beside her chair, Chuck dipped a pen in the inkwell on his father's oak desk and handed it to her. "Just sign the papers right there." He pointed to a line that appeared to waver as she leaned forward.

She had trouble making her hand obey her commands. The room seemed a little fuzzy, the men's voices hollow. She guessed she was still a little groggy from the long train ride and her lingering illness. She scratched the pen across the paper as best she could, then handed the pen to Chuck.

"Good girl. Now let's go into the parlor. The minister's waiting."

She nodded, accepted Chuck's hand, and leaned against him for support as she moved into the other room.

Henry Dawson talked quietly with the Reverend Mr. Dickerson, then turned to Elaina. "Well, daughter," he said, "let's git this show on the road. You've kept my boy waiting too long already."

She smiled inanely and clutched Chuck's hand. The housekeeper and the two men who had helped bring her back to Keyserville stood by as witnesses, along with Henry and Dolph.

The minister began to intone the familiar marriage vows she'd heard since childhood, and an image of Dan Morgan flashed across her mind. Why should she be thinking of Morgan at a time like this? Chuck was the man she was marrying. She looked at Chuck's face, his sandy hair, the slightly crooked nose and dark eyes. She pictured blue eyes so light she could barely make out the color and black hair graying at the temples. Ren. Where was Ren?

"Say 'I do,' " Henry prodded.

"I do," she whispered.

The minister's voice droned on. She felt a wave of dizziness and leaned toward Chuck to steady herself.

"You may kiss your bride," the preacher said.

Chuck tilted her face up and captured her lips. She could barely feel his kiss. Her own lips felt cold and numb.

"Congratulations, daughter," Henry said.

"Maybe I'd better sit down a moment," she whispered. "I'm not feeling too well."

"Of course, my dear." Chuck helped her over to the settee.

She watched Henry and Dolph pour the minister a snifter of brandy. He smiled gratefully and sipped the amber liquid. She wasn't quite sure how much later it was that he and Dolph Redmond left.

"Well, son," Henry said, "you and yer new bride goin' upstairs fer a while?" He winked and grinned broadly.

Chuck just looked at him, his dark eyes unreadable. "She's been with Morgan. As far as I'm concerned, she's nothing but a whore. I just want this little charade over with as soon as possible."

Elaina's head throbbed. Her eyes buzzed and her stomach heaved. What had Chuck said about Morgan? What did Morgan have to do with their wedding?

"Chuck? What's happening?"

Chuck ignored her. "Mrs. Knudsen." He motioned the broad-shouldered, thickset woman over. "Take Elaina upstairs for her nap; Let her sleep as long as she likes. The trip was very tiring."

Beulah Knudsen just nodded. She guided Elaina toward the stairs.

Chuck Dawson watched his new wife leave the room and lifted a corner of his mouth in a satisfied smile. Everything had gone as planned. They'd had Elaina sign over her shares — and execute her last will and testament making him the beneficiary, just as a precaution, since he would be anyway.

"How long you gonna keep her on that stuff?" his father was asking.

"She only had a mild dose this morning. I didn't want the preacher getting suspicious. When she wakes up I'll give her another. We need to get people used to the idea of our marriage. Once they're convinced it's for real, Mrs. Dawson will have an unfortunate accident. Then I'm a free man again — and a whole lot richer."

"Damn shame. If the girl had just done what she was supposed to, none of this woulda happened."

"Yeah, well she didn't."

Henry Dawson sighed and shook his head. "Damned shame."

Ren Daniels stepped off the Lehigh Valley train and gratefully stretched his lanky frame. Nine long days since he'd left California. Nine days of cramped conditions, hot, airless weather, and the wearying, bone-jarring rumble of the train. And nine sleepless nights of worrying about Elaina.

Ren retied the thong that held the black leather holster to his thigh and eased the Colt into his hand. From force of habit, he checked the cylinder, then slid the revolver back in place. Lifting his broad-brimmed hat, he mopped his brow with the inside of his elbow and settled the hat back on his head. A quick check of his surroundings confirmed that Dawson and his men weren't expecting him.

According to the message Chuck had left with Herbert Thomas, Chuck had discovered that Dan Morgan was Ren Daniels, though Ren didn't think Dawson had made the connection to the youth Henry and Dolph had left to die in the coal mine. He had known that Daniels was to marry Melissa Stanhope. In fact, Chuck had planned Elaina's kidnapping to take place while Ren was at his wedding. Dawson was counting on the fact that Ren was marrying into one of the wealthiest families in California. He was convinced Ren would no longer be interested in Elaina — and that was where Chuck Dawson was wrong.

Ren tossed his satchel over his shoulder and headed toward the Hotel Keyserville. Ada Lowery was the first person he wanted to see.

"Why, Mr. Morgan," she greeted him warmly, extending a meaty, veined hand, "good to see you!"

"Hello, Ada." He accepted the hand, leaned over and kissed her plump cheek.

"What's wrong?" she asked, guessing there was trouble by the tone of his voice. "It's Elaina, isn't it? Lord a'mighty, what's happened to her now?"

"Dawson took her, Ada. I believe he's brought her back here. I was hoping you could tell me where." He plopped his satchel on the front desk.

"Chuck got in early this morning," Ada told him. "Hasn't been in town, but somebody seen him get off the dawn train. That's all I know."

"Where's he most likely to take her?"

"My guess'd be his father's house. The old McAllister mansion. There's plenty of room, and it's far enough outta town so's nobody'd be likely to stop by."

"Thanks, Ada. Watch my satchel for me?"

"I'll put it upstairs. Get a nice room ready for you. Let me know if there's anything I kin do."

Ren smiled, but his eyes looked grim. "I will." He pulled open the freshly varnished double mahogany doors of the hotel and headed into the street.

"Be careful," Ada called after him.

He nodded and headed toward the livery. He knew the old McAllister place well. It was out near the patch town, out near the mine. He would need a way to bring Elaina home if she was there, so he rented a buggy and headed in that direction, passing few people on the street and fewer still on the road out of town. A break for his side. He didn't need somebody recognizing him and, thinking he still worked for Dawson, taking another potshot at him. This time, if there was any shooting, he intended to be the man behind the gun.

Elaina sat still while Mrs. Knudsen brushed her hair. She was feeling a little better after her nap, a little more in charge of herself. Her mind was still hazy, but she was comfortable here in her room, though she liked her butterfly wallpaper better than the red magnolias that covered her walls now. She wondered why her mother hadn't let her choose, as she always had before.

The door opened, and she swung her gaze around just as Chuck entered, carrying a glass of water. Time for her medication. She was beginning to hate the bitter liquid, even though it did make her feel better — as if she hadn't a care in the world.

She rose as Chuck walked up to her.

"Here," he commanded, "drink this."

"I don't need it, Chuck, really I don't. I'm feeling much better."

He grabbed the back of her neck and forced the cup to her lips. The sudden movement threw her off balance. She swayed crazily, bumped into Chuck, and sent the glass crashing to the floor.

"Idiot! Now look what you've done." His navy blue suit was soaked down the front and shards of glass littered the floor of the bedroom.

"Don't worry, Mr. Dawson," Mrs. Knudsen said. "I'll clean it up." She left to fetch a broom.

"I'm sorry, Chuck. I didn't mean to stumble. It's just that I'm so dizzy all the time."

"Never mind. I'll get you another." Chuck walked to the door, but the sound of footsteps thudding rapidly up the stairs brought him up short. Panting from exertion, Andy Johnson cleared the landing at a dead run.

"Morgan's in town!"

"What! He can't be."

"Jimmy Stevens over at the station saw him get off the train. Jimmy got out here as fast as he could, just like you told him."

"Damn! Why in blazes would the man leave in the middle of his honeymoon and come all the way out here? Surely the blasted woman can't mean that much to him."

"I don't know, boss. Jimmy said he was wearing his hog leg. We'd better get Bill Sharp back out here right away. He's still in the patch town. Over at Jennings's Saloon. I'll go get him."

"Wait a minute. We'd better hide the girl first. We can't afford to let him find her in this condition." He paused for a moment. "Take her out to the mine. There's nobody around today. Take her into the main shaft, that old tunnel on the right. Go in just far enough so no one will see you. I'll send someone to get you after Sharp finishes Morgan off."

"You're taking me into the mine?" Elaina asked. "What for? I don't want to go to the mine, Chuck."

Chuck took a steadying breath, setting his mouth in a hard line. He wished she'd taken the laudanum — now there wasn't time to mix another dose. Clenching his fist, he punched her — one quick, sharp blow — and she crumpled to the floor.

"Grab that blanket." Andy did as he was ordered, and Chuck wrapped Elaina in the folds. "Take my buggy. It's sitting out front. Make sure no one sees you. And don't get impatient. We don't know when Morgan will show. Whenever it is, Sharp had better be ready."

Chuck carried Elaina down the stairs to the front door. Johnson loaded her onto the floor of the buggy. Then Chuck returned to the house to dismiss the housekeeper and find his father. He needed to warn Dolph and send for Sharp. He hoped the gunman was all he claimed to be. Chuck damn well knew *he* was no match for Morgan.

Ren skirted the patch town and headed straight for the mansion. The sooner he got to Dawson, the better his chances. When he spotted the chimney of the house just over the next rise, he halted the buggy. Tying the horse in the shade of a sycamore, he took a shortcut across the field. In minutes he reached the fence behind the Dawson house.

"It was quiet — too quiet. Moving closer, he climbed the stairs to the back porch, entered the mansion with as little noise as possible, and flattened himself against a kitchen wall. He could hear Chuck's shrill voice coming from the parlor, as well as the raspy, uncouth voice of his father.

Ren moved into the dining room, his gun drawn and held to his chest, ready for any sudden movement.

"Why don't you join us, Mr. Morgan?" Chuck said as if inviting him to tea. "That's what you're here for, isn't it?" He stood in the doorway, calmly indicating Morgan's welcome.

Aiming his gun at the center of Dawson's chest, Ren moved into the parlor. "Get over there" — he motioned toward Henry — "next to your father." Chuck complied.

"She's that important to you?"

"She's that important. Now, where is she?" Ren remained tense.

284

Sharp was here somewhere, but where? His glance kept straying to the stairway.

"I don't believe my wife's whereabouts are any of your concern, Mr. Morgan."

Ren took a step toward Dawson, his temper barely in check. "I swear, Dawson, if you've laid a finger on Elaina, I'll kill you with my bare hands."

"Steady, now, Morgan — or is it Daniels?"

"Daniels?" Henry spoke up for the first time. "His name's Daniels?"

"So I gather," Chuck said. "Mean something to you?"

"Not unless he's Ed Daniels's son. Now, that couldn't be, could it, boy?"

"One and the same," Ren told him, regaining some control. Henry's ruddy complexion paled noticeably. "I believe you and I have some unfinished business," Ren told him. "And I haven't forgotten Dolph Redmond." His mouth thinned to a grim line as the muscles of his face grew taut. "Now, where is Elaina?"

"As I said before, my wife's —"

In two long strides Ren reached Dawson and grabbed him by the lapels, hauling him to his feet. With grim purpose, he forced the gun barrel between Dawson's teeth, the long muzzle gagging him. Henry Dawson started to rise.

"I wouldn't do that if I were you," Ren warned. "Now, I'm tired of asking. Where is she?" When Dawson didn't answer Ren cocked the hammer, the ominous click sending beads of perspiration running down Chuck's brow.

"She's . . . she's . . ."

"Where is she?" Ren rammed the gun in farther.

"The mine," Chuck gagged out, the words barely discernible with the revolver down his throat.

Ren slid the barrel out from between Chuck's teeth. "Where in the mine?"

"Near the entrance. On A level. The old tunnel to the right."

"That's all I wanted to know." He let the hammer down easy, but kept the gun pointed at Chuck's heart. He opened Chuck's coat and removed the revolver that had been tucked in the top of his trousers, then did the same to Henry. After tossing the guns out an

285

open window, he holstered his weapon. A shadow in the doorway caught his attention.

"Hello, Morgan. I've been waiting for you." Bill Sharp stood poised on the threshold. Tall and well built, he stood confident and smiling. "I was hoping you'd show up sooner or later." He faced Ren with his feet spread wide and one hand just inches from the butt of his revolver, a Smith and Wesson Schofield .45.

Ren straightened. "You want it here?"

"No time like the present. I don't trust you, Morgan. You might be a back shooter. A man never knows."

Sharp's eyes hadn't moved from Ren's face. It was an old trick — watch your opponent's eyes, wait for the telltale blink — but it wouldn't work this time. Ren forced himself to relax. Here in the parlor he stood at a definite disadvantage. Sharp's back was to the sun, his eyes in shadow.

"Make your move, Sharp," Ren baited, hoping to force the gunman's hand.

Sharp remained cool. "Uh-uh. It's your move, Morgan. When I kill you, I want to know I gave you a chance to draw first."

Ren willed himself to be calm. Don't think of Lainey, he warned himself. Think only of the feel of the gun. Of your finger as it touches the trigger. Just like the old days — just like always.

In a split second blue metal gleamed in the sunlight. The roar of shots echoed wildly across the room, and the acrid smell of gun smoke filled the air. For a moment both men stood stock still, each eyeing the other as if the last few seconds weren't real. Then Bill Sharp crumpled to the floor, his blood running red on the thick Persian carpet.

"Chuck!" Henry Dawson's raspy voice sounded brittle.

Ren turned just in time to see Chuck Dawson slump to the rug, a growing red stain darkening his lapel.

Henry leaned over him, then knelt to cradle Chuck's head in his lap. "He's dead," Henry said, his voice thick with emotion. His eyes were filled with tears. "Sharp's bullet went wild. He killed Chuck instead of you."

Poetic justice, Ren thought as he slid his weapon back into his holster.

"I wish I could say I'm sorry." The words Chuck had spoken

burned in his mind like a white-hot poker: *my wife*. Ren didn't doubt Dawson's words, but if she was his wife, then she was his widow now. Ren just prayed he'd arrived in time to stop Dawson from consummating his vows — or worse. He wouldn't let his mind linger on the grim possibilities. He had to find her — and soon.

"How long have we been here?" Elaina kept her gaze focused on the kerosene lamp next to Andy Johnson's feet. The lamp gave off only a dim, wavering illumination, but it kept her demons at bay. She was sitting on a blanket on the floor of the mine, her back against a thick, rough timber. This seemed to he an older part of the mine. The timbers looked dry and half rotted. She shuddered to think of the miners working in such unsafe conditions.

"Couple of hours. Guess Chuck hit you pretty hard."

She tested the bruise on her jaw. She knew it must be swollen and purple. Chuck hadn't lost his touch. Her head throbbed unbearably, but at least her dizziness was finally gone and her mind crystal clear.

Andy Johnson kept his revolver aimed steadily in her direction, but even if he'd been unarmed, she wasn't sure she had the strength to run. She'd lost weight since she left California, and the laudanum — she figured that must have been what Chuck used — had left her weak and out of sorts.

She wondered if Ren knew she'd been kidnapped. Probably not. He'd gone away on his honeymoon. It was doubtful he'd left word where he could be found. Even if he did know, she wasn't sure he would come. He had a new set of responsibilities now. He was a married man.

For the first time in days, her mind felt something besides numbness. Wretched loneliness for Ren. Even her forced marriage to Chuck didn't distress her as much as the thought of Ren with Melissa.

"Why do we have to stay here?" she asked, wishing he'd let her go back to the house. "Why in God's name are we here at all?" So far she'd been able to keep her mind off her fears, been able to keep the walls from closing in. Having someone with her, knowing she could get out, and being able to see, even just a little, had kept her in control. God help her. If Chuck ever discovered her fear of dark,

287

confined places, he wouldn't even need the laudanum.

"Look, Mrs. Dawson, I just follow orders."

"Don't call me that!" she snapped.

Andy Johnson smiled for the first time. "You know, I think you and yer husband feel just about the same way toward each other. What you need is a good man."

She rolled her eyes at the repugnant thought.

Andy looked at her as if she were a morsel of dessert. "I've seen your breasts," he told her, and she felt the prickle of a new kind of fear.

"They're beautiful, all white and creamy. And so round. Just the kind a man loves to touch." He left his perch and moved toward her, still pointing the gun in her direction.

"You'd better get away from me," she warned. "I'm Chuck's wife, remember?"

"You just told me not to call you that. Besides, Chuck says you've been with Morgan. He thinks you're a whore, but I don't." He ran a slender hand through her thick mass of hair. "I think you're beautiful."

Elaina felt her stomach roll. She focused her eyes on the light as his fingers touched her cheek. Her weakened condition, her fear of dark places, and her revulsion for the thin little man combined to overwhelm her.

"Get away from me," she ordered.

"Bet you didn't say that to Morgan."

Elaina felt a pang at the sound of Morgan's name. Dan Morgan the gunman. Ren Daniels, San Francisco gentleman. She loved both sides of the man, always would. She felt Andy's fingers tighten around the back of her neck, felt his too-moist lips suddenly thrust against hers. Struggling to free herself, she pounded her fists against his chest. He laid the revolver aside as he pushed her down on the blanket and rolled on top of her.

Groping for the gun, her fingers clawed the earth, but the weapon was too far away. She had to stay calm. She relaxed a little, letting his hand slide up her leg, his probing tongue invade her mouth. Then she bit down as hard as she could.

Andy screamed and rolled off her. When she sat up, he glared at her murderously. "You could have just said you didn't want to."

"I didn't think you'd believe me." Determinedly she climbed to her feet. She could feel her strength already beginning to wane, but she didn't dare risk letting him get close again. Watching him warily, she waited for just the right moment.

"That wasn't very nice of you," he said, wiping blood from his tongue with the back of his hand. "I thought you were a nice girl." His eyes searched the tunnel floor for the gun. "Maybe Chuck was right about you, Duchess." He spotted the revolver and leaned over to pick it up just as Elaina charged into him, hurling their two bodies into the dirt. They landed with a resounding thump against the rotting timber, Elaina's ribs hurting unbearably, the snap of the dry wood echoing off the walls of the tunnel.

Andy Johnson grabbed for the gun, but she knocked it from his hand. When it hit the ground, the gun went off with a thunderous bang.

Elaina swallowed hard. She knew the next sound. Her mind would never forget it. A slow, deep rumble that echoed and grew.

"The mine's caving in! We have to get out of here! Which way do we go?"

Andy Johnson ignored her, the terror on his face even more distorted by the dim light of the kerosene lamp as he picked it up and ran toward the entrance of the mine. Elaina grabbed up her skirts and ran along behind him, dodging falling rocks and grinding timbers.

"Hurry!" They rounded a bend in the tunnel, and Elaina glimpsed sunlight. They just might make it. Then she heard Andy's frightened scream, saw a wall of dirt and debris fall from the ceiling to cover his body, and hurled to the ground atop the trembling earth. Covering her head with her arms to ward off the rocks and debris that fell like hailstones from the roof of the tunnel, she forced herself to breathe the stifling, dust-filled air.

For a moment she lay unmoving, trying to blot out the grisly image of Andy's thin body being crushed under tons of debris. Then she forced herself to sit up.

Blackness. Nothing but terrifying, mind-twisting blackness, so dark she couldn't even make out her own hand. She shuddered, a tremor running the length of her. Her heart pounded and her chest constricted against the suffocating, dirt-filled air. How much time did she have before she ran out of oxygen? Could she last till they found her? Would they even bother looking? Maybe this was what Chuck had planned all along. She grasped the wall of the tunnel, feeling the crumbling dampness, laboring just to stay upright on the tunnel floor.

She could feel it coming — the heart-stopping, mind-numbing fear. Soon she would be paralyzed, frozen with her terror of the darkness, the mine rats, the decay. the stench of death — only this time her nightmare was real.

# Chapter 29

With awful, gut-wrenching clarity, Ren recognized the mounting rumble coming from the mine. He raced toward the entrance, praying Elaina would come running out of the mine ahead of the wall of debris, but he knew it was already too late.

By the time he reached the main tunnel, it was completely sealed off, and Ren knew a despair greater than anything he'd ever dreamed. He stifled the cry in his throat. Too late! How could he be too late? It was impossible. Unthinkable. It couldn't be happening to them again!

He forced himself under control, forced his mind to think clearly. He knew she was in there. Chuck had said so, and even if he hadn't, Ren could feel it in his bones. Either Dawson had planned the cave-in or someone had accidentally done something to set it off. Whatever the cause, it would take a mammoth effort to open the mine. He had to get help.

A few long strides carried him to the emergency bell. He tugged the dangling cord, and loud clangs issued from the bell's wide mouth. The eerie sound, which signaled death and destruction, sent shivers down his spine. The bell could be heard all the way to the patch town. There it would be echoed by another similar bell outside the general store so that every miner for miles around would be alerted to the cave-in.

In minutes men began to arrive at Blue Mountain. Each took one look at the still dust-smoking rubble and knew what had happened. Some of the men looked at him distrustfully, but he held his ground. He waited until twenty miners, milling and muttering among themselves, surrounded him; then he climbed atop a coal car and asked for their attention.

"I want to thank you for coming. As you can see, there's been an accident." He could hear the slight quaver in his voice and willed himself to subdue it.

"What are you doing here, Morgan?" a burly miner wanted to know.

"Yeah! Why should we help you? Who's trapped in there anyways? None of us was working today."

Ren fought down his anger, fought to keep his control. Every second was important, every minute could mean the difference between life and death. But without the miners' help, seconds wouldn't matter.

"First of all, my name's not Morgan. It's Daniels. Reynold Daniels. My father was Ed Daniels. Some of you may remember him — or me." Ren pulled off his hat, hoping someone would recognize him.

"I remember Ed." It was Josh Colson. "But Ren was killed. He and his brother been gone nine years."

"Take a good look at me, Josh. Elaina McAllister dug Tommy and me out of that mine nine years ago. Now she's buried in there. She needs our help."

"Are you tellin' me our duchess is in there?" a German miner wanted to know.

Ren knew everyone in Carbon County would have read about the duchess, but he was surprised at the pride in the miner's voice as he laid claim to her for the others.

"What the hell would she be doing in there?" someone asked.

"Chuck Dawson put her in there," Ren said. "It's a long story. Right now the most important thing is to get her out."

Colson eyed Ren strangely. "By God it *is* you, Ren. I'll be damned! Well, men, what are we waiting for? Let's get the duchess out!"

There were cheers of agreement and the shuffling of booted feet as the men moved toward the toolhouse. In minutes they were shoveling, readying coal cars to receive the dirt and debris, and more men were arriving. Word of mouth and the small boy now ringing the bell were quickly spreading the news of the cave-in.

Ren made his way to the head of the crew.

He'd been doing ranch work, digging post holes, pitching hay. His muscles were hard and his body lean, but nothing could have

292

prepared him for the grueling, backbreaking labor of clearing the mine entrance. He'd forgotten the blisters, the screaming muscles, the heat and the stifling air. Shovel after shovel of the heavy dirt and coal were tossed over work-hardened, muscular shoulders into the waiting coal cars. When each car was filled to capacity, it was rolled away and another was brought to take its place. Once the men could dig their way into the tunnel, mules would be hitched to the cars. Luckily their stable near the entrance had been spared.

Ren put his back into his work, but kept his thoughts carefully controlled. Few words were spoken. Every ounce of effort was put toward the singular task of clearing the entrance to the mine.

Ren's thoughts were of Elaina. He prayed she wasn't hurt. Prayed she'd been able to elude the tons of rock that filled the tunnel. He knew what it was like to be trapped; he remembered the awful, terrifying fear of being buried alive — if she was alive. He refused to acknowledge the possibility of her death. He would know if she was dead, he told himself. Somehow he would know.

He shoveled harder, pushing himself beyond the limits of his endurance. More coal cars were loaded and rolled away. Men hauled in timbers to shore up the opening as soon as the space was cleared. Miners spelled one another. Women arrived to carry water and supply the men with food to keep their strength up.

"Better rest a spell," Josh Colson warned. "You'll be no good to her if you work till you drop."

Ren mopped the sweat from his brow with the back of his hand. He'd discarded his shirt after the first hour and worked in his breeches and boots. "Not yet, Josh. But I'll be careful. Thanks."

A nagging memory kept him working: the sight of Elaina McAllister huddled on the floor of the potting shed, her eyes blank, her body trembling with terror, plagued by her desperate fear of the darkness, of being trapped in dark places. Now her worst nightmare was real. What would it do to her? Would her mind be able to cope with the long hours alone in the mine? Or would the terrible fear cost Elaina her sanity? Ren swallowed the lump in his throat and hoisted another shovelful of dirt. Please, God, let her be all right.

Twelve hours of bone-crushing, backbreaking labor. Twelve hours of not knowing whether Elaina was alive or dead, whether

293

she had enough air to breathe, whether she was injured or bleeding, whether she was still sane.

"We found something, Ren," Erik Winston, a miner from Ren's old crew, called out to him.

Ren's heartbeat quickened. He made his way through the throng of dirty, sweating bodies to where Erik waited. The miner held a lamp near the ground and pointed. Two booted feet protruded through the dirt and coal dust. The rest of the man's body lay buried under hundreds of tons of debris.

"Got any idea who he is?" Erik asked.

Ren just shook his head. His throat was so dry he couldn't speak. If this was the man who had taken Elaina into the mine, wouldn't she be with him? If she was anywhere near the man, hers would surely be the next body uncovered.

"Why don't you sit down a minute?" Erik said. "You look a little pale."

"I'm all right," Ren told him, his voice thick. "I'd better get back to work."

Erik nodded, understanding Ren's need to keep busy. Every miner had experienced the same kind of agony at one time or another while waiting endlessly for news of a loved one or waiting behind a mountain of debris, hoping and praying to be found before it was too late.

The digging seemed interminable, hour after agonizing hour crept by, each one longer than the last, yet no one complained. Every man focused his total effort on piercing the insurmountable barrier that lay before him. It was dark outside, though within the tunnel there was no night or day, only the blackness. At least the cool night air brought a little relief from the heat.

Ren heeded Josh Colson's warning and paced himself. He was sure the big redheaded man knew more about mining than anyone else at Blue Mountain. He was glad to have Josh alongside him to direct the rescue operation.

More hours passed. Ren's hands were bloody, his face and torso black from the dust and the coal. His mind had long ago blotted out the pain in his aching body; he refused to acknowledge its existence, denying it as he did the possibility of Elaina's death.

They dug for two more hours, some miners from Hazleton having arrived to spell those who'd been working without pause through the long hours of the night. Ren refused to quit. As long as he was able to stand, he would keep working.

"We're through! We've broken through!" The cry sent shudders of relief — and dread — the length of him. He rushed to the right side of the tunnel where several miners were digging furiously, the tiny hole growing with every shovel full of dirt.

"Lainey!" He yelled through the opening, his voice thick and strained. "It's Ren." He didn't know if she could hear him, didn't even know if she was alive. But he wanted her to know he was there. "Hang on, pretty lady. We'll be there in just a few minutes."

When the hole was big enough, he squeezed through the narrow opening, the feel of the dirt cold against his bare skin. Someone passed him a kerosene lamp, and he moved into the darkness.

Elaina held her breath, trying to identify the sounds she had heard. Was it the fear again? She had conquered it so far — at least she thought she had. Maybe the long aching hours in the darkness were making her delirious. She thought she'd heard Ren's voice, but she knew that couldn't be.

"Lainey? Lainey where are you?"

She swallowed and tried desperately to make her throat work, but no sound would come. If she was delirious, she didn't want to wake up. Didn't want to leave the sound of his voice.

"Lainey, if you can hear me, move something. I'll find you."

She wet her parched lips. "Ren?" she called out weakly, still not believing her ears. "I'm here." If he was an illusion, maybe she could conjure his image, imagine the feel of his arms around her. Maybe she could die convinced she was with him one last time.

She felt strong arms around her, her body held against hard, muscular flesh. She felt his tears on her cheek. "Ren?" she whispered.

"Are you hurt?" he asked, his voice low and husky, and for the first time she dared to believe he was real.

"Ren?"

"I'm right here, Lainey. Tell me where you're hurt."

"Oh, God." She clutched his neck so tight her arms ached. He kissed her cheek, her neck, her lips.

"Tell me you're all right," he said.

"Please . . . take me out of here."

"Just as soon as the opening is big enough."

"You're really here?"

"Right here, Elaina. Right where I should have been all along."

For the first time she heard the clank of shovels, the joyous shouts of the miners. Still clinging to Ren, she heard their heavy footfalls as they made their way through the opening, bringing more light and a stretcher into the tunnel.

She recognized Josh Colson's red hair and broad, comforting grin. "You all right, Miss McAllister?"

Ren released his hold on her.

"Don't leave me!" she cried. "Please!"

"I'll never leave you again, Lainey. We're going to be married."

"Married?"

"Yes. You'll have me all to yourself until you can't stand another minute of my company." She heard the catch in his voice. "Right now we need to be sure you don't have any broken bones."

She clutched him a moment longer, then let him lift her onto the stretcher. As he walked along beside her, tightly holding her hand, she could feel the strength he willed her. When they reached the outside of the tunnel, she breathed deeply of the fresh air and silently thanked God for sparing her life.

Dirt-covered miners surrounded her, wishing her well, obviously pleased that they had cheated the greedy tunnels of another victim. They loaded her into the back of a wagon, and one of the miners climbed atop the seat. Ren climbed in beside her and gently cradled her head in his lap.

"How do you feel?" he asked.

"Now that you're here, I feel fine."

He brushed several strands of thick, dark hair from her face. "I know exactly what you mean, but humor me and tell me the truth."

She smiled tremulously, her hand resting against his thigh. "I feel a little weak, and my ribs are hurting again, but I don't think anything's broken." They were both covered from head to toe with coal dust. The only parts of his face she could clearly distinguish were his light blue eyes and flashing white teeth.

"How did you know I was in there?"

"It's a long story. I'll tell you about it after we get you to the hotel." He kissed the top of her head. "I was worried about your fear of the darkness. How did you manage to control it?"

Elaina swallowed hard. "At first it overwhelmed me. But somewhere down deep, I knew if I didn't conquer the fear, I'd have no chance to survive."

"I'm so proud of you. I was afraid . . ." His voice trailed off, and he looked away.

"I'm safe now," she told him. "And I love you."

He smiled at that, a gentle smile that touched her heart. "We came so close to losing each other. I love you so damned much."

"Did you mean what you said in the mine?"

He kissed her forehead. "Every word of it. We're going to be married — if you'll have me," he teased.

"But what about Melissa — and Jacob?"

"Melissa is happily married to Stewart Pickman, the man she loves. Jacob says to tell you he'll be proud to have you in the family."

Tears gathered in her eyes. It was more than she could ever have wished for. Then with a flash of clarity she remembered she was Mrs. Chuck Dawson. Oh, God, what would Ren say when he found out? What would Chuck do? Imagining the consequences, she tightened her hold on his hand.

"What is it, Lainey? What's the matter?"

How could she tell him? How could she shatter their illusion of happiness? "I'm . . . already married . . . to Chuck. He gave me laudanum, Ren. I didn't know what I was doing. I . . . oh, God, what am I going to do?"

"Hush, Lainey," he said, touching her cheek. "Chuck Dawson is dead. Even if the marriage was legal — which I doubt — you're a widow now."

For a moment she felt confused. "A widow?"

"Yes. Bill Sharp was waiting for me at Henry Dawson's house. He drew down on me. I killed him. Dawson was killed by the bullet from Sharp's gun."

Elaina felt the sting of tears, not for Chuck — never for him — but for the burden that had been lifted from her heart. Then she noticed Ren's uncertain glance.

"You're wondering if Chuck . . . took advantage of me."

"It isn't important. We're together now, and that's all that matters."

"He didn't," she said. "He knew I'd been with you. He wouldn't touch me."

She caught the flash of a white-toothed grin. "Then I did something right after all." Even covered with dirt and coal dust, he looked handsome.

Lifting a hand to his face, she felt the hard planes of his cheekbones beneath her fingers. "More than one thing, my love. Much more."

He kissed the palm of her hand. The wagon hit a pothole, and she winced a bit at the jolt to her ribs.

"All right?"

"I will be, just as soon as I wash off this coal dust."

"Nothing would please me more, pretty lady, than to assist you in that task." Even in the darkness, she saw the heat in his eyes, heard his soft groan as she snuggled a little deeper against his thigh.

"I see you're not as tired as you look," she teased, feeling the hardened length of his manhood pressing determinedly against his breeches.

"Apparently not," he agreed. When he cupped her breast, she felt a shiver of pleasure that overrode even her fatigue.

The wagon turned down the main street of Keyserville, heading toward the hotel. Gaslights illuminated the front, and Elaina barely recognized the freshly painted exterior and the new hand-painted sign above the door.

Ren jumped from the wagon as Elaina sat up.

"I'm feeling much better," she told him. "I can make it on my own."

"Not a chance," he said, his coal-covered face breaking into a grin. "I haven't held you in days. I'm not about to let you spoil my chance." He scooped her into his arms, careful of her bruised and battered body, and waved his thanks to the miner who had driven them into town. With long strides, he carried her toward the hotel.

Clutching his neck as if she'd never let him go, Elaina was asleep in Ren's arms before he cleared the doorway.

# *Epilogue*

Elaina lifted her silk chiffon skirts and climbed the last flight of stairs to their suite.

Ren had stayed in the lobby to talk with the federal marshal who had investigated the Redmond-Dawson partnership and the Blue Mountain Mining Company swindle — and that was just what it had turned out to be, a swindle from the very beginning, ten years ago. Lowell McAllister had been led to believe the mine was going broke when in actuality it was producing a steady stream of income all along. Dawson and Redmond had been behind the string of disasters that had forced him to take on partners in the first place.

In the long run, the swindle that had cost Lowell McAllister his life had been for nothing. Now Chuck Dawson was dead, and Dolph Redmond and Henry Dawson would spend the rest of their lives behind bars. Though the investigator had been unable to link the two partners to Edward Daniels's death, the outcome was the same — it was doubtful either man would live to see the outside world again.

Elaina crossed the landing and stood before the wide, freshly painted double doors to the third floor suite. Fitting the key in the shiny brass lock, she turned the knob and stepped through the doorway. Mauve silk draperies hung at wide windows behind the settee, and elegant William and Mary walnut tables nestled in front and along the sides.

She moved gracefully through the room, the swish of her petticoats and the tick of a lovely old grandfather clock the only sounds. She was still amazed at all Ada had done.

"I saved this suite especially for you," Ada had told her, beaming with pride at her accomplishments. "We're still working on the rest of the rooms, but it won't take long to make the old place shipshape again."

"Papa would be pleased," Elaina said.

Ada grinned with pleasure. "No more pleased than I am. You're a good friend, Elaina."

Elaina had hugged her, thinking how fortunate she was to have a friend like Ada.

Pausing in the bedroom doorway, her mind occupied, as always, with thoughts of Ren, Elaina seated herself at the walnut dressing table, determined to ready herself for his arrival. She fingered the lovely diamond and topaz necklace at her throat — his wedding gift to her. It matched her golden eyes, he'd told her.

They'd spent the evening at a party held in her honor. The townspeople had wanted to thank her for founding the hospital, a delegation of miners had shyly accepted her praise for their courage and hard work after the cave-in, and Ren had announced the purchase of Blue Mountain Mining by a company he and Jacob Stanhope controlled — the Anthracite Mining and Colliery Company, the outfit that had been negotiating with Blue Mountain from the start. With the shares Elaina still owned — discovered during the investigation — she and Ren would be partners. They planned to make a great many changes.

The familiar cadence of his footfalls on the stairway set her heart to pounding. He'd watched her all evening, his light eyes speaking his hunger. He had smiled rakishly, lifting just one corner of his mouth, while his fingers lightly traced a pattern on her arm that sent shivers racing up her spine. She knew he wanted her, could hardly wait for the evening to end. Her own eagerness made her giddy with anticipation.

Forgetting her promise to be ready for him, she sat motionless on the stool, the sound of a key in the lock increasing the tempo of her already fluttering heart. As his booted footsteps drew nearer, alternately muffled by the carpet, then ringing against the polished wooden floors, bright heat flooded her cheeks while a more languorous fire began to warm her blood.

When he stepped through the doorway, she swung around on the stool, feeling the same sweet yearning as always. He looked so ruggedly handsome, so tall and virile, his black hair and brows emphasizing the lightness of his eyes and the strength of his cheek-bones. She loved the soft look he saved only for her, the way his mouth curved with pleasure while his eyes moved over her body. Wordlessly he dipped his head to nuzzle her neck, then kissed the place behind her ear.

"I've missed you," he said. "I should have insisted you stay."

"I meant to he ready for you," she told him, "but I didn't realize how difficult unfastening this gown was going to be — or how soon you'd be joining me."

He grinned, even teeth flashing against dark skin. "Then I'm a fortunate man indeed. You're giving me my favorite gift. There's nothing I like better than to unwrap a beautiful package."

He turned her back to him to gain access to the diamond clasp of her necklace.

"How does it feel, Mrs. Daniels, to be merely a businessman's wife instead of a duchess?" He slid the jewels from around her throat and laid them in their satin-lined box, the warm touch of his fingers against her skin leaving her breathless.

She moistened her lips. "More wonderful than anything I could have imagined." She rose from the stool, turning to face him. She rested her hands on his shoulders, then slid her arms around his neck. "I feel like the luckiest woman in the world."

He dipped his head and claimed her lips, at first softly, showing his love, then, as his arousal strengthened, demandingly. She parted her lips to allow him entrance, and he used his tongue deliciously to explore the inside of her mouth. She savored the faint taste of brandy on his breath. When she softly sighed, a plea for more, he pulled away.

"I'd better finish my task, or your beautiful gown will end up in shreds." He kissed her again, quickly this time, then turned her around and began working on the buttons at her back. She fidgeted, eager to be free of the cumbersome clothing that kept her body chaste when she yearned for his touch.

"Hold still!" he commanded. "You keep wiggling like that, Mrs. Daniels, and your husband will be forced to bed you fully clothed."

She lifted a smooth dark brow and smiled seductively, suddenly intrigued by the idea. They'd made love endlessly since their wedding six days ago, their joy at being together constantly demanding release. Once their union had been sanctioned, both by law and by God, they'd been unable to tear themselves away from each other for more than a few hours at a time. He'd taken her gently at first, aware of her bruised and battered body. He'd held her and loved her and said the words she longed to hear. Now both, like playful children, were eager for something more.

Ren unbuttoned the back of Elaina's sienna silk gown and pushed the slippery fabric away to expose her shoulders, forcing himself to ignore the tremor in his hand. She always had that effect on him, as if each glimpse of her flawless skin was the very first. When he pulled the pins from her hair, the thick, gleaming strands cascaded down her back. He loved the silky feel of it, had wanted so many times to linger just as he did now. He lifted the heavy mane out of his way and kissed the nape of her neck, then pulled her back against his chest, surrounding her in his arms and pressing her cheek against his face.

"I love you," he whispered. He could feel the curve of her smile.

"I love you, too."

His hand slid along her body to cup the heavy weight of her breast, still hidden beneath her chemise. The nipple pressed through the lace to harden against his palm. Her whimper of pleasure increased his attention, his fingers pushing the fabric aside to stroke bare flesh, his lips moving to her shoulders. She started to turn, but he gripped her firmly around the waist and held her in position.

"We have all night. I'm through with hurried embraces. Each time we've made love, I've wanted you so badly, I fear I've rushed us a little. You're staying right where you are until I tell you to move. Tonight," he teased, drawing a finger along her jaw, "I intend to torture you with pleasure until I drive you mad with desire."

She laughed softly, and he thought again how he loved the sound of her voice. But then, he loved everything about her, from the arch of her neck to the dimple behind her knee to the curve of her slender ankle.

He unlaced her corset, pushed the dress and the fluffy petticoats down over her hips, then bade her step free of the confining garments. She stood and turned to face him, in sheer pantalets, a delicate lace chemise, and milk-white stockings. The sight of her set his blood on fire.

"I think it's time your husband inspected his property." Lifting her fingers to his lips, he fixed his gaze on the quickening rise and fall of her breasts and ran a brown hand along her shoulder, then lower, until it dipped beneath the lace and covered the hard bud of her nipple. His swollen manhood threatened to speed the game, but still he refused to hurry. A tiny shiver and the catch of her breath told him his touch was affecting her just as he intended. With slow, deliberate movements, he stroked the flat spot above her navel. Her golden eyes reflected his own heated look, and her pink tongue moistened her full red lips.

"I think you've tortured me enough, my husband," she said breathlessly. "Surely you can't mean to deny me much longer."

"The night is young, my wife," he replied, continuing the game. "Let me enjoy the rest of you."

Elaina swallowed hard, wanting to touch him as he did her, wanting to feel his lips on hers, craving the heat of his tongue, but reveling in the sport.

He inspected her arrogantly, circling her as if she were one of his finest brood mares; and her mind recalled the story he'd told her that day on the ranch, the story of the one fiery filly who could please him for life.

He stepped in close to nibble her ear, his tongue warm and moist against her skin. He ran a hand from behind her knee, up her thigh to her bottom, where he kneaded the lush roundness through the thin fabric of her pantalets. She moaned and reached out for him.

Ren only shook his head, enjoying these few moments of power. She was his now. His and his alone. He would protect her with his life, love her forever, and give her the pleasure of his passions. He unhooked her stockings one by one and slid them down her shapely calves. The game was beginning to wear thin, but he intended to continue as long as his body could withstand the torture. Though he ached with wanting her, in the end the pleasure would be worth it.

As he unbuttoned the front of her chemise, he noticed her face was flushed, her eyes nearly closed. He removed the garment and lowered his mouth to the taut peak of her nipple. When she shuddered and swayed against him, it almost ended the game.

"Ren, please," she begged, and the husky desire he heard in her usually gentle voice renewed his determination.

"Soon, pretty lady. Soon the game will be over, and we will both be winners." He slid his hand inside the waistband of her cotton pantalets to feel the silken triangle above her womanhood. She moaned and arched against him. His practiced hands moved between her thighs, stroking, heating; then his fingers slipped inside to find her wet and ready. As he slid the last of her clothes down her slender legs, he stroked the cleft of her womanhood until she writhed against his hand.

With a last long kiss, he knelt in front of her, his hands gripping her buttocks, holding her immobile.

"Ren?" she whispered, a little unsure.

"Let me love you, Elaina." Then his tongue was touching her navel, leaving a hot wet trail as it moved down her body, through the tangle of soft black curls below, to settle determinedly on the cleft of her womanhood.

"Oh, God, Ren," she whispered and laced her fingers in his hair. His mouth followed his tongue, and before Elaina could protest he had her writhing and moaning, begging him for more until she felt the first ripples of a climax that drove her beyond the brink of this world and onto another plane.

Ren came to his feet even before the delicious sensations had ended. She trembled as he scooped her into his arms, moved across the room, and placed her on the canopied bed. He left her only long enough to discard his own clothes, then returned and eased himself down beside her.

He nibbled the curve of her neck, kissed her deeply, using his tongue as a moist probe to renew her desire, which in seconds flamed to a blazing heat greater than before. Wanting him desperately, she reached for him, seeking his swollen member. He claimed her mouth, gently at first, then with driving need. She felt the tension in his body and knew the sport had ended. He was no longer her master, no longer in control. Now it was she who played the game.

She kissed him passionately, determined to provoke in him the same fever he aroused in her. She felt his hands caressing her thighs while she stroked his torso, nibbled his earlobe, nipped his shoulder. Corded muscles rippled beneath her hand as she moved lower until her fingers circled his huge pulsing shaft. She reveled in his deep, urgent groan. Taking his nipple between her teeth, she tugged gently, entwining her legs with his and feeling the prickly hairs of his sinewy thighs.

When she kissed him again, with tender, kiss-swollen lips, his tongue, hot and seeking, tangled with her own. She trembled and moaned and lost control of the game. Words of love tumbled from her lips as she pleaded and begged him to take her. He was her world. Her love. Her life. Flames of passion scorched her soul. She had to have him. She could play the game no more.

Ren positioned himself above her, pressing her into the mattress, controlling her body as he always did, knowing just where her pleasure would be greatest. With trembling fingers, she guided his shaft into her heated flesh, craving the fullness of him, begging him to make her complete. He buried his thick length inside her, and his powerful strokes, at first measured and controlled, soon turned reckless. He slammed against her, each thrust deeper than the last. She met each one with abandon. He was her husband. He was her love.

The waves of pleasure she felt with each surge amazed her, promising new and greater pleasure than ever before. She clawed his back and called his name, and he lifted her, grasping her buttocks to drive even deeper inside her. Fiery heat flamed through her, turning her liquid, melting her to silvery swirls of fulfillment. She cried his name, arched against him, then felt the warm wetness of his seed spilling inside her.

His kisses gentled as his mouth caressed her eyes, her nose, her mouth. It was a promise of things to come, of love and passion, of giving and receiving, of happiness and home. She knew theirs was a rare love, the kind only a fortunate few ever found. But it hadn't been given to them. They'd had to reach out and take it. They'd each overcome vast obstacles before they'd been granted this love. They would never let it elude them again. Ren rolled to his side and pulled her against him.

"I love you," he whispered. "I always have. I always will."

She blinked at the tears of happiness she couldn't hold back and gently kissed his lips.

"I'm so fortunate. The most fortunate woman in the world."